D0250848

THE POWER PLAYERS

HANK LANCASTER. All-American golden boy. A killer in bed. Willing to kill for success.

DOROTHY LANCASTER. Gorgeous socialite. With a porn act on the side.

GEORGE POWELL. New-style company man. With the goods on everybody.

SUSAN POWELL. Her sex life makes her ripe for blackmail.

MARK SCOTT. The idealist. Betrayed by his own ambition.

ANNE SCOTT. Torn apart in the game she's forced to play.

THEY KNOW ALL THE RULES . . .
AND HOW TO BREAK THEM.

"AN EXCITING PICTURE OF CORPORATE IN-FIGHTING"

—*Los Angeles Herald Examiner*

"GRIPPING FROM START TO FINISH"

—*Publishers Weekly*

THE POWER PLAYERS

A Novel by
ARELO SEDERBERG

BANTAM BOOKS
TORONTO · NEW YORK · LONDON

THE POWER PLAYERS
A Bantam Book

PRINTING HISTORY
William Morrow & Company edition published January 1980
2nd printing .... January 1980
The Literary Guild edition published October 1979
Bantam Edition | January 1981

*Grateful acknowledgment is made for lines from Collected
Poems of Wallace Stevens, copyright © 1954 by Wallace
Stevens. Reprinted by permission of Alfred A. Knopf, Inc.
Also for lines from T.S. Eliot's "The Love Song of J. Alfred
Prufrock," in Collected Poems 1909–1962. Reprinted by per-
mission of Harcourt Brace Jovanovich, Inc., and Faber and
Faber Ltd.*

ISBN 0–553–14141–4

Published simultaneously in the United States and Canada

Dedicated to several persons without whose aid and support this book might not have been possible—Ellis Amburn, Charles Bloch, Dorris and Reece Halsey, Stella Zadeh, and James, my son.

PART ONE
THE REMBRANDT

I

Looking back on it later, Harold Long would blame himself. Obviously someone had slipped aboard the Breedlove International, Inc., executive jet that humid July day at O'Hare in Chicago to post the ominous message. Security wasn't exactly Long's job—the company had squads of blank-faced, tight-lipped operatives in that function—but he was BII's chief pilot and therefore responsible for the bird's safety. So, after the Chicago experience, he'd kick himself, admitting he'd goofed. Also, he would fly the BII 727 jet with a twinge of fear, wondering if something would go wrong in the cockpit, his hands occasionally trembling just slightly as flash pictures of an explosion in the hold and the jet plummeting earthward in flames shot through his mind. It was a nightmare he could not drive away. He'd been tired that day, overworked, and certainly he'd received no sign that would make him more cautious than usual. Long was a careful, veteran pilot, a former United Airlines captain, and he'd never felt anything remotely akin to fear in the cockpit before, despite the fact that he'd once had a close call. That day in July, coming in empty from Newark, he had touched down at O'Hare exactly at noon.

"What's the cargo here?" asked Russ Chambers, the copilot.

"Valuable cargo. We're picking up the big three."

"What big three?"

3

"Scott, Lancaster, Powell."

"Do we get Breedlove, too?"

"Nope. Not today."

"I've never even *seen* Breedlove. Is there a Breedlove in this company?"

"There is a Breedlove in this company, that is one thing for sure."

"Well, you couldn't prove it by me."

Long grinned. "You don't have to see him. You can feel him, his presence."

"Do I have time to go into the city?"

"No way. We'll check the bird over."

"We did that in Newark."

"So we'll do it again."

A truck marked "Midwest Caterers" pulled up, driven by a redheaded youth in uniform. He jumped from behind the wheel, wiped sweat from his brow with the back of his hand, and shook a cigarette from a crumpled pack.

"BII 727?" he asked.

"Put the smoke back," Long said.

The youth crammed the cigarette back into the pack. "You're BII 727, then I got some goodies for you."

Long wrinked his brow. "Who ordered it?"

"I dunno. All I know is I got a consignment slip. Some food and booze for BII 727 O'Hare."

"Okay," Long said. "Put it inside. Russ, you go with him."

Long gave the airplane an exterior inspection, checking the nosewheel and the skin on her belly. A-okay. This bird was always A-okay. She was a superb flying machine with a touch and feel he loved, and sometimes he regarded her as his own. The caterer, returning, agreed she was quite fantastic.

"Jeeze, I never seen anything like *that*," he said, his eyes wide.

"Her interior, you mean?"

"Is this an airplane or a flying palace?"

"Both," Long said.

The redhead gazed at the plane. He whistled. "Jeeze," he mumbled in awe, tipping his hat back.

As he hurried from the hotel, an out-of-towner seeking his home, Mark Scott stopped abruptly. Between him and a taxi was a group of sign-carrying demonstrators, flanked by a row of helmeted Chicago police. The group apparently was protesting in behalf of have-nots during a convention of the World Food Congress featuring David Rockefeller, head of Chase Manhattan Bank, as chairman and keynote speaker. Scott felt a surge of nervous apprehension.

"Here, go on past," a policeman told him, holding back a bearded young man who, despite the heat, wore a thick poncho. "You, that's far enough now," the cop warned the demonstrator.

Scott stepped forward. For a few seconds he was in the midst of the sign-carriers, jostled by them. He did not look at them. The taxi driver came over to meet him.

"Want me to put them bags of yours in the trunk?"

"No, the back seat will be all right. I'll keep them with me."

"I can put 'em in the trunk, no sweat."

"I'll keep them here, thanks."

"Awright. Suit yerself."

Scott paused. He turned. The demonstrators milled slowly behind him, a silent moving force of potential explosiveness held defused by the nightsticks and black-butted holstered pistols of blue-uniformed authority. From the lake came a moist wind that smacked of rain and brought ripe summer city smells to Scott's nostrils. He got into the taxi.

"O'Hare," he said.

A tall young black wearing dirty tennis shoes and pants laced with rope thongs broke from the group of demonstrators and jogged to the taxi. He pressed his nose against the window and stared menacingly at Scott until a policeman wrestled him away.

"Punks, hippies," the driver snorted, edging into Loop traffic. "Doped-up pack rats. Shit on 'em. That's what I say. Shit."

"What do they want?"

"Want? Who knows? Maybe they want dope made legal. Maybe now there ain't no war on, maybe they want a war on now so they can have somethin' to raise hell over." The cabby snapped his head around. "Why they pick on the bankers, that's beyond me. You a banker?"

"It's not a banking convention. It's a food convention."

"You in the food business?

"Well, as a matter of fact, I am. But I'm not in Chicago to attend the conference."

The driver turned to the front, studied traffic openings, and then said, "What's your opinion right now on this Jimmy fellow in Washington?"

Scott sighed. *Here it comes again,* he thought. Something about him seemed always to transform even morbidly silent taxi drivers into garrulous word fountains. This driver mumbled unintelligible monosyllables as he maneuvered through the Loop, but once on the expressway to O'Hare he opened up, both in speed and verbal outpour.

Scott didn't respond. He sat stiffly. He was in no mood to discuss politics with a taxi driver. Right now he had only one desire—to get home as quickly as possible. He wanted to see Anne, touch her, talk with her, make love to her; he wanted to play softball with the kids, to sip a martini before dinner, to sag in an easy chair in front of the television set, to read a book. The smell and touch and sight of home. Over the past few months he'd constantly been on the road. Airplanes and taxis and hotel suites and lonely, unfamiliar streets. He was tired and tense and alone.

The cabby's voice flowed around him. He tried to shut it out. Exhaustion closed in on him. His eyes hurt and his back ached. He needed a rest. He'd wormed just three weeks of vacation from the company over the past decade, and two days of that had been spent looking over the farm-machinery licensee near Rome. Now he was scheduled for a week off, and that week had become the most important immediate consideration in his life. He was to take Anne and the kids to Disney World on Monday, a trip that had already been postponed twice.

When the diver began to play tag with a speeding Mercury, Scott leaned forward and said, "I would appreciate it if you would slow down. There's no hurry. I'm catching a private plane and it will wait."

"Oh. I see. Awright. You looked like a man was in a hurry. I make this trip in sixteen minutes from downtown."

Scott leaned back. His hand brushed his suitcase. Looking down, he discovered a small white piece of paper taped to the handle. Something was scrawled in red ink on it. Scott felt a sudden inexplicable apprehension, an electric surge through his nerves that seemed like a warning, like a flash of fear. He peeled off the paper and read the note. Then he sat stiffly, numbed. The note read, " 'Tis the season for the slaughter of the blood-bedewed fattened hogs." Scott found that his hands had no feeling.

The driver was talking again. "Where you from? No. Lemme guess. I'd guess New York."

"W-what?"

"You okay back there?"

"I'm all right, yes."

"I said I guessed you from New York."

"You're three thousand miles off target."

"California?"

"Yes."

"L.A.?"

"Right again."

"Ronnie Reagan's territory, California. I see him on the Late Show playing a cowboy and I see him again on the morning news. He's gonna become President someday. You watch and see. He's got the gift of gab, and that's about all it takes. Brown, my money's not on him. What'cha do? In California?"

"I work for Breedlove International."

"Breedlove? I heard of it. My brother drives a cab in Jersey, he's got stock in it. What do you think of ITT?"

"I think it is a large company."

"Bigger than Breedlove?"

"Slightly, yes."

"What d'you do there, if you don't mind my askin'. Salesman?"

The third degree annoyed Scott, but he felt compelled to answer truthfully. "I'm a vice-president, I'm afraid."

"No kiddin'?"

"No kiddin'."

"I had Joe Kennedy in the cab once," the driver said, and lapsed into respectful silence, his speed now seeming absurdly low.

The windshield wipers squeaked and the rain purred around them. The day had been windy and hot, an unpleasant Chicago July that seemed to symbolize the futility of the trip. Scott tried to relax. He could not. Again he read the note. He realized he'd been speaking mechanically, answering without really hearing. A short surge of anger went through him. He crumpled up the note and stuffed it into his pocket. It meant nothing. Obviously one of the demonstrators outside the hotel had put it there, a sick joke by a mindless, immature would-be revolutionary too lazy to find work, too directionless to channel his energies into useful endeavors. *Forget it. Think about home.* There had been too many alien hotel bed and suites with an antiseptic sameness over the past few months. Many of the trips, like this one, had been fruitless. He and two other Breedlove International, Inc., executives—Henry Lancaster of marketing and George Powell of finance—had been sent to Chicago by the old man himself, Lewis Anthony Breedlove, founder, chairman-president, and chief executive officer of BII. Their task, in Breedlove's words, was to steal an insurance company. But merger talks with National Casualty had quickly broken down. They had invaded an unknown beachhead uninvited and unwelcomed—a too morose Mark Scott filled with foreboding about the chance for success, an intense George Powell insufficiently familiar with the peculiarities of insurance accounting and drained by overwork in a hurried preparation of a merger proposal, and an amicable, smooth, boundlessly energetic, but somewhat insincere Henry Lancaster, who relied on the sales appeal of his reputation as a former backup quarterback for the Chicago Bears.

A deep malaise filled Scott's mind. His eyes were heavy. His arms ached. He'd never been able to sleep well on business trips; he seemed constantly a victim of raw nerves and jet lag. He thought of the demonstrators outside the hotel. He thought of Anne and the kids. Then, inevitably, his thoughts returned to Lewis Anthony Breedlove. "Get 'em," Breedlove had said. "That company's cash rich and must be looking for a merger in fear of a raid. Give this one your best shot." An invisible Breedlove crouched beside Scott—a commanding, impish presence with sagging shoulders and piercing dark eyes, a being defiant of age, even of mortality.

They could have done it. Had the old man chosen to join them, most certainly they could have pulled it off. But Breedlove had not gone. He'd dispatched his three key corporate troopers and had stayed home, no doubt spending most of his time in the library-den of his Pasadena home, surrounded by his Greek tapestries, his Rembrandt, his Mo-

nets and Cézannes, and his pre-Columbian masks and statuettes resuscitated from centuries-old kingly graves—kings
now violated, treasureless, and anonymous in history.

The driver turned on the radio as O'Hare came into view.
He turned the dial. Country-western music. Cubs in the last
of the seventh, trailing the Cards 3–1. News. Dollar slumps
overseas. Consumer prices up. Terrorists demand $2 million
ransom for a kidnapped Italian businessman. The cabby,
outmaneuvering an encroaching Chevy, was moved to words.

"It don't mean nothin'. Sooner or later everything's history.
Even them bonehead Cubs."

A marvelous attitude, Scott thought. Let nothing worry
you because soon it will be history. He was so relieved to
escape the taxi that he tipped nearly five dollars. He was at
the airport, a symbol of homegoing, and he felt better. But he
couldn't get his mind off the crumpled piece of paper in his
pocket.

Henry Lancaster was in the terminal lobby, reading the
Chicago *Tribune,* nibbling a Baby Ruth candy bar, and
having his shoes shined by a sweating black man who listened
to the Cub game on a transistor radio. Lancaster saw Scott
enter and pause by the bar, looking around. Buckner of the
Cubs had just hit a ball over the right-field wall.

"Whee-ee!" the shoeshine man said. "Them Cubbies, they
playin' *ball* this year."

"That's enough," Lancaster said.

"Huh?"

"When I buy a service, I expect some concentration upon
the vending of that service."

The black flashed a look of hate. "Doan push it," Lancaster
said. He smiled, gave the black a dollar, jumped from the
stand, and ambled toward Scott. A young woman glanced at
him with appreciation and he favored her with a nod and a
smile. Another time, another place, she'd be available to him;
they were all available to him. Past, present, future. He'd
scored them at will during his jock days, his rise in advertising in New York, his career at BII. Last night he'd planked
the wife of a Pittsburgh steelman in Chi on a convention, a
hungry lay who'd thanked him and had suggested a continued
liaison.

Approaching Scott, Lancaster changed. He assumed his business pose. "You look like you've lost your wife and family, not just an insurance acquisition," he said.

"What do you suppose went wrong?" Scott asked.

"They weren't ready. When they are, they'll come to us."

"I don't think so. I got the feeling during those meetings that they know something about us. Something even we may not know."

"I don't understand what you mean."

"Neither do I. Not exactly. But there was a tenseness there that gave me the feeling that no matter what sort of a stock package Powell came up with for them, they'd reject it out of hand. They were courteous, yet still cold. Unreceptive. And why did they keep asking about Breedlove?"

"Well, he's still the boss of this circus."

"That doesn't explain it. Not the way they were asking questions. His health. His future. His connections."

"We lost them because the climate is not right. It's as simple as that. A year ago we would have got them. But this merger boom has peaked now."

"I have a wild idea about something, Hank. There's talk again about federal regulation of insurance companies. Do you think they turned thumbs down on us because they think Breedlove no longer has such strong contacts in D.C.?"

"No way," Lancaster said, waving his hand. "That insurance gang is cunning enough to realize Breedlove is going to have contacts upstairs no matter who's in. Demos, Republicans, Commies, or Mafia. Let's get out of this damn town, Scottie."

"I second your motion, my friend."

And that very possibly was right, Lancaster reflected as they started down the corridor to the gate where the BII executive jet waited. They probably were friends. He knew Scott liked and respected him. He liked and respected Scott. He respected Powell, too, but it would take a saint to like him. Powell was an introverted worrier who chattered about depreciation and amortization even at social gatherings. He was intense and seemed devoted to the company, a little man of fifty-three whose innovations in finance astounded even Breedlove at times. But he was a cold s.o.b., cold as his computers.

In its industries—principally food processing, farm equipment, and drugs—BII was known as a company under very firm one-man rule. But recently Breedlove had shown uncharacteristic willingness to subordinate important responsibilities to others, stirring rumors that the old man, now nearing eighty, was at least considering retirement. Everyone at executive level thought about it. But no one discussed it.

Walking the corridor with his peer and friend, Lancaster felt a strong surge of well-being. He had a sudden premonition. He felt that something very important was about to happen to him. Sizing up all matters, he decided he looked very good.

He knew only one field thoroughly—selling and advertising —but he also knew that he had a remarkable, almost intuitive grasp of finance. At first he'd watched Powell with respect, but lately he'd begun to believe Powell's acquisition packages had been too generous. Some of the acquisitions, rapidly absorbed in the merger boom of the '60s, were generating insufficient cash flow to cover the per share profit dilution resulting from the exchange of stock. Eventually that would show, no matter how creative the accounting, and the responsibility would settle on Powell. Also, BII's accounting procedures were quite liberal; one security analyst had termed it "hot pants" accounting, designed to make profits look better than they were. It could add up to scandal, descending upon Powell.

Scott? His specialty was administration, advance planning, and industrial and shareholder relations. He'd learned his job well, Lancaster had to admit, and he had a real ability to get along with people. And, at thirty-nine, he was the youngest BII vice-president–director. So Breedlove obviously thought a lot of him. If Scott had any weaknesses, they were his occasional displays of almost boyish naïveté and his too gentle attitude toward the unions. Those traits could hurt him. Also, he wasn't well grounded in finance.

But Scott certainly had youth on his side. The executive market today was a youth market. Fifty was old, especially if you were out, résumé in hand, tramping the cold sidewalks, looking for work. Oh, they'd come to Lancaster, onetime smart asses and bright comers showing their year-old mentions in the advertising column of the New York *Times* but seeming to forget the time or two when they'd snubbed Lancaster at the club—overnight down-and-outers reduced to snivelers and beggars with obligations like country-club dues, Park Avenue apartments, and sons at Yale. He'd turned them down with pleasure.

Lancaster also had youth on his side. He'd made vice-president—director at forty, four years ago. It was his second successful career. He'd been a millionaire at thirty-two, when his New York advertising agency, the Lancaster-Masters Group, had been billing over $100 million a year. Now most of the million was gone. Money had little staying power with him.

He touched Scott's shoulder. "You look a little uptight, sport. Something bugging you?"

"Did you see the demonstrators at the hotel?"

"You mean a pack of pothead punks worries you?"

"Well, I—"

"Scottie, stop worrying about things you can't control. Like the insurance company turning us down. There are other insurance companies we can stalk. The world's full of companies ripe for raids."

"I still think they didn't trust us."

"You mean they know about the Bolivian slush fund? The political contributions?"

"What Bolivian slush fund?"

"Oh, come on, Scottie."

"Now, look, Hank. I'm not some junior partner in this organization."

"Indeed you are not. You're one level removed from the top. Therefore you know. The political contributions. The slush funds. The lobbying. The entertainment."

Scott's face showed irritation. "Should we call Breedlove and tell him we flubbed the insurance deal?"

"I've called him."

"You did? What was his reaction?"

"He said, and I quote, 'Fuck the insurance gang. Let somebody raid their ass.' "

"All right, let's go home," Scott said.

"Right on, parson."

"You could have gone all day without calling me parson."

"Then don't preach."

"I'm not preaching."

"Your eyes preach." Lancaster said.

* * *

The BII Boeing 727 had been so completely customized that Long sometimes thought he should go back to school to learn to handle her right. There was a joke around that Breedlove had had a secret passage built into her belly where he could hide from the IRS. Russ Chambers once cracked that there was a chamber in her hold where Breedlove showed dirty movies to congressmen. Long stood in the rain, watching George Powell, the first of the big three to board in Chicago. Long mentioned the weather. Powell, as usual, hardly acknowledged him.

"But a small sprinkle won't hold down a bird like this one, Mr. Powell." Long glanced at the Chicago *Tribune* in Powell's hand. "Anything new in the world?"

"No."

"*Time* says we're getting colder with the Commies."

"*Time* often is inaccurate."

Long would almost rather talk than fly, but he decided not to push it. He was—what the hell—only a bus driver to the BII bosses he hauled around the world. The only executive with whom he was able to talk human-to-human was Mark Scott, the kind of man your New York taxi jockey would call "regular people." Powell settled into his seat, opened the paper, and chewed on the stem of an unlit pipe. He looked beat. Long went to the cockpit, his home. Another Chi–L.A. run. He could fly it blind in a Jenny. He'd logged over 20,000 hours in the left seat of airplanes, everything from DC-3s to 747s. He'd flown Chi–L.A. and L.A.–Chi hundreds of times. Every railroad station, town, hill, boulder, and even tree along the route was stamped on his mental map.

Powell's eyes closed. His head slipped forward. Well, he wasn't the only tired one aboard. Long had just logged his busiest week since he'd joined BII.

The 727 was clean now, but she'd been a mess yesterday. You'd think he'd been flying the Mafia, not a load of Wall Street stock analysts who'd been touring company plants in California. Long had dropped the analysts in Newark yesterday, had arranged a cleaning for the bird, and had left for Chi that morning, ordered to make an executive pickup at O'Hare. He grinned, thinking of the analysts. A great bunch; a great drunk airborne party. They loved to disagree. The market would hit 1,000 by December; the market would drop to 500 by December. Gold stocks were solid; gold stocks were too high. Bonds were high risk; bonds were a safety hedge against the coming depression. A gnomelike man from Lehman Brothers with a cigar the length of his arm informed Long in whispered tones that a now shadowy Mafia chieftain would be president of the country within six years. They played knock poker, told J. P. Morgan jokes, cursed the SEC, and expressed alarm about the rise in short interest on the Big Board. A man from Loeb, Rhodes did a passable imitation of Jimmy Carter. A Merrill Lynch man, smashed on twelve-year-old Chivas, offered to handle the Boeing's left seat for the Newark landing.

It always happened when an uninitiated group came aboard the 727. Her interior did something to them. She'd been bought (at Breedlove's behest, Long had heard) from the bankruptcy court of a wheeler-dealer named Gordon Sterling, who, chased by federal authorities, had fled to South America with only his Swiss bank account number and his Japanese mistress. Long had flown her for well over a year, and he still marveled at her extraordinary accoutrements. Her interior seemed more like a Bel Air bachelor's pad than an airplane. She had two elaborate bathrooms, a sauna, a bar with a built-in quad stereo system and overhead strobe lights, a kitchen with a microwave oven, refrigerator, and garbage disposer. There was a sunken marble tub in one of the bathrooms, with a mirrored sliding door; the water taps were gold-plated and the walls were decorated with sheets of green onyx. The salon, often used for mid-flight conferences by key BII executives, had a gun locker that contained a .45 automatic, a 30–30 rifle, and two 12-gauge shotguns.

The 727 was Long's mistress, but his relationship to her was one of love-hate. She handled like a dream, yet he detested her finery. Someone had dubbed her the Taj Mahal, a name that stuck. She was a saucy lady, decked out in seductive party clothing at all hours, reflecting the near-decadent excesses of her former owner. She seemed always to incite her guests to hedonistic revelry. The Taj Mahal worried him on occasion, but he really didn't doubt her safety. He loved her design. He trusted her. She was a little overweight, like many enchanting mistresses, but her weight didn't affect performance, or worry the FAA. She probably could fly herself. Perhaps, with Long in the right seat, the Merrill Lynch drunk really could have set her down at Newark.

He stopped short of the cockpit. Scott and Lancaster had come aboard through the specially installed rear ramp entrance. Long walked back to them.

Scott grinned. "Will this opium dream get off the ground today, Harold?"

"We can practically guarantee that, Mr. Scott."

"I suppose you realize by now that I'm a gray flier. Sweaty palms."

"A stiff martini is a fast cure for that."

Lancaster slumped down beside Powell. "Let's roll," he said. He looked at Long. "Now?"

Long didn't hurry. He took his good time. He meandered to the cockpit, squeezed by the flight engineer's jump seat, and got into the left seat. Russ, always eager to go, was already in the right seat. Chambers was twenty-two, but looked about eighteen.

"Check," Long said.

Slowly they went through the routine. Hydraulic-pump lights. Generator brakes. Overspeed warning. Pilot-static heat. Fuel-valve fire switch. Parking brakes. Parking lights. A-okay. Chambers glanced at Long. The is-this-necessary glance. Yes. It was necessary. He fired up the power plants. Engine-pressure ratio. Okay. High- and low-pressure RPM. Okay. Fuel flow, oil pressure, oil temperature, pneumatic pressure, exhaust-gas pressure. Okay. Russ Chambers recorded. He looked eager to take off. It was likely that a miniskirted, booted chick would be waiting for him at LAX. Russ constantly complained about the long hours, which deprived him of bedtime with his girls. He also complained about what he considered inadequate pay. Hell, the kid should have been around when Long had handled the right seat. You flew just for the joy of it then.

One thing was certain. The 727 had the best navigation equipment Long had ever seen. She was equipped with a new AiResearch computerized AirNAV-100, a solid-state computer with a magnetic memory alphanumeric keyboard programmer and a 17-register alphanumeric readout, providing her pilot with automatically computed distance, course, and time to a selected way point, ground speed, flight-path angle, course-offset information, cross-track and altitude error. She also had extraordinary operational redundancy, an elaborate system of fail-safe devices that cut in if the original ones failed. She was so automated she made her pilot feel redundant.

So why worry? Are you getting old?

Perhaps the young new college-educated hot-stuffs in the cockpits of today, like Russ Chambers, did consider him a Curtiss Jenny seat-of-the-pants flier, an ancient bird who clung to the past. And, in some ways, maybe he was old-fashioned. But he wasn't the old stuff they probably thought he was. He understood the modern way, too. And he flew jets by the book, not by instinct.

If he hadn't flown that 707 by the book one night a few years ago, he and his crew and sixty-three passengers might be dead. For Long had gone down once; he'd damn near bought the barn.

They were on the runway, two jets ahead of them. The windshield wipers dashed in front of Long. Like that night. *Jesus, why do you think about it before every takeoff?* The first jet, a 747, lifted into the rain. Now they were second up. Long edged the 727 forward.

It had been weather like this, at this airport. He'd been twenty minutes out, at 30,000, when radar had picked thunderstorms over Iowa. He buckled the passengers down and got Air Traffic Control clearance to climb to 40,000.

As they rose, increasing turbulence chopped the 707 from side to side. Long felt imprisoned, encapsulated in a metal tube driven by a greater power, nature's unpredictability and capriciousness. A powerful updraft bounced the jet a thousand feet higher. A downdraft hurled it down a thousand. Then they were in an updraft again, caught, shoved, buffeted, the fuselage trembling and the wings shuddering like a model plane in a wind tunnel. The airspeed indicator hovered at 220 knots, precariously close to stall speed. Long shoved on full power. The indicator danced, then slipped back.

They strained in the thin air, seeming not to move.

Then the 707 stalled. Dead. It poised in space, its turbines howling above the wind. Silence. Two seconds? Five seconds?

It went down on its side, absolutely out of control.

For the first time in his flying career, Long saw death

staring at him in the windshield, a creature that seemed to crouch like a man, laughing at him with its yellow face and broken teeth.

He cut back the throttles. Air speed: 350 knots. Not 400. The Mach warning bell clanged, roaring in his ears.

Out of the overcast, then, and plunging.

Pull back.

No. Not yet.

The copilot's eyes were desperate. The eyes said, "Get the nose up, nose up, now, *now!*"

But not yet. She'd break up at this speed and altitude.

500 knots. 20,000 feet. Howl of the engines. Mach bell alive. 15,000.

Now! Power!

The copilot handled the throttle. The bird's nose came up, slightly. They both struggled with the control yoke. Slight response.

10,000 feet.

They were leveling.

They were coming out of it.

At 7,000 they'd been nose up, climbing again. They had made it.

Now, turning the 727 for takeoff, Long found himself full of sweat. How many times would he relive it? He nodded to Chambers. The 727 moved down the runway.

"V-one," Chambers said. The takeoff point of no return. Then they were off. "Rotate!" Chambers said.

It was an easy, effortless climb to 30,000.

There was no company stewardess on this flight, a fact that didn't bother Scott at all, for he loved to ramble around the jet after they reached cruising altitude, making marvelous discoveries. Last week he'd determined that the carpeting in the johns was real mink. He'd also found a sending-receiving shortwave set in the salon. It was simply too much. The ultimate corporate perk. Sometimes he thought they worked not for salaries and bonuses but for the perks—the expense accounts, the drivers who met them at airports with Cadillacs, the mountain lodges and seaside resort homes, and the polite youthful underlings whose manner in their presence seemed dictated precisely in relationship to their rank and status. It was not title, not really. Status was measured by the thickness of the carpet in your office, your number of private lines, the way your secretaries dressed and acted, and, at BII, your closeness to Lewis Breedlove. Now, probing around, Scott again felt the old man's presence. Breedlove wasn't given to excesses, yet the 727 had become one of his favorite playthings. It had been bought on his orders, after he'd personally inspected it. Its cost and maintenance outlays were a tax write-off against BII income; Scott wondered when the IRS would begin looking into that. He sighed. *Forget it,* he thought. *Accept it.* He mixed a light vodka martini and switched on the strobe light. Red patterns danced on the wall.

"Cheers," Lancaster said, a Beefeater-rocks in his hand.

"Cheers."

"You look tired. Relax."

"Sometimes I think I've forgotten how to relax."

"It's simple. Lean back. Sip your booze. Close your eyes. Think of ocean waves. The sun. Tit nipples."

"When I close my eyes, I see Breedlove."

"I drink to our leader. The corporate Godfather. Don't let him send shivers down your spine, my man."

"I'm not afraid of him, Hank. It's not that."

"Then you have more courage than most of us. Or foolhardiness. He is both a lion and a teddy bear, our Mr. Breedlove. I fear his teddy-bear manner more than his lion's." Lancaster shook the ice in his glass. He grinned. "You suffer it all too much, Scottie."

"What is that supposed to mean?"

"You think you can be husband and father, Little League coach and preacher, authority on Rachmaninoff and Shakespeare—"

"I am not an authority on Rachmaninoff. Or Shakespeare."

"Whatever, whatever. You can't do it. Not and work high up for this company. Or any company." Lancaster drank. A ray of sunlight flashed in his eyes as the 727 banked. "I do not think our Mr. Scott is too complex a man. I think I can cut squarely to the inner truth of him."

"All right. Cut away."

"He has a conscience. He's a dreamer, an idealist. He cannot abide ruthlessness. Yet he knows he's in a game that is not serene. He witnesses ruthlessness. He is torn. He grieves."

"Hank, you're in the wrong business. You should shrink heads."

"I do that, too," Lancaster said. "I have a collection."

Scott touched the crumpled paper in his pocket. He'd wanted to tell Lancaster about it, but he knew he would not. He was frightened, but he did not want Lancaster to know it. Besides, it was silly. There was no reason for the fear. The note meant nothing. Just a sick joke, he told himself again. Yet his hand was unsteady and a hollow feeling danced in the pit of his stomach, a feeling almost of dread.

They brought their drinks into the salon and sat in silence. Lancaster leaned back. Liz, Scott's twelve-year-old daughter, had once breathlessly declared that she thought Henry Lancaster was the coolest, dreamiest, and handsomest man she'd ever been fortunate enough to cast eyes upon. Lancaster was six-two and about one-eighty, with light wavy hair and deep blue eyes. He had extraordinary hands—long, thin-veined, and very strong. Once Scott had seen him bend an iron fireplace poker, a feat he still could hardly believe.

Powell came up, tapping his pipe on a copy of the *Wall Street Journal*. "Our Mr. Carter is somewhat less than an economic genius," he said.

"Please," Scott said. "I just had a cabby's lecture on the economy."

"George heads the Nixon-in-'80 drive," Lancaster said. "Nixon has three friends—George, Lewis Breedlove, and a Chinaman."

"You are an extremely amusing person, Henry," Powell said.

"Around this company, we need comic relief," Lancaster said.

Powell continued to tap his pipe. "It is my opinion that Richard Nixon was treated unfairly. In addition, it is my opinion that he was a good president. His accomplishments in foreign relations were extraordinary. Nixon opened China, not Carter."

Lancaster clapped. "Hear, hear," he said.

Powell stalked away, plumped down in a forward seat, and opened a report by the Senate Finance Committee on U.S. multinational corporations. Immediately he was engrossed in the report. Powell had been putting on weight; in his dark suit and white tie he reminded Scott of an overfed, forlorn penguin. Scott was feeling better. His uneasiness was gone. *The two-martini cure,* he thought, strolling toward the lavatory. His step was sprightly. He was thinking of Anne and the kids.

He opened the lavatory door and peered in. He gasped, feeling blood drain from his face and his arms run cold.

"Hank," he said, his voice strained. "Come here. Now!"

The airplane swayed. Minor turbulence cracked its side. Lancaster moved slowly, his shoulders square, his chin high. The lavatory mirror was cracked down the center, a sharp, clean crack. It was clotted with a sticky red substance that looked like blood. Pinned to the wall was a message on cardboard, its letters scrawled in red paint.

> BREEDLOVE HOGS
> TO DIE IN FAT
> HOG'S AIRPLANE

"Get Long back here," Lancaster said.

The seat-belt sign was on. The turbulence increased. "He might have all he can handle up there," Scott said.

Lancaster scowled, peering at the mirror. "That bastard hasn't done his job."

"You can't blame Long."

"I can't? Like hell I can't. It's his job not just to fly this airplane but to guard it as well." Lancaster paused, stroking his chin, as the 727 trembled. Then he said calmly, "We're going to set her down at the nearest airport. There could be a bomb aboard. We're going to land and have this mother searched from tail to nose."

"All right. We land."

The 727 jumped. Scott swayed for balance. He followed Lancaster toward the cockpit. Powell sat absorbed in his reading. Scott's knees were unsteady. The airplane pitched roughly under continuous sharp thuds of turbulence. Scott gripped a seat and stood swaying against it, his fingers clawing the fabric. He heard a sharp crack that seemed to come from below. Powell turned, regarded Scott with a dispassionate glance, and turned back. A new blast of turbulence tossed the 727 up and then sideways in a ragged zigzag pattern. Scott lost his balance and found himself thrashing on his back. He kicked. He could not rise. The ceiling whirled above him. Lights darted around him. The terrain flooded into view. He saw a twinkle of lights below. The door of an overhead compartment opened, spilling clothing and magazines. Lancaster, also on the floor, was trying to crawl toward Scott, but he couldn't make progress. He slid backward, away from Scott. He grinned, his eyes bright.

The engines screamed, a shrill, painful howl in Scott's brain. His vision was blurred. He writhed in a timeless void, hearing tiny pops in his ears, his heart thumping, his throat dry. He felt as if he'd begun to float. He had no balance. His body had no substance, no feeling. The tendons on his hands stood out. His knuckles were white. He grabbed for a seat, but it seemed to spring away from him. His fingers dug deeply into the carpeting, clutching for an anchor. Another shock wave struck the 727, a tremor that reverberated through its interior in small, rippling waves.

Then it righted. They were flying evenly.

Scott gulped air. His hands were tight balls, still clutching the floor carpeting.

Lancaster got up. He stood brushing his coat.

Powell turned in his seat. His face was expressionless. Then he slowly donned bifocals and returned to reading his report.

Soon Harold Long was there, flustered and apologetic, mumbling something about "clear air turbulence," which, he explained, doesn't show up on radar.

"Where are we?" Lancaster asked.

"Just west of Omaha."

"Can we land there? Omaha?"

"Is anyone hurt?"

"You didn't answer the question."

"Yes. Yes, we can land in Omaha."

"Then we will do so," Lancaster said.

Long returned to the cockpit. He walked slowly. Scott slumped into a seat. He felt his heart squeeze. Powell wet his finger and turned a page in the report. He sat as if nothing had happened. Now the flight was perfectly smooth, streaking on a clear path opened by a sky darkly sullen above and around them.

The 727 banked sharply, heading down.

2

LEWIS ANTHONY BREEDLOVE HAD LIVED AT NO. 1162 ON
Arbor Road in Pasadena, California, since 1938, when he had
bought two acres, sold off one, and built a house almost
exactly in the center of the other. The house was large, but
not ostentatious. Many Arbor Road residents less rich than
Breedlove had homes of greater splendor. The Breedlove
residence was one of the few in the area that had no
swimming pool or guesthouse. Three servants lived in—the
cook, Mrs. Lamson; the butler, Scoggins; and the chauffeur,
Morris. There were two full-time black maids and two Japanese gardeners. These four lived off the premises, coming to
work at 9 A.M. each weekday, like employees. The live-in
servants actually were employees, too, but had the status of
staff.

Breedlove's builder had been a domesticated Russian with a
massive walrus mustache who said he'd twice escaped from
capture by the Japanese and who claimed his degree was from
the University of Heidelberg. His ideas were avant-garde in
the extreme for his time, although Spanish-influenced. The
house was constructed on three levels and featured a center
area the builder planned as a court with a giant skylight.
Breedlove had rejected the idea out of hand, forcing the
builder to roof the court, and the result was a great enclosed
area with one row of windows and walls almost forty feet
high. For years it was used as a dining room, lighted by an
elaborate fluorescent system, but when Breedlove's art passion had burst on him in 1968, he'd had banistered walks
built from the walls at various levels and had hung his
paintings near them. The room now had the appearance of an
art museum.

The house was surrounded by huge level lawns of St.
Augustine grass, a thick, tough blade that discouraged en-
croachment by weaker species. Interspersed on the lawns
were circular beds of red-purple geraniums, a strong flower

22

that thrived and dominated with little care. Ivy constantly crept close on all sides, only to be thrust back by the chopping sickles of the Japanese gardeners. In the back or south side was a natural shelter of elm and palm trees. The other three sides were enclosed by brick walls. There was a tall outer wall on Arbor and a less substantial inner wall some thirty feet up the driveway.

Arbor Road had a culture and snobbery of its own, existing without a deliberate origin or plan. Most of its residents were unknown to each other, because they preferred it that way. It was common knowledge that a salt heir existed behind the curved window of the white house on the knoll, and that a Huntington survivor had three bulldogs behind his gate at 1172, but neither was sought out or became an object of anything but the curiosity of visitors. If the Red Cross or heart or cancer fund recruited a volunteer from Arbor Road, that volunteer solicited funds elsewhere. Real estate agents knew which people should and should not be shown homes on the road. Besides, properties on Arbor seldom came up for sale, except when estates were liquidated, and perhaps not even then, because the houses and land often passed on to descendants who took possession or sold to relatives or associates. The average value of Arbor Road properties had increased from $125,000 in 1960 to $450,000 in 1975, although that was not the official estimate of the Pasadena Realty Board. Average income was impossible to compute, and indeed unnecessary; it was assumed that few families on Arbor had net worths under one million.

Neighbors from adjoining San Marino generally regarded Pasadena people with disdain, but the resident of Arbor Road was regarded as almost a peer. Few sightseers came—the movie stars, after all, clustered in Beverly Hills or Bel Air—but those who did discovered little, for the Arbor homes lurked behind locked gates, tall hedges, and ivy-overrun fences. Dogs were there, their attitudes toward strangers seldom tested. Postmen dropped letters into fence slots. They could ring bells for attention if they had parcels too large for the slots, but they usually preferred to leave notices.

There had never been a sociological jolt on Arbor Road. When the blacks began moving into Pasadena, Arbor residents were tolerant because they were totally unaffected.

Their children were either grown and married or at SC or Stanford; if younger, they were at private schools. As for the city itself, it could handle its own problems. Arbor Road was not Pasadena. It was Arbor Road.

It was a curving lane, not widened when the autos grew wider, with narrow sidewalks on both sides and grass patches sectioned with streetlights and palm trees. The utility lines were underground, something accomplished just after the war in one of the few uniformly supported co-endeavors of the residents. The road started just south of the California Institute of Technology and twisted on to Arroyo Seco, which led to the tortuous curves of the Pasadena Freeway. At night Arbor Road was so quiet that barking dogs miles away could be heard. Arbor dogs seldom answered.

The road was a haven of business opportunities for Mexican or Japanese gardeners, but none came unsolicited or unrecommended. Only the most foolish or sophisticated of burglars would venture onto the landscape. Salesmen found it impenetrable. Its auto population was a strange mix of Chevies, Porsches, Fords, and Mercedeses. There were three Rolls-Royces, but fully a dozen Volkswagens.

Here Lewis Breedlove lived, and, in recent months, also maintained his business office. An elaborate communications system of telephones, telecopiers, and TWX receiver-senders linked him to BII headquarters in Century City and to other key offices and plants around the world. He went to his headquarters office only about once a month. Usually he worked out of the library-den of the house, surrounded by stuffed heads of deer and elk. A mounted eagle perched on the mantel, its wings spread and its talons hooked like iron claws. Breedlove's one Rembrandt was always in the den, on a tall stand before his desk.

This Sunday he'd slept past 6 A.M., an hour later than usual. Dull pain throughout his body had kept him tossing all night. He'd spent the forenoon with a company table of executive organization in a multicolor chart before him. It was difficult to concentrate. The pains came and went. He had medicine for the pain, but he feared addiction to its use. Pain, he had discovered, was somewhat a product of a man's mind. He took in a deep breath and held it. He let it out. The pain had lessened. He glanced at the Rembrandt. It seemed to help; it seemed to speak to him.

The private telephone on a stand beside his chair buzzed. Its button turned yellow. Only five persons in the world had the number. Breedlove picked up the receiver.

"Yes, Scottie," he said. "I heard that you three had an unscheduled stop on the way home from Chicago."

"I was calling to tell you about it," Scott said. "I see now that it's unnecessary."

"We do have a security department, you know. One that's overpaid to keep me at least slightly informed."

"Well, as it turned out, it was only an unpleasant scare. No bomb. Nevertheless, I think we should keep the plane under constant surveillance for a while."

"Scottie, it is under surveillance. I've done that. I don't like this any more than you do, but we'll just have to chalk it up to a sign of the times. Now, I'm not going to let myself be intimidated by a bunch of hippie would-be revolutionaries, and I don't want you to be intimidated either. I have people to handle it. I'm sorry you didn't make it with the insurance company."

"And I, too. They—"

"Say hello to Anne for me."

He hung up. A sharp pain twitched in his bowels. He ignored it and returned to the chart. A few minutes later he heard Scoggins clearing his throat.

"You enter this domain at high personal risk, Scoggins. Everything in here is dead. There are only ghosts here."

"The senator has arrived," Scoggins said.

"Scoggins, tell me something. What is it that you see here?"

"The chart, sir?"

"Does it make sense to you?"

"Mr. Breedlove, I am hardly competent to judge."

Breedlove pointed, his finger jabbing. "What you see here is a company. An organization. In some ways it is almost human. Call those lines veins. They all lead up here, to the main heart."

"Where your name is, Mr. Breedlove."

"It is a system of leadership. If a line clogs, the entire system can break down. Without leadership and without organization, nothing can function. It is then merely chaos. It is directed by a single mind. But, Scoggins, suppose. Do you think the leader's mind can be splintered, can become a centralized force of several men, and still be as effective?"

"I really could not express an opinion, sir."

"I may test the idea. I may test it soon."

"Where will you and the senator be dining?"

"We will dine where diners dine. In the dining room."

"Very well, sir."

"Was that comment unreasonable? Cantankerous?"

"No, sir."

"Would you tell me if you thought so?"

"I believe that I would, Mr. Breedlove."

"And I believe that you would not. I think you expect me to be unreasonable and cantankerous. It is seldom—is it not?—when I am otherwise. You are inhumanly patient, Scoggins. You withstood Mrs. Breedlove's rages with remarkable calm. How many servants did that woman go through?"

"I remember Mrs. Breedlove as a fine woman."

"A fine woman. A fine woman who produced a fine son."

"Yes, sir."

"I'm a rambler today, Scoggins. But a goddamn liar I'm not. Mrs. Breedlove wasn't always a lady and what she produced and called Lawrence some forty years ago reflects some of that. We are born with our seeds. Tell the senator I will see him now. And Scoggins?"

"Yes."

"I placed you in charge of the cigarette rationing. I now relieve you of that responsibility."

"Mr. Breedlove, the doctor said—"

"I no longer employ that doctor."

"Very well. I will get the cigarettes."

He hadn't smoked since yesterday noon and now was undergoing the irritation and light-headedness of withdrawal. The doctors had been trying for decades to cure him of nicotine addiction, with absolutely no success. His longest abstinence had been six days—time spent two months ago when he'd undergone a checkup at the Mayo Clinic.

He chain-smoked Luckies through the prime-rib lunch with the senator, as Scoggins hovered near them, serving, emptying ashtrays, and scowling at Breedlove's bad manners. Breedlove chuckled inwardly. Scoggins, the ultimate English snob. Horrified to see his boss in robe and slippers entertaining a senator who'd once made a run at the presidency. Appalled to hear the boss being rude, grumpy, even childish before a guest who was a national figure. Shocking bad form.

The senator was not from California. Breedlove had long ago given up on ever raising a decent, cooperative, and inexpensive California senator. Nor was this senator any longer young. He was thin and pale-faced, with fringes of gray hair around his red scalp. His White House fever eighteen years ago had won him some important primaries until he'd been swept to oblivion not by scandal or lack of funds but by the greater appeal of the Kennedy machine. He'd been on the decline ever since.

"Excellent," the senator said, sipping private-label Burgundy from Breedlove's Fresno vineyard.

Breedlove waved at Scoggins, and the butler slipped away. "You will have to taste for me," he said. "I have my brandy after dinner but I have allowed the doctors to take away my wine." He lit a Lucky Strike. "They want my cigarettes, too, of course. I tell them, 'Go fuck a duck,' an expression so crude it works. If you spill any more, Senator, Scoggins will spank you."

The senator's hand trembled as he put down his glass.

Breedlove said, "Here I am in this art-laden mausoleum with Homer and Manet and Cézanne and I can't even enjoy them because there's always some piss-ant problem no one can take care of but me. In the Senate, when you're not on vacation, you have a decision-making body. I think that's the reason—because it's a body—it takes so long to do anything there."

"It's the democratic process, Lewis."

"Lewis? Jesus, d'you know how few people call me that?"

"Then I am a privileged man."

"I named myself. There were no Breedloves where I was born."

"Where were you born?"

Breedlove scratched. He sucked his teeth. "Wisconsin," he said. "A part of Wisconsin close to hell. I ran, hopped a freight at fourteen, or I would have died. There was an old man on the freight who called himself Tony the Breed. That's where I got part of my name."

"Interesting," the senator said.

"When that old half-breed started feeling around between my legs one night, I shoved a rail spike into his belly."

The senator blanched and turned away, but he recovered quickly. "Wisconsin is a fine old state," he said.

"We can peas there," Breedlove said. "Peas and corn. Why I keep that plant open is beyond me. It was our first integrated plant and I don't think we've had a capital improvement there since we opened it. Senator, what's on your mind today?"

"Well, I realize you are a busy man."

"I am a busy man. But I agreed to see you."

"I'm grateful that you did."

"It has been a long time since we have seen each other. Much has changed, Senator, as you well know. Tell me. Are your relations with the White House cordial?"

"Yes. Very much so."

"I don't believe you."

The senator's jaw dropped. "I assure you, Lewis, that this man in the White House today has the ability to get along with everyone."

"Is he an honest man?"

"Perhaps that is his strongest point."

"And is honesty important in politics today?"

"Of course. It has always been true. Integrity—"

"I agree, Senator. I agree that in this day and age we need integrity more than anything else. I think that is more than obvious."

The senator was nodding. He avoided Breedlove's gaze. He seemed suddenly quite nervous.

"I believe this myself with strong conviction," Breedlove said. "We need trust around the world. A trust that has been lacking. We need an *image* of straightforwardness and honesty. We need a Teddy Roosevelt galloping over the hill, brandishing his sword. And not in politics alone. In our companies, too."

"Yes."

"All right. That is why I am no longer going to support you."

The senator's head snapped up. "I don't understand."

"Of course you understand. You've been on my payroll for twenty years. We have used every trick possible, you and I, and while not all of it has worked, much of it has. But nothing will work now. It's being watched too closely. Now you can go back home and spill the beans, but I don't think you will. You'll find the beans spattered all over your face if you do."

"You will be hurt, too."

"I will not be hurt, Senator. I have a company of three hundred thousand employees and five hundred thousand stockholders. It's beyond getting hurt. It's too important to this country and to the world to get hurt. As for me personally, Senator, you see that I am an old man. Old men cannot be hurt very much. I do not care too much about myself personally. I have a company that will go on. It is more important than I am. No. *You* listen!"

Breedlove was on his feet, pacing. "Senator, I'm of an age where my views are not supposed to change. But mine do change. I have a lot of years to look back on. They were years of incredible change and opportunity. Depressions. Wars. Upheaval. You have to change with the times, grow with them, or you die. I haven't read the books on philosophy or history. I've experienced them. I've lived them."

The senator's mouth was moving. He wanted to say something. He squirmed uncomfortably. Breedlove watched him. He chuckled.

"No," he said, waving his hand. "I'm the talker now, because I'm an old man, but I used to be the listener. I learned from listening. I can sum it up. You're born with a head and a body, but also with something else that is more important. It is your wanting. Your will. Mine was to create this company. It was all and it is all. Some people want children or to write books or paint pictures. Some want to be President. In the same way, I wanted this company. I have it. It cannot come down. Not now. And it must be guided by someone who sees the temper of the times. You've done your service for it. There is nothing more you can do, except damage it. You cannot go to the White House now and it's likely that you couldn't have gone at any time in the past. You can only hurt us, a man of your reputation. It may also be true that I myself can do little for the company now. Except one thing. Assure its immediate future by managerial selection. All men have their ends, Senator, but if in their time they create something that is vital, that entity lives beyond them. Perhaps our times are over. A gracious exit is the measure of a man."

The senator's jaw moved. No words came out. Then he said calmly, "I believe, sir, that you are mad."

"It is possible," Breedlove said. "And now Scoggins will show you out."

After the senator had left, Breedlove sat for a long time in front of the fire in his library, listening to his heart pump, breathing rapidly, and studying his Rembrandt. Scoggins appeared, carrying a silver tray with a glass of milk and three large pills encapsulated in thin yellow plastic. He stood guard until Breedlove swallowed the pills; then he slipped out, leaving Breedlove with his fire, his Rembrandt, and his thoughts. Slowly Breedlove ran his hand over the painting. He felt the fine brushstrokes. His eyes rolled. He chuckled. He let out a rush of air that whistled in his teeth. His heartbeat had slowed. There was no pain.

Mad? Yes, perhaps mad. But, if mad, a fine madness, a controllable madness. He'd been in control before the senator. He'd merely told the truth. The senator had come to him prepared to beg; a man reduced to beggary was of no use to anyone or to himself. Breedlove snuggled closer to the fire. He rubbed his thin white hands together. The fire was hot on the back of his neck, warming his brain, making him conscious of the rush of blood in his temples. Lately he'd found himself given to quick, short bursts of temper, an exploding impatience that brought heat to his face and quickened his pulse. Even small matters bothered him. He'd never been a patient man, but he'd always been able to control his temper. Now he raged easily—at an inoperative light bulb, at inefficiency among his domestics, at business subordinates who were less than perfect in the execution of their duties. The rages usually subsided quickly. No doubt many persons thought him to be odd, eccentric. But only the senator had called him mad.

Again he chuckled. He felt calm. Mad? Well, he had lunched with the senator in slippers and a blue robe, a sharp contrast to the senator's tailored gray suit and thin maroon tie. Breedlove had intended to change, but, when the senator had arrived, he'd decided it would be a delicious prank to greet him in lounging attire. A tactic the aberration of a madman? No. The senator had been made to realize at the outset that Breedlove was receiving him with disdain. The message had been plain and effective.

Breedlove donned thin bifocals and peered at his Rembrandt. It was a little-known work, purchased for $440,000 in his behalf by Andre LaMont, the Paris art dealer. It was a portrait of a man in a greatcoat, wearing a red shawl. LaMont believed it to be an early version of Rembrandt's Jan Six portrait, perhaps about 1650. LaMont said he'd stake his reputation on its authenticity. The man in the portrait stared from a dark background with a defiant, knowing look. He was a man undefeated and unconquerable. As he gazed without, he seemed to be also gazing at himself within. The hands, clutching gloves, were extraordinary. They seemed warm to Breedlove's touch. He could almost feel the outline of the tendons, the skin texture, the veins. This was a man of mystic background and of significant stature. He was a man who saw death, but defied it; he was a man who felt pain, but ignored it.

When Breedlove looked at the portrait, he saw himself. The figure gave him strength. He was himself a man of advanced age and of varied experiences, one now with false teeth and hollow cheeks and a red pate where hair once had been, but he was not a defeated man. He did not see death, nor did he fear death. Death could be met and overthrown. He saw life. Life as in the bright landscapes and durable figures of the Cézannes, life as in the sea-defiant men of Winslow Homer, life-rage as in the unyielding eyes of the Rembrandt man.

Breedlove did not regard himself as an art expert—he hadn't the time—but he bought art for more than just investment. He bought only what appealed to him. It had begun on a trip to Paris in 1968, when he'd acquired his first Monet. After that, art acquisition had become a minor obsession. The colors and the patterns of the Impressionists—with the exception of Van Gogh, who'd gone too far—caught and held him. His taste in art was catholic and tolerant unless the painting was of a religious nature. He even had a small store of modern American art, which he kept crated. Rembrandt, to LaMont the king of the world's painters, hadn't at first appealed to Breedlove; he'd found the tones, the dark backgrounds, the figures themselves depressing and uninspiring. But when his Rembrandt had arrived nine months ago, Breedlove had known almost immediately that he had to have it, and more. *The blind Homer? Aristotle and Homer? Danaë?* No no no, LaMont had insisted. Unreachable. Yes yes yes, Breedlove had answered. Find me the unreachable.

He arose and slowly made his way up the main staircase to his bedroom. He admitted to a touch of emphysema, an inevitability brought on by decades of heavy smoking, and he bowed slightly to the disease by pausing for breath. The bedroom was cold and vast and austere; as he entered it, Breedlove paused and glanced around, as if he expected to see someone there. He had scheduled another appointment for that afternoon, one with a man he hadn't seen for many years but had known intimately in his youth—Philip Mendenthal, a New York proxy fighter who'd learned his trade as a self-made lawyer on Robert Young's staff. Mendenthal had called the office for an appointment last week, and Breedlove, receiving the message, had said, "Tell him Sunday, two P.M." Now he found himself almost completely incurious about Mendenthal's wanting to see him. He had, in fact, forgotten Mendenthal, just as he'd put all the struggles of his early years out of his mind. It was history.

Before the meeting, Scoggins served him two more pills, this time with water, and stoked up the flames in the library fireplace. He said, "While you were bathing, sir, there was a message. A Mr. LaMont."

"What does LaMont want?"

"He wants to see you, sir."

"He's in L.A.?"

"Yes. He left a number. He said that it was extremely important. Something about a painting, sir."

"Of course it would be something about a painting. He's a dealer in paintings."

"I'm sorry, Mr. Breedlove."

"Is Mendenthal here?"

"Yes, sir."

"All right. Send Mendenthal in. Then call LaMont and tell him I'll see him here at six. What else is it?"

"Mr. Lancaster called, sir, to remind you to watch"—Scoggins referred to a notebook—"to watch a CBS special at nine. The Drug Division is the sponsor."

"Can you remember to tape it instead?"

"Of course, Mr. Breedlove."

Breedlove slumped into his chair before the fireplace. He sat perfectly still, his fingertips joined, his eyes half closed, awaiting Philip Mendenthal. For the first time that day, he concentrated on Mendenthal. It stirred memories of his start—a leaky tent in a San Fernando Valley apricot orchard, visions of land primeval and rich and unviolated, the first tomato cannery, the Mexican pickers stooped in the fields like machines. It had not become big by accident or luck; it had become big by design. And now Mendenthal was before him again, a man he could not shake, a foolish man who dissipated time and energy by nourishing hatred; a tall gray man in a dark suit, unrecognizable from the past except for his penetrating hawk's eyes and large curved nose with its thin nostrils that dilated with a tiny hollow rattle as he breathed.

They did not shake hands. "Time has served you well," Breedlove said.

"I cannot say the same for you."

"I shouldn't expect you to, Philip. From what I recall of you, you are not a person given to exaggeration or flattery."

"What else do you recall of me, Lewis?"

"That I learned from you. That you aided me when I was young. That we learned together. And that you were once a person of foolish emotional makeup."

Mendenthal shrugged. "May I sit down?"

"If you wish. If I appear unattentive, it is from the pills. Do the doctors have you on pills?"

"My health has remained very good."

"Will you tell me now what your business is with me?"

"I want your child."

"I have no child," Breedlove said.

"I don't mean your sons."

"My son has left, long ago."

Mendenthal was seated, his hat on the arm of the chair. "As you know, I have followed your progress closely. I trust you have followed mine."

"You are here to tell me that you are wealthy."

"National Casualty turned you down."

"I am startled to discover you know about that."

"You are a mask, Lewis, an iron mask," Mendenthal said. "I spoke with the chairman of National Casualty before your representatives met with him."

"Your recommendation to him may have hurt him."

"I made no recommendation."

"You should not lie, Philip. Your eyes betray you."

Mendenthal drew a white handkerchief from his pocket and mopped his brow. "When I mentioned your child, I did not mean your offspring. I meant your company."

"It is not in your league."

"I have a merger proposal."

"Is that what you've become? A merger broker?"

"You know full well what I am, and what I do."

"I do, yes. You're a Jew who chases me for his living."

"My associates and I control Dimension Corporation. Dimension, in turn, controls seven companies. We're in retailing, steel, shipping, cosmetics, construction. It would fit well with BII."

"It would not fit. You're leveraged to high heaven. For every dime in your treasury, you owe thirty."

"I propose to merge BII into Dimension."

"BII *into* Dimension?" Breedlove sighed tolerantly. "Philip, my poor Philip. I'm four times your size."

"Mayer Drugs was bigger than you when you acquired it."

"That was years ago. You can't merge like that now."

"I believe that you can."

Breedlove allowed himself a luxurious crudity—a prolonged, deliberate fart. "Philip, your proposal isn't worth what I just did," he said slowly. "Now tell me the real reason why you're here. And spare me the dramatics."

"You leave me no choice. We will gain control of BII by proxy solicitation."

"You tried that before. You failed. Miserably."

"We are much stronger now."

Breedlove felt his heartbeat rise. He must not lose his temper. It was so foolish. He had admitted a man to his home he hadn't talked with for many, many years, an old enemy who had publicly vowed he would someday gain control of BII, a statement so asinine, so foolish that Breedlove ignored it. This must end. But Mendenthal was making it even worse now. He had begun to talk about the past. Breedlove closed his eyes. His chin dropped. He felt the warmth of the fire.

"If you don't mind," he said, "the pope will take a nap. You jabber on as much as you like."

"I'm as wary of a sleeping lion as of one who growls,"

Mendenthal said. "You see, you no longer deceive me, as you once did. When you came on my land, asking for work, I saw only a sick person who repaid me by ravaging not only my land but also my niece. Do you remember Rebecca?"

"No," Breedlove mumbled.

"She is still alive."

Breedlove opened his eyes. Had he dozed off? No longer did he feel tired. He glared into Mendenthal's eyes.

"Philip, we have nothing to discuss. I do not dwell on the past. It is the now which is important, the now and the future."

"I see no future for you."

"You have never seen very much of the future."

Mendenthal glanced around. "I had heard you've become a collector of art. Is that a Rembrandt?"

"It is a Rembrandt."

"An obscure, early Rembrandt. Is it your favorite?"

Breedlove snapped his palms together. "Philip, our business has ended. Ask Scoggins to show you out."

"You are not afraid?"

"Of you? Of course not."

"You have other enemies."

"We all have enemies."

"Your enemies are personal. They are from your seed."

"A man who has enemies also has protectors."

"You are in danger, Lewis."

Breedlove belched ceremoniously and began an exaggerated sucking of his teeth. Blood surged hotly in his brain. He jabbed his little finger violently into his ear, digging so hard he brought a tiny blot of blood to his nail. He stared at Mendenthal, his hands locked, his thumbs rotating rapidly around each other.

"I am going to tell you something, Philip, something you should know by now," he said slowly. "I want you to listen carefully to me, and if you do listen I think that you will end this nonsense right here. First of all, let me say that I believe you. I do believe you are willing to commit a million dollars or more in a proxy fight to gain control of my company. And you have apparently convinced your associates that it is not a useless undertaking. But, deep down, you yourself know that it is. I have already reminded you of your previous failure."

"Young didn't get the Central on the first try, either."

"That was years and years ago. It was another period. And, I might add, after he succeeded, where did it get him? But I'm not going to push that point, Philip. But I am going to say that proxy fights are not for people like you and me. Not any longer. They're for movieland people. You do not take over big companies by proxy contest any more. Do I have to tell you that? You're a foolish man, Philip. You are guided by your emotions, not your head. You have some personal whim, some decades-old grudge, and apparently you think you can satisfy it by making trouble for me. But you cannot make trouble for me. It's too big, Philip. It's far too big for you. Give it up. Now. Can I put it any simpler for you? Philip?"

Mendenthal leapt up. "I am filing our intention to engage in proxy solicitation for control of Breedlove International with the Securities and Exchange Commission in Washington next week."

Breedlove gazed into the fire. He spoke calmly. "I want you to realize something, Philip. I want you to realize that your threats may well backfire if you attempt another proxy fight. You will risk your organization, your personal funds, and your life."

"So now you threaten me?"

"Did you not threaten me?"

"I did not threaten. I merely warned you."

"Bullshit. Jewish bullshit. You are a child, Philip."

Mendenthal paced. Perspiration ran down his face. "We have a good chance. You realize that. Look at your *real* profit record at BII. Not what you tell the stockholders, but what you're *really* earning. Look at the acquisitions that went sour. And look, look at you. You're old. You're sick. You're almost finished. Another big proxy fight with me certainly would be the death of you."

"Or, as I said, of you," Breedlove said.

Andre LaMont arrived an hour before his appointed time, and Breedlove let the art dealer pace excitedly in the reception room while he finished his early dinner, a fillet of salmon with a green salad followed by a quarter glass of Felipe II, a Spanish brandy. He never saw a man until the exact moment of the appointment; if a man arrived late, he found his appointment canceled. The reception room, adjacent to the library, was a small, high-ceilinged square with bare yellow walls and a single window. It was furnished with four high-backed chairs of indeterminable vintage, a glass coffee table stocked with back copies of *Barron's* and *Fortune,* and two artificial potted plants. It had originally been used to store visitors' hats and coats.

When LaMont was admitted to the library, Breedlove saw a man so visibly agitated that he was at the point of collapse. LaMont's face was white and strained. His miniature hands jerked spasmodically. His mouth twitched.

"I've come from Paris only today," he managed to say slowly, his English precise.

Breedlove said, "What about the Rembrandts? Have you located any more?"

"No, no, no, no," LaMont said. "Mr. Breedlove, it is about the Rembrandt that I have come here today."

"My Rembrandt?"

"May I look at it?"

"You see it there."

LaMont moved across the floor in little dancing steps. Then he retraced his steps, opened his briefcase, and removed a small zippered leather case. He unzipped it with an exaggerated effort and took out a magnifying glass and a steel tweezers. Then he scurried back to the painting and began to examine it under the glass, probing delicately with the tweezers. Finally he looked at Breedlove.

"A forgery," he said.

"What?"

"A forgery. Not even a good forgery."

Breedlove was up, bending near LaMont. "What are you talking about? A forgery? You certified its authenticity."

"I certified the authenticity of an authentic Rembrandt. This is not the painting I certified. Almost to the naked eye it is a forgery. This is not the painting I brought to you, Mr. Breedlove."

"Jesus Christ, LaMont, will you make sense?"

"I cannot make sense of it. The authentic Rembrandt, the Rembrandt that was here, in this house, has been offered for bidding by a Venice dealer, a disreputable dealer, I must add." LaMont's knuckles hit the frame of the painting. "This, it is worthless. Worthless! You have been robbed."

"I have not been robbed. I could not have been robbed. It

would be impossible. That painting hasn't been out of my eyesight for more than—" He paused. His heart was pounding. He felt rising anger. He turned on LaMont. "You! You are the fraud, the forgery! What do you take me for? What is your game?"

"My game, Mr. Breedlove, my *game,* as you put it, is the location, sale, and delivery of authentic masterworks of European art. I delivered to you, sir, an authentic Rembrandt. It was in this house. It has been removed from this house and a cheap forgery has been substituted for it." LaMont lifted his eyebrows and regarded Breedlove with a dignified, haughty stare. "You may rant at me, you may rave at me, but I am not a man capable of duplicity, sir. And, in works of art, I do not make mistakes. I have come here from Paris, across your country to this city, this disorganized, uncultured citadel of *gasoline pumps,* and I have called repeatedly, been forced to pace in a square waiting room, and—"

Breedlove sighed. "All right, LaMont. We'll make a pact. You calm down and I will."

"So you now believe me? This is a forgery?"

"No," Breedlove said.

"No? No? No?" LaMont stomped to his briefcase, deposited the magnifying glass, stroked his mustache twice, and assumed a military stance. "Good night, sir."

"LaMont. Before you leave."

"Yes?"

"I want you to do something for me. I want you to remain silent about this matter. I do not want it investigated."

"I will notify the proper authorities, of course."

"No. No, you will not. If, as you claim, this painting is a fake, it is I who have been victimized. So any complaint would be mine to file. If you want to do business with me in the future, you will not mention this matter. Look into it for me only. Perhaps I will want to repurchase the painting."

LaMont considered. Then he said, "Very well."

The staff of domestics at the Breedlove estate operated under the principle of decentralized management. Scoggins had his area, Mrs. Lamson hers, and the chauffeur, Morris, his. A housekeeper named Mona Luce had once been there, bossing the maids and anyone else submissive enough to take it, but the position had not been refilled after Mrs. Luce had left the Breedlove service in 1962. She'd quit finally in a huff, over some disagreement, after having left and returned several times. The present staff still talked about it, but no one, not even the inquisitive Mrs. Lamson, had been able to determine why Mrs. Luce had departed so suddenly after nearly twenty-five years of service. The maids now operated without direct supervision, something unheard-of when Mrs. Breedlove had been alive. Scoggins thought their effectiveness was questionable indeed.

Despite the autonomy, there was a status ranking in the household, and, with Mrs. Luce gone, it placed Scoggins at the front. He led in age and time of service. His quarters consisted of two upstairs room and a private bath. Mrs. Lamson had only a single room. Her bathroom was down the hall. The maids were known to use it. Morris had a comfortable loft above the garage.

Scoggins was an authentic Englishman who could trace his heritage back to the Battle of Hastings. He'd been at Dunkirk; he'd watched Spitfires and Hurricanes over London. He'd joined Breedlove in 1947, his only position in the States. Now, at sixty-two, he was pondering retirement. His wife had died in 1950 and his daughter, a singer in a touring European band, seldom communicated with him any more. They used to write long letters to each other. He'd urge her to come to America; she'd urge him to retire to a cottage in England. Now he hadn't heard from her for a year. He still wrote long letters to her.

He knew his role. He played it well. He was efficient, imperturbable, humorless, genuinely morose—perfect foils to Breedlove's irascibility and frequent temper tantrums. Long ago Breedlove had advised him to buy BII stock, but Scoggins considered all American securities dangerously speculative. His salary was $285 a week, which he deemed adequate. He had $44,500 on deposit at Home Savings, Pasadena branch. His status entitled him to a weekly cleaning of his rooms, but he was an intensely private man who regarded the maids as incompetent snoops, so he cleaned his area himself. His principal amusement was derived from English mystery novels; he sincerely believed them to be vastly superior to

American ones. On Mondays, his day off, he donned a black derby, and, with an umbrella staff to ward off dogs and children, both objects of utter detestation, he marched stiffly down Colorado Boulevard from Pasadena City College almost to the Rose Bowl, a spectacle so predictable and punctual that local merchants set their clocks by its appearance.

Breedlove was always in bed by 9 P.M., rising at 5 A.M., but tonight he changed his pattern. About eight, Scoggins saw him emerge from the library and enter what was now called the art room. Breedlove inspected the paintings on all levels. Once he crouched on his hands and knees like a sniffing animal, peering at a Cézanne landscape. Then he returned to the library, trailed by cigarette smoke, and closed the door. At ten he summoned Scoggins through the house intercom. Scoggins drew on his coat, tapped lightly on the library door, and entered. Breedlove's appearance gave him a momentary start. He seemed to have aged in a few hours. The firelight danced on his face, emphasizing the deep shriveled creases and yellowed skin. He sat slumped in his chair. Then he spoke. His voice was clear.

"Tell me, Scoggins. I was in Philadelphia for a few days a month or so ago."

"Sir, it was Minnesota. Rochester, Minnesota."

"Yes, I was there, too. You were here, were you not, during the time I was gone?"

"Yes, sir."

"The entire time?"

"Yes."

"Were there any visitors during my absence?"

"Only Mr. Lawrence, sir."

Breedlove's head snapped up. "Lawrence? What do you mean? You allowed Lawrence to stay here?"

"Why, you remember, Mr. Breedlove, I telephoned you when he came here, asking to stay a few days, and you granted permission."

"I did not."

"Very, well, sir."

"So you assume, because you have been with me for a while, that these rooms are apartments for rental?"

"No, sir. I do not assume that, Mr. Breedlove."

"Did he stay in his old room?"

"No, sir. Mr. Lawrence slept in the room once occupied by Mrs. Luce."

"How long did he stay?"

"Three nights."

Breedlove worked his fingers into a tightly intermeshed ball and regarded his servant with a cold, fixed stare. "I will tell you this only once. Lawrence is never again to come into this house. We do not operate a hotel for outcasts and expatriates. Lawrence had his chance. He did not take it. Is that clear to you?"

"Yes, sir."

"Once I thought the boy had a brain and some spunk. Now I know he is dim-witted and lazy. He does not belong in this household. He has not belonged here for many years. Now tell me this. While he was here, did he have visitors?"

"No, sir. None."

Breedlove turned away and closed his eyes. Scoggins slipped quietly out. Mrs. Lamson swooped to his side as he fumbled for his key outside his rooms, her large prying eyes twisted in a narrow squint.

"You ask me, I say he's actin' mighty queer, Mr. Breedlove is. I think he's gone slightly balmy, you ask me."

"I do not recall asking your opinion on any matter, Mrs. Lamson."

"Well! Well, you have it, never mind askin' or not."

She stalked away.

Downstairs at midnight, deep in his enormous bed under layers of blankets, Lewis Breedlove lay shivering and fighting sharp incursions of pain and anger. The pills no longer fully stopped the pain. He fought the pain with anger. Now he was convinced the Rembrandt was a forgery. Its texture, color, and lines spoke to him of its falseness. Yet once, in this house, he'd had an authentic Rembrandt. He had been robbed; he had been tricked. It would not go unavenged. He had private means of discovery, which he would soon set in motion. He knew this much. It was more than the mere theft of a painting. There was a developing plot against him, perhaps even against the company. Apparently Philip Mendenthal knew something about it, had at least some hint of it. Perhaps Mendenthal, Breedlove's severest and most enduring enemy, knew quite a bit about it. Perhaps the old Jew had come to him, his chin high and proud, not really to suggest merger or announce his plan to start another proxy fight, but instead to drop hints that would frighten him into acquiescence and compliance. If so, Mendenthal was truly a fool, one who grossly underestimated his antagonist.

He would find out. He would find out soon.

The pain thumped in his groin and stomach. He lay stiffly. He heard the far-off cry of a bird. He feared nights because he could not be sure at his age of living to see another day. Yet now, in the darkness, he felt a strange clairvoyance. The past ran before him in a hundred bright, shifting phantasmagoric scenes. He saw himself in the strength of his youth. Before him stretched the land in the California valleys which he'd acquired to use as the base for his grand design. BII. He had created it. He had not given up before. He would not give up now.

Finally he slept. His hands were clenched.

A light rain began to fall on Arbor Road. The houses behind their iron fences were dark and indistinguishable from the street. The guard dogs stretched their chins on their forepaws and slept lightly. A she-rat in a nest high in a palm tree cuddled her young, pink forms squirming for nourishment. The rain was as soft and as quiet as death.

Victoria Scoggins took the steam-powered *vaporetto* across the Grand Canal to the island of the Piazza San Marco. In her pants suit from a Piccadilly shop she stood breathless and squirming amid the chattering Japanese tourists with cameras and bags slung across their chests like protective armament. It was a bright day, cloudless and hot. She passed through St. Mark's Square, walking with a determined stride, pushing through the tourist horde now maneuvering for position to be photographed with their favorite prop, the clusters of pigeons that held sway over the area with a territorial dominance at once imperial and innocent. She was thinking of a time when she'd been fifteen. Her father, now butler to a rich man in the States, had taken her on a motor trip from London to Dover. They had passed through vast green stretches of English countryside and had stopped at a cottage at nightfall. The cottage had been in her dreams ever since. She wanted to be there now. Perhaps she soon would. After this business. The medieval buildings rose around her. She passed the dank, sagging palaces of the old lords, now settling into the ooze like hulks of grounded ships, and turned up a crooked little street where merchants sold trinkets to foreigners with lira-swollen pocketbooks. She went into an art shop.

"*Buon giorno,*" she said to the proprietor, a fat, ashen-faced old man.

He looked at her. His thick lips curled upward. "*Buon giorno,*" he said. Quickly he ushered her into a back room. He stood wringing his hands. His eyes were sunken into the fleshy folds of his face. "There is no doubt," he said in English. "It is an authentic Rembrandt."

"That I told you when I brought it to you."

"But we must check, you understand."

"How much will it bring?"

"That is yet to be determined. There will be commissions, you understand."

"And commissions on commissions, no doubt."

"Your father is a very fortunate man to have received such a legacy as this."

"He took enough shit for it," she said. She lit a cigarette, an American Salem. "When will you know about the money?"

"Soon."

"How soon is soon?"

"A week. Perhaps two."

"Well, you do your goddamnedest to hurry it up. Our group is leaving this pigeon-shit place pretty soon."

She left, hurrying to the square. The sinking palaces of the past were etched against the sky.

The bearded man in the tattered green coat came out of the fog in Venice, California, into the noisy crush of people at the Oarhouse bar and restaurant, thinking that this was an ideal place for conspirators to meet and plot. He was thinking clearly this evening. Often he did not think clearly. He pushed past the hanging fishnets and other sea symbols—oars and anchors and model ships and splintered mast poles—directly to his target, a clean-shaven man with an ugly, pitted face who might be older than he and who might be younger.

The man was eating a fish that still had its head on and was drinking red wine in great gulps. The fish's eyes looked alive.

"To Lewis Breedlove," the man said, raising his glass. "We will drink to the start of a successful journey."

"I don't want to drink."

"You drank in Paris."

"That was Paris."

"It is operation go. The English lady you met in Paris now has the old man's Rembrandt. The Chicago trick was done by amateurs, but soon we'll have professionals."

"What Chicago trick?"

"It is unimportant. The important is what will come, my brother."

"Stop calling me that."

"You are Lewis Breedlove's son."

"I don't know whose son I am."

"You are afraid."

"I still don't like this. I don't know. Sometimes I want to get out of this. I don't know."

"You need confidence in yourself. I will give you purpose and confidence. He is only a man, a weak old man."

"You do not know him."

"I know this," the man said. "We cannot stop now. It is only beginning. Phase the first is over, phase the second begins." The man ate heartily, smacking his lips as he drank wine. "For both of us, it is a rebirth," he said. His eyes were very bright, burning out of a ruined face from a brain that very likely was mad.

3

THE COMPANY HAD OPERATED OUT OF SEVERAL LOCATIONS, AND under three different names, since its founding in the San Fernando Valley in 1923. Breedlove had incorporated it as Coast Foods Company, and initially it had been headquartered wherever he'd hung his hat—in a cellar room with a single slant window below the first tomato-canning plant, in a back room of a Van Nuys warehouse, and, by 1927, in leased offices on Wilshire Boulevard. The 1920s, the 1940s, and the 1960s had been the company's most prosperous decades. Its name had been changed to Sterling Foods in 1928, to reflect its principal brand name. Also, Breedlove had sold stock to the public for the first time that year, and the investment banker, Sutro of San Francisco, agreed that the name change would help the stock's marketability. During the depression, headquarters had shifted rapidly, from a succession of offices reconverted out of inoperative plant space to, in 1934, a deserted railroad station in East Los Angeles. New bank financing in 1935 gave Breedlove a burst of life. Then World War II came. Business increased sharply. New plants were opened. The staff was moved back to leased offices on Wilshire. The postwar international expansion, coupled with a domestic acquisition binge, necessitated a vast buildup of headquarters staff. Additional space was leased, and soon the line staff was splintered in three different areas. Studies began on centralizing the staff in 1965, and it was decided that the company, now called Breedlove International, should construct its own building. The banks and oil companies were staying downtown, putting up high rises, but Breedlove personally abhorred downtown Los Angeles. The Realty Division recommended Century City and Breedlove bought the idea. Construction of the Breedlove Building began in 1969, and the headquarters staff was comfortably settled in by the spring of 1972. The location had several advantages, such as proximity to the major airport and to a first-class hotel, the Century Plaza.

The building was not within the development; it was on the fringe. It was a straight, bleak thirty-story tower, square and sleek, directly in the center of a five-acre plot. There was a fountain in the lobby, a heliport on top, and parking for 4,000 autos underground. Nothing distinguished it from its counterparts in the area. It was functional, solid, and inconspicuous in the maze of buildings around it. Breedlove International occupied the top five floors; the rest was leased to real estate developers, mortgage bankers, stockbrokers, mutual funds, law firms. The Pacific Ocean was in clear view from offices to the west and south.

This was BII's command post, directing thirty-six domestic and twenty-one foreign plants, housing top executives for marketing, finance, industrial relations, production, and foreign operations. BII had three main domestic divisions—Drugs (both prescription and non-prescription); Food (including soft drinks, pet food, and dairy products); Farm Machinery (including trucks, camping equipment, and mobile homes). During its 1966–73 acquisition binge it had absorbed companies in factoring, auto rental, electronics, and printing. Some had been acquired through a "cut the offer" technique inspired by Breedlove. He'd offer shareholders a certain amount for their stock, and if the company's directors balked he'd cut the offer, resulting in class action lawsuits from shareholders who reasoned they had lost a chance to sell at a higher price. Often, threatened by court action, directors of target companies capitulated, recommending a sellout to BII at a compromise price.

The building's night life consisted of black and Chicano cleaning crews shuffling lackadaisically through corridors and suites, pushing carts and toting bags, mechanical as robots, bored, incommunicative, morose. Weekday activity began about 7 A.M, when night guards gave way to day guards. The first day guard to arrive was usually pudgy, red-faced Tim Hooten, a former Waldorf doorman who'd come west when the Dodgers had deserted Brooklyn. Hooten was a keen observer of status. He could tell class by the cut of a suit or by stride. BII employees were different from the employees in leased offices. They seemed to have more style. They took separate elevators—two of the seven stopped only on the top three floors—but a sharp-eyed observer could tell them even if he didn't know about the elevators. No sports coats or pants suits went into Breedlove elevators—even, it seemed, on visitors. Breedlove shoes were shined. Breedlove clothing was unwrinkled; Breedlove secretaries were prettier, Breedlove executives trimmer.

So, this Monday morning, Hooten's normally alert antennae sent loud bells clanging in his head when the slovenly bearded man in a dirty green coat and Levi's wavered into his ken and slumped toward the sacred Breedlove elevator. The coat wasn't a cheap one.

"Jus' where you think you're headed, eh?" Hooten said.

The man cowered back. "Breedlove," he said. "Breedlove." His eyes were hidden under sunglasses. He said, "Breed—"

Hooten heard no more. The man offered no resistance, as if he were used to collaring, as Hooten ushered him out.

Except for arrival at work and for claiming his Dodger Stadium box seat each home-game night, Hooten was not one to follow precise routine, but he liked to observe the routines of others. His favorite was the Henriette Tompkins phenomenon. Exactly at 7:30 A.M. each weekday, as punctual and as predictable as the sun, she parked her Mercedes coupé in the downstairs garage, clicked her heels across the concrete to the elevator, pushed the button, waited for five seconds, and rode to the lobby to catch the express to the thirtieth floor. Hooten could tell her exact location below by the movement of the second hand on his watch.

He snapped his fingers. The elevator opened.

"Good morning, Miss Tompkins," he said.

She nodded curtly. Today she was in black and was wearing a wide-brimmed hat. It was her Monday purse, the patent leather. And the gloves; always the white gloves. She was in the tower elevator. The door closed.

"Fuck you, Miss Tompkins," Hooten said, opening his *Sporting News*. "No one else has."

He was wrong. Someone had fucked Henriette Tompkins, although it had been many, many years ago. The man was Lewis Breedlove. There had been some close calls, after Breedlove, groping hands and even a few kisses that had quickened her pulse rate and heartbeat; yet, since him, she had never gone all the way with a man, perhaps not even close to it. She'd always been able to maneuver away, to mount effective excuses or resistance before it was too late. She'd had one man. She needed no other. She was entirely self-sufficient. She did not think about happiness or a social life or friends. She had not thought about sex for decades. She thought only of Breedlove International, and of Lewis Breedlove. She had been his private secretary since shortly after the company's founding. It was entirely possible that he had said more words to her than to any other person he'd known in his life.

It took forty seconds for the elevator to reach the top floor. Henriette Tompkins had her keys out when the door opened. She turned on the pale fluorescent ceiling lights in the

Breedlove International reception area. She inspected the potted plants for dust, the chairs and sofa for spots, the carpet for ashes, the magazines for ripped pages. She noted with disgust that a small crack still showed in the wood paneling. Maintenance had been alerted last Friday. Nothing had been done. Feeling slight rage, Miss Tompkins opened the door and entered the corridor to the executive offices.

This portion of the thirtieth floor was an inner sanctum for officers of vice-presidential rank or above. Along the corridor were seven oak-doored suites without nameplates. Each suite contained a separate office for secretaries—vice-presidents had two each, Lewis Breedlove had three—and, deeper within, the executive's office. Breedlove's, at the end of the corridor, was no larger or better furnished than any other on thirty. On both sides of Breedlove's office were huge double doors, of darker oak than the others. One led to the boardroom, a long, narrow enclosure with practical nylon carpeting and Swedish mahogany paneling dominated by a giant oval table of Washington redwood; the other opened to the executive dining room, a pale-blue room with a bar and signed Picasso lithographs on the walls. Both areas had identical washrooms, except that the dining-room washroom had silver-plated taps and the taps in the boardroom had 14-karat gold plating. Nothing was fake on thirty. The wood was real, the plants had life, the desk pads were leather, the ashtrays and bud vases were Irish crystal.

The vice-presidents—called "corridor executives" behind their backs by staff members on twenty-nine and twenty-eight, a phrase Miss Tompkins abhorred—were entitled to furnish their offices to their tastes, with a $21,000 budget, but boundaries were outlined in a corporate manual personally edited by Breedlove. The manual prescribed the thickness of the carpeting and established general rules of taste on such matters as paintings, desks, guest chairs, and filing cabinets. No bright colors were allowed. No coat racks were allowed. Individual bars were outlawed. Bookcases were encouraged, if built in, but it was suggested the books be of uniform size. Elaborate art books were furnished from central purchasing for display on tables. An executive could bring in his own art books, as long as they were not the Time-Life series or anything on Walt Disney or pop art. A vice-president could have pictures of his wife and family on his desk, but not on the walls. Wallpapering was permitted only in the individual washrooms. Wood paneling was allowed, but discouraged; if used, it was limited to one wall and to dark woods. No pictures of BII facilities, even the portfolio that had once been featured in *Fortune,* were permitted. During the heat of the first proxy fight with the Philip Mendenthal forces, Breedlove had been on the cover of *Time* once and on the cover of *Business Week* twice. BII's public-relations director had ordered hundreds of covers framed, and they had begun to appear on executive-office walls. The office decorum manual stopped that, prohibiting the display of Mr. Breedlove's photograph or likeness. Only Miss Tompkins knew the reason for the rule. Mr. Breedlove had not liked either picture, particularly the *Time* one.

It was widely suspected that the office rules had been authored by Miss Tompkins, but that did not matter, for it was known they had Breedlove's sanction. Everything Miss Tompkins did, in fact, had Breedlove's sanction, and as a result she knew she was feared by many and hated by some. This gave her neither satisfaction nor concern. She was concerned only with her own efficiency and effectiveness—both considered extraordinary—and with the health, image, and progress of Lewis Breedlove and Breedlove International.

Now she was in her own area, an office adjacent to Mr. Breedlove's, removing her hat and gloves, running a cloth over her desk (maintenance men dared not touch it), opening the drapes to the morning's sunlight. These were moments she enjoyed, alone on the thirtieth floor and perhaps the only person in any office of the Breedlove Building, and it gave her a secret sense of possessiveness. But she was not really possessive. Except for her Mercedes, her furnishings from Barker Brothers in the Westwood apartment, a small Goya sketch Mr. Breedlove had given her, and an excellent Saks wardrobe (including a treasured Gucci bag she carried only on trips overseas), she had accumulated very little during her years with Mr. Breedlove. There was money, of course; quite a bit of money. But she neither wanted nor needed that. She wanted and needed proximity to Lewis Breedlove. She had been with him, had listened when he spoke of his dreams and visions, had watched as he turned them into reality. She had intimately known a great man. It was enough.

Her private line buzzed. "Yes, sir," she said.

He did not say good morning. Usually he was courteous, but today he was gruff. She didn't notice. She was used to his moods. She listened.

"I'll begin immediately, Mr. Breedlove," she said.

She sat behind her desk, totally within her space. Hers was an undefined space, a perimeter around the desk that no one entered. Even Mr. Breedlove avoided it. She sat in a ray of sun perhaps cruel to her complexion and coiffure, but she did not care. Miss Tompkins dressed with precision and taste, but she wore very little makeup and had never dyed her hair. She despised older women who did not dress their age or who'd obviously had face lifts or any other form of cosmetic surgery. She believed such tampering caused disruptions of the circulation and metabolism.

Slowly she removed the telephone receiver from its cradle, tucked it under her chin, and began to push the buttons. She knew the numbers. Mr. Breedlove had asked her to call all fifteen BII directors and tell them there would be a special board meeting at 2 P.M. that afternoon. There hadn't been a special meeting for several years, yet Miss Tompkins was not even mildly curious about it.

Electric impulses rang in her ear. Her mind was on the boardroom. She would personally supervise its preparation. Pencils. Pads. Water glasses, crystal and antiseptic. The temperature would be exactly sixty-five. No lint on the chairs or speck of dust on the table would be tolerated.

"Is Mr. Scott there, please?" she said into the phone.

4

THE BEARDED MAN IN THE DIRTY GREEN COAT STOOD ACROSS the road by the Volkswagen, watching Mark Scott. Scott was at a Little League diamond on the bench in a sweat suit, cracking out grounders to Tod, who wore his Solon uniform. The kid was learning to go to his left pretty well, but his throwing arm was unpredictably erratic. Liz, who wanted to play in Little League herself, handled Tod's throws from short to first.

Actually, Scott admitted to himself, she was the best coordinated person on the diamond. She short-hopped Tod's wild pegs, foot on the bag; she leapt for the high ones, pulled them down, and tagged the mythical runner. Scott looked over at the road. He saw that the Volkswagen was gone.

"Safe," he said, as a throw from Tod sailed past Liz.

"Error on the first basegirl," Tod yelled.

"On short," she said.

"We don't stick out our tongues, young man," Scott said.

"You're throwing all *wrong*," Liz told Tod, her tone not scolding but genuinely instructive. "Watch your follow-through. Like this. Not like *that*. See?"

Tod dropped his glove. "Oh, gross," he said.

"Back to your positions," Scott said.

"Dad?" Tod said. "You play first, okay?"

"Who'll hit?"

"I'll hit," Liz said.

"Aw, she can't hit."

"Who says I can't hit?"

"I said so," Tod said.

"You're the one can't hit."

"Oh, yeah? I can hit. Dad, can I hit?"

"Do you mean you want to hit grounders now or are you asking my opinion on your hitting ability in general?"

"I want you to tell her I'm a good hitter."

"He's a good hitter."

"See?"

"We do not stick our tongues out," Scott said. "Have you ever seen Steve Garvey stick his tongue out?"

"I've never seen Steven Garvey, period," Tod said.

Scott sat down on home plate, the bat across his knees. He felt a pang of guilt. He'd never taken the kids to Dodger Stadium, despite the fact that the company had twelve box seats right behind the catcher. They had planned to go many times, but something had always come up with him.

He said, "Well, we'll go see Steve Garvey."

"When?"

"Right after we get back from Disney World."

"Promise?"

"Promise," Scott said.

But he was not quite sure. Although he seldom worked late at night in the office, he was prone to take work home. And there always seemed to be a project, some matter that demanded immediate action, a problem solution needed tomorrow, today, now. Breedlove hadn't helped, particularly in recent months, assigning him to tasks and missions Scott believed a person of far lower rank could handle. Yet Scott seldom complained. Breedlove had a way of testing a man. Often Scott had come home too tired to do much but eat and slump into his leather chair in the den. And, always, there was the briefcase by his side, demanding to be opened. Also, the trips. New York. Milwaukee. Rio. Paris. He'd set a record last month—in the thirty days, he'd slept with Anne three times and had seen the kids together only once, a Saturday.

"Look," he said. "You kids. I'm pooped."

"We just *started*," Tod said.

"We have to get packed."

"Mom was doing the packing," Liz said.

"Dad, is Disney World like Disneyland?" Tod said.

"I hear it's even better."

"Do they have a Small World there?" Liz asked.

"They don't," Tod said.

"How do you know?" Scott said.

"I read up on it."

"Oh. Well, I will, too. On the plane. C'mon."

He stood up. From the beach he could see their home—a rambling, six-bedroom ranch house with a red tile roof and a white rail fence on a hill above the Pacific. They had lived here in Palos Verdes Estates just over a year, the culmination of a dream for him and Anne, one planned almost two decades ago, when he'd still been a law student at the University of Wisconsin. At that time neither of them had ever seen an ocean; they'd been landlocked Midwesterners, yearning for horizons beyond the Mississippi or Lake Michigan. It had taken them a long, long time to reach the ocean after he'd joined BII, however; since 1960 they had lived in nine different states and in fifteen different cities or towns, averaging one move every thirteen months.

A long flight of blue wooden steps—exactly eighty-four, he knew—led from the dirt road along the beach to the house. When the kids saw their mother waiting on the first landing, they dashed ahead, Liz in the lead, Tod scrambling to beat her. Scott puffed slowly up the steps, the bat over his shoulder. His legs started to ache on step twenty-one. He wasn't overweight—not much, at least; certainly not like, say, George Powell—but he could stand to shed a few pounds, especially around the middle. Henry Lancaster, the company athlete, was fond of teasing Scott about the developing paunch. When they had moved to Palos Verdes, he'd planned to run four miles a day along the beach. That had lasted exactly two sessions. Other plans also had never been fulfilled —beachside marshmallow roasts, camp-outs with the kids, twilight barbecues, volleyball games.

Anne came down to meet him. "Hi. They wear you out?"

"No. I'm just fine."

"I see."

"Are we all packed?"

"There was a call for you," Anne said. "Miss Tompkins."

"Did she say what she wanted?"

"She wants you to call her. Mark?"

Their eyes met. He could read her moods, her expressions. This one said chin-up acceptance, whatever it was. It said disappointment, too, and fear. Anne was a small woman, recently turned thirty-five, so tiny the obstetrician had expressed doubts about her childbearing ability, a caution that proved unwarranted. She weighed just over a hundred pounds in a snowsuit, an outfit she'd been wearing when he'd first met her in Madison. Now he had a vision of that day—the bright winter sun, the packed snow glistening with ice crystals, and Anne laughing under her parka hood. He shook the vision from his mind.

The kids had scrambled to the top. They peered down at them. Scott started ahead, using the bat as partial support.

Anne said, "Don't answer the call."

"I'm afraid I have to answer it."

"Why?"

"You know why."

"Yes. I know why. And I'll be a good girl. I *will*. But I want this trip. For us. Now."

"We'll have it. I promise."

"You promised Tod about the baseball game, too."

"Are we going to get into that again?"

"Well, you shouldn't promise if you're not sure."

"I'll take him. I'll take all of us."

"Oh, I don't care."

"Of course you care." He stopped. "It's important. Don't you realize I know it's important?"

"Shhh. They'll hear."

"Anne," he said, and took her hand.

He made the call to Miss Tompkins from the den while Anne resumed her packing. He listened, hardly hearing, not wanting to hear, looking through the bay window near the fireplace at the ocean, a vast green curling wave topped with white, rushing on the sands. A small boy was there, hurling a stick into the surf. The stick was retrieved by a dog. Scott thought he could hear the boy laughing. No. Of course not. A trick of the mind. He hung up. Anne was seated on a divan amid the suitcases, her tiny ankles crossed.

"Tell me," she said.

He looked at her, at her soft blonde hair and into her large blue eyes, now reflecting almost childlike disappointment. It was a face he'd seen in all its phases—radiant and sad, loving and moody, laughing and sobbing. She did not hide her feelings, particularly from him. She was his, yet not his; she was independent, yet dependent. She'd never known her father, who had been killed in a factory explosion. Her mother, who had died four years ago, had once told Scott, "It's a tiny package you're getting, but it has some TNT in it. She needs love and attention, yet on occasion she also needs loose reins." He had taken her with love and, he thought, understanding. Her face had inspired him to write bad poetry and to pour out his innermost thoughts. Yet now, for a long time, no poetry, no secret thoughts.

"There's a board meeting today," he said.

She sighed. "Well, scratch one Miami trip. It's all right. I hear Miami has loads and loads of chiggers, anyway."

"It won't affect our trip. We'll go later."

"Sure," Anne said. "Later."

"Don't say it in that tone. I mean later today."

"Or tomorrow. Or next week. Or next year."

"Anne. Listen."

"No. No, I don't want to listen." She was doing things with her hands, gesturing, smoothing the bed, opening and closing suitcases. "Where are the kids?" she said.

"They're out."

"Where is Mike?"

"He's still sleeping."

"You know what time he got in last night? After eleven."

"I'll talk to him," Scott said. "Right now—"

"No. I'm all right. I'm getting over it. I'd better cancel the plane reservations. Oh, the hotel, too."

"Anne, I tell you we'll go just a little later."

"I don't think so. Something will come up."

He turned away. "I suppose you're right," he said.

"Something always does, you know. Well, I suppose I'd better tell the kids."

"We'll both tell them. I need your support."

"Just like I need yours."

"That comment has a double meaning."

"Well, without you we'd be in the poorhouse, wouldn't we? The kids and me?"

They did not look at each other. Despite her expressions of stubborn independence, Anne occasionally revealed feelings of basic insecurity, which Scott traced to her childhood. She had known poverty and despair, at least for a time, after her father's death. Her mother had been totally unprepared for it. One incident, mentioned to Scott once when Anne was trying to explain her one phobia to him, clung indelibly in her mind. When Anne had been about five years old, she'd seen an old woman in a park feeding cookie chips and bread pieces to the birds. After the woman had left, Anne had approached the feeding birds, planning to take some of their food home to her mother, who'd complained bitterly that morning about their almost empty cupboard. Two of the birds had attacked Anne, severely pecking her hand. She'd run, holding back her screams. She still had a phobia about birds. And, despite Scott's high income, she remained a saver and almost a penny pincher.

Now she said, "I'm going to get myself involved in something. Something besides kids and PTA and Tupperware parties. I'm sick of it. Oh, not the kids. I don't mean that. But I want to *do* something. I want to be involved in your life, but I'm still a person myself. Maybe I'll get into politics."

"Do it. I encourage you."

"I will. After all, you're gone half the time anyway."

Scott felt himself drifting. His eyes were heavy. He was thinking of an elevator in the Sears Building in Chicago. Last Friday. As the elevator doors had closed, he'd glanced around to see three businessmen about his age, wearing gray suits and carrying briefcases. Like him. Like Mark Scott. Four Mark Scotts away from home, seeking something. He'd stopped the elevator and had fled from its confinement, fleeing from himself.

He hadn't told Anne about that. Nor had he told her about the incident on the airplane. It held vividly in his mind; he'd relived it a hundred times. The slow descent. The landing. The search. Lancaster had taken charge, ordering Harold Long and the copilot to conduct the search, swearing them to silence. No police. No FBI. No publicity. Lancaster had taken color photographs of the mirror and the cardboard sign, saying he'd turn them over to the security department. After a ninety-minute delay, they'd been airborne again. The flight to Los Angeles had been smooth.

"Mark?" Anne said.

"Yes."

"You're away. Are you coming back?"

"There was a demonstration outside the hotel in Chicago," he said idly.

"Against what?"

"Against everything, I suppose. South Africa. Money."

She sighed. "Too much goes on in the world for me." Their eyes met. Anne bit her lower lip. "Oh, good God," she said. "Here I am, complaining like a little brat, when you're the one who has all the pressures. Mark? Hold me. Please?"

She came warmly into his arms. He felt her face against his neck. She held him tightly, strongly, and he realized that she was crying.

Finally he said, "Give me forty cents. I'll walk away from it."

"I don't want you to walk away from it."

"No. I know you don't."

"I just want you to walk away once in a while."

"I'm afraid that's not possible."

She moved away from him and began to dab her eyes. "Well, crybaby's finished her bawling," she said. Again their eyes met. "Mark? There's something else, isn't there? Something you're not telling me."

"No. What else?"

"There is."

"No," he said. "Nothing." But he was thinking of the BII 727.

They found Mike in the kitchen, eating burnt toast. "That was quite a date," Scott said. "Where did you take her?"

"Movie. Drive-in."

"What movie did you see?"

"I don't know what it was. It was a drive-in. You got a girl at a drive-in, you don't watch the movie too much."

Anne laughed. Scott said, "I don't regard that as too very funny."

"I haven't even got a *car*, Dad," Mike said. "So I couldn't go to a drive-in. How's a guy going to go to a drive-in without a car?"

"I see. Already, at fourteen, you want a car."

"I know four kids at fourteen with cars."

"You don't say."

"I do say."

"Stop it," Anne said. "Mike, go wash your hands."

"I did."

"Do it once again. And now?"

"I guess we'll have to admit it," Scott said after Mike had left. "He's starting to grow up."

"You noticed."

"That comment had a little sharp edge to it."

"I've noticed myself," Anne said, breaking an egg on the pan. "I noticed, in fact, a few months ago, when I saw him in the bathroom."

"Doing a no-no?"

"No. But he could have."

Scott smiled. "I guess I'd better have a talk with him."

"Well, it *is* your job. I've already talked to Liz."

"And?"

"She knew . . . well, a little. No. Quite a lot."

"How do they find out?"

"At school. Where else?"

"I guess old dad has to face it. They're no longer babies."

"They'll be in college before you know it. Or know *them*."

"I think we're going to have our talk," Scott said.

"I'm saying it only because I know what a good father you can be."

"Anne, when I said forty cents, I meant it."

"No. No, you didn't mean it."

"What you don't understand is that I think it's going to get worse. I think something is going to happen to me at the company."

"A promotion?"

"Maybe."

"What's wrong with that?"

"When we were earning two hundred a week, between us, I think we were happier, closer."

"We didn't have three kids then."

"Or a big house to support."

"I still don't see what's wrong with a promotion."

"I'll try to tell you. Lancaster said something to me on the plane coming back from Chicago that got me thinking. He called me an idealist."

"Are you an idealist?"

"What do you think?"

"I don't think you're an idealist. Perhaps you'd like the world to be different from the way it is, but I don't think you believe you can change it." She paused. She smiled. "Although you are a very good man. Good and loving."

"I'm afraid it's not a good man's world. It's a survival world, at least in corporate ranks."

"I think you're a survivor."

"Maybe. We'll see."

"I don't want you unhappy, brooding. Let me be the brooder."

"Maybe I am brooding. It's just that I don't exactly revel in competition. I hate firing people. And I hate to make decisions that cost jobs. It just might be that I'm not tough enough."

"I think you let it bother you too much."

"You sound like Lancaster. He said I suffer it too much."

"Maybe you do."

"I'm sure Lancaster doesn't suffer it. He enjoys it."

"He gives me the chills."

"What do you think of his wife?"

"Dorothy? Beautiful. Perfect."

"She's hardly perfect. I'll wager grocery money on that."

"But she's beautiful."

"Are you being jealous?"

"Well, not of her looks."

"Of what, then?"

"Of her freedom, maybe."

"No kids? Only hairdressers and fashion shows? I think that's an empty life. So do you."

She flipped the eggs, breaking the yolks. "Oh, I don't know what it is, Mark. We're not getting anywhere with this talk. Maybe it's that I sometimes think I can't live up to your strict moral sense. For example, what Mike said about the drive-in and the girl was perfectly normal. But you were going to make a federal case out of it."

"I hadn't had any idea what a strict moralist I am. No wonder Hoffa always ran over me."

"Oh. Sarcastic now."

"I've got to run," he said.

He'd driven a company car until his promotion to a vice-presidency at BII, when he'd found out that at some point in the past Breedlove had decreed that vice-presidents earned enough to buy their own cars. Instead of a car, he'd been given a $150 monthly transportation allowance. His salary had jumped from $43,000 a year to $88,000, but he'd lost his company Ford. Now he drove a year-old Buick. This morning, however, the Buick was low on gas, so he took Anne's Chevy station wagon. In the garage, Liz greeted him with wide eyes.

"We leaving already?"

"No. Not yet. I have to go in to the office first. But I'll be back early. Then we'll leave."

She adjusted her baseball cap to the brim-rear catcher's position. "What's Rembrandt?" she said.

"Rembrandt? The painter Rembrandt?"

"I dunno."

"Why do you ask?"

"A hippie said it."

"You're not making sense."

"Well, the hippie was here when we were playing catch. He said, 'Tell your dad I know about the Rembrandt.'"

"What was that? Again?"

"'Tell your dad I know about the Rembrandt.'"

"Where is this man now?"

Liz shrugged her shoulders. "He left. A hippie."

"Why do you say he was a hippie?"

"Hippies have beards and they take dope."

"Dope? What do you know about dope?"

She chanted, "Downers, uppers, reds, agates, bennies—"

"That's enough."

"Oh, Daddy," Liz said, smacking her glove. "I guess you think I don't know *any*thing."

5

HIGH IN UPPER BEL AIR, IN A HOUSE OF HEAVY GLASS ABOVE the smog, lived Dottie and Hank Lancaster, a couple famous for their beautiful-people good looks, their fantabulous all-night parties, their racy humor, their fun clothing, their zest for life, their walls laden with Charles Bragg originals, Roger Price droodles, and Salvador Dali lithographs, their sporty den with its slot machines, twin pool tables, and real live growing indoor tree, and their wow of a swimming pool, a heart-shaped, constant-temperature fifty-footer that could be completely covered over by an electronically controlled aluminum dome. Visit Dottie and Hank on a Sunday afternoon and you might find the likes of Ronald Reagan, Bob Hope, Willie Shoemaker, Otis Chandler, Arnold Palmer, Harold Robbins, Sandy Koufax, or even Alfred Hitchcock. The Lancasters were doers, getters, organizers, adventurers, climbers, joiners, jet-setters, fad creators, name droppers, table hoppers. And they were beautiful. When Hank headed down winding Stradella Road in his baby-blue Cadillac coupé de ville with its customized white leather top, young girls in the neighborhood felt faint flutters not even Elvis Presley or Clint Eastwood could invoke; when Dottie approached the pool in her latest bikini, old men felt stirring in their loins they hadn't experienced since the reign of Clara Bow.

The house wasn't all glass, but it was largely glass. It had been designed with California outdoor living in mind, and also to conform with and to blend into its environment—hills of gnarled shrub and retarded elm and oak alive with birds, chipmunks, raccoons, deer, and invading predators such as bobcats and wolves down from their mountain haunts in search of easier, more domesticated prey. Large oak doors at the front of the house opened into a giant living room with a deep green carpet and a vast brick fireplace. The living-room ceiling was a massive sheet of glass, slanted from only a few feet off the ground on the west side to over forty feet at the peak of the roof. A green tint in the glass filtered the sun, so that the room by day was bathed in a soft, mellow glow. At night guests could lean back in adjustable leather chairs and view the stars, like vicarious travelers in a mystic planetarium. The open ceiling could be converted to almost normal by closing a series of drapes on various levels. Sliding glass doors led to the pool area. Carpeted stairs led to glass-enclosed upstairs bedrooms. Farther up, in a progressively shrinking area, was the den and a loft study with a wall of books immobile and silent in their uncracked eighteenth-century bindings. The house had four bathrooms, plus a swimming-pool dressing room. It had wet bars poolside, in the living room, and in the den. The kitchen was all electric and modernistically microwaved. The dining-room walls were filled with conversation-piece pop art posters—Smilin' Jack talking to Downwind, a can of Heinz 57 tomato soup, a blob of green paint on a white fence, and blown-up photographs of Mao Tse-tung swimming in the nude and Nikita Khrushchev pounding his shoe at the UN. On its floor was a Moroccan rug so preciously ordinary that Dottie liked to say she'd bought it at an Akron auction. The decorator agreed it was a nice touch. He also insisted that living-room art be limited to Miró, Calder, and Chagall; it *integrated* the house thematically, he explained.

Visitors said the house was fabulous. Some made jokes about living in glass houses, but they all agreed that Dottie and Hank did know how to live. And that Dottie and Hank themselves were fabulous. Hank, decked out in sports clothes from Mr. Guy, could talk football and he could talk stock market. Dottie, draped by Hermès of Beverly, was hep on the latest fashions and on the latest best sellers. Party guests to the home said it was like taking an LSD trip. There, sipping rare wine from glasses of Waterford and Baccarat crystal, you could discuss anything freely—women's lib, homosexuality, abortion, free love, sexual technique. Dottie and Hank made one thing clear, however. They did not swing. They wanted only each other.

Beyond that, not much was really known about them. People knew that Hank was an advertising executive, one of the best paid in the nation, but they were always forgetting the name of the company for which he worked. They knew he'd once been with the Chicago Bears, and it was said many times over drinks that he probably would have been as great a quarterback as Luckman if he hadn't been hurt in his rookie year. Right now, he was one of the top amateur golfers at Lakeside and his tennis partner often was Rod Laver, no less. Dottie's background was much more vague. They knew she had been a top fashion model at one time, of course, and it was said she had once been in pictures. After all, movie stars and producers were always visiting the Lancasters. It was said that Dottie had given up a promising career to marry Hank. How sweet and loving and unselfish of her that had been.

They had, in fact, been married five years ago, in Las Vegas, by a legitimate Methodist minister and in a legitimate church. His second. Her third. Johnny Carson and Tiny Tim had been there. Joe Namath and Howard Cosell had been there. From Madison Avenue had come old pals from N. W. Ayer, Benton & Bowles, and Dancer Fitzgerald Sample. When they asked Hank how he'd found a beauty with brains like Dottie, he said he'd picked her name out of the Pittsburgh social register. It was half true. Dottie had been born in Pittsburgh, thirty-one years ago. But she'd never been in a social register.

"Have you?" he said, turning in the bed.

"Have I what?"

"Ever been in a social register."

"Hank, I'm tired. Can't I sleep?"

"You were tired last night, too."

"Can you blame me? What time did they leave?"

"I think some of them are still here."

"Oh, Christ."

"Headache?"

"Splitting. What was that social-register crack?"

"Nothing. I was just think of something Boots Harlan asked me the night we got married. Of Ayer?"

"Oh."

"Let's take a swim."

"Now?"

"Good for a hangover."

"It's not a hangover."

"You said you had a headache.'

"This pillow is the best thing for my headache." She turned over on her back, a great golden animal with her flowing blonde hair and smooth tanned skin, and Lancaster began the preliminary inroads to sex. "Hmmm," she purred.

"Like that?"

"You know I do. Lower. There."

Slowly he pulled the straps of her nightgown down. He ran his hand over her stomach. Then he touched her breasts. She stiffened. His thumb stroked her nipples. She did not respond.

"Turn over," he said.

"Hank, do you think someone really *is* still here?"

"No. They're gone. I saw Bugner out at two. He's always the last."

"Could he drive?"

"There was a taxi."

Lancaster took her shoulders, turned her roughly, and peeled back the sheet. She lay with her hands over her breasts, her eyes wide open. He leaned forward and ran his tongue over her nipple. His hand stroked the dry opening between her thighs.

"I'm no good for you now," she said.

"Do you want me to do what I do to you? Here?"

"If you want."

"You do it to me, too."

"I can't. Not now."

He put his hand under her chin and forced her head back on the pillow. Her eyes looked suddenly frightened. Her thighs quivered and she lay stiffly, cold and unresponsive.

Lancaster said, "Touch it."

She did. He felt a surge of pleasure. Her hand moved slowly. Then she let go of him.

"Hank, I'm just not in the *mood*."

"I'll get you in the mood."

"I can't. Not now."

"I'll find a director. A cameraman."

"You bastard. You son of a bitch."

He drew back his hand and struck her in the face. Blood trickled from the corner of her mouth. She drummed his face and neck with her closed fists. He held her wrists together with one hand and began to stroke the mound between her legs with the other. His hand moved roughly.

"Shall I stop?" he said.

"Would it matter?"

"No," he said.

"No," she said.

He said, "Do you give a good blow job?"

She said, "The best."

"Is sixty-nine your favorite number?"

"Seventy. A sixty-nine with one watching."

"Do you want it now?"

"Yes. Now. Right now."

"Ask me."

"Give it to me. Give it to me."

He entered her deeply with a single rapid stroke. She winced. He raised her legs and placed them over his back. He began to move slowly, then rapidly. It was approaching already. His want. His need. He stopped his movements, trying to hold off, but she now seemed suddenly aroused and began to pump her pelvis hard against him, rotating her hips rapidly. He exploded within her. It was over. It was out of him. He withdrew and sprang up. She lay with her eyes closed, her knees raised and spread.

"I'll have a swim before Marie gets here," he said.

"Tell her what a great lover you are."

"She wouldn't understand."

"As far as I'm concerned, you're a meatball as a lover. A meatball."

"Don't tell me. Tell your shrink."

"You tell yours."

"I'm going to have a swim."

"Sure, you have a swim. And fuck you."

"You just did."

"I wouldn't know about that."

"Tell me it was lousy. Tell me."

"It was lousy. It always is lousy with you."

"Sure," Lancaster said. "Tell me you hate it. Tell me that dirty talk makes you blush. When it's true the talk turns you on."

"You're so sure it's the only thing?"

"Fail-safe," he said.

"You haven't tried any other way."

"Should I try flowers?"

"You son of a bitch."

"I'm going to have a swim."

"Have a swim, you shit, you bastard."

"Sure," Lancaster said.

He swam in the nude, quickly, twenty laps of the pool, and he emerged not breathing hard, his thighs tingling and relaxed, his head clear, his body now primed for the work ahead. The sun crept through the trellised glass that formed the roof over the swimming area and birds began to sing in the trees up the hill. Lancaster stretched out beside the pool, wrapping a wool blanket around his legs and shoulders. He breathed deeply. He let out a rush of air. His pulse rate and heartbeat were soft and regular. He felt strength in his legs and back. His mind was blank. He closed his eyes and slept for exactly four minutes. Then he got up. He was ready.

For the day's war, he selected a plain gray suit, a light pink silk shirt, and a maroon tie. When he came into the kitchen, dressed and shaved, Marie looked at him with slight reproach.

"Party?" she said, gesturing at the stacks of stained dishes.

Lancaster tapped his temple. "Heap big headache," he said, although he hadn't drunk last night.

"Learn lesson?"

"Learn heap big lesson. No more firewater."

It was their routine. He didn't speak Spanish and she spoke only a few words of English. He guessed she liked Indian talk, for she reacted to it with a smile. He went to the living room and found Dorothy lounging in a chair, studying the horoscope in the *Times*. She wore a blue robe.

"Did you know July was named after Julius Caesar?" she said.

"No. Honest? Julius Caesar? No kidding."

"So you don't know everything."

"Augustus, *septem, octo, novem, decem*," he chanted. He winked. "Janus, Februalia, Mars, *aperite*, Maia, *juventis*. But who would know old Julie Caesar?"

"All right. You're smart. The big man. Well, you may be a big man at the office, but you're not around here."

"What am I around here?"

"To me, a perfect bastard. A shit."

"Dottie's upset. Why Dottie upset?"

"A perfect, Class A shit."

"Dottie has advanced vocabulary."

"All right. You're so smart. Define a word for me, Define the word love."

"Love is," he said.

"Love is what?"

"Love is a hard on. A good blow job."

"Oh, Christ."

"Love is making it. Owning it. Getting there. Getting more. Controlling it, running it, directing it."

"Oh, good Christ," she said. "You're sick." Lancaster caught her hand and squeezed it tightly. "Hank, now *don't!*" she said. "That *hurts!*"

Lancaster pressed her knuckles together. "I will say this one more time. We do not pretend to each other. We know where we're from and what we are. I picked you for your ass but also, thanks to me, because you know how to act. You know when to keep your mouth shut and how to sit and glow when you should. You are stupid, but they do not know that at the company. They think you can read and write. They accept you. They're old fashioned, like most companies, embracing the notion that a wife is helpful to the man. Now we know each other. We're alike. We've both come from deep down. Now we have something. We'll go higher. We're in together, in conspiracy. Do you understand?"

"Yes."

He released her hand. "I have a board meeting today. Then it's out of town again."

"You did hurt my hand. I want you to know that."

"The house up the hill is for sale," he said.

"The Greer house?"

"Yes."

"I'll have a look at it," Dorothy said.

Before he left, Lancaster checked the security system and made sure all of their weapons were in place and loaded. They kept a .38 pistol in the bedroom, a sawed-off shotgun in a locker by the pool, and a .45 under the living-room couch. There was a private security patrol in Bel Air, yet the wisest residents stocked in their own protection. Dorothy said she hated guns, yet had become pretty proficient in their use in practice at the Police Academy, particularly the .38. Lancaster went outside. Birds sang in the bushes. He backed the

Cadillac out and lowered the top. It was a good day to drive with the top town.

Dorothy Lancaster spent a half hour in the shower after he'd left, scrubbing the smell of him off her body. She came out and stood naked before the steamy mirror. She wiped a spot clear on the mirror and examined the cut on her mouth from his blow. Her lip was swollen and there was a bruise on her cheek. She ran her hands over her damp body, feeling her hips, her buttocks, her breasts. She had firm, large breasts, the pride of her body—equipment no man rightly sexed could keep his eyes off, or his hands off, either, if she didn't discourage him. And she seldom had discouraged them. There had been a brief time in the past when sex had been beautiful for her, but, after that, it had become nothing, merely a fumbling around and a thrust, and when it was over the men became sleepy and unconcerned, their proud cocks limp and ugly. She'd taken that from them, at least, deflating the erect cocks that made them strut and crow. When she'd met Hank, sex had changed again for her, neither gentle nor impassive but rough, sometimes close to brutal. She detested him, yet was drawn to him; she didn't know what it was, and couldn't analyze it. Oh, maybe she was dumb, a fool. If only once she could bring him down, down just a peg. She hated him, yet she knew she could not exist without him. It wasn't his money, nor was it her fear of him. She didn't know. She only knew that if he left, she'd beg him to come back and on his own terms, too. He owned and dominated her, and for that she hated him, but she knew she could never escape from him.

She put on a robe and slippers and went into the kitchen, where Marie noisily clanked dishes. Marie was an enormously fat woman with a strong body odor, but she had kind eyes.

"Don't break any, Marie, Hank'd get mad at us. He'd beat on us. Look at my face, what he did. And my hand still hurts. You got a fat greasy taco husband but I'll bet he's gentle."

"*Sí*," Marie said. She didn't understand.

"I'll tell you what, you can have this house, that's what," Dorothy said. "You can have him with it. Him and his always-hard cock. Someday I'm going to cut that cock off with a butcher knife."

"*Sí*," Marie said, smiling as she washed the dishes.

"For ten cents, I'd kill him," Dorothy said. "I'd kill the son of a bitch bastard for ten cents, believe me. He thinks I'm stupid. Do you think so? Marie?"

"*Sí*," Marie said.

"Oh, shit, you don't understand. That's why I talk to you, because you don't understand. I'll tell you this. Someday I'll see that bastard suffer. Someday he'll get his. I hope I'm around when he does. Maybe I should just walk off. Walk off right now. I'd find somebody else, somebody gentle. Just a gentle man. Maybe there aren't men like that any more. At least men like that who can support you. Do you think I'm right?"

"*Sí*," Marie said.

"You don't understand. You're lucky because you can't understand. It's good not to understand."

6

THE CALL FROM HENRIETTE TOMPKINS INTERRUPTED AN IN-tense discussion between George Powell and his daughter, Sophia.

"Father, I *do* respect you and your views," she said. "But they are not necessarily for me."

"Father?" Powell said. "That is a new designation for me. Am I that stuffy?"

"You're not stuffy. I didn't say you were stuffy."

"The word is in your mind, however."

"I know that I'm disappointing you."

"An apt word. Disappoint."

"But I am twenty-four years old now, whether you realize it or not. I've had my nose in textbooks for almost six years. Now I have my life to live."

"I see that you are twenty-four. Yes. I see that you have your entire life ahead of you, despite your contention of advanced age. Your leaving this household would not disappoint me, of course, if you were leaving to establish one of your own. Instead, however, you are leaving to experiment with a style of modern living that is antagonistic to your upbringing and position in life. And, meanwhile, until you decide that marriage is not an outdated concept in our society, you do have a good home here with me and your mother."

"Father? May I interrupt? A good home? May we face the truth of that?"

Powell lit his pipe, avoiding Sophia's eyes. He felt relieved when a housekeeper in gray shuffled in to inform him of the call with gestures of her dry old hands and repressed, diffident movements of her thin lips. The interruption would give him time to gather his forces. His argument was going badly; Sophia's experience in debate at SC was telling. Powell scowled tiredly. Tiny surges of pain twitched in his forehead. He excused the housekeeper, picked up the phone, and listened as Henriette Tompkins coolly informed him there would be a board meeting that afternoon. When he hung up, he saw that Sophia was at the window, her back to him.

"Have you already made arrangements with this young man?" he asked.

"Yes."

"Justin Clifford? Have I met him?"

She turned sharply. "Of course you've met him. He's in law school at SC."

"I see."

"You really do not remember, do you? Honestly, I don't know how you run a big company the way you always forget things."

"I do not *run* the company. And as for my memory—"

He hesitated. Was his memory slipping? It had once been his greatest asset. Now he found himself jotting notes to remember appointments. It wasn't age. He had too much to do. To Sophia he must appear an old stuff indeed, black-suited and gray-mustached, a spreading frame antediluvian as Cro-Magnon and anachronistic as Julius Caesar. She was the laughing girl with dark curls and great asking eyes he was losing. He had tried to find time for her, and for Timothy, but he had not found enough. It was useless to analyze it. He would blame change. Change rushed around him in tight, choking convolutions, undoing his contributions and maneuvering him toward premature obsolescence. Not long ago he'd been considered a leader in the avant-garde ranks of financial creators, an innovator honored by universities and envied by competitors, but now his work was being destroyed by a perilous economy shaky at its political roots and perhaps even at the brink of collapse owing to the asininity of incompetent regulators and a government that displayed shocking indifference to international monetary conditions and advance planning in domestic fiscal policies.

"Sophia, I am going to say this as clearly as I can." He put down his pipe. They faced each other in the vast living room of the massive house, cold with its unused bedchambers, its austere upstairs halls, its mechanical daily cleaning by hired help in dark uniforms. "There is nothing I can do, or will do, to prevent you from doing as you wish. You call it, I believe, doing your thing. I am consistently appalled by grotesque expressions that have degraded our language, but that opinion is merely an aside. It is not the point."

"Henry James," she said.

"Henry James? I do not understand."

"You speak like Henry James writes. Roundabout."

"Then I will go to the point. You want to move in with this young man, to live with him out of marriage. As you say, you are no longer a child—"

"Nor am I a virgin, if this is turning into a confessional."

"I believe your mother and I realize that, yes, without your having to articulate it."

"I'm not trying to be nasty, or shocking. I'm trying merely to be honest."

"Then tell me why you want to live with this young man. The honest answer."

"It's hard to explain."

"To me, or to anyone? Could you explain it to your mother, for example?"

"No. Never."

"Try to explain it to me."

"I think that I want to marry Justin someday, but I simply do not *know*."

"You want to see if you're . . . compatible?"

Her hands moved. She did not look at him. "I'm not doing it because it's the new thing, or the thing to do. It's not that. I love Justin, yes. Now. But suppose it doesn't work? I mean, why should I make a total commitment to a man? Isn't that taking a chance?"

"Somehow I think you have in you the spirit of chance-taking."

"Well, I can't explain it any other way."

It was not working. He would try another approach. "Sophia, regardless of your current political leanings, you are not an ordinary or average person. I do not think you really realize that. Or perhaps this revolt is—"

"I think I know what you're saying. You're telling me that you're a successful man."

"Does that reaction have a hidden meaning?"

"I suppose that it does."

"Explain."

"Elucidate. A favorite word of the professors. You make a point in class, they say, 'Elucidate,' and stand with their arms crossed."

"All right. You don't have to explain."

"I can't! I don't *know!* But there are *people* out there. Hundreds. Thousands. Perhaps hundreds of thousands that go to bed hungry while we ... we sit here with all this. I want you to look at the profile of this city. Just one city."

"I'm not unaware of this."

"You're not unaware."

"We do what we can. Companies are not philanthropic organizations, but they do what they can. Our minority employment is—"

"Zilch. Almost zilch."

He picked up his pipe and tapped it in his palm. He stood up. "You know so much," he said. "You profess to know so much. How much do you really know? I mean, about living itself."

"About living, very little, I suspect. Perhaps I'm about to find out about living."

"At expense to your mother and me."

"Financial expense or social expense?"

"Sophia, a young woman of your station in life simply does not do this."

"We arrive at the point. It is the social stigma."

"Yes. Frankly, yes. That is part of the reason, yes."

"Tell me, Father. Are you worried because I'm doing this or because I'm doing it in the open?"

"I am concerned because I do not think it is right."

"Do you want me here? To finish school? Then marry, properly?"

"Of course."

"And you want Tim back, too?"

"I do. Of course."

"He might come back. If you'd ask him. If you'd go talk to him. But I will never be back."

"You will not have my help."

"I only half believe that."

"I mean it. Do not come to me for help."

"If Mother had said that, I would have believed her one hundred percent. I believe you only fifty percent."

"Unkindness toward your mother is uncharacteristic of you."

"I don't like to be unkind. But, you see, I do know about her. I realize she needs help."

"You know about her? What is that supposed to mean?"

"Shall we pretend? Very well, let's pretend."

"I think you've said quite enough."

"It hit me, too. The truth can hit hard. Sometimes I think I hate the truth as much as you do."

"I see now how useless it is for me to attempt to talk to you," he said.

"There was a time. There was a time with Tim, too."

"I suppose that you are right. I tried."

"I know you tried."

"You had better go."

Sophia stood up. She faced him, a girl—a woman—not really pretty, he realized, one with nibbled nails and a sharp, thin mouth like her mother's, dressed in unattractive slacks that revealed the breadth of her hips and the lack of symmetry in her figure. He could not be proud of her, he knew, and he was not sure, then, that he loved her. But he had. He had.

She said slowly, "Daddy, I'm not sure that what I'm doing is right. I'm sure it's not *correct* to your way of thinking. But I have to find out. I don't want to become a divorce statistic. You and Mother—"

"I think I've heard enough from you," he said.

"Will you come to see us? If I call?"

"Please leave the room."

"I love you. I want you to know that."

"Then stay."

"I can't."

She kissed him lightly on the cheek and went away. Powell

sat down on the couch. He sighed deeply. He held the pipe in both hands. The grandfather clock bonged the hour. He heard a sharp snap and looked down to discover he'd broken the pipestem. Looking up, he saw his wife, Susan, standing across the room, staring at him.

The Powells lived at 82 Sherman Place, Los Angeles. The entire fifty acres had once belonged to Mitchell Lawson, a Canadian wildcatter who'd struck oil near Signal Hill. He'd staked out a center claim, named it after his hero the general, and had eventually allowed rich friends to build houses on leased plots as long as none came within an acre of his front lawn, which he protected with a Civil War cannon. The area languished after Lawson's death, his magnificent genteel mansion decaying because of probate court delays, but when his heirs did get control, they promptly disposed of the land to a real estate syndicate. Sherman Place was slowly parceled out in quarter-, half-, and full-acre lots. With time, some of the exclusiveness passed. Lawson would set off his cannon to signal his gang of oil-rig roughnecks if he even smelled a Mexican or a black in the area; now Mexicans and blacks were permitted to enter, as long as they were maids, mailmen, dog walkers, or of embassy rank. High brick walls had been erected around the area in 1922, because the residents agreed that the previous iron fence with spear-top poles gave Sherman Place the look of a cemetery. Thick ivy covered the walls. There was one avenue of ingress and egress, an iron gate just off Wilshire between two large concrete posts. The gate had a sign threatening trespassers with arrest and prosecution. Guards kept it open during the day, but it closed automatically at 9 P.M. A motorist without a key could get neither in nor out.

When Sophia Powell left Sherman Place, a trunk and a suitcase strapped in her top-down MG, she accelerated too rapidly, hit a bump in the street, and almost lost the load. *Easy,* she thought. Her hands were weak. Her arms trembled. She reached the gate, stopped, glanced back, and turned left on Wilshire, through the red signal. The MG sputtered and coughed. It had been a high school graduation present from her parents; it had been well used and seldom tuned. She used it often to escape, heading alone aimlessly at high speeds down freeways to places like Barstow or Bakersfield or Fresno. Now, turning up Crenshaw to the Santa Monica Freeway, she felt as if she had stolen the car. West on the freeway, exceeding the fifty-five limit, chewing her nails, she looked into the rearview mirror for cops. Nothing. Only a battered red VW, which seemed to be straining to keep up with her.

She had done it. Had she? Really? Yes. She had.

She felt like shouting. She felt like getting high. She felt like crying. Her senses seemed heightened. Truck noises roared in her brain. The smog was acid-strong and the exhaust fumes were nauseating. Wind streamed in her hair. She turned off in Santa Monica before the tunnel and headed west to Venice. Tim's place was a sagging hippie pad, a three-story apartment that had once been a summer rental for vacationers. Now the paint was peeling and the screens were rotted. She double-parked and hurried up the stairs. A bare-chested black in bright green pants answered her rap on the door to No. 9.

"Social worker?" he said.

"No. I'm looking for my brother."

"Who you the sister of?"

"Tim. Tim Powell. Is he here?"

"Tim? Well, he's here, sure. You his sister, huh? Well, who could tell. You know?"

"Tell him to come out, will you?"

"Go on in."

"No. Tell him to come out."

She returned to the MG, leaned against its fender, and lit a cigarette. Ocean smells were strong in her nostrils. The sun was obscure behind a mist. A couple paraded by, laughing—a young black girl of perhaps fourteen or fifteen in sandals and shorts holding hands with a much older white man in Levi's. Tim finally came out, wearing dirty tennis shoes and green bathing trunks. There was a tattoo of a cobra on his forearm.

"I see you have a new roommate," she said.

"Who? Hunk? A temporary with us. From Frisco. He says. A scream. That boy's a scream. He could stud a horse."

"I don't doubt it."

They didn't look at each other. They looked away. Their appearance, close up, was strikingly similar, especially now since he'd grown long hair after leaving home; looking closely at each other was somewhat like looking into a mirror. She did not like her looks—hated mirrors, in fact—and did not like to be reminded of the face the world saw by scrutinizing her twin. Yet they were very close. They'd had long talks, conspiratorial talks, mostly at night.

"Well," she said, lighting another cigarette. "I did it."

"Moved out?"

"I told him just now."

"How'd he take it?"

"Hurt," she said. "More than anything, hurt."

"I'm saddened."

"I see."

"But I am. I really am."

"Tell me something. Would you move back?"

"No," he said.

"Honest?"

"Are we not honest folk?"

"Between us, yes. I think so."

Now his back was completely turned to her. He said, "Who's your admirer?"

"What do you mean?"

"The cat in the VW. He's looking right at you."

She turned. "Good Christ, do you suppose he *was* following me?"

"Want me to get Hunk to take him?"

"No. Forget Hunk."

"Let's go talk to the guy."

"I think I've seen him before. I *know* I have."

"You may have. He's a stranger to me. And freaked out."

"I'm going to go talk to him."

"I'll get Hunk."

The VW fired up. The driver made a sharp U-turn and sped away.

"That cat's smashed," Tim said. "Heavy stuff."

"How can you tell?"

"There's ways. His eyes, for one."

Now she looked at him. "You're using, aren't you?"

"A little."

"How much?"

"Not much."

"But hard stuff?"

"I'm not hooked."

"Don't they all say that?"

"I'll never get hooked."

"Tell me," she said. "Are we afraid of words?"

"No way."

"Then answer me. Are we fucked-up people?"

"The whole world's fucked up," Tim said.

The Powells had been living in Boston when the twins had been born in 1954. They had been love children, or at least children of passion, but yet a mistake. The births had been difficult for Susan, so excruciatingly painful that for months and even years after she awoke at night experiencing dreadful psychosomatic contractions. But it had been she who had conquered him, not vice versa. He'd been in his final months at Harvard Business School when he'd met her—a full-breasted, dark-haired woman from a Scarsdale-bred family who'd earned her master's from NYU at twenty. It was a proper introduction, at her mother's Park Avenue apartment. His experience with women was limited—heavy teen-age fondling on the Staten Island Ferry, a few whores in Jersey City, Vassar girls set up for him by fellow students—and she, it turned out that first night in a Boston motel, was actually a virgin. They'd known each other three weeks. She had suggested the liaison. He'd never thought such passion could exist in a woman.

"If we ever get married," he said, "we'd kill each other in bed."

"You wouldn't marry an older woman, would you?"

"Age isn't important."

"Do you like that?" she said. "When I touch you there?"

"I'm afraid I'm too sore to feel anything."

"Come on. Come on."

"Aren't you worried?"

"About what?"

"You know."

"Just do it. *Do* it!"

After the birth of the twins it had died so completely that he wondered if he'd married a woman absolutely different from the one who had seduced him. They'd been married at a small Catholic church in the Bronx six months before Sophia and Timothy had been born. Two weeks after the births, he had graduated with honors from Harvard. A position as an accountant with her father's firm awaited him. Their love-making continued, but with little passion from her. She complained of burning and pain. Doctors could find no physical malfunctions. When Powell hinted that she see a psychiatrist, Susan flew into a rage. He was not opposed to raising a large family, but she made it clear she wanted no more children. She hired nurses and tutors to look after the twins. At the time, Powell still clung to the Church doctrine that sex was for impregnation, so he refused to use contraceptives. Nor would he do it the one way she seemed to enjoy; that disgusted him. Sex festered between them coldly in their twin beds for over a year, and then it was gone. He sublimated it with work. They became companions and conspirators for success.

Powell's top-floor bedroom-bath at the Sherman Place residence was the only area in the house where he enjoyed absolute privacy and felt contentment. He had two telephones, a television set, a desk, and a shelf of books on corporate finance, computerization, and the international monetary system. He was an orderly man with a logical mind, a brain that functioned in precise algebraic symbols and geometric designs, and these were books of order. Interspersed among them, almost hidden, were some volumes by poets he'd recently discovered. He sought sanctuary in the poets and found order in their rhythms; yet, inevitably, they all seemed to write of disintegration and a world run to anarchy and decay.

He fought anarchy in his personal life, but he could not bring total order to it. He tried to think of it as ordered. It was entirely possible, for example, that his marriage was better than most. They were civil to each other, if formal; they seldom had a spat or altercation. They did not question each other. Money was plentiful. They talked, at least of surface matters, and they sometimes watched television together. Occasionally they went out, especially to the concerts and plays they both enjoyed. Their social life was limited, but certainly did exist.

Now she stood before him, a still handsome woman of fifty-six. He rose from the couch.

"I'm afraid the Chrysler is still in the repair shop," he said.

"Are you planning to go to the club?"

"I have a luncheon scheduled, yes."

"Then I'll take a taxi to the office."

"You and Sophia had your little talk. What did she say?"

"About you?"

"About her future."

"Simply that she is leaving home."

"She'll come back."

"I'm not so sure she will, Susan."

"Did you give her money?"

"No. I'll send some money to her."

"Not yet, please. Let her find out what it's like."

"As you wish," he said.

He was in his room, changing into the gray suit he often wore to board meetings, when his private line rang. He let it ring three times, his hand on the receiver.

"Hello."

"Me," Carol said.

"Where did you get this number?"

"You gave it to me."

"Oh. Yes, I remember. With instructions not to use it."

"Then why did you give it to me?"

"I do foolish things with you."

"My afternoon is free."

"Unfortunately, mine isn't. Board meeting."

"How about a drink later on, then?"

"If I can get away."

"Same place?"

"Yes. If I can get away."

"You can."

"I will," he said.

7

A CHARGED ATMOSPHERE PREVAILED AT EXECUTIVE HEADQUARTERS on days when the board of directors met. Office boys wore white shirts, receptionists assumed matronly poses, secretaries made sure their lipstick was modestly applied and their skirts were below their knees. The show was not just for board members. It was largely because board-meeting days were sure to produce the physical presence of Lewis Anthony Breedlove. Breedlove's office, guarded by Henriette Tompkins, awaited him at all times, dust-free and orderly, but he was in it only about three days a month. His average so far this year, in fact, had been even lower than that.

Today the atmosphere was unusually tight. The meeting had been so suddenly called that normal preparations were impossible. And surely, because of the haste, something important was going to happen. Public relations had been alerted to the possibility that a press release would be needed. Rumors ran from office to office. A major acquisition was being discussed. The Food Division—Breedlove's founding base but one that now had the slimmest profit margin of them all—was being sold. Richard Nixon had been offered a post at BII. After all, he was a friend of Breedlove's.

But the most discussed rumor of all: Mr. Breedlove was going to announce his retirement.

Nine BII directors were internal, executive of the company. Six were external, employed elsewhere. Secretaries on thirty seldom gossiped, but there was a communications network among them. They had likes and dislikes. Mark Scott, for example, was universally liked. Henry Lancaster was a puzzle, viewed with suspicion except by his own secretarial pool, who remained somewhat distant from the others. George Powell was regarded as stuffy, but tolerated. Five of the outside directors (a current and former commercial banker, an investment banker, a lawyer, and a realtor) were considered dull and similar, taciturn and efficient robot-like men in gray suits and sincere ties, but the sixth was a zany live wire. His name was Carter Mannering, an auto dealer. He sold Fords and Pontiacs from four lots—Redondo Beach, El Monte, Encino, and Lakewood. He'd accumulated more TV time than Raymond Burr and James Arness combined; flip to Channel 9, 5, or 13, days or nights, weekdays or Sundays, and the chance was excellent you'd see Carter Mannering in his act, moving out shiny new cars. He had tall, rugged good looks, a friendly Texas twang, and at least fifty beautiful cowboy suits. He would do anything to make a deal. He'd do handstands and backflips. He'd sing, recite poetry, tumble, dance, weep, plead. He'd come on dressed as a clown, as the Frankenstein monster, a magician, a waiter; he'd ride steers, Shetland ponies, St. Bernard dogs, water buffaloes. There was a joke in the TV stations that the little old ladies in Pasadena were waiting for him to expose himself. Lancaster had recruited him to the BII board; the man obviously could sell. His volume exceeded that of his closest competitor in the Los Angeles basin by threefold.

Carter Mannering was usually the first outside director to arrive for a board meeting. He maneuvered among secretaries and staffers, handing out discount stickers, tickets to plays and concerts, ball-point pens, Blue Chip and S & H Green Stamps. Normally he wore a business suit to the meetings, but today he'd shown up in a white cowboy suit and hat. He'd received Miss Tompkins's call during a taping session for an auto commercial.

"C'mon down to the car ranch," he told Joan Leeky, one of Scott's secretaries.

"I'm afraid my old VW will have to do for a while," she said.

"With pretty ladies, we don't take no for an answer."

"Why, Mr. Mannering!"

Miss Tompkins didn't loosen up for Mannering's smile. "C'mon down!" he shouted at her.

"Mr. Mannering, do you wish to wait in the boardroom?" she said coolly, drilling him with an owl-serious stare.

"Wal, I think I'll jus' wander."

"As you like."

"C'mon down!" Mannering told a passing office boy, dropping leaflets and tickets into his mail basket.

Breedlove regarded board meetings as one aspect of the company's business that was totally private, so no official minutes were taken. Regular meetings were held on the first Tuesday of each month. There hadn't been a special meeting, like today's, for almost eight years, when a hurried vote on the Mayer Drugs acquisition had been taken. The meetings were limited to the fifteen directors, unless a representative of a division or a subsidiary was making a proposal, yet on occasion Miss Tompkins had sat in as an observer. They were conducted on a first-name basis, with any director having the right to interrupt a speaker with questions, yet they were usually formal and orderly under Breedlove's firm guidance.

Informal discussion came only after adjournment. Coffee or tea was often served, and sandwiches were ordered from the executive dining room if morning sessions continued through the noon hour, but no liquor of any kind was permitted.

Fuming at Mannering's obstreperousness, Miss Tompkins entered the boardroom at 1:45 to make her final check. To her mind, Mannering symbolized the eccentricities and outrageous abuses characteristic of Southern California's consumer-economy lowlife, even if he was rich and had Mr. Breedlove's respect (something that was undeniable); he was as gross and undignified as the giant tires, ten-foot doughnuts, and inflated balloons that screamed their wares along the freeways, as alien to good manners as a motion-picture premier or a flea-market sale. Today it wasn't his manners that infuriated Miss Tompkins. It was his dress. To arrive for a meeting of the board of directors of Breedlove International in a flamboyant cowboy suit! It was unthinkable. Infuriating.

She started her careful inspection. The board members always sat in the same chairs, Breedlove at the head. She made sure that ashtrays were in place for those who smoked. She thumbed through the legal-size yellow pads. Once she'd found scribbling inside one. The pencils were new and freshly sharpened. Their erasers were untouched. The water glasses were sanitized. The lights were all working, including the high-intensity fixture Mr. Breedlove often used for close-up reading. The temperature was precisely sixty-five. Miss Tompkins ran her fingertips over the smooth surface of the table. She was satisfied.

She left, quietly closing the doors.

Scott was late.

Perspiration crawled on his back as he parked the Chevy in the office garage. It was 2:10 P.M.; the board meeting was scheduled for 2 P.M. He'd been delayed by the manager of the Torrance cannery, where he'd stopped on his way to the office to discuss upcoming labor negotiations, and by a truck accident on the Harbor Freeway. He hurried toward the elevator. Then he stopped. His heartbeat picked up.

A man in sunglasses stood twenty feet away, gazing at Scott, dimly crouched in the shadows of a concrete pillar, as if hiding. Scott realized, in an electric flash of recognition, that he was looking at Lawrence Breedlove, the old man's son.

"Larry?" he said. The other stood slumped and disheveled, his hands gesturing. His hair was long, braided down the back. "You're Lawrence Breedlove," Scott said.

The man's lips twitched. "Yes."

"You've been following me. Why?"

"I've been all over. Trying—"

"Trying what?"

"Will you listen to me?"

"I'm afraid I'm already late for a meeting."

"Go ahead to your meeting then, man. Like—you know?—you just go ahead." Lawrence stepped back. He staggered. An unkempt beard and the sunglasses hid part of his features. "I talked to you once," he said. "Do you remember that?"

"All right, Larry. I'll listen. What is it?"

Lawrence took off the glasses, and Scott saw that his eyes were like his father's. His face twisted into a cunning, knowing grimace. The words tumbled out.

"There's danger. The airplane. There's danger for him and for all of you. Oh, they'll get him. Believe me, they'll get him. I didn't start it. The one who started it is *like* him. So much so like him, it's like he's in his skin. He looks like him. He acts like him, talks like him. He formed the group. He got me to help. I helped get some money for them. Now they have money. Money for professionals. They'll be hitting soon. Here and there. Small hits, then bigger ones. You see, they want to *show you* that they're capable. They want you to squirm a while. The big hit will be the airplane. It's mapped out, man. A plan."

Scott stood silently, stunned. Then he said, "It's a group of extortionists?"

"I won't say any more. I said too much already."

"Larry, I want you to come upstairs with me. Talk to him. And I think we should get a doctor for you."

"No. I don't talk to him."

"I believe what you say. I want to know more."

Lawrence began to back away. "I won't tell you any more. You just tell him it's *personal*. He'll understand that. That's the key to it. I got in, nothing can get me out. I did my bit, coming here. They'd kill me if they knew."

"We'll protect you."

"You can't. Nobody can."

"You want to get out. Coming here indicates that. Following me around indicates that. Talking to my daughter—"

"I didn't talk to her. I'm not here. You didn't see me." Lawrence tripped as he backed, sprawling on the cement. He scrambled up. "I didn't come here. I didn't talk to you. I didn't follow you."

He ran up the ramp toward the street, his voice fading as he fled.

As Scott entered the boardroom, Breedlove looked up and said, "Well, we're all here now. Sit down, Scottie. I'm making a speech and you've misssed only the preamble, which was largely bullshit anyway."

"There was an accident on the freeway," Scott said lamely.

Seat assignments at board meetings were strictly observed, a matter of tradition rather than discipline. They had been made by Miss Tompkins, to whom a director wishing a change would have to appeal. Since his election to the board, Scott had sat between two outside directors, Clemson Hawley, a retired banker, and James A. Wright, senior partner in a Los Angeles law firm. Positions near Breedlove at the head were meaningless in terms of rank or status. Clemson Hawley obtained Breedlove's right flank because of a hearing impairment, not because of his importance, although he outranked everybody in seniority as a director. Lancaster held Breedlove's left flank, and Powell's seat was next to Lancaster's. Scott, Hawley, and Wright were nonsmokers, a factor in their placement. Across from Scott was Carter Mannering, who presented him with a flashing smile and, of all things, a wink. Mannering was not a habitual winker.

Breedlove was talking. "Something I want you all to promise me—here and now, I might add—is that when they put me toes up into a pine box nobody is going to make a motion to this group that a bust of my face be sculpted to put into the lobby. It isn't because I think I'm not handsome. You all can see what a handsome s.o.b. I am. It's because if you have some fairy sculptor make a bust of me when I'm dead, I can't control the thing, you see. I'll come out like the Roman busts. Those bastards used to make busts of their generals in helmets looking mean as sin and send them around to the provinces they controlled so nobody would think about getting out of line. All we need in this day and age where the workers sit down at the drop of a hat is to have this old face sent around in an iron bust to put in all the individual lobbies."

He was in a rare light mood, Scott saw, but he really didn't look well at all. His cheeks were sunken, his eyes were hollow. Scott hadn't seen Breedlove in almost a month; it seemed as if he'd aged a year in that time. The eye sparkle— his most characteristic feature—was no longer there. Scott thought again of Lawrence Breedlove; he saw Lawrence's tortured face before him, and again he heard the inarticulate mumblings. Danger. The airplane. What had he meant? Well, he would talk to Breedlove about it as soon as he could corner him after the meeting.

Breedlove paused. He cleared his throat, adjusted his bifocals, and glanced out the window. The boardroom was still. Scott looked at the directors. Lancaster tapped his pencil. Powell folded his arms over his chest. They waited silently for Breedlove to speak. To Scott the atmosphere seemed unreal, not a board meeting of a giant multinational conglomerate company but a gathering of conspirators called by their aging leader for a purpose known only to him. He had been invited, he realized, to a surprise party, and he knew, in an intuitive flash, that he might well be the guest of honor.

Breedlove turned. He got to his point.

"As the joke goes, you're all wondering why I've called you here today. It's for a single purpose. I'm going to recommend a change in management. I've thought about it for some time and I decided just last night to go ahead. I apologize if the suddenness of this meeting has disturbed your plans, but I'll make it quick. Effective immediately, I am stepping down as president of Breedlove International."

The reaction was absolute silence. Breedlove didn't pause long.

"I plan to stay on as chairman, unless you gentlemen mount effective resistance against that. I hope it will be a very active chairmanship. I will remain as your chief executive— that is, I will remain unless someone here wants to stand up and declare me infirm and senile and nominate a more effective candidate for that post. As I indicated earlier, this move is not a sudden whim or impulse of mine. I have thought long and hard about it. I am going to recommend the establishment, effective today, of an Office of the President for Breedlove International, with three members of equal rank. They will be Mr. Lancaster, Mr. Powell, and—" He paused, looking away. Then he looked at Scott. He said, "And you, Scottie."

Murmurs rose. Breedlove silenced them with a quick wave of his hand. "I realize that, in making these recommendations, I am bypassing consultation with the Nominating Committee. I hope I will be forgiven this one time. I set up these committees and I believe in the committee approach in the management of a large business. But time comes for all of us, and it's best to move quickly. I have some personal business that's come up which is going to take time and energy. But I'm not ready to be carried out of here. Understand that, please. I plan to be around raising hell for quite some time. As you no doubt know, the idea for an Office of the President is not an original one in corporate history. It has been tried before. Some of you might wish to argue that it has never been done successfully. Perhaps it has failed in some cases. But that doesn't mean it will fail at this company. Are there any questions?"

There were none.

"Then we'll vote," Breedlove said.

The vote was quick and unanimous.

It was Lancaster who first called it the Troika.

The meeting adjourned to the dining room and the bar was opened. Scott, a Coke in his hand, found himself surrounded by subordinates from the lower floors. They shook his hand, brushed against him, chatted briefly, and went on to corners held by Lancaster and Powell to congratulate them. Lancaster was the master of a corporate cocktail party. He knew where to stand, what to say, how to react. He never made rounds. He never broke in on a conversation. He treated everyone in a manner his position deserved. He was neither curt nor supercilious. He had only one drink, that a light martini, which he sipped slowly. His presence was clearly the dominant one in the room. Breedlove didn't attend the party, and Miss Tompkins made only a very brief appearance. She congratulated Lancaster, Powell, and Scott, in that order. There was some thought among executives from the twenty-ninth floor that the order of her congratulations had some significance, but the fact was that Lancaster had stationed himself closest to the door and Powell had taken a position second closest. One had to cross the room to reach Scott.

The only secretaries admitted were those from the thirtieth floor. Joan Leeky gave Scott a pretty smile and said, "Well."

It appeared as if she'd known about this before he'd found out himself. Had they all known?

In the latter stages of the party, Scott found himself next to Lancaster. He'd crossed the floor slowly, interrupted regularly by assistant vice-presidents and assistant treasurers who insisted on discussing problems and situations with him they had never before mentioned.

"What do we say to each other?" Lancaster said. "Congratulations?"

"Something like that," Scott said.

"Do you think it will work?"

"I think it *can* work, yes."

"Troika," Lancaster said.

"What?"

"We're now the Troika. It's Russian. Means three horses pulling a vehicle together. Look it up."

"I'll take your word for it."

"A drink after work, Scottie?"

"If you like."

"Harry's Bar?"

"Fine," Scott said.

He looked around. Carter Mannering was passing out cards. Powell stood in an intense discussion with the BII treasurer. Lancaster shuffled away from Scott and took up a new position.

8

THE THIRTIETH FLOOR AT BII HEADQUARTERS, THE PINNACLE, had a culture and atmosphere of its own. It officed the elite of the elite in BII's world. Decisions made on thirty had destroyed and anointed politicians, had toppled foreign dictatorships, had influenced thinking in the U.S. Congress. The decisions had made poor states self-sufficient and rich states less viable. Thirty was an arena of power, moving in palpable, noiseless waves. The power was ostensibly vested in the board of directors, but in reality it was exercised almost solely by Lewis Breedlove. He could ruin an executive with an offhand comment, discharge a thousand employees with a nod, or turn a young riser into a potential millionaire with a tap of his knuckles on the boardroom table. When Breedlove slumped down the corridor, looking deceptively harmless, a hush came over the area, secretaries issued respectful smiles, and office boys prone to wisecracking or humming stood in pale awe, like pages to a king. Below, across the country and around the world, bare-armed BII workers slaved in can factories, BII-hired Mexican green-carders humped down rows in sun-scorched fields, and assembly-line employees queued up to punch time clocks, lunch pails under their arms and identification badges on their shirts, each waiting to turn a thousand bolts over the next seven hours.

Executives on thirty were secure, shielded, feared, and honored. Headhunters, recruitment firms that survived by stealing talent for other companies, seldom approached its residents. Middle management—young men and women with M.B.A.s from Harvard, Wharton, or Stanford—hovered on the floors below, their briefcases smelling of new leather, their faces turned eagerly upward, their minds consumed with plans and schemes that would allow them to spread their wings and soar to thirty.

The status of thirty applied not only to executives but also to secretaries, who drew power from their bosses. Secretaries on thirty seldom lunched with their counterparts below. Excluding Miss Tompkins, who was in a classification by herself, they averaged forty dollars a week more than those in lower offices. They were also better dressed, better groomed, better educated, and older. They were well adjusted, close-mouthed, and exceedingly efficient. They seemed to know the rank, order, and even the potential of all BII executives; they knew which calls to put through and which to block. Most were married. None was a divorcée. This was not a rule, but it was helpful in being promoted to thirty, for marriage discouraged fraternization with executives. The idea had once been committed to memo form by an ambitious personnel aide. The memo had been destroyed, the aide had been fired. Only the idea remained.

Since BII had a policy of internal promotion, most top-floor secretaries were graduates from below. They were selected by the executives they served. The two who worked with Miss Tompkins were not called secretaries to Mr. Breedlove. Only Miss Tompkins had that title; the other two, whom she'd hired, were her aides. One was a widow of forty-three, Mrs. Hazel Culbertson; the other, Hannah Brown, who was thirty-nine, had never been married. Neither attended the Troika party, as it was already being called.

The party was brief; by 3:30 P.M. the office had settled into its normal routine. Secretaries returned to their desks, smoothed their skirts, and resumed their poses behind noiseless IBM electric typewriters. The switchboard glowed, desk phones buzzed, office boys picked up memos from outbaskets. A maintenance man began to repair the tiny crack in the receptionist's paneling. The office life droned on quietly under the pale white glow of overhead neon, shielded from the bustle of the outside world by drawn drapes.

A messenger interrupted the order for a moment, skirting the receptionist and slouching down the executive corridor, issuing a strident whistle and twirling his cap over his finger. Somehow he found Miss Tompkins's office and unknowingly committed a capital sin. He violated the sacred space around her desk.

"Oh," said Mrs. Culbertson, peeking in. "Come away from there. Please."

"Letter for Lewis Anthony Breedlove."

"I'll take it."

"Oke. Sign here."

She did. He left, whistling. When he got back to his office, he discovered he'd been fired.

The Troika was placed on alert by Miss Tompkins at 4 P.M. Mr. Breedlove, she said, wished to see each member that afternoon, one at a time. Powell came first, moving slowly down the corridor, tapping his pipe in his hand. He was an astonished man. He had considered himself a very unlikely candidate for promotion; he had, in fact, believed for some months that he'd soon be pushed aside. He'd feared the new treasurer, a man with vast international experience, had been brought in from Brussels to replace him as vice-president—finance. Now, suddenly, he'd been promoted to at least a share of the presidency of the company. It was perplexing and stunning. Powell felt as if he'd been given new life.

Breedlove waved him to a chair in front of his desk and got right down to business.

"Philip Mendenthal is on our ass again," he said. "I just got his letter here. It's the formal declaration of his plans to start a proxy fight."

"Again?" Powell said, reaching for the letter.

Breedlove stood up. He walked to the windows and stood with his back to Powell. He lit a Lucky Strike. His back still turned, he said, "I want you to go see him, George. I want this s.o.b. off our backs, once and for all. I don't care what kind of tactics you use. There are more skeletons in his closet than in a graveyard, and you dig some of them out if you have to."

"Maybe he's willing to listen to a compromise," Powell said.

"No. No compromises." Breedlove turned. "I don't want two or three of his lackeys on this board, and neither do you."

"The letter asks that we send him our shareholder list."

"I have read the letter."

"Should I do it?"

Breedlove didn't answer immediately. He walked briskly across the carpet. The old sparkle was back in his eyes. He opened a closet door, probed around inside, and returned to Powell with a pair of red suspenders dangling in his hand, a boyish smirk on his lips.

"Send him the shareholder list," he said. "Tie it up with these."

Powell was flabbergasted. "Are you serious?"

"Yes. I am serious."

"Then you're not taking Mendenthal seriously."

"I sure as living hell am. Much more so this time than the last time. But I don't want *him* to know that."

Powell took the suspenders and slowly folded them. "I'll leave tomorrow."

"You'd better make it tonight. You fish around there in New York. See what his strength is. See how much of our stock he's got. See if anyone of substance is backing him this time. Hell, I don't have to tell you these things. You know what to do. And something else."

"Yes."

"I want to market some of my BII stock."

"How many shares?"

"From a hundred thousand to two hundred thousand, depending what the market will take. Will you see about that in New York?"

"You're thinking of a secondary offering?"

"Not unless you have to go that route. I don't want to take the time to get up a prospectus. There are other ways, are there not?"

"I could try the third market. But I don't know. That's a sizable block. You realize that you'll have to file an insider's report with Sec."

"I understand that," Breedlove said, exasperation in his voice. "You just get rid of the stock for me."

"I'll do my best."

"You have that confused look on your face, George. What is it you want to know?"

"Well, you realize that this isn't the best time to dispose of stock."

"I realize that, of course."

"And you've just told me you believe Mendenthal has a chance this time."

"I didn't say that. I said merely that I'm taking him seriously."

"Then why sell two hundred thousand shares? If this does come down to a proxy contest, we may need every vote we can get."

"If I do sell, it may stop this thing before it starts."

"Please explain that."

Instead, Breedlove began to laugh, followed by a spate of red-faced choking. He sat down behind his desk.

"George, I want to tell you something. I think you're the best goddamn financial man in the country, and I'm very glad that we have you. You took us through some terribly difficult maneuvers when we were buying every fucking thing in sight. But you don't have the slightest iota of understanding when it comes to human psychology. You can't read people. I want to flaunt this stock sale in Mendenthal's face. It's just like the red suspenders. He's going to be thinking what I want him to think. That we're not afraid of him. The truth is that we are. If this proxy fight comes off, we're going to be working our asses off to stop him. But I want him to think, for now, that we consider him just an old fool who's trying to get his rocks off by satisfying an old grudge. I want him off balance. He may reconsider."

"I must tell you that I do not think what you say adds up well."

"Still, however, it is what I say."

"Very well. I'll go to New York."

"If you go with a chip on your shoulder, I might as well send an office boy."

"There is no chip on my shoulder. It is a matter only of disagreement."

"Instead of disagreement, I want harmony with you on this. And something else. In your estimation, how well will we do this year?"

"The forecast is for six billion dollars sales, about three dollas per share net profits."

"Can you jack it up? Say, to three-fifty?"

"Not with income from operations. And not unless the accounting methods are changed again."

"I'm not satisfied with our price/earnings ratio. That's our real measure. I'm not satisfied."

"This is not a good stock market."

"It is for IBM. You look at IBM. Their growth rate is under ours, yet their PE is higher. I want you to think up some ways to get ours higher. We'll need it with this fucking proxy fight coming up. Give me a report on the PE matter."

Breedlove tapped a letter opener on his desk, a signal for Powell to leave. "Very well," Powell said, rising.

"My best to Susan," Breedlove said. He was looking away.

Powell left. He felt confused and slightly intimidated. He carried the red suspenders. Absurd. Did Breedlove actually expect him to use them? It was asinine. Childish. He had never really liked Breedlove. He'd never tried to get close to him. Now he realized something else. He actually despised the crude, abusive old man.

* * *

Entering Breedlove's office, Henry Lancaster knew immediately that the meeting would be short. Breedlove kept a three-minute hourglass on his desk, a device he used to limit phone calls and also to signal visitors that their meetings with him would soon be terminated. Now he slapped it over; the sands began to run. Lancaster grinned. He sat down. It was a crude device, but at least more honest than the secretary's phone call to tell the boss he was late for another meeting.

"I saw the CBS program," Breedlove said. "I had it taped and saw it this morning. In my opinion it was not worthy of our sponsorship. Did it get a rating?"

"A very low rating, I'm afraid."

"Then we threw a half million out the window."

"I'm not ready to accept that conclusion. When you sponsor these specials on important subjects you might get a low general rating but you get a high profile of important people. A high-quality audience."

Breedlove waved both hands. "Hank, where do you live? You live in Bel Air, don't you? That's what we'd call high quality. Yet I'll wager that your consumption of aspirin and toothpaste is no greater than the average nigger in Watts who was watching 'Hollywood Squares' or the ballgame when we were educating the world about the tragedy of Vietnam."

Lancaster began to feel a little uneasy. Breedlove was red-cheeked and animated, a sharp contrast to his relatively spiritless performance in the boardroom. Somehow, a massive dose of adrenaline had been pumped into his veins.

"I think we need a new ad agency," he said. "At least for the Food Division. You go to New York, Hank, and shake up things. Fire the agency if necessary."

"I have been considering changing agencies."

"I'm happy to hear you have. I'm sorry that nothing has been done about it."

"I wanted to discuss it with you first."

"When we acquired Mayer Drugs, we got our hands on a magazine in New York."

"Yes. *Fortnightly Comment.*"

"Do you read it?"

"On occasion."

"I read the red ink in their balance sheet. I want you to do something about that, too."

"Fold it?"

"As you see fit. And my congratulations. Can you work with Powell?"

"I'm sure that I can."

"I know you can work with Scottie. I want to mention that I liked—very much—the way you handled the plane incident."

Lancaster beamed. He glanced at the hourglass and left.

A nervous and courageous Joan Leeky kept Miss Tompkins under the hold button as Scott talked to Anne. Then she entered Scott's offce with a note that read, "Miss Tompkins says Mr. Breedlove will see you now." Scott took the note. Joan left.

"I don't know what to *say*," Anne said. "Did you tell me you've been made *president?*"

"Office of the President. Three of us."

"Shall I tell the kids? Oh! We'll have a party for you, the kids and the neighbors."

"Your mood has changed."

"Not because of this. You know my moods change. So do yours."

"Are you still going to go into politics?"

"I'm still going to go into politics, yes. But first we'll have a party. Will you invite George Powell?"

"How about Hank?"

"All right. I'll wear my armor. I wonder if this has cheered up George. He's so . . . well, so immeasurably *sad*."

"Have you forgotten Disney World?"

"Hardly. The kids and I may go alone. When will you be home tonight?"

"I think I'll be a little late."

"I want to love you."

"Then I'll hurry." Scott looked up in astonishment to see Breedlove wandering into his office. "Gotta hang up."

"Will you marry me?" Anne said.

"Immediately."

Breedlove waved his hand. "No, go ahead, talk," he said. But Scott had hung up. Breedlove walked to the door, closed it, and slumped down on the couch. Scott could not remember a time when Breedlove had been in his office. He'd always been summoned to Breedlove's. Now Breedlove was scrutinizing the walls. "Your taste in art, Scottie. It leaves something to be desired." He said it with a smile.

"To each his own."

"I'm sorry we missed the insurance company."

"I'm sorry, too. Believe me, we tried."

Breedlove leaned back, his hands behind his head, his eyes closed. His weight loss now seemed even more apparent to Scott, especially in the neck and arms. He seemed frail and unsubstantial, with dry, splotched skin and extended veins. His eyes opened. A sparkle appeared.

"Those fucking insurance companies," he said. "You make a claim and you discover you're undercovered and still your rates go up. You don't make a claim and your rates still go up because others are making claims. And *they* claim underwriting losses are eating them up. Christ, what a racket they have. I still want in in that business."

"Perhaps we should give it another try."

"No, I don't think so. Not now. We're fat with acquisitions already, as if you didn't know. What you three have to face, and iron out, is the digestion phase."

Scott stood up. He still felt somewhat timid in Breedlove's presence, an awe or an almost-fear that he had tried to overcome. Perhaps now was a good time to start.

"If I ask you something personal, will I get a straight answer?" he said.

"You can ask."

"You've been to Mayo. What did they tell you?"

"That I'm a dying man. Can't you tell by looking at me that I'm a dying man?"

"You do not look like one. Nor do you talk like one."

"Death is the least of my worries, or my fears. I'll tell you exactly what they did and what they said. They told me to quit smoking. I've cut down to less than a pack a day. They told me to reduce my work load. You saw today at the board meeting what I've done about that. Then a bunch of shit-faced specialists in rubber gloves looked up my asshole for two weeks, pumped me full of green piss and took pictures, back and front and sides, and then shot me so full of what was probably some poison that I got so sick I had to leave. Because they knew I don't give money for medical research, they made it as painful as they could. Now that I'm out of that jail, I feel great. You should see the bill. Will you go to Olen?"

"What was that?"

"I want you to go to Olen. Wisconsin. Home week for you."

"You have a way of introducing a subject, don't you?"

"I want you to go pretty soon. Tomorrow. Just snoop around. That plant's having labor problems again and I'm not sure we should keep it, at least not there."

"Why not send Adamson?"

"He wasn't raised in Wisconsin. And he hasn't worked a canning line and he's a fuck-up when it comes to working with people. He doesn't think. You do." Breedlove's face now seemed paler. His voice had weakened. "I know what you're thinking. It's too small a job for a president."

"I'm not the president."

"That meeting just now, Scottie. Bullshit."

"What do you mean?"

"I set it up like this because I don't want to lose them. Not now."

"Who?"

"Lancaster and Powell."

"I'm afraid I don't understand."

"What I'm saying is that I didn't set up this three-man thing hoping it would last. And I'm also saying that I want it to be you who comes out on top. Why? For a reason you'll understand later. It's not that you're smarter or more experienced than the others. I'll tell you later what it is. What I'll tell you now is that it *can* be you and that's the way I want it. You can have it, if you want it badly enough."

"Is that what you told Lancaster and Powell too?"

"No. It's what I'm telling you. But you've got to want it. More than a home and a family. More than anything. I want this company in your blood. I want it so that you can't separate your gut from it, so it becomes like a person to you. So it *is* you." Breedlove paused, looking away. "The trouble with most people is that they really don't know what they want. Or who they are. When this is over, I think you'll know who you are. There are some things you have to show me before this ends up yours, but I think you will show me. You've got to learn to look at things more realistically and to wield a big stick more often. Now you go to Olen for me."

"All right. I'll go to Olen."

"I'll admit, to you, that that Olen plant was somewhat of a whim of mine. I came from there, and that area damn near killed me, so I suppose returning there was a way of showing them I couldn't be erased." Breedlove fumbled for a cigarette, found none, and started to get up. His face showed strain, as if movement caused him pain. "I'll tell you this, Scottie. This old fart's not gone yet. He's going to be around to pester for quite a while. Now it's time I took another one of those horse pills."

Scott stepped forward. "There's one other matter."

"You want to discuss the airplane incident." Breedlove had a way of anticipating, of knowing what was on someone's mind. He eyed Scott squarely. "All I know is security says an underground revolutionary group got aboard in Chicago."

"No." Scott met Breedlove's stare. "I don't think so."

"Scottie, exactly what are you trying to say?"

"I think Lawrence knew about it."

"Lawrence? Lawrence is in Europe."

"He is not in Europe. He's here. I saw him just a few hours ago. He was wild, almost incoherent. He was trying to warn me—us—of some danger. Something to do with the 727. He said for me to tell you that it's personal."

"I thank you for telling me this but I don't want you to concern yourself with it," Breedlove snapped. It was not a request. It was an order. The old man rubbed hard at a spot in his back, rubbed almost viciously with his knuckles, as if he could eradicate a pain by creating a greater pain. "You have enough to worry about now without worrying about a company airplane. I'll take care of that matter myself. It is nothing, but I'll continue to look into it."

"One more thing. Do you own a Rembrandt painting?"

Breedlove clapped his palms together. "Yes," he said. He added sharply, "I don't know how, but you've gotten yourself into something that is none of your concern. I want you to stay out of it. Now understand that."

"What if Lawrence contacts me again?"

"Tell me." Breedlove's eyes seemed to grow dim. "Scottie, in today's times I'm not sure we have much control over our offspring, and I'm not sure that we're responsible for their actions when they're grown. I see no sense in discussing personal matters. If you're frightened, I assure you that the fear is unjustified. You see, you are like the leader of a nation now, and you will be protected as they're protected. I don't think you really realize yet what a big day this has been for you. What I'm doing, in effect, is handing you a company. But not for free. I didn't get it free." He paused. He struggled for his breath. "I didn't," he said. "Not for free. I lived in a tent for three years. I scrimped and I didn't work only when I slept. Some people would tell you I also schemed and raped and robbed. If I did, it was for this."

"And that is what you want me to do?"

"No. That's past. But if you want it, you will do things you do not want to do. Now, if you'll let me go, I'll limp out and down that fucking horse pill. My luck to you, Scottie. Say hello to the family for me."

He left. He nodded at Joan Leeky as he passed her desk and moved slowly down the corridor, walking in a stoop-shouldered, shuffling posture characteristic of a very old man. Miss Tompkins waited for him at the end of the corridor.

As he passed Powell's office on his way to keep his appointment with Lancaster, Scott heard a sound like glass breaking from within. He paused at the door.

"George? Are you still here?"

There was no answer. The door was ajar. Scott pushed on it carefully and stepped into the office. Powell sat behind his desk, glancing into a book—an upright, studied position that appeared to have been assumed for effect. There was a smear of liquid on the wall. A broken cocktail glass lay on the carpet.

Powell looked up. "Scottie. Come on in. I was just catching up on some matters here. Waiting for the traffic to subside."

Scott picked up the glass. "Join us for a drink. I'm meeting Hank."

"No, thanks. I've had my one a day."

"It looks as if you threw it out."

"A little celebration party," Powell said. "A celebration for myself, by myself. Like the old college days. Take a sip, toss the glass into the fireplace." His eyes widened. "And, ah, there were fires then. Fires in the brain."

"What are you reading?"

"Wallace Stevens. Have you ever read him?"

"I'll have to plead blind ignorance. I've never heard of him."

"He was a poet. And an insurance executive."

"I wasn't aware you had an interest in poetry."

"Shall I read this to you?"

"If you like."

Powell did not read. He closed the book and quoted:

> *"Let the lamp afix its beam.*
> *The only emperor is the emperor of ice cream."*

"Your Mr. Stevens?" Scott said.

"He is saying no ruler rules over anything really significant, at least not endlessly."

"I begin to see. We're getting closer to the subject. Lewis Breedlove."

Powell stood up. "I think Breedlove is ill. An illness that approaches dementia."

"Dementia? Hardly. He's as sharp as a firecracker."

"In my opinion, he is a m~ who fears something."

"Why do you say that, George?"

"Call it just a hunch."

"Anything to do with the airplane incident?"

"I don't know. Perhaps. I said it was just a hunch."

"Breedlove did say he had some personal business to take care of. Do you have any idea what he meant by that?"

"No."

"I'll bet my bottom dollar it has something to do with the incident on the airplane."

"I don't know," Powell said thoughtfully. "I'm sorry, in fact, that I brought it up. You know that I dislike surmising or guessing." He looked up. "I believe that I have not yet congratulated you."

"Nor I you."

"It will be a pleasure working with you."

"I feel the same way, George."

"We should have that meeting. But I must leave for New York."

"I'm off, too. Wisconsin."

"He has sent us all away on missions."

"Hank, too?"

"I understand Henry is going east soon."

Scott smiled. "Have we been throned as co-presidents or as errand boys?"

"It's far from an errand I'm undertaking. We might be facing another proxy contest."

"A proxy fight? Tell me."

"I'm afraid I'm late for an appointment already. I'll tell you what I know in the elevator." Powell went to his desk, picked up a photograph of his twins, and placed it face down in a drawer. He looked at Scott with dim eyes. Scott thought of Anne's phrase. The immeasurably sad Mr. Powell. Powell said slowly, "I rather suspect you realize I threw that drink not in exhilaration but in frustration." He looked away. "You know that I am not a man who unburdens his personal problems on others."

"Perhaps you should."

"How is your family?"

"Very well, thank you. Anne and I want you over."

"I fear our social life these days borders on the nonexistent."

"As Mannering would say, c'mon down."

"Mannering. I fear we'll have to do something about Mannering. The company clown."

"I regard him as welcome relief."

"Scottie, if I were to ask you to name the one factor in America and perhaps the world that characterizes the times today, what would your answer be?"

"I'm not sure. Atomic revolution? Social change?"

"No. I nominate something else. The decline in religious faith."

"Agreed."

"You are a man with religious convictions. I am one who once had such convictions. I would like to say that I admire you for maintaining yours. And I would like to add that I greatly respect your executive abilities."

"Thank you. The feeling is mutual. May I now officially offer my friendship to you?"

"I'm afraid it's too late for that now."

"I don't accept that, George."

Powell turned abruptly and gazed at Scott, his eyes again dim, far away; he spoke in a strained, halting voice, as if the words came with great difficulty.

"Scottie, I would like to tell you something I hope you'll

accept in the spirit of friendship. It will be the last of this outburst. Somewhere along the path of our lives, we do things that cause us great losses. It is the haste of things. We wake up one morning to discover we are no longer young or even middle-aged, and we realize, in a flood of panic, that we've lost not only those we have loved but perhaps even our ability to love. It is too much to pay. It is too much to pay. In our haste, we do not face things. There does not seem to be time. We run too fast. My Mr. Stevens said it more meaningfully: 'We live in an old chaos of the sun.' If we look back, I think we can see times where we could have changed matters if we'd acted differently. But we can't go back. Or perhaps it would do no good to go back. Maybe it has all been planned, started those aeons ago when the sun threw off blazing rocks to form our earth. I don't know. It becomes too late with the quickness of snapping fingers. I am sorry. It is a strange mood to be in after news of a promotion. I fear I've said quite too much. Yes, quite too much."

Scott returned Powell's gaze. He felt a surge of genuine affection for the man. He realized he was seeing an entire new side of him, a hidden side of a sensitive and even highly emotional man who, to the world, presented a front of reserve and, on occasion, intellectual snobbery. Except for superficial comments, Powell had never before discussed personal matters with Scott; now, in a few seconds, he'd revealed more of himself than he had over the past decade.

"C'mon," Scott said. He grinned. "C'mon down."

They walked the executive corridor to the elevator together, carrying briefcases, friends at that moment.

Despite the fact that Harry's Bar was within walking distance of the Breedlove Building, Scott had never been there. It was a replica of the Venice bar of the same name and catered primarily to theater-goers at the Shubert directly above it or tourists visiting the nearby ABC Entertainment Center. Scott entered it, squinted, and finally spotted Lancaster at a far-wall table, drinking Beefeater-rocks. With him was a young woman in a semiformal blue gown. When Scott approached, the woman stood up. She was, he saw, a stunning beauty.

"Allow me to introduce Mr. Scott," Lancaster said. "Mr. Scott, this is Miss—"

"Lois Frankel," the girl said, smiling.

"We have changed her name," Lancaster said, sipping his drink. "From now on, she is Lola Layne. That's spelled L as in love, A as in ache, Y as in yearn—"

"I'm pleased to meet you, Mr. Scott, but I must run," Lois Frankel said. "Goodbye, Mr. Lancaster."

She waved her red-tipped fingers and left. Scott sat down. "You look half gone," he told Lancaster. "How many you had?"

"A couple."

"Who was the girl?"

"A conversation piece, that's all. She's a stand-in upstairs in the theater."

"I see."

"It is all theater. All theater. We ourselves have our small drama. The king is abdicating, the kingdom is being divided. And who shall prove his love the greatest, that man shall gain the realm. It is drama. Real drama. We have the king, his kingdom, and his castle, and we ourselves, we are the knights, dispatched on our crusades to gain favor with the king. We have, even, a court jester."

"That reference, I'll assume, is to Carter Mannering."

"The reference was indeed to Carter Mannering."

"Powell wants to get rid of him."

"So, already, on day one, we have conflict. I'll fight to keep him. And I'll tell you why."

"Because he can sell."

"Because he is a genius at selling." Lancaster shifted closer to Scott. His eyes sparkled. "And that's what it is really all about in most companies. Selling. On the bottom line, scrape away the bullshit, it's selling. We're not far removed from the old hawkers who sold cure-all medicines at the county fair. Step right up, folks, and for a dollar get your cure for dandruff, bad breath, headache, liver ailments, TB, and cancer. The only difference is that we peddle scientifically. We have six hundred people with M.A.s in peddling."

"And they live in San Marino. Or Bel Air."

"Well, we welcome anybody in Bel Air as long as they have money. In Bel Air, we welcome niggers, spicks, wops, kikes, polocks, even Chinks, Japs, and gooks. As long as they have money. Well, we do rule out all pyromaniacs and mad-eyed hippies. All other maniacs are welcomed, especially money maniacs. We writhe with maniacs of all descriptions."

Lancaster drank. Scott peered at him—at the exterior man in his Brooks Brothers suit and Gucci shoes, wearing gold cuff links and a 23-jewel Cartier watch—and he wondered if he'd ever be able to penetrate to the interior of a man so complex, many-sided, so flexible and quick-changing in attitude and outlook. He was revealing, yet inscrutable. The waiter arrived. Scott ordered a vodka martini; Lancaster ordered another Beefeater-rocks, a double. Scott found himself amused and somewhat startled. He'd never seen Lancaster even slightly tipsy before; now the man seemed quite drunk. The drinks came. Lancaster lifted his.

"Not to me, nor to you, nor to Mr. Powell. We will drink to us three. To the Breedlove Troika. From the same glass, we drink."

"To the Troika."

"To the three musketeers, the three stooges, the three blind mice. To Percival, Gawain, and Galahad."

"You left out King Arthur."

"Oh, many omitted," Lancaster said, and, to Scott's amazement, he chanted, "Oh, Agravaine, oh, Gaheris, oh, Gareth; of Pellinor, of Lamorak, of Aglovale, of Durnarde; up Labor, up Pellam, up Pelles and Elaine; down Launcelot, down Ban, down Bors and Lionel. And Lionel number two."

Lancaster paused. He drank. He flashed his smile. His eyes were wide and very bright. "No," he said. "I am mistaken. We are not knights. We are gophers. We are high-priced gophers. You work directly for Lewis Breedlove, you are a Lewis Breedlove gopher. But it won't be like that forever. He can't live forever."

"Sometimes I wonder about that."

"Have you told Anne?"

"About what happened to us today, I've told her that, yes. But I haven't told her I have to go to Olen."

"I pine for you. They will eat you alive there when you close that plant. The hometown boy with the big double cross. Bring a bodyguard. I can get the Swedish Angel on rental from Abbey for six bucks an hour plus nine pounds of raw red horse meat per day."

"We might not close the plant."

"If you don't, you may end up not president gopher but office-boy gopher."

"Whatever we do, we have time. After all, we're holding the annual meeting in Olen next year."

"If we live so long."

"What do you mean by that?"

"Nothing. Except that life has no guarantees." Lancaster peered at Scott. "This Troika malarkey. It won't last. This will come down to one of us. Breedlove hasn't the slightest hope that it will work."

"Did he tell you that, Hank?"

"No. Did he tell you that?"

Scott hesitated. "No," he said.

"We're placed not in a band but in a ring." Lancaster waved. "Waiter! Another round."

"Not for me. I'm fine."

Again he peered at Lancaster. He thought not of Lancaster, however, but of Lewis Breedlove. He saw the external Breedlove before him—the hollow cheeks, sallow face, the deep, penetrating eyes. He knew only the outer Breedlove; he'd never been able to reach to the inner man. What of his background, his associations, his mind, his feelings? Scott did not know. It was said around BII that Scott was personally closer to Breedlove than any other executive, yet Scott could not recall a time when the old man had really revealed much of himself to him. Certainly Breedlove had taken an interest in Scott's progress at BII; he'd been the dominant factor in Scott's series of rapid promotions. And now, apparently, Breedlove had picked him for the top spot, a prospect still overwhelming to him. What did he know about his benefactor? He knew that Breedlove had founded and built BII into a giant multinational conglomerate, that somehow he had clawed and fought and exercised the powers of his mind to forge, tear, create a living empire. A genius? It was very likely. A monomaniac? Perhaps. Breedlove had been born to abject poverty; he'd had very little formal education. What explained it? Timing? Genes? Mere desire? Scott had seldom pondered the questions before. Yet now Breedlove's force haunted him. An insatiable curiosity gripped him, heightened by today's encounter with Breedlove's son.

Earlier he'd intended to tell Lancaster of the encounter, and of Breedlove's reaction to Larry's warning. Now he decided he would not mention it. Nor had he mentioned it to Powell.

Why? He did not know.

Would Lancaster or Powell use the 727 soon?

He'd call Harold Long. Tonight. Make sure the plane was grounded.

He felt cold. It was a feeling of quiet anxiety, almost of terror.

Lancaster's lips moved. The inner Lancaster, Scott realized, was also an unknown quantity. Only his surface showed. New York-born, Penn State athlete; briefly, a professional quarterback. Once owned a New York ad agency. Married to beautiful Dorothy. Also, he had great personal magnetism, untiring energy, wit and intelligence, and a tremendous speaking ability. Once, receiving an SC management award, he'd been given a five-minute ovation at the Beverly Hills Hotel after delivering an extemporaneous speech that had lasted forty minutes. Scott had listened in awe. Yet, driving home that night, he'd been unable to recall one concrete point Lancaster had made about anything.

"Scottie, I'll tell you what I think you should do with the rest of your life. You shouldn't get any deeper into the shit world than you are. You will lose your reality and perhaps even jeopardize your life. I'll tell you what I think you should do. Get yourself a backing, buy a radio station, and go into the evangelist's business. You're a natural for that. You'd make 'em forget about Aimee and forget about Billy. And you'd have the best of all worlds. You'd be healing sinners and you'd get rich to boot."

Scott sipped his drink. "Are you telling me something?"

"My man, you may be the best of us all. The best of us all. But you're not a risker. Do you know what a risker is? He's the guy who'd put his life on the line for a dime. Like that fellow who jumps fourteen buses and rivers on his motorcycle. He's crazy, you see. So was Columbus. So were the Vikings. So are war volunteers. I'm a risker. Breedlove's a risker. So, by the way, is Mannering. Last week that nut flew upside down strapped to the top wing of a biplane to publicize an air show in a town where he operates. It made every TV news program in L.A. We'd do it for a dime. For a penny. Because if a man would not risk his life for a penny, he wouldn't risk it for a million dollars. Smart people, sure, try to balance risk against the potential reward. But those who really make it have more than smarts. They have balls. They'll take the risk, the risk of their lives against the penny. You don't, then you lose your nerve. You won't risk it for a million. You don't believe my way."

"Yet I'm listening to you."

"He may ask you to take the risk."

"Who? Breedlove?"

"He has extraordinary instincts. He has poetic instincts. He can read minds. About people he cares nothing. That is his great power. His advantage. The Breedlove advantage. He is an animal in the trees, with a cunning *Homo sapiens* mind. Is this pop psychology?"

"I think you're wrong."

"About what?"

"That he cares nothing about people."

"Then I am wrong. Maybe he has only developed his non-caring more than most others. Because if you bottom-line it, my man, none of us really cares for people. Do our hearts bleed when we see them suffer after a disaster? No. We thank the stars we were not involved. We water at the mouth when we see falling buildings and consuming fires at the movies. Tell me that I'm wrong."

"I don't know, Hank."

"When I add that we all, perhaps even you, are just a slight step above the jungle world, then also I'm wrong."

"Shall we adjourn this? Do you want a ride home?"

Lancaster's eyes narrowed. He sneered. "Look around you. The ladies. The gentlemen. Us. Us in our three-hundred-dollar suits and the women in gowns and jewels. But Capone wore three-hundred-dollar suits, too, and strip the women and they all fuck like animals. Out there, fish eat fish, eagles prey, and jungle bunnies stick knives in each other. And whores crawl in the night with festered pussies, hating the world. Say it's not so."

"All right," Scott said, feeling uncomfortable. "It's so. Now may I ask you something?"

"You may. My man, you may."

"There are two matters. One is your postmortem thoughts on the airplane incident."

"That's simple. Somebody is after us, baby. I don't know who or why, but I won't let it trouble me. Question two?"

"You mentioned an overseas slush fund. Where is it accounted for in the balance sheet?"

"Ask Powell."

"I will."

"On second thought, don't ask Powell. He won't answer. It's between Powell and Breedlove."

"I was under the impression that even Breedlove had a board of directors to whom he is responsible."

"Were you? Were you really?"

"Hank, I simply will not take any more of your abuse."

"You call this abuse?"

"I call it abuse, yes."

"Very well, my man, no more abuse. Let us shake. Soon we will come out fighting."

"I'm not a fighter. I'm remarkably uncoordinated."

"Then you had better go into training."

"I think you should take a cab home, Hank."

"We see ourselves in war. Did you go to war?"

"I'm afraid I missed all of the wars."

"It's extraordinary how easy it is to kill. It's extraordinary how interesting combat is. We should be grateful for wars. Breedlove built this company on war contracts. Without wars, we would be a dot on the map." Lancaster drank. "Scottie, you are not a bad executive. I think, when I am on top, that I might keep you on. If you grow some balls."

"Then I promise I will do the same for you when I go up."

"No. You have yet to really see me. When you do see me, as you will, you will not want me. I will be revealed to you in stages. Here is a hint of me. Look over there. See that black buck in a suit? No, behind you. Now he's all dressed up, sure, but that is a mask. Suppose we're in his territory. You're with your wife. Anne? Up to you comes this black bastard and says he'd like to screw Anne. 'I desire to fuck the lady,' is what he says. What do you do?"

"I'll get you a taxi."

"First, let me tell you what I'd do. I'd grin at the guy. I'd say, 'Hey, man,' grinning. Then I'd stand up. I'm in their territory, so I'm ready. I have a ten-inch blade under the table. Before this cocksucker knows what hit him, I have the blade under his chin. He backs off. He runs. There isn't a nigger born who's not scared shitless of a knife."

"Is that your fantasy of the day?"

"I deal in fantasy, most certainly." Lancaster extended his hand. "Shake," he said.

"Shake," Scott said.

9

ALONG THE MIRACLE MILE DISTRICT ON WILSHIRE BOULE-vard in Los Angeles, adjacent to the County Museum of Art, there is a sticky, treacherous bog known as the La Brea tar pits. It bubbles and oozes blackly, stinking of oil and sulfur, within a few steps of the placid Manet landscapes and amorous Rodin love sculptures in the museum. Tar from the pits was once used to pave Los Angeles streets, an early contribution to the city's mania to become overwhelmed by automobiles. Here paleontologists have excavated the largest collection of prehistoric fossil bones ever discovered in North America. Replicas of saber-toothed tigers, mammoths, mast-odons, and sloths raise their woolly heads in angry defiance before visiting schoolchildren from Watts and San Marino alike, depicting the struggle with each other and with nature that led to their extinction ten thousand years before Christ.

Just before midnight, the chauffeur, Morris, stopped the Breedlove Cadillac on the Sixth Street side of the pits and waited for a signal from the lights of a Lincoln Continental to flash behind him. Lewis Breedlove sat slumped in the back seat, wearing a black topcoat and a hat. It had begun to rain, a firm patter that chilled the air and streaked the wind-shield.

"Should I stay, Mr. Breedlove?" Morris asked into the auto's intercom tube.

"Have I asked you to leave?"

"No, sir."

Morris leaned back. In the side-view mirror he saw the Continental stop about five car lengths behind. Its lights flicked twice. Soon Morris heard footsteps on the sidewalk. He did not turn. They were the footsteps of two men, he knew. The back-seat locks clicked open. The two men got in beside Breedlove. No one said a word of greeting. On other occasions when Breedlove had met men in his auto, Morris had been instructed to keep the intercom on and to record the conversation on a portable tape recorder under the dash. This time he had not been asked to make a recording. He'd left the intercom on, however—not out of curiosity but simply because he'd forgotten to turn it off. Now he feared to do so, thinking the little clicking sound might give Breedlove and the others the impression he'd been deliberately listening.

He heard Breedlove say, "I have my own security department, but I don't want to use it on personal matters."

"That's understandable, Mr. Breedlove," one of the men responded. "The man, by the way, he sends his regards. He will be here personal, he says, if that's what'cha want. He ain't been feelin' up to snuff lately, but he'll be here if that's what'cha want. He ain't a man forgets, Hudson ain't."

Morris perked up. He'd heard of a man named Hudson before, a Hudson who'd liked boxing and horse races and was rumored to be a dope dealer and whore supplier. Managers and trainers had talked of him around the gyms, especially on the West Coast. Hudson was a big man and a feared man. When word came down to a fighter from Hudson that you sit down your next bout, you sat down; if you didn't, you'd find yourself without a license or, worse, with broken hands in some dark back alley. Could this be the same Hudson? Well, probably not. A man with Breedlove's money wouldn't be a meeting with people who knew Hudson. They must be talking about another Hudson. Morris heard a few more scraps of conversation—something about a painting and an airplane—and decided to hear no more. They were talking now about something he had knowledge of; the talk frightened him, so he tuned it out. Instead, he fantasized. He had stopped Bolin in the sixth round that night, not the other way around.

It was a fight he'd relived a hundred times. He'd been seventh in *Ring*'s middleweight rankings at the time, and Bolin had been fifth. It was a status Morris had never even dreamed he could reach. Seventh ranked in the *world*. The winner would get a crack at the title, and, for both contenders, the white boy and the black boy, it had been a long road getting there. For Morris, it had been reached through an interminable succession of back-street gyms reeking of sweat and blood smells, sheetless motor-court mattresses crusted with yellow stains like hardened slime, hitchhikes, freight trains, managers and promoters with bow ties and suspenders calling him "kid" and "boy" and, to anger him, to rev him up for the kill, "smartass nigger." And it had been reached through the living pain of taped fists bashing the heavy bag, eye cuts sewn and iced like meat, push-ups, rope dances, sit-ups, roadwork, blood urine, spit pails like toilet foam, ringing earaches after bouts won or lost, beer-logged crowds frenzied at first blood, swabs of fat cutmen on a face squashed numb. Niggers bleed black. Never hit a nigger in the head; take him out with body punches. Cut the nigger and he'll run. It was a world of deals, fee-splitting, pills, dives, setups, publicity men, resin smells, and ring bells that bonged far into sleepless nights.

But he was up now. He'd reached the near top. He was main event, the Garden. He was 41–6 as a pro and he'd been down only three times and he'd been KO'd only once. He had only eight KO's himself, for he wasn't a puncher. He was a dancer, he knew how to counter, he could use both hands, he knew how to use the ropes, he could go fifteen without tiring, he knew tricks like kidney jabs and rabbit punches when the ref wasn't alert, how to cheat in the clinches, how to psych out opponents with long nigger stares at the weigh-ins and introductions.

Bolin, the white boy, knew them too.

The fight was for real.

They felt each other out in the first two rounds. Morris got in a few good body punches. Bolin trapped him on the ropes in round two and scored heavily with a right cross that Morris somehow couldn't shake. But his knees held sturdily. His legs carried him well. They clinched and pushed a lot in the third, and Morris again felt the dizziness from the hard right cross, a feeling that he wasn't here, he was away, drifting and bodiless. But he wasn't tired. His counterpunches were sharp. He got the jab in repeatedly. He opened a cut above Bolin's eye in the fourth. He would work on the cut, open it again, obscure the white boy's vision, blood him, scare him, show him nigger power. Because it was for the niggers that he fought, for the mamas and the chicks, for the little boys with noses squashed against candy-store windows; here, in the ring, he could lash out at the white world, at sneering whitey in red trunks, at he mob shrieking for whitey, at the promoters wanting whitey to win. But the strangeness in his vision after the second-round right; it was like looking at everything through jagged glass. This was the Garden. It was on TV. Mama has kind eyes. Papa never remembered to zip his fly. Preacher's got shiny pants. Catch a nigger by the toe. Sambo. tiger. black boy. sweet tits in sultry summer no' cant go home

Sixth-round bell.

Breedlove and the men had left the Cadillac. They strolled in the park. "I know something about it now," Breedlove said. "I have a fake Rembrandt. I want to know how the real one got out, where and by whom it was sold. I think it goes way beyond the theft of the painting. I think they're using that painting to raise money to hire some heavies to push me around. Maybe scare us into coughing up some money. You people know how to do this. My security department doesn't. They'll be working on it, too, but you work independently. When you find out what's behind it, let me know. I want all of them taken care of. No matter who it is. You might find family in this."

"Family?" one of the men said.

"I have a son. If you can call him son."

"Maybe we'll start there, lookin' for him."

"Let me know before you do anything."

"Sure."

"Hudson will back me on this."

"You two go back a long ways, don't you?"

"Some forty years or more."

"He ain't feelin' so good, like I said."

"I'm sorry to hear it."

"Well, he's still boss, I'll tell you that."

"Tell him I'm still boss, too," Breedlove said.

Morris had thought he'd had Bolin down. It was a sweet one-two, Bolin coming in, flush on. Then he saw faces above him. He had no hearing. He saw Bolin's hairy legs. The ref was above him. He felt the canvas. *He* was down. Was it six? Seven? He strained to rise. Then he was up. He was all right. Where had that punch come from? He couldn't feel his legs. He moved mid-ring, his gloves up, and watched Bolin lurch in for the kill.

Later they told him he'd been down five times before the ref had stopped it. He could not remember it. He'd showered and dressed and had gone by taxi to his hotel. The headache had begun about midnight, burning needles deep in his brain that blackened his vision and opened his pores to gush out thick globes of hot sweat. He weathered the night, but was admitted to Bellevue·in the morning and operated upon for a blood clot in the brain. He didn't die, to the amazement of the doctors. His manager didn't visit. An elderly black trainer who said he'd once fought Jersey Joe said the ref had been suspended for not stopping it sooner. No medical board would certify Morris to fight again. He'd wandered, broke, for almost two years, visiting gyms and empty arenas, thinking of the battle up from Mississippi, where mama and papa had laughed and loved, and where a warm-bodied girl had met him in tall grass on hot nights filled with bird sounds and lonely train whistles. He couldn't go home. A man once ranked seventh couldn't explain. Then, one day, someone from California named Scoggins contacted him, offering him a job of driver for a rich man in Los Angeles.

Morris had discovered several months ago that the rich man had owned a piece of his contract in his boxing days. Other owners were men like those who were now returning with the rich man to the back of the Cadillac.

He opened his eyes. To his right lay the dark slime of the tar pits. The rain made patterns like faces on the windshield.

A thick, moist fog had replaced the rain by the time Lawrence Breedlove stopped the Volkswagen near the porch stoop of the apartment building in Venice. It was close to dawn. He couldn't think clearly, but he knew this was the right place. He'd been here recently, perhaps only yesterday or this morning. His body ached. He fought nausea. The need cried out shrilly in him, deep in his flesh; it said fix me, fix me, fix me. He opened the car door. He was too weak to get out. The fog swirled around him, encasing him like a chill blanket. *Test yourself,* he thought. *What day is it? What time?* He did not know. Time no longer had meaning to him. It fled by, days and nights blending into each other with the swiftness and unsteadiness of dream sequences. He leaned forward. He must move. But the fog held him; he was frozen in its clammy embrace. He'd been in a fog, it seemed, most of his life, his occasional square-jawed resolve always shaken and defeated by indecision and vacillation. Fear trod behind him; fear slept with him. The old man had said it, time and time again. He could never do anything right. Today he'd tried. But he had failed. He'd come back to his benefactor in the apartment with the light in the window that beckoned to him through the fog. It would be warm in the room. All he had to do was get out of the car, walk up the narrow side street, go up the stairs, follow the worn velvet hall carpeting to the yellow door. There was peace behind the door. When had he met his benefactor? He could not remember. Nor could he remember where. It had been in Europe, he was sure, perhaps Rome or Paris. *Test yourself. Remember where.* But he couldn't. Not now. He would remember later. Besides, it really didn't matter. All that mattered was that he *had* met the man.

He felt slight shame. The man probably had saved his life and, today, Lawrence had almost betrayed him. But now he'd returned to him. To confess? To beg forgiveness? To plead for mercy? He didn't know. It seemed he was always confessing, always begging. His life was a circle. He couldn't make up his mind. *Go away. Now.* But he couldn't move. He shivered. Faint images appeared in the fog. He saw a shape like a woman in a white shroud. It was his mother. She moaned, calling to him. He closed his eyes. Dizziness overwhelmed him. *Test yourself. Shake it off. Think.* But he didn't want to think. Thinking only reminded him of hopelessness, of a dead-end past—Greyhound bus depots, rot-decay odors in cheap hotels, failures of Methadone and Synanon, queer queens, freaks in purple pants pushing dandelion H. It would have been better to die. His benefactor had done him no favor.

Now it was worse. Dark leaves seemed to be swirling past him, leaves that smelled of the sea. His shoulders ached. His stomach turned. Bile choked him. He began to retch, shaking with dry heaves. He thought he heard laughter in the fog. A bat with red eyes darted toward him. He screamed, his hands over his eyes. Strong arms reached out from the fog and seized him, holding him tightly.

"I'll help you," a familiar voice said.

Soon it was all right again. He was in the little room, under covers on the bed, cared for by his benefactor. A hamster ran on its treadmill in a cage near the window. It was warm in the room. Perhaps he had gone back in time and was in his father's house, in his bed on the edge of sleep. Sleep seemed to be his only joy in that house, sleep and dreams. Was this shadow-shrouded man seated across from him his father? Sometimes he feared the man like he'd feared his father. Yet, unlike his father, the man gave him comfort and spoke in hushed tones.

"I believe that you tried to warn them," the man said. "Was that an intelligent action? Why did you do it?" His tone was firm, almost scolding, but not angry. "Do you know why?"

Lawrence did not know why. That morning, awakening to see a giant man with tattoos of dragons on his arms squatted on the floor like an animal, his eyes twinkling like a child's play-twinkle as he adjusted the mechanism on a homemade bomb, he had realized for the first time since it had started that he was deeply involved in a matter very sinister and dangerous. He'd wanted to get away, away to anything—to do a charcoal etching, to build a sand castle on the beach, to write a poem about the sky. He was too sensitive for this. For years he'd been running from the tests and weights and manacles that always seemed to be thrust at him. Yet now, in warm comfort, fixed and serene, he did not understand why he'd acted as he had. Nor could he remember fully what he'd done that day. He was confused.

"You have shown unsteadiness," the other said. "You have not honored your pledge to me. Perhaps you have done no harm, for now they will writhe all the more, but you have disappointed me. He always said you were weak, did he not? I thought that I had shown you your strength."

"You did."

"I helped you."

"Yes."

"Like a brother."

"I have no brother."

"We will call it a brotherhood in spirit. Alone, we could not do this. Together, we are a man who can. You will gain from it. You will exchange that ragged coat for a silk gown. You will have a manservant to dress you. We have gone this far. We will go on. It is in motion and cannot be stopped. The girl has sold the painting in Europe and our professional mischief-makers have arrived. A wondrous pair."

"Swine," Lawrence said.

"Hardly swine. The German, when he is not doing his one-handed pushups, can touch a bolt in an airplane and tell you to the minute when its wing will fall off. The Italian, I do believe, could build an atomic bomb in a bathtub." The man paused. There was silence in the room, only the faint rustling of the hamster. "I must leave for a few days, taking one of them with me. The other will stay here. The car you have belongs to the black man who helped us. Does he want it returned?"

Lawrence pulled up the covers. He did not want to talk. The covers were warm.

"We will keep the car for now," the shadowed man said. "The black man has done his part. My mischief-makers now will do theirs." His voice droned on, a low, almost soothing voice. "We will move slowly, carefully. We will deal in the grotesque, high adventure, and in risk. The grotesque has always delighted me, and risk to me is as intoxicating as drugs are to you." The man leaned forward. Lawrence saw his face in the light. It was a face like his father's. The man opened the hamster cage and took the animal out. He stroked its fur. Again his face was hidden. Lawrence could see only his hands. His fingers moved slowly. "We will lull them, just as I lull this animal. When I touched him, his heart began to beat rapidly, but now he is calm." The man's fingers tightened on the hamster's throat. Lawrence heard a small, sharp crack. The hamster lay limply in the man's hands, its neck twisted. "Now he need run uselessly no longer," the man said.

Lawrence felt a twinge of disgust, almost horror. The hamster had been his pet, brought from Europe. Sometimes, alone, he had talked to the animal. He felt powerless to react. He was caught in the grip of the other man. He closed his eyes. Sleep was near. It was good to sleep. All things slept. Even the fog slept, slipping from the lampposts to nestle against the curb to sleep and die.

The Hudson organization's first business venture was a speakeasy on the Sunset Strip, now a famous nightclub that the group still owned. The organization was widely diversified and operated divisionally like a corporation. Kenneth Hudson had come to Los Angeles from Philadelphia, where he'd promoted boxing, in 1924. He'd quickly branched out into bootlegging, prostitution, pornography, loansharking, and narcotics; later, after the war, during which he'd distinguished himself by organizing rebellious dockworkers on the West Coast, he'd further diversified into resort hotels, apartment houses, shipping, insurance agencies, and investments. Lawyers, accountants, and security analysts were on his payroll. He maintained a cadre of bodyguards, investigators, and enforcers. He did not have an office; his staff usually conferred with him at his home in Beverly Hills. Hudson seldom left the house. He maintained an association with other organizations similar to his, mainly to enforce agreements on territory division, yet he was known to his world as a loner. To the outside world he was known as an enigmatic but successful businessman with high-up contacts—including the U.S. Senate and, once at least, the White House—and also as a devoted husband and grandfather.

His chief enforcer was an ex-policeman named McKeen, who had experience in police intelligence, narcotics, and internal affairs. He'd been profitably employed by Hudson for almost a quarter century. McKeen, who'd left the force under a slight cloud when a robbery suspect was beaten to death in the interrogation room, considered the organization just another business. He generally reported to Hudson by phone, and, until summoned to the house this humid night in July, he hadn't seen Hudson for three years. He was surprised at the old man's appearance. He looked just like that—an old man—whereas three years ago he'd been tall and dashing, with distinguished gray hair and a handsome puss, one handsome enough to cause even young dames to squeeze their legs together. He never shook hands.

"Sit down," he said.

"Jerry's gettin' careless," McKeen said. "No frisk."

"Well, Jerry knows you."

"For all he knows, I coulda changed sides."

"No. Jerry knows those things. Have a cigar."

McKeen took one from the box, a genuine Havana, and stuffed it into the breast pocket of his suit. He never smoked. Hudson's voice was creaky and his face was pale. The room was hot. McKeen was drenched with sweat. He was feeling uncomfortable for another reason. Usually when Hudson ordered a man to his home it was to call him on the carpet. This year the take in the territory was sharply lower, with the cops cracking down on the sports cards, the retail protection racket, and, suddenly moral, busting whores right and left, particularly in Hollywood and the West Side. McKeen expected a strong ass-chewing, at the least. Hudson wasn't looking at him. He sat slumped in his green robe and black slippers, breathing laboriously. McKeen had heard that the old man hadn't been feeling up to snuff; now, looking at him, he wondered if perhaps the board hadn't begun to look for a successor.

Hudson stirred. His hands moved. "There is an important task I want you to do." Now he looked at McKeen. He said, "Only you can do it."

McKeen felt a flood of relief. "I'm honored."

"I don't like doing work outside the organization, but this is a special case."

"What sort of job is it?"

"Protection. Investigation and protection. A man who operates a company believes he is in danger. Look into it. Find out the circumstances. Then we'll see if we'll take action."

"What company is it?"

"The information is in an envelope Jerry will give you when you leave. Proceed on your own from there. It is a high-priority job."

"How high?"

"The very highest," Hudson said.

"This friend of yours, he must be some friend."

"It is a business arrangement. We've done favors for each other in the past."

"Anything else you can tell me?"

"Report directly to me. When you discover what we are up against, do not take action until I tell you. Take your time. Work carefully. You may pick anyone you want to help. Money is not an object."

"Like I said, this must be some friend."

"I know that I can count on you."

"You can." McKeen was elated. Not only wasn't he getting chewed out, he was being put on a job that promised relief from his recent boredom. He was sick to the gills of knocking heads to collect pennies from pimps and welshers. It would be like being back on the force again. He still missed the force on occasion. He'd been one helluva good copper. His old buddies downtown envied him, thinking he was one of the biggest private eyes in L.A. (he was listed under private investigators in the Yellow Pages, a good cover), working exclusively for lawyers and insurance companies. "I'll get rollin' on this right away."

"One other thing," Hudson said. "It's top secret."

"Goes without saying."

Jerry handed him the envelope in the hall. "Hudson's sicker than I thought," McKeen said.

"He'll be okay."

"I ain't so sure, Jerry. Do you know a priest?"

Jerry stuck out his lower lip. "Do I know a priest? What kind of lousy remark is that? Eh? What kind of stinking lousy remark *is* that?"

"Sure, Jerry. Awright. Don't get uptight."

Was the fat bodyguard actually holding back tears? Jesus. Well, you never know about things. McKeen left, looking forward to excitement in the coming weeks, wondering if old Hudson would live to see the outcome of it.

PART TWO

THE MISSIONS

10

ABOUT TWO HUNDRED MILES UPSTATE FROM MADISON LAY the town of Olen, watered by a branch of the Wisconsin River and nourished by surrounding flat stretches of rich loam and clay land. It was almost precisely in the geographic center of the state, a fact its townsfolk publicized with pride and used to attract an annual autumn fair promoted by an amusement entrepreneur from Milwaukee named Clark Buzzey. The Indian bones and arrowheads that occasionally surfaced on both sides of the river spoke dimly of Olen's prehistory; its more recent history could be found in the yellowed pages of the *Weekly Record*, which once had printed an article tracing the town's modern inception to the establishment there of a flour mill in 1877 by a Canadian trapper named Garth Olen. Evidence of the mill still remained—a jagged cement foundation near the Milwaukee Road tracks infested in spring and summer with milkweed, ragweed, and thistles. Olen had languished with a population of barely one hundred, supported by the mill, a co-op creamery, and a pickle factory, for almost a half century, hidden by deep snow in the winter and sometimes overrun by floods from the thaw in spring, until Lewis Breedlove had located a large cannery there in 1928. Now it had a population of almost three thousand, fully two-thirds of which worked at the cannery. The Breedlove plant was Olen's center and reason for being. Following it had come a Ford dealership, two motion-picture theaters, a half dozen grocery stores, a hotel, a thriving newspaper, four bars, a high school with a basketball team that had once been runner-up in the state championship tournament.

Clearly the area was Breedlove-dominated. The cannery, which manufactured cans for its own use as well as for other BII food-processing plants around the nation, employed an average of 1,500 full time, swelling to almost 3,000 during harvests. The extent of BII ownership of land surrounding Olen was a subject of constant debate in town bars, but everyone agreed it was substantial. Breedlove farm machinery plowed the fields and reaped the harvests. Breedlove milking machines drained the cattle, Breedlove wire fenced the land. Olen residents consumed Breedlove old-age tonics, aspirins, and diet pills. They seldom paid retail prices for canned goods; ample supplies of dented or mislabeled tins were available at the plant for a nickel each. Olen grocery stores stocked only limited quantities of canned vegetables, and brands competitive to BII's Sterling were seldom displayed.

The town had produced some notable persons, including an all-American tackle at the University of Wisconsin, a World War II Medal of Honor winner, a poet whose work won a National Book Award a month after he leaped to his death—and, bar talk had it, an international business tycoon now named Lewis Anthony Breedlove. That fact, or rumor, had never been noted in the *Record*, although it was generally believed to be true, a tale passed on by old-timers who claimed they had known the family, a family called Tyson then, pioneer stock who'd lived nearby in the '90s, lived in a hole in the ground with a tar-paper roof. It was a family who'd come to a tragic end, the old-timers whispered mysteriously.

The town had also produced Mark Scott, whose father had taught a one-room grade school there in 1937 and 1938. And now, again a prisoner in an erratic public conveyance, Mark Scott was returning home. He was a passenger in a sputtering Piper Cub with yellow wings and a red body piloted by a toothless man in overalls named Hanson—an adventure caused by a mix-up in car rentals in Madison. They were five thousand feet above vast stretches of flatland now full of crops for summer harvest. Hanson wasn't a talker; he was a nodder and a grunter. Since takeoff, their conversation had been limited to two exchanges.

Hanson: "Nice weather."

Scott: "Yes."

Hanson: "That Carter, he ain't no JFK."

Scott: "No."

The Cub's engine coughed and backfired sharply. Gas and oil smells from the cockpit drifted into Scott's nostrils. Hanson guided the plane with the stick between his legs, his head lowered. A second backfire jarred him upright. The Cub began a slow, circling descent. Below, BII fields stretched in all directions. Scott rubbed perspiration from the back of his neck.

He admitted to himself that he wasn't quite sure of the nature of his mission. Breedlove, typically, had been vague— a tactic he often used, thinking it would inspire a subordinate to creativity. He'd been asked to look into the plant, see if it should be kept open; it had been suggested to him that there might be some labor problem developing in Olen, which, if so, was news to Scott. Since Scott handled labor relations, Breedlove no doubt expected him to concentrate on that aspect more than on an assessment of the plant's future, which would be a function of the advanced planning group. Perhaps, however, Breedlove was now increasing Scott's functions, and this was the start of it. He was sure of one thing—he'd been dispatched on this mission as a form of test. Lancaster and Powell, also, had been sent on missions—jobs no doubt related to their specialties, marketing and finance, and perhaps they too were being tested. It had begun already, the race against each other that Lancaster had forecast. The old man certainly had not stepped down. He had merely changed titles.

Anne had surprised him. He had dreaded telling her he'd been dispatched to Olen, again cheating them out of a vacation, but when he'd blurted it out, she'd taken the news without protest. She'd said she and the kids would go to Disney World, suggesting he join them later. He wondered if news of his promotion hadn't had something to do with her reversal of mood. He hadn't yet told her of the even bigger news—Breedlove's admission that the Troika was temporary and that Scott was his personal choice for the top chair—

partly because he had difficulty in believing it himself. Now, grasping his seat as the Cub swooped down, he wished he'd fought harder with the couple who got the last rental car in Madison. He found himself thinking about the BII 727. When he'd called Harold Long to suggest that extreme caution be taken before flying again, he'd learned that Breedlove had ordered the airplane grounded, at least for a while—news that only intensified Scott's concern.

"Lookit that there down there," Hanson said.

"What?"

Hanson tipped the left wing. Scott gulped, fearing a wing-over. It didn't come. A tree-fringed clearing below was filled with unpainted shacks and scattered tents.

"The Mexicans," Hanson said. "Come up here for harvest work at the cannery."

The tent city seemed devoid of life. "Where is everyone?" Scott asked.

"Ain't there," Hanson said, apparently judging that answer to be adequate.

They soared over trees, now barely two hundred feet off the ground, and Hanson pointed the Cub toward a lake, cutting power as if he intended to land on water. Somehow he missed the lake, dropping the Cub to a four-bounce landing on a short slab of weed-ingrown tar. The plane stopped. Its engine clanked.

"Close as I can get'cha to Olen," Hanson said.

"How far away is it?"

"Three, four mile. Up the road."

"I don't relish walking four miles in this heat. With two bags."

"See out there that buildin' near the strip by the lake?"

"Yes."

"Fellow named Joe Casper's there. Joe's got a car he'll rent'cha."

"Thank you." Scott got out, took his bags, and stood with his hair blowing in the slipstream of the propeller. Hanson called him back. "What?" Scott said.

"You Breedlove?" Hanson said.

"Hardly."

"Naw, I don't mean the old man hisself. I know he's dead, years ago. I mean, you work for the Breedlove combine?"

"Combine? Is that what you call it?"

"What it is, ain't it?"

"I work for Breedlove, yes."

"Wal, you work for Breedlove, lemme tell you, brother. You got a mess on yer hands right now."

"How so?"

"How so? You work for Breedlove, you don't know? I tol' you them Mexicans, didn't I?" He squinted. "Where you from?"

"Here," Scott said.

"Here? Olen?"

"Yes. I was born here."

"Jesus Christ, I'll be danged," Hanson said.

He opened the throttle and sent the Cub hurtling down the runway, leaving Scott in a backwash of exhaust and hot wind. The Cub rose, streaked toward a grove of trees, barely cleared them, circled back, passed overhead, and rose unsteadily. Scott felt relieved, fortunate to have survived. He removed his coat, loosened his tie, and walked toward the building Hanson had designated, dragging his bags.

It was an unpainted, sun-punished shack, a structure so frail and desolate that it looked like a refuge for derelicts. Scattered around it were motorless, tireless cars, chipped porcelain bathtubs, rusted pipes, pails, broken pottery, stove lids, and battered sofas with exposed springs. An old man with a single front tooth lounged in a musty chair, his hands over the back of his head. He consumed most of the shade. His feet were up on a flour barrel, his shoes cast off on the ground, and he appeared dead except that his toes twitched flies away.

"Are you Joe Casper?" Scott asked.

"Gone to his reward," the man responded without opening his eyes. "Dead."

"I was told—"

"Wal, people round here's always tellin' things."

"I wonder if you can help me."

The old man opened one eye. "You the Baptist?"

"I'm Mark Scott. I'm from—"

"They's a Baptist comin' in I'm waitin' on. A Baptist for the church."

"Do you have a car I can rent?"

"I got a Corvair."

"A Corvair would be fine."

"Holdin' that for the Baptist."

"All right. I'm Mark Scott, the Baptist."

"It's twelve cents a mile, six bucks a day, twenty-five deposit, no credit cards, you pay gas."

"Fair enough."

"You ain't the Baptist," the man said. "The Baptist, he'd dicker."

Scott put down his bags and withdrew his wallet. "Do I get the car?"

"You explain it to the Baptist then," the man said, standing up.

It was a red convertible with bald tires and a broken headlight, but it was transportation. Driving it down the narrow two-lane pavement toward Olen, Scott felt his mood lighten. The wind was in his face, the air was clean, the sky was bright blue. As a boy Scott had lived in a succession of small midwestern towns, names like Ladysmith and Shell Lake and Wausaukee. His father had been an itinerant schoolteacher with the dedication and restlessness of a preacher, an extroverted organizer whose trade tools—microscopes, replicas of human skeletons, a scratchy record of Thomas Edison's voice, and beetles, walking-sticks, moths, and scorpions mounted and categorized with the patience of a Linnaeus—had lured boys in patched overalls out of the woods and away from swimming holes. His parents now lived retired in a cabin near Eagle River. They fished all summer and read all winter. Dad Scott felt his son had become a corporate slave; to him, success was being happy. Scott knew they would never settle in California; his parents became nervous when more than fifty miles away from Eagle River.

He wondered about the anonymous Baptist, deprived of transportation by the country boy turned city slicker who'd dropped from the sky in the yellow-winged Cub. The Baptists had held sway in most of the towns of Scott's youth, running out the Methodists and the Presbyterians but occasionally succumbing to bloodless coups d'etat subtly crafted by the Church of God, and many of the preachers had been hellfire, wrath-of-God Bible pounders who ruled and fought progress with sanctimonious righteousness. But one, a man named

Paul Stevenson, had been different. Stevenson ran out faith healers, patched up domestic quarrels, held down third base on the ball team, and read and discussed Stendhal, St. Augustine, and even Spinoza and Darwin. He'd once brought Scott to the very edge of studying for the ministry. Instead, Scott had studied law, inspired by a vision of Darrow in the tepid southern courtroom attempting to rescue mankind from victimization by its own ignorance. He'd never made it to a courtroom. He'd married Anne and joined BII in St. Paul, specializing in labor relations. His fieldwork in settling a strike near Mankato had brought him to Lewis Breedlove's personal attention. The succession of moves and promotions followed; they'd been on a whirlwind of settlement and abandonment, on a pattern that in retrospect seemed almost an inexorable flight to the top. And now, there or almost there, he found himself slightly overwhelmed—and, strangely, more insecure than ever before.

He stopped the Corvair at the peak of a hill and got out, leaving the engine running. The road was lined with giant oak trees. Vast fields of ripening corn stretched to the horizon in all directions. Ahead was the river, calm as glass, spanned by the old bridge that led to Olen. The Breedlove cannery was just on the other side of the river, near the bridge. It was a series of low buildings interconnected by cement paths. Even at Scott's distance, it looked neglected and run-down. He detected some activity on the river side of the cannery. He could make out a group of people in bright clothing, standing motionless in a line before the plant's main entrance. He was too far away to determine the exact nature of the activity, but he assumed employment applications were being taken for the harvest buildup.

Scott stretched. He took in a deep breath of air. Birds sang all around him. A squirrel sat on its haunches, eyeing him. A slight breeze came up, dissipating some of the heat, and he felt a sudden and complete contentment. The serenity of the valley below him seemed to transfer its force lazily into his mind. He was not a stranger to valleys such as this. They were home to him.

He heard the roar of an auto. His head snapped up. The squirrel darted away. The birds rose. A blue Ford streaked toward him, swerved to avoid the Corvair, and screeched past. A red-faced man in a sheriff's uniform clutched the wheel; beside him was another uniformed man, younger and thinner, holding a shotgun with both hands. The Ford moved down the hill at high speed, braked for a sharp left turn, and headed over the bridge toward the cannery. Scott watched it for a few seconds, frozen to inaction; then he hurried to the Corvair and began to follow the Ford. Halfway across the wooden bridge, he realized the group outside the cannery was picketing, or at least demonstrating. They formed a two-deep chain, their arms linked. Their number was much greater than he'd thought; there were perhaps four or five hundred. Women and children were among them. Obviously, they were the Mexican workers from the deserted labor camp he'd seen from the air. Fronting them was another group, about thirty or forty men in overalls and caps. As Scott drew closer, he saw that some of the men held rifles. The sheriff's car had stopped between the two groups. Its front doors were open. The two officers held shotguns. They lounged near their car in an attitude of almost lazy indifference. Scott turned onto the dirt road leading to the cannery, pressed the accelerator full down, and raced bouncing and skipping directly toward the sheriff's car. Then he braked, skidded to a stop, and got out. He'd been acting like a fool, rushing toward what now appeared to be a tense confrontation; a sudden, reckless entrance, he realized, might trigger violence. He stood in the sun, calmly appraising the situation. A hundred yards ahead, the demonstrators began to sway, a linked line that moved in unison, casting a long, undulating shadow. The men with rifles sprang forward, advancing in quick steps, pausing to squat like soldiers. The fat sheriff glanced at Scott. There was no sound. The scene played quietly before him, a strange group pantomime etched vividly in the sun, moving in ominous stillness. Thick heat rose in visible waves. Scott stood— detached, indecisive, not yet involved. Then he began to walk toward the demonstrators.

The sheriff's shotgun snapped up. "Awright, awright!" he shouted at the armed men. "That's close enough."

The men stopped. The demonstrators ceased their sway.

A rifle shot rang out.

Scott sprinted over dry yellow grass, running with his knees high, and plunged into the melee. He tripped. He rolled over. He was in the midst of flailing arms and legs. An elbow thumped into his back. Men and women tramped above him. He crouched on his hands and knees, trying to rise. He was hurled violently back to the ground. The soil seemed moist. A woman lay next to him. Her shawl was stained red. Scott looked down and discovered that his palms were covered with blood.

11

A YEAR BEFORE THEIR MARRAGE, DOROTHY LANCASTER HAD bought Hank an orgy for his birthday present. It had been a delicious prank. She selected two starlets from the bevy sent to her by Tip Hearn, the Hollywood agent, and paid them five hundred dollars each to show up at a Palm Springs hotel. They were examined by a doctor, at her expense, before the trip. Hank was with the agency then and always coming to the Coast. The orgy began on Friday night and ended on Sunday afternoon, with the girls exhausted and Hank napping. Dorothy, who'd taken a next-door room, had spent most of the time by the swimming pool, reading Gothic novels.

"Whew, I pity you if you hope to handle that stud by yourself," said one of the girls, a big-breasted blonde named Kitty. "I think I popped that big cork of his ten times myself."

"I don't want to handle him alone," Dorothy said. "Ever."

It was still true. She had sexual needs, of course, but she could never match his. She let him have his women. There wasn't much she could do about it. She didn't care. Hank was discreet about it; too much was at stake not to be discreet.

Now, alone in the Bel Air house, she drew on a robe after a bath and mixed herself a Chivas Regal and water. It was a pleasant evening, full of stars and soft breezes. She thought about calling some friends, but she couldn't come up with a name; Hank, with his sometimes brutal frankness, had driven away almost all her friends. They really didn't have friends for the sake of friends. Their parties were for people who were seeking jobs or contacts. And they were really Hank's parties. He selected the guests, his secretaries handled the invitations.

An electrician was tinkering in the kitchen, a fat, red-faced man with a pleasant smile. Dorothy sipped the Scotch. The cat came into her lap. Loneliness swept over her. She sat huddled and shivering. She needed a friend, a real friend, man or woman. Hank ran her life, telling her it was a good, comfortable life. He selected her clothing, hairdressers, etiquette teacher, voice instructor. He used to take her with him on business trips, but that quickly became a bore. Hank would go off to his meetings and she would find herself talking to bartenders and taxi drivers. She couldn't go shopping for fear of buying something he didn't like; she couldn't go to the plays or movies because, at a moment's notice, he might need her for display. To him, she just ass and tits. Maybe that was all men had ever seen in her. Ass, tits, and cunt. Meat. A slab of meat.

The electrician came in. "That's it, Mrs. Lancaster. Just a minor circuit failure."

"I thank you for coming at night. I'll get you a check."

"That's all right about that, missis. We'll bill you."

"Would you like something? A drink?"

"Oh, no, but thanks. I'd better scoot on home."

"It's interesting work you have."

"Well, it keeps me busy, that's for sure."

"I'll bet you have children. A family."

"Six kids, as a matter of fact."

"Six? That *is* a family. Do you have photographs of them?"

"No, I don't carry no pitchers, missis."

"You should. Tell me about your family."

"Well, no, I think I gotta run now." He was backing away.

"Do you have a barbecue? A backyard barbecue?"

He nodded.

"And a boat? A camper?"

"As a matter of fact, I do. Both of them."

He left. She returned to the drink and the cat. She looked at the telephone. Maybe she'd go out to a movie. There wasn't much on TV. Loneliness and sadness gripped her in rising, consuming undulations. She wasn't the sensual sexpot people thought. She'd merely wanted to talk to the man and he'd escaped as if he feared rape. She'd been put into a category, because of her body and her face, and also because of Hank. Secretly she yearned for tenderness, for understanding, even for a family. Looking at the silent phone, she began to weep bitterly and uncontrollably.

Lancaster made a stop at Las Vegas on his way to New York. He checked in at the hotel, changed into a blue blazer and gray slacks, and went to the casino. The cards began to turn well for him on the first hand. By midnight he was up almost a hundred thousand dollars.

"Too many," the dealer said.

Lancaster smiled. His audience, a group of about a dozen, issued a cheer. The dealer paid off in black chips, five hundred-dollar chips for each of the seven spots Lancaster had played. The hand had been a total sweep for him. He hadn't busted on any spot, and he'd doubled down on three, meaning a win of five thousand dollars. The last spot had been a crowning triumph. He'd doubled a soft eighteen, drawing a three to twenty-one. If the dealer had taken the three, he would have had nineteen, a break-even hand for him. Instead, he'd been forced to hit his hard sixteen with a ten. Bust. Player wins all. The pit boss drifted by the table. A black hooker, trying to pass off as a mere chip hustler, patted Lancaster's arm. She was a light-skinned black in a velvet gown that showed her tits almost down to the nipples. Lancaster hadn't screwed a nigger since his teen-age days in Brooklyn, where he'd planked them right and left—whores who'd hump in cars and alleys for two bits, young ones with undeveloped breasts and unbroken cherries, musky mamas who'd bang all night and take on all comers for a dollar. Maybe he'd take this one upstairs. Change his luck.

"Shuffle up," the dealer said.

Lancaster motioned to the pit boss. "I'd like to move up to a thou a spot," he said.

"Would you like to try baccarat, sir?"

"No. Blackjack's my game."

"I'll call the casino manager."

"You do that. We'll hold the game."

He leaned back in his chair. He did not touch the stacks of black chips in front of him. He did not even look at them.

Lancaster never counted his chips when he gambled, nor did he ever engage in chitchat with the dealer. Both were bush-league. He usually knew pretty well where he stood with the house, however; now he estimated he had about a hundred and ten thou in blacks before him. He'd brought seven thou cash into the game. For almost two hours straight, he'd been blowing them out of the tub.

He glanced back. The black hooker was still there. She smiled. He felt a surge of blood in his loins. He wanted the whore. She knew it. She figured she had her trick for the night all wrapped up. He grinned at her. It was entirely possible that she had the surprise of her life coming later on.

"Play one for you," Lancaster told the dealer.

He placed a black chip on the dealer's side of the table and put out five blacks on the middle spot. The cards came out. The dealer showed a seven. Lancaster looked at his hand. A two and an eight.

"Double," he said, sliding out five more chips.

The dealer gave him one card, face down. Lancaster did not look at it. The dealer exposed his hand. Seventeen. Lancaster flipped over his hole card. Ace. He didn't gloat. He didn't smile. The dealer paid off ten black chips. He was a young dealer, and looked somewhat nervous. Perhaps he'd never been in a game this big. Lancaster tipped him a black. The dealer tapped the chip on the table and dropped it into his shirt pocket.

The pit boss returned. "It's all right, a thousand limit," he said.

Lancaster nodded. He liked this place. He always came here. They knew him, yet they did not know him. Only the casino manager knew his real name, and affiliation. He was a cash player. He'd never cashed a check or signed a marker. His biggest win in one night had been about fifty K. For all his Vegas gambling, he was down perhaps a hundred K. So right now he was about even on a career basis.

But he wasn't going to stop. Not now. It was going to be a two hundred K win night. At least.

He had registered under a pseudonym, Henry S. MacKay from San Francisco, and at that moment he really was Henry S. MacKay, the Frisco importer. Lancaster did not delude himself about identities. He knew he was not one person but several. Sometimes he slipped so totally into another identity that when out of it, when back to Henry Lancaster, he found himself alarmed at a change so absolute and so uncontrollable. When he changed, he even looked different. He was confident that if someone who knew Lancaster were to watch the man in the blue blazer playing blackjack, he would not recognize him as Henry Lancaster. Upstairs in his baggage were four suits—a plain gray, a gray pinstripe, a plain blue, a blue pinstripe—and six shirts, white and light blues. The ties were thin. Two of them were black. It was the clothing of Henry Lancaster.

He had ten chips out on each spot.

Seven K on the line.

The dealer showed an ace. "Insurance," he said.

MacKay-Lancaster said, "No insurance."

The dealer looked at his hand. He didn't have the twenty-one.

MacKay-Lancaster hadn't had to look. He'd known it.

He wanted a drink. But MacKay-Lancaster never drank when he gambled.

His first hand was pat. Two lovely tens. The second was a hard sixteen—a king and a six. Against the dealer's ace. MacKay-Lancaster always played the game by the book, yet an ace showing often confused him. The dealer could have anything from two to twenty. But he had to figure the dealer for a good hand. If he didn't have it in the two cards, he could easily draw to it. So MacKay-Lancaster hit the sixteen. He got a four. Two twenties, two lovely twenties, back to back. The third spot had an ace and a nine. Three lovely twenties. He held on the fourth spot, a hard seventeen, and hit the soft fifteen on the fifth spot with a deuce. Six and seven were both hard fifteens, a hand he hated against a good dealer's card. He hit them both and busted out on both. The dealer showed his hole card. Another ace. Two or twelve. He hit it with a four. Five or fifteen. He hit again. A queen. Now it was a hard fifteen; he had to hit again. The card came over.

Six. The dealer had twenty-one.

MacKay-Lancaster's audience groaned. The hooker eyed his remaining small fortune in blacks. MacKay-Lancaster didn't wince. He smiled. He put out another seven K.

But the feeling was no longer there. He was growing tense.

He knew he should quit. The run was over. The cards had turned against him. He should, at least, cut back. The pit boss stood with his arms folded. He'd just gone up to a thou; it would be chicken shit to cut back.

The dealer showed a face card, a sneering jack.

MacKay-Lancaster looked at his hands. Most of them stank. He busted on one and two. He held the hard seventeen on three. Four and five were twenties. Six and seven were shitty fifteens. He busted on six, hit seven with a four. The dealer turned over a second jack.

It wasn't good. It was turning. It had turned. He should stop now. Have a drink. Bang the ass off the whore. Get out of town. Catch the red-eye flight to New York.

It was all right.

He had control.

Another seven K went out on the spots.

"Jesus, honey, lookit *here,*" squealed a broad in a yellow print to her boyfriend or husband, the skinny punk with pimples and horn-rimmed glasses she held by the hand. "Are they hundred-dollar chips?"

"Black chips, hundred dollar," said the punk.

MacKay-Lancaster viewed the broad and her punk with a wilting stare, backing them away into the crowd toward the nickel slots where they belonged. He looked around to see that the fuckhead dealer was showing another goddamn king.

Now he realized that he *was* losing control. His hand trembled. The pit boss no longer seemed concerned. He had his back turned to the game. He went to the phone. MacKay-Lancaster hesitated. Then he looked at the first hand. Twenty. Better. Improving. The second was another shitass fifteen. He busted it. Eleven on the third. He doubled down. He didn't look at his card. Hands three and four. Fourteen and sixteen. Shit hands. He busted on both. Six. Eighteen. Hold. Seven. Nineteen, soft. Hold. Not bad.

The dealer had two fucking kings.

Cut back. Cut way back. Better yet, leave the game. Screw the hooker. Take her humped and backwards, where he could get his hands on her soft black throat. Oh, Christ. Come back. Come back. Quit   split   move out

"Tough run," said the hooker.

She was seated legs crossed on the edge of the oval bed in

his room, a martini of straight Beefeater in her hand, curling her long red fingernails around the glass, smiling at him with her thick sensual red lips, batting her fake eyelashes at him.

"Take it off," he said.

"Why you ain't even paid me, honey."

"You got the two chips."

"But I'm a three-chip girl, honey. On an all-night basis."

"What does two buy me?"

"A roll."

"Then let's roll."

"Can't a girl even finish her drink?"

"No."

"No? You're nasty."

"Take it off."

"Do you want to take it off?"

"No."

"Then watch." She took off one shoe, slowly, looking up at him, the glass still in her hand. The eyelashes seemed to droop almost to her cheeks. She shifted the glass to her other hand and removed the second shoe. She held the shoes up on the palm of her left hand and dropped them noiselessly to the carpet, sipping her drink as she did so. "You gonna like this, baby."

"For two chips, I should."

"You got a come per chip a-comin', honey."

"Don't call me honey. Don't call me baby."

"You're upset. I understand. I'll take care of you."

He lurched into the bathroom. For the first time since his football accident, he was feeling sick. His bags were stretched out open before him. He saw the suits, the ties, the shirts. He looked into the mirror. His eyes were bloodshot. His face was pale, almost white. He needed a shave. He decided he'd shave. He washed his face in ice-cold water. He turned on the hot water. Steam gushed up. The face in the mirror was a blend of Henry Lancaster and Henry S. MacKay.

He'd lost it all.

His winnings had disappeared in an incredible succession of rotten hands, fifteens and fourteens and twelves he'd hit and busted. When he'd come up with decent hands, the dealer had had twenties and nineteens. He'd blown his winnings, the seven grand cash he'd brought, plus almost twenty grand in checks and markers, approved personally by the casino manager. He was out some twenty-seven thou. But that part was all right. He could afford it. The Compensation Committee would soon raise his salary to well over two hundred thousand. His bonus would be bigger this year, and he had a couple of hundred grand in stock options. He didn't owe much. So he could hack it. The loss didn't bother him. Not Henry Lancaster. But it bothered Henry MacKay. MacKay raged in him, a man who'd lost when he'd been sure he'd win. This time, Lancaster had difficulty in coming back, in shaking MacKay. And MacKay had ideas, a way to take out his frustration and anger. When he left the bathroom, he was going to murder the nigger hooker. He was going to undress her, lie on top of her, and put his hands on her throat. He was going to watch her eyes as he squeezed. Scratch one leeching black whorecunt, as a service to humankind. Lancaster looked at MacKay's face. He smiled. Lancaster. Mac-Kay.

Take a slow shave. Take a cold shower.

The hooker tapped on the door. "Is everythin' all right in there, handsome?"

"I' . all right."

"I'm ready for you."

"Go away." Lancaster fought MacKay's image. "Get out."

"Go away? We ain't started, hon."

"Get *out!* Get the fuck out of my room. Now!"

"Well, that's the way you feel, it don't make me no never mind. No never mind a'tall."

"Don't talk. Leave."

"I'm leavin,' hon. I'm jus' leavin' now. That noise you hear, that's me leavin'."

Lancaster began to shave. He wiped steam from the mirror. The face he peered at was the face of Henry Lancaster. It was streaked with sweat. But he was back. MacKay was gone.

Dorothy had made up her mind about something. She wanted to go to the beach alone, and she did, heading to Santa Monica on a fine day full of sun and a bright sky fringed with giant white clouds so marvelous and free that she gazed at them in childlike awe. She felt on the edge of tears. The driver was a young black with fine thin hands. He was polite and quiet. She wanted to talk to him but she decided that would not be in keeping with her role, a Bel Air executive wife in a three-hundred-dollar pants suit carrying a hundred-and-fifty-dollar Gucci bag (containing a romantic novel, a hundred dollars in cash, credit cards, her cigarettes in a gold-plated, initialed case, suntan lotion, and a red bikini). She got out on Coast Highway near the pier, tipped the driver, and stood in the sun, breathing deeply, tingling with well-being. She and Hank belonged to a private beach club in Malibu, but she did not want to go there. She didn't want to see any of their so-called friends and listen to them talk about the servant problem, gold speculation, which marriages were on the rocks, who was sleeping with whom, coke snorting, and plastic surgeons. She wanted only to lie in the sun and smell the ocean. She changed into the bikini in the public lounge and walked along the beach, swinging the Gucci bag. The sand was moist and warm. Kids shrieked in the waves. A dog chased a ball. A white-haired old man, his trousers rolled up, waded in the surf. She loved the kids, the dog, the old man. She was naked by the sea, an innocent child's nakedness, a free nakedness. Only when she passed the volleyball game and noticed that the players stopped to look at her did she become aware of her body. She was used to stares from men. She expected them. She began to run, again free, and then stopped and spread a towel and lay down. The sun was perfect. Sea smells filled her nostrils. She did not want to think about Hank, yet she found herself unable to avoid it. The stares of the beachboys had somewhat disturbed her day. Hank and Dottie; Dottie's Hank. Well, one thing was sure. He underestimated her. She was smarter than he thought and one of these days he'd go too far. She knew she was beautiful and she knew that at any given party she had the best ass and the men knew it, too. She knew how to flirt, using her eyes and mouth, and she wanted men around her and enjoyed arousing them with movements of her body. It was something she couldn't help, something instinctively learned in the struggle to escape Pittsburgh. She was considered chic, carefree, modern, extroverted, and she knew that other women envied her. But she had her fears. Strangers terrified her, especially well-dressed, moneyed strangers, men who were both smart and shrewd, primarily because she was afraid she'd say the wrong things, use improper grammar, or reveal her ignorance. She needed Hank for protection. But she didn't need his sex, not the way he did it—fierce, hard, rapid, almost angry, with no gentle words or touches. Often he came just as she was getting warm. Yet Hank was very good in social situations. People grouped around him at parties and women literally swooned in his presence. She needed him. He was right about that.

But why think about Hank? She was free now, at least for a day, perhaps into the evening. Sometimes she thought he had her followed when he was out of town, but there was no evidence of that today. She found herself peeking around. Only more kids, more dogs, a fat woman reading a novel, two young men running and throwing a football. She wouldn't think about Hank. She would think about the pleasant things of her past. She remembered going to the movies as a girl, cutting classes to slip away to matinees, sometimes sneaking in through the back door, yearning to get a job as an usher or behind the concession counter so she could see the shows free after work. There were triple features on Saturday afternoons, plus a serial and a cartoon. She remembered the smells—popcorn, must of the old creaking seats humped with hard dried gum wads underneath, sweet candy wrappers she'd find and lick. Then the theater darkens. On screen is the doomed, wide-eyed Bette Davis, the sad Joan Crawford with a scar on her cheek, Claudette Colbert laughing and crying as she runs through tall grass into her lover's arms, and the oh-so-handsome, oh-so-successful Robert Taylor and John Payne and William Powell in tuxedos. She always cried at the movies. She still cried at the movies. And she thought about something else, something so special she did not often think of it because, saving it for the right moments, it became sharper and more lovely in her vision. It had been the time sex had been gentle for her, the first few times, with a boy who dreamed of being an architect, the first boy she'd kissed, so gentle and soft, on a hayride near Dublin, Ohio, when she'd been fifteen. Her mother had saved for months to send her to camp. Now there were smells and tastes and sounds of the camp deep in her senses, as if she were there again— apricot smells and the protective, friendly birds in the trees at night and a sky that was filled almost totally with moon. And the boy who had touched her hand on the hayride and who'd stroked her cheek and then, shyly, so gently, so softly, had touched her lips with his, causing her to sleep and to dream for a long second of beauty unmeasurable, beyond human explanation. She had loved him instantly with a love that could not be expressed in words or even in song, a love with the beauty of innocence and the promise of permanence. He would be the first to have her and she would be the first to have him. It was like the scent of the apricots and the light of the moon, neither awkward nor painful but gentle and lovely and natural. Like snow. Oh, gentle, down gentle, down gentle on me, down soft, down gentle, down gentle on thee.

She heard a whistle behind her. Her head snapped up. She saw the boys who'd been throwing the football standing a few yards away, staring at her and giggling. Only then did she realize she'd been slowly rubbing one of her breasts. The nipple was aroused. The boys ran away, laughing. Dorothy got up and wrapped the towel around her shoulders. It now seemed chilly on the beach. The people had changed. A child was crying. A couple were squabbling. The seaweeds lay coiled like swollen, diseased animal innards and stank like decayed garbage. She walked toward the street, hurrying; the good feeling was gone, the day had darkened, and she thought she could see Hank in his Cadillac on Coast Highway, waiting for her.

She stopped abruptly on the edge of the beach, near the hot-dog stand. A young man in a dark bathing suit lounged by the stand, sipping a Coke. He had blond hair and his face was sunburned. He looked so much like her first lover, her only lover—his name had been Gary; yes, yes, Gary—that she thought at first it might be him. But, no. That was many years ago. How many years? Gary would be in his thirties, his mid-thirties. The boy by the stand was trying not to stare at her. When she looked at him, he turned away, his head down. She wanted to talk to him. She *had* to talk to him. No. It was silly. She should get a taxi and go home. Read a book. Call a friend. Instead, she walked over to the boy.

"Pardon me, but I'm afraid I've lost my way," she said.

He looked up. "Eh?" he said. He looked down.

"Do you know where Wilshire comes in here?"

He didn't look at her. "Sure. It's a mile, like a mile. Up."

"Which way?"

"That way."

Dorothy looked at him and he looked away. He was about sixteen, maybe seventeen. She saw something clean and innocent in him, in his clear reddened face and strong young body, so hairless and smooth. She wondered if he were a virgin. He probably was.

"Thank you," she said. "Well, it's not really Wilshire I want, I guess. I was hoping to try Huntington Beach, but the bus takes so long."

"You ain't got a car?"

"I don't drive."

"You don't *drive?*"

"Do you drive?"

"Sure I drive."

"Well, I guess all the kids your age drive these days."

He seemed less shy. "I'll take you, you want. Huntington, I mean."

"Do you have a car?"

"Sure I got a car."

"Someday I'll learn to drive."

"Well, it's never to late, they say."

"I think I just might take you up on that offer. The ride to Huntington, I mean. Will you wait here until I change?"

"I'll wait in my car. It's that blue car, right over there. The Chevy."

"I hope you don't think I'm some pickup. I want you to know that I'm not some pickup."

Again he looked away. His face was so red she couldn't tell if he was blushing. He stared at the sidewalk.

"The truth is that I'm a writer," Dorothy said. She found herself amused, having to make up an excuse. "I'm writing this article for a magazine on the beach area here."

"Oh," he said.

"Maybe you can be in it. You seem to know the beaches."

"Sure."

"If you wait, I'll just get changed and we'll be off."

She hurried, fearing that when she returned he would be gone. But he wasn't. He drove barefooted. She got him to talk. He was so much like Gary it was uncanny—same voice, same boyish shyness, same laugh. Sometimes he stuttered;

Gary occasionally had stuttered. He told her about the times when the kids would flock to Balboa Island around Easter, pushed together in a great carefree laughing youthful tangle, and again she felt a pang of regret for the lack of good times in her youth. His hands were thin and soft; gentle hands, like Gary's. She knew this was foolish, risky, but the need for it in her cried out for it. She was in a dream. Again the day seemed lovely. The sky was bright and the clouds were immense and billowing—giant pillows filled with laughing, happy spirits, souls that knew no pain or duty or the meaning of time. She removed her watch, putting it into her bag. The boy said his name was Tom Keeton. His father and mother were divorced. He had a younger brother named Jerry. He said he was eighteen. He had a nice smile and white, even teeth and a very attractive mouth. Gary, oh, Gary. She lit a cigarette, a Virginia Slim.

"Do you smoke?" she asked.

"Ah, naw, none of the kids smoke."

"How about pot?"

"Well, the kids'll smoke pot. But I don't like it."

"I can tell you're a good person, a decent, clean-cut young man. And you're very . . . well, you're very cute."

He smiled shyly.

"Do you have girl friends? Or am I prying?"

"You ain't prying. I don't have a girl now, no. I did, but we broke it up."

"I'm sorry."

"Don't be. It wasn't that heavy. She wasn't that hot."

"What do you mean, not so hot?"

"Oh, you know."

"You mean, not so hot in bed?"

He gulped. "Yeah, I guess so, I dunno."

"You don't fool me, Tom. You've never been with a girl."

He was silent.

She said, "Would you like to? With me, I mean?"

His gulp was tremendous. The car swerved. "Jeeze, I—"

"I'm not trying to be forward, but I don't think you'd ever break the ice. If you want to, I'll make love with you. You can stop right up there, at that motel."

"Jeeze, I just don't know, lady."

"I told you my name. Connie. Use my name."

"Connie."

"I'll register us at the motel, if that bothers you."

"You sure it's okay?"

"Sure it's okay."

The dream, the fantasy continued. The motel room was dark and musty and the bedspread was dirty. There was a dresser with a cracked mirror. He would not look at her, and when she came to him, running her tongue softly over the nipple of his breast, he gasped and stepped back. Then he reached out awkwardly for her, trying to kiss her, and she avoided him.

"I'll show you," she said.

He cleared his throat and gulped. He tried to respond, but no words came out.

Slowly she removed her blouse. Her breasts tumbled free from her bra. The boy's mouth was open and his eyes were wide.

"Do you think I'm attractive?" she said.

"Lady, I think you're somethin' else."

"Connie."

"Connie," he said, biting his lip.

Then for her it was not here, not now; it was then, there. He'd be gentle; she'd show him how. She went to him, her shoulders square, her breasts erect and firm, her lips parted. He leaned forward to receive her kiss. Now she was fully back in time, Gary's soft and warm mouth, his hands gentle; it was not a dirty motel where bodies had clashed before to rid frustration and to achieve temporary, uncommitted joy. She held him, her Gary-Tom, her boy-lover, feeling her breasts come alive and the blood rushing in her loins. She touched him between his legs and he groaned with pleasure. She went to the bed, taking him by the hand, and lay back with her legs spread. She laughed.

"It works best if you take off your clothes," she said.

She caressed the nipples of her breasts with her fingertips, feeling languid, almost sleepy, away and drifting, coming from a deep place to slow sexual awakening. He removed his pants with trembling hands. He was wearing boxer shorts, something that amused her, causing her to repress a little girl's giggle. She could see the head of his swollen penis, a pink protuberant flower bud he tried to hide. She felt inward mirth and rising desire. Naughty. Boy and girl behind the barn. But she didn't care. She raised her arms and he tumbled in beside her, now anxious, seeking to kiss her hard, pressing against her body. His penis was long and thin, nowhere near Hank's size (why think about Hank?), but it was beautiful, warm and alive. When she touched it, stroking it gently, he stiffened and moaned, his eyes shut tightly, his neck veins standing out. She was feeling more than naughty. She was feeling fully aroused. She must not stroke too hard. He'd come. Then maybe he'd grow frightened, start thinking about his girl friend. Dorothy turned, crouching, and took the head of his penis in her mouth, moving up and down slowly. The boy lay back, gasping. She was certain he'd never had a woman, much less a head job, and the thought aroused her even more. She could tell by his breathing that he was close. She stopped abruptly, stretched her body over his, and plunged him inside of her. She moved rapidly, feeling immediate surges of climax in her thighs, her stomach, her forehead. It was not gentle. It was hard, rapid, seeking.

"Come on, come on, come on," she moaned. She felt his climax in her, fast hot spurts, but she was not ready. Already he was getting soft. "Come on," she said.

"I can't. Not now." He was wet with sweat.

"I'll turn over. We'll do it that way."

"I can't."

She wanted him some more. It was revenge, revenge against Hank, who had probably planked a half dozen whores on this trip already. But he turned away, as if in shame, trying to reach for his clothes. He would not look at her. She sat up and saw their reflection in the cracked mirror; and, above the mirror, she thought she could see Hank's face. His face was glaring at her from a misty cloud. She gasped. Then the phone rang.

"W-what is it?" the boy said.

"Nothing. It's nothing. Oh, I don't know."

"The phone—"

"Don't touch the phone."

He was dressing, rapidly. The phone stopped. *Hank. It's Hank. He knows I'm here. He doesn't care. He just wants to remind me of who I am. Who am I? I don't know. The bastard, the son of a bitch. Oh, how I hate him. How absolutely I hate him. I want this boy to stay. Do it again and again. Come twice, three times, four times. Get me pregnant, good and pregnant. Swell up my belly so I can show Hank.* Again the phone was ringing.

She felt dead inside. She picked up her bra and slowly drew it on. The phone was silent. She noticed fat ripples around her waist, and her thighs seemed too thick. The boy was leaving.

"Don't go," she said.

"Lady, I got to."

He opened the door a crack, peeked out, and then he was gone. Dorothy sat alone on the bed, staring at the unclean room, trying to feel. She had lured the boy here, seeking an allusive tenderness, but it had been false. She had tricked only herself. It was impossible to go back. She was not a teen-age girl at a camp. She was like Hank said, a demanding sexual woman. Hank's woman. Again the phone was shrieking. Dorothy picked up her Gucci bag and went to the office of the motel to phone for a taxi that would take her back to Hank's house in Bel Air.

12

EXCEPT WHEN HER HUSBAND WAS OUT OF TOWN, SUSAN POWell seldom drank before noon. Sometimes she made early luncheon engagements, permitting her to have a martini at eleven-thirty, but when George was gone there was no pretensc. Today even the maids were gone. She had a quickie at ten; then, after her shower, a stronger one. The gin went quickly to her head. She sat before her dresser in her slip, peering into the mirror. It was a strong face, and still attractive. She'd let her hair grow out, but she didn't really like it that way. She sipped her drink. It was just after eleven. She decided that she would make the call.

"All right," Maxine said. "If you want to, come on over then."

"Are you sure?"

"It's been a while, you know. You haven't called."

"I'm sorry. I've been very busy. It's not that I don't love you any more."

"Are you coming over, then? Or not?"

"Don't be cross."

"I'm not cross."

"You know that I've wanted to call."

"When shall I expect you?"

"Would an hour be all right?"

"I suppose so," Maxine said.

George Powell had been nicknamed "Gloomy Gus" by the men in his dorm at Harvard. To them he was humorless, serious, and utterly pessimistic. Yet he wasn't teased, for he could always be called upon for counsel. He was older than most of his classmates, even his fellow veterans, for he'd spent a full four years as a naval supply and payroll officer during the war, never leaving the States. He'd enjoyed Navy life so much he'd thought about making a career of it. Upon graduation, he was considered a behind-the-scenes campus leader, a most-likely-to-succeed, but still known as Gloomy Gus. The reputation followed him into his business life; office boys called him Raincloud and management trainees called him the Computer. But now, helping Carol into a taxi at the TWA terminal at Kennedy Airport, Powell's step had a light spring. He hadn't felt quite so good in months.

"Remember, you're paying only half of everything," she said. "Even taxi fares."

"No. I won't hear of that."

"You will. This may be an affair between us, but I'm not a mistress."

"Of course you're not a mistress. In our culture, there are no mistresses."

"Then why are there convertible cars?"

"What do convertible autos have to do with mistresses?"

"A man's convertible reminds him of his mistress. A psychologist told me that. Only last week."

"Oh, bosh!"

"Bosh, bosh, bosh," Carol said. She smiled at him.

"You will not pay half. Not where I'm taking you."

"Where might that be?"

"Fonda los Milagros, La Scala, le Vert-Galant, Quo Vadis, O. Henry's."

"O. Henry's?"

"The steak house, O. Henry's."

"Then I'll pay him. O. Henry."

"Very well."

"And another thing. I will not register as Mrs. Powell. I want to sleep with you, but I won't register as your wife."

"I've arranged for an adjoining room. They do not know me at the Americana. An associate of mine is coming to New York, or is already here, so it wouldn't do for us to be discovered in a love nest. I'm afraid we must play hide games. May I tell you that it is worth the risk? I'm not often daring."

She leaned closer to him. "How long will I have you?"

"I should return to Los Angeles on Friday."

"Stay the weekend. Now that you're president, you can do those things."

"I'm not president. Not really."

"But you will be."

"No, I fear I haven't the drive for it."

Her hand touched his. "Let's not talk of ambition. Mine is off target these days. Instead, because of you, I'm a happy woman. I'm not a security analyst. Not now."

"You're much more than a security analyst."

"When I'm by myself, I am what I do for a living. When I'm with you, I define myself differently. I'm a woman."

"You are always a woman."

"Will we talk?"

"Yes. About everything."

"Except business."

"I will try not to discuss business," he said.

"I do love you. I want you to know that."

"And I love you, Carol. Very much."

Inevitably, despite their vows when they met, they did discuss business, for it was a subject they both knew well. One thing they did not discuss, however, was where their relationship was leading. He'd known her for two years. They had shared a dozen weekends, places like Santa Barbara and San Diego; once, in a conspiracy daring for him and exciting for her, they had shared a week in Paris. They also now shared confidences, secret touches, and remembrances. She had brought out in him what she called the gentle poet behind the mask of the financial mind; he had brought out in her what he called the loving woman under the mask of cold ambition. He'd seen both moods in her, extremes that sometimes shifted from week to week. Her full name was Carol Lynn Reynolds. Her father was a professor of biology at Harvard who'd seldom looked up from his microscope long enough to touch her hand; her mother was a French-born milkmaid-housewife given to flights of romantic fancy, ceaseless chatter, and the smothering of her one offspring with attention and affection. Early in life, she had shown an interest in business, a calling her father tried to discourage (he opted for medicine) and her mother viewed with fear (she opted for marriage). She'd entered Harvard Business School, graduated with honors, and thrust herself into the arena full of resolve, liberation, and energy. Her goal was high: to become the second woman in financial history to own a seat on the New York Stock Exchange. She'd started as an analyst with Bache and now, a twelve-year veteran of financial combat, was portfolio manager for a group of West Coast mutual funds. She'd worn the right clothes, slept with the right men, and sought out the right contacts at the right conventions. She'd never really wavered from her goal. A love affair with a banker had ended in disaster; the banker had wanted not only her heart but also her time. At thirty-five, she had found her goal still in sight but her life empty. Then she'd met George Powell, a man she had long admired by reputation, at a luncheon meeting of the Los Angeles Society of Financial Analysts. They'd had coffee. It had started. Powell found himself amazed. He also found himself preening before mirrors, seeking ways to cover bald spots, exercising to reduce his chin fat. With her, he'd rediscovered his sexuality.

He lit his pipe as he watched Carol unpack in her room—a tumble of summer clothing that seemed enough for a month-long trip. He found himself thinking of Sophia. If Sophia knew of this, he thought, she might well approve.

"I think you are a beautiful woman," he said.

"Oh, nonsense," Carol said, but she smiled.

"When we first met, I didn't think so. But I've said that to you before."

"Several times. But I like to hear it."

"I've half decided something."

"But you won't tell me what it is now. I see that expression

on your face. You're going to arouse my curiosity—and you
know I have curiosity—and tell me when you choose."

"Exactly," he said. He kissed her cheek. "Pick you up at
six for dinner?"

She looked at him. "Nothing doing," she said. She was
turning back the bedcovers. "Get in," she said.

His mood changed completely. He felt years younger,
almost light-headed. She was marvelous. When he was with
her, all things seemed marvelous to him. The weather had
been miserable when he had arrived—the sultry heat of summer misted with uncertain rain that turned to steam on the
streets and held full and heavy in branches of the wilted,
dispirited trees—but now, with her there, it seemed almost
pleasant weather to Powell. It brought back the stirrings and
wantings of his youth, when his vision had been clear and his
mind receptive. Sights and sounds that previously had gone
unnoticed, surroundings he had passed through in preoccu-
pied, blind depression, now pressed sharply on his awareness.
He moved in a glowing sea of miracles—glittering store
windows, skipping children, the subway-bound crowds, mailmen with puffed cheeks and sweat on their shirts, darting
taxis, and the view of the city from the Rainbow Room at
Rockefeller Plaza.

"I'll have a manhattan," Carol said. "Appropriate."

"Make it two," Powell told the waiter.

The drinks came. Menus were distributed. Carol put on
thin-rimmed glasses and studied hers, a slight frown on her
face. Powell found himself staring at her. Not a beautiful
woman. No. Perhaps not even pretty. But a fine face, one
with delicate bones and flawless skin, clear blue eyes offset by
long lashes, and long dark hair that now was curled over her
cheeks like a little girl's. The drink went right to his head; he
ordered seconds. He felt soft and contented. There was no
world but this one. There was no demanding Lewis Anthony
Breedlove, no company named BII, no loveless aberrant wife,
no errant offspring confused and lost in the impossible transi-
tion from childhood to young adulthood. The lights of Manhattan danced before him like stars. He asked for the wine
list.

"Oh, I can't make up my mind," Carol said. "Everything

on the menu seems attractive. What is that couple over there having?"

"Veal Oscar?" Powell said.

"Oh, no. Not that. It's—"

"I want to thank you."

"Thank me for what?"

"For coming here. For being with me. For that time in bed just now."

"Shall I sneak into your room tonight, or will you sneak into mine?"

"I'm afraid you're going to discover what an old stuff I really am."

"Oh, nonsense."

"Oh, nonsense. Your favorite expression."

"Have we vowed not to discuss business?"

"Yes."

"One small violation of the vow. I want to tell you that our growth fund is preparing a report on BII. It will not be a favorable one, George."

"Why?"

"Too much dilution of equity due to acquisitions."

"May I ask you a favor? May I ask you to attempt to delay the report for a few months?"

"I think I'm just slightly in a conflict of interest position here."

"I'm sorry. I don't want that."

"Well, I'll try to delay it." She smiled. She leaned forward. "Now let's talk nonsense. Nothing serious."

"There is something I want to say now."

"Will it be serious? You have that serious look."

"It is indeed serious. I want to say that I'm a very happy man right now. And a startled and amazed man. Happy because of you, startled and amazed because I really think I do have you. At least for now. You are the only woman— perhaps the only person—with whom I have been able to speak of love. I've been afraid of the word. Love."

"I have, too. In the past. That's changed now."

"At least you have experienced it. I have never experienced it. I have never had time for it. A business associate of mine is fond of telling me that I was born a stuffy old man."

"Oh, that's—"

"Nonsense?" Powell said. He reached for his pipe, tapped the bowl on the table, and replaced the pipe in his coat pocket. "Carol, you are twenty years younger than I, so perhaps you will not see, at least now, the truth of what I'm about to say. I had a boyhood of school uniforms and desks and books. I've had a business life of airplane trips, ledgers, and offices. I've had a marriage of convenience. I cannot count on one hand the really happy days of my life. I've had happy days only after I met you, but even they have been tinged with some despair. Fear of discovery is one. I've become literally neurotic about that. I always think someone is following us, looking at us. Even today, I thought I saw someone."

"You imagined it."

"A man in tweeds. At the hotel."

"Oh, sure." She smiled. "CIA. FBI."

"Please don't joke. I'm quite serious about that."

"I'm sorry."

"And, with us, there are other matters that bother me. Often when I'm with you I have a hopeless feeling that is almost as bad as the anxiety I feel between our meetings. I love you. I believe that you love me. Yet we can do nothing about it. Or, rather, we have not done anything about it. I feel I might be holding you back. You could marry. Have children."

"I have never thought about children. Until just recently. Now that I think about them, I fear it's too late."

"You know that mine are disappointments to me."

"And you blame yourself. I know that, too."

"I'm afraid I do feel guilt about it, yes."

"Do you feel guilt about us?"

"No. I do not."

"Good. You shouldn't."

"Carol, I'm not thinking now of the present, or the past. I'm thinking of the future. This relationship of ours, eventually, must be all or nothing."

"I don't like it the way it is now either, George. This is a new Carol. I do want more of you. But I'll take what I can get."

"I want you to go away with me," Powell said.

He reached out, seeking her hand. He upset a water glass and looked away in foolish despair while the waiter cleaned it up. They ordered dinner and then sat silently for a long while.

"I realize I've sounded somewhat like the impetuous young lover," he said finally. "The sighing furnace."

"You haven't. It's a lovely thought."

"I've been thinking about it for some time. I have the money. Enough for a lifetime."

The food came. Again they lapsed into silence. A slight irritation tinged his nerves. Carol seemed distant and unresponsive. The talk of love—a subject so difficult for him— might have frightened her. Perhaps she did not want him permanently; perhaps she wanted him only periodically, for times like now. Disgust and small anger replaced the soft contentment that had gripped him. His silence became morose. He felt tiny surges of something that approached desperation. He squared his shoulders. He gulped air. The food did not taste good. He did not know what to say and he could not read her mood. Manhattan's lights seemed blurred, merged, a haze of shifting neon that obscured his vision and sent dull pain to his forehead. Then he found his voice and began to talk rapidly, blurting it out.

"I am sorry if I have disturbed or upset you. No, please don't interrupt. Please hear me out. I want you to know me. I want you to know the feelings that are inside of me. We all live in shells these days, I fear, in protective shells with ourselves, bound up with dreads that we dare not express and which impede our actions and serve only to turn us more inward. That is not good. To the world, perhaps to you, I am a successful man, but to myself I am only a man. An aging man. There is not much left of me. No. Do not say, 'Oh, nonsense,' for what I am saying is the truth. I am going to speak with absolute frankness to you, something I have done before with no one. I have given myself absolutely and completely to an organization and I have done things for that organization no man with moral rectitude could rationalize as expediency. It amounts to moral failure. But this is not a confessional about my business life. It is a confessional about me. I am now circling helplessly like an airplane that cannot land. I am on the very edge of breakdown. I want to leave it all. I want you to join me when I do. I have said that I have money. I have almost a million dollars, safely on deposit in a foreign bank. It is money I feel that I have earned. I want to leave the country. I want you to go with me. I am not a man approaching middle age, but a man who is approaching old age. I may now be on the verge of being forced out, after long years of total dedication and despite newspaper accounts heralding my promotion. I respect only a few of the men who work with me. And, perhaps most important of all, I want to acknowledge something else. I want a life with a woman. A sexual life. A man-woman life. I have not had that, and now I feel that I have missed much. And I also feel that there is not much time left. When a man is twenty-two, he has nothing but visions of the future. But at my age the visions become obscure. At least this is so with me. I want you, for as much or little a time as you will give the all of yourself to me."

"Now may I interrupt?"

"Yes. I'm sorry. I've said too much."

"Please do not apologize. Not to me." Carol took his hand. Her eyes were misty. She smiled. "Now may I make something clear? As they were wont to say in Washington, I wish to make something perfectly clear."

"Yes. Yes."

"Whatever you want me to do, I will do it. You have me in a rare, rare mood. Maybe this isn't the real me. But you're not in this alone. I'm here. I'll be here until you no longer want it that way. I won't make a pact, a promise, right now, and I don't want you to make a pact. I don't fully believe you, for I think your organization, as you call it, still has you. And I don't think it's like you to give up in the middle of a fight. We're not kids. We're intelligent adults. We've both had disappointments and felt despair. Yet I'll go. If you decide that's really what you want, I'll go. Now or tomorrow or next week."

He turned away. He did not want her to see. There was a tear on his cheek. He fumbled for his pipe. He felt total relief, perhaps for the first time in his life.

"I'm going to have dessert," Carol said, glancing into the redistributed menu.

They hid their faces from each other, like children.

After dessert, they went for a walk, skirting dangerously dark Central Park, then heading lightly towards the glitter of Times Square. Again the sights were marvelous to Powell. He noticed everything; he noticed nothing. They window-shopped, they paused at theater entrances, they ignored taxi beeps. They stood in dazzling lights, alone in a crowd. He plucked two carnations from the gnarled hands of an old crippled woman, gave her five dollars, and threaded the red one through the lapel buttonhole of his suit and pinned the white one on Carol's dress. He purchased all the papers from a news vendor. He gave two quarters to a beggar who sold pencils. He gave a dollar to a blind man. Carol said she would not share the cost of his charities, but, feeling the empathy and goodwill he felt, she found some of her own, including a white-eyed black lad who hawked cheap silver charms. The sky was clear and the moon was almost full. Now Manhattan seemed magnificent to Powell—alive with colors and sounds and smells that tingled in his loins and rendered him deliciously intoxicated.

They walked back, their arms linked. At Fiftieth, a tall, unshaven man in a low-visored cap blocked their path.

"Yer wallet," he said. "Da lady's purse. Like, quick."

A white flash moved in the man's hand—the steel blade of a knife reflected in the streetlight. Powell stood stunned. Carol clutched his arm. He looked around. People milled on the other side of the street, hurrying away. A man approached them, stopped, turned, and walked rapidly in the direction from which he'd come. A cruising taxi sped up and darted away.

"Now," the man said quietly.

Powell reached for his wallet. He heard footsteps behind him, clumping rapidly. The man with the knife took a quick step toward Powell, then turned and began to back up. A big man in a tweed jacket pushed between Powell and Carol, his arms raised, and pounced on the man with the knife, driving him to the curb with a sharp chop of his hand. The knife clattered to the sidewalk.

"Go ahead, go," the man in tweeds said to Powell. "Go!" He stood over the fallen man.

Powell took Carol's arm. They hurried across the street. He looked back to see their attacker fleeing into a side street. The man in tweeds was no longer there. The street seemed suddenly busier. People rushed about, minding their business.

*   *   *

The incident jarred them to full awareness. They had a brandy in a bar at the hotel and went to their separate rooms. About midnight Carol called and soon she was knocking on his door. He let her in.

"Well," she said. "New York. Mugger's paradise."

"Yes."

"I don't want to return to my room."

"I want you here," he said.

"Who was that man?"

"I don't know. I honestly do not know."

"Well, we will thank the good Lord for him."

"Yes."

"Tweeds," she said.

"You noticed. I noticed, too. It wasn't my imagination."

"What shall we do?"

He shrugged. "What can we do?"

"Go to bed, I guess," Carol said. "Is the door locked?"

13

THE DEAD WOMAN WHOSE BLOOD HAD SPATTERED SCOTT'S hands was named Margarita Sanchez. An old Mexican man said that as a girl she had danced every Saturday in the square at Hermosillo, twirling her red skirt and tossing her hair until exhaustion had overcome her. In her leather pouch were a statuette of the Virgin, some rosary beads, and a small gold locket with photographs of two children. The old man, who remembered well, said the children were hers. Her husband was dead; the children lived now in Sonora with relatives. The woman had first come across with her husband in 1963, to work in the California fields under the extended Bracero program. Mexican men brought their wives, unlike the Filipinos, who left their women at home. She and her husband were green-carders; they had visas, permanent resident alien status. They were not *alambristas*. They had no fear of *la Migra*. Then the husband had died; the woman had become the provider. She came, worked, and returned. All this the old man related in slow, halting words, speaking in broken English. He said years ago Sanchez had been active in the union; he had, in fact, once been a submarine, crossing picket lines to agitate and slow non-union pickers in the fields. But Margarita was not an agitator. She merely wanted to work and return home with money. She had come to Olen with the group assembled for harvest work by the Milwaukee supplier. The old man had been standing behind the woman when she had been shot. The bullet had struck her in the throat. She had died instantly.

"Not a agitator," said the sheriff, wiping his nose with the back of his hand. "Why's she out there then, she ain't no agitator?"

The old man didn't answer. He sat on a chair, wearing patched overalls and a red shirt with sleeves that extended to his knuckles. He was growing uncomfortable. His eyes were beginning to show fear. He wanted to leave. He would not speak any more.

"Awright," the sheriff said. "Talk at'cha later."

The old man left. Now there were four in the room. The sheriff. The plant manager, J. B. Toms. A young Mexican in a red shirt and black trousers whose name was Arthur Rodriguez. And Mark Scott. A Mark Scott who had yet to recover, a man uncertain and confused, with a stimulated heartbeat and pulse rate and adrenal-gland flow. He closed his eyes. It ran before his consciousness like a slow-motion film—the two groups, the sheriff between them, the shot, the scuffle, the tramping shoes, the woman dead by his side, the blood on his palms. They were in the plant's sole office, a narrow room with feed-mill calendars, paper-scattered desks, and a slow-moving overhead fan that ticked against its wire-mesh enclosure, a room full of sticky heat and sweat smells and a brine odor from the plant pungent and unavoidable. Through the window Scott saw the river, rolling placidly. The sun was going down. The fields were pink.

The cannery had been closed for the day. An ambulance had come and gone. Four persons had required hospitalization for minor injuries. The Mexicans had returned to their camp. The armed men had dispersed, racing to trucks that escaped over the bridge. Scott hadn't identified himself to the sheriff—Johnny, they called him—until the ambulance had left. Then the sheriff had called Toms over to them and they had gone to Tom's office. Rodriguez had brought in the old man five minutes later.

Toms squashed a fly that had settled on his sleeve. "Get'cha a drink, Johnny?" he said.

The sheriff considered. "Naw, not now."

"Mr. Scott?" Toms said. "A drink?"

"Yes. Please."

"Bourbon whiskey okay? The Old Taylor?"

"A Coke, please."

"Oh," Toms said. "I'll get it at the machine."

"Get me one, I'll spring," the sheriff said.

Toms went out. Scott looked at the sheriff. "What will be the next step?"

"Wal, there'll be a inquest, you know. It'll be up at Indian Falls, no doubt. Papers'll be here. From the cities? Paper here, that's okay, you know what I mean, but if the city guys come in, then you don't know what can happen. I ain't gonna have nothin' to say to 'em, you can count on that."

"Why?"

"It don't do no good, talkin' about it. We got a problem, this county, we can handle it."

Toms returned with three opened bottle Cokes. He gave one to Scott and to the sheriff.

"You're not thirsty?" Scott asked the Mexican, Rodriguez.

"He knows where he can get it," Toms said.

"Wal, I don't see no need for me to hang around here no more," the sheriff said. He had drained his Coke. "Mr. Scott, I was pleased to meet'cha."

"Wait," Scott said.

"Eh?"

"I want you to hear this."

"Sho," the sheriff said.

Scott turned to Toms. "I met you for the first time only a half hour ago, but I know your record. It's a good record. I'm saying that because I want you to know I have no pre-formed prejudice. All I want, for now, is information."

"Min' if I have a drink?"

"Go ahead. Then tell me who the men with rifles were. And who hired them."

Toms poured a trickle of Old Taylor into a glass. "I hired 'em," he said, and he drank.

"Then you know who they are."

"Not personal, no."

"Why were they here?"

"I had information there'd be trouble." Toms glanced at the Mexican. "Mr. Scott, I don't think he should be in on this."

"Your name is Arthur Rodriguez?" Scott said to the Mexican.

Rodriguez nodded. He had not spoken a word.

"Do you speak English?"

"I do."

"Do you want to stay?"

"I want to talk to you."

"All right."

"I'd prefer to talk to you alone."

"Now?"

"No. I will leave now. There has been enough for this day. Will you have the time tomorrow?"

"Yes."

"He's a stinkin' shit, that Mex," Tom said after Rodriguez had left. "Man like that get his rocks off stirrin' up trouble."

"Were any of the Mexicans armed?" Scott asked the sheriff.

"Sho," the sheriff said.

"How do you know?"

"They'll always have a knife."

Scott turned back to Toms. "Why were your men armed?"

"Wal, they ain't my men, you understand. They come from all around here, farmers and National Guard people up from around Indian Falls and thereabouts, where there's a post. I didn't ask for no rifles. I told Stetson that if anybody carried a rifle, he should make damn sure they weren't loaded."

"Who is Stetson?"

"That's Colonel Stetson, up at Indian Falls. I got a bothersome problem, I'd call him."

"He is the unofficial militia?"

"Sir?"

"The private army?"

"Wal, no, Mr. Scott, not that. He'll stop a problem b'fore it starts, you see. A show of stength, you'd say."

"What started the demonstration?"

"You jus' saw 'im. Rodriguez. I'll tell you for a fact, Mr.

Scott. That's a bad Mexican. Some of his own people, they'll even tell you that. Am I right, Johnny?"

"Sho," the sheriff said. "You say it, J.B."

"All right," Scott said.

He left.

It was now twilight, a soft glow between darkness and bright sun. It seemed even hotter—not the burning heat of noon but a motionless damp penetrating heat that seemed to seek out and cling to a moving body. Dragonflies appeared in thick squadrons. Scott started the Corvair, turned, and drove slowly toward Olen. He was just out of the plant area when the sheriff's car overtook him. He stopped. The sheriff clumped up in a noisy, exaggerated stride and jutted his sweaty face in through thet Corvair's open window. Scott really saw him for the first time—the hard black eyes underlined by puffy dark circles, the flat nose with large nostrils that dilated as he sniffed, the wet skin sagging in rolls under his chin like kneaded bread dough.

"You'll need to fix that headlight, Mr. Scott."

"It's not my car."

"Don't matter, long's you drive it."

"I'll see to it."

"You might have the wrong idee about somethin'."

"What would that be?"

"I'm on the county's payroll. Not J. B.'s. And, in there, I was actin'."

"How so?"

"I gave the movie act of a typical county sheriff. That was for him, not you. Around here, they expect it."

"I see."

"You enjoy the stay in Olen," Johnny said.

J. B. Toms, fifty-nine years old and thirty-three years with the Breedlove company, was one of the biggest men in Olen. He was far from the biggest in stature, standing only chest-high to most of the nearby farmhands, sun- and windburned men who proudly displayed the permanent black marks on their backs ingrown from harness straps used in the days when men and beasts were linked with two-furrow plows in constant struggle with the earth. Nor was he by far the most intelligent man in the area, although no one underestimated his shrewdness. His power base was simple. He hired the town. Growers depended directly upon him, merchants depended indirectly upon him. He received free drinks in bars, free meals in restaurants, and told the newspaper what to print. If he was not liked, he was tolerated. His disposition was dominated by his poorly molded false teeth; when they hurt, he could be mean. He was called, always, "J. B.," his real name, not initials. He was a Baptist, attending church every Sunday, pushing a wheelchair that contained his silent, birdlike wife. It was well known at the plant that a Baptist had a better chance for promotion than a Church of God member or a Methodist.

Toms could barely read and had no conception of how to spell. But he shaved every day, bathed at least twice a week, and seldom had liquor on his breath at the plant. Experience had taught him how to fix machinery and organize. The town considered him a petty thief when he was, in truth, almost a major thief. He withheld a percentage of the fees paid to harvesttime labor suppliers, and he invariably underestimated when he reported social-security deductions of temporary workers. He had the wisdom to avoid communication by the written word—not because of his inability to spell but because he knew documents could be used as evidence.

Seconds after Scott had left, Toms was on the phone to Cotton Mecks, Olen's auto dealer and acting mayor.

"Name's Mark Scott, an' he's a top man from California," he said. "Why he's here, that he ain't tol' me."

"Perhaps they're going to modernize the plant. Expand it."

"Could be. Needs it."

"It was unfortunate an accident occurred there this afternoon."

"You hear about that? Jesus Christ."

"Thank you for telling me about Mr. Scott, J. B. I'll follow up."

He did, immediately, and the chain reaction started. He called a lawyer and a doctor and two merchants. He called a banker in Indian Falls. The lawyer, doctor, merchants, and banker called farmers, ministers, innkeepers, food-product wholesalers, amusement vendors, train dispatchers, traveling salesmen, and schoolteachers. They told their wives, their girl friends, their children. Rumors ran. The executive from California was in Olen to double the plant's capacity. BII was buying up all of the land within a twenty-mile radius. They've discovered oil and soon would drill. They're going to dam the river. A boomtown is in the works. The governor of Wisconsin and a senator from Washington will be in town tomorrow. Reporters are leaving Milwaukee for Olen.

It was all out, spilled, by the time the executive signed the register at the Madison Hotel.

"Oh, Mr. Scott," the clerk said. "Your room is ready."

"I have some bags in the car."

"The boy will get them, sir. Boy!"

An old man in a bellboy's uniform shuffled up, stared out the open door in disbelief at the executive's battered Corvair, and then limped obediently toward it.

"Did my wife call?" Scott asked.

"No, sir."

"Would you have someone try to reach her, please? Mrs. Anne Scott, the Four Ambassadors, Miami Beach."

The clerk darted off. The ancient bellman returned, sagging under the weight of Scott's bags. Scott gave him a dollar and asked him to take the bags to his room. The bellman moved toward the stairs. Through the door galloped two sweaty fat men in suits, who paused, tapped their heels, wiped their faces, and then streaked directly at Scott.

"Welcome to Olen, Mr. Scott, welcome, welcome," said one. "I'm as much of a mayor as you'll find around here— Acting Mayor Cotton Meeks, sir, and *acting* only because the CPA died countin' the vote in '74, and here with me in the backbone of the Town Council and our leadin' retailer, Polk Anderson. We'd like you to know that anythin' you might need—and we mean *anythin'*—well, all you have to do is ask, that's all."

"Thank you."

"We mean it."

"Thank you."

"I'll send you over a car with a driver in the mornin'. An' you get in some fishin' when you're here. I got a private cabin up on the Wisconsin."

"I'm afraid I haven't the time. And I already have a car, thank you."

"Your call, Mr. Scott," said the clerk.

He excused himself and took the call in his room, which was probably the best in the hotel, despite its smell of stale air, hard bed, and invasion by a swarm of healthy flies.

"No, it's just ten here now," Anne said. "The kids are asleep, though. Worn out."

"I miss you," he said.

"I miss you. How soon can you get here?"

"Anne, I want you to try to understand something."

"You're not coming here. Is that it?"

"I'm afraid it is."

"Well, I guess I really didn't expect it."

"There's something I haven't told you. Something Breedlove said to me. He said I could have it all. He said this Troika idea is just a sham. He has me in mind for the top job at BII."

There was a pause. Then Anne said, "Do you believe him?"

"Yes. Yes, I do."

"What do you have to do for it?"

"I don't know. Work. You sound unimpressed."

"But I am impressed. I'm just trying to digest it all. Quite a bit has happened to you in the past few days."

"To us," he said.

"To us," Anne said. Again she paused. "Mark? Listen, because I'm going to blurt something out. I've done a lot of thinking. I know I've waffled all over the place. But I'm not going to waffle any more. I want you to have it. I know you want it and I know you can do it. I want you to do it."

"Sudden change."

"No. Just rethinking. It might be a lifetime opportunity."

"Then I'll go for it. All out."

"But don't change on me. Promise me that."

"I won't change."

"Please love me."

"I do," he said.

He dozed off and came awake fully dressed at about 11 P.M., sensing something in the room, a hovering presence. He shook his head, thinking, *Breedlove*. He went to the window. Olen lay below him. Across the street a man slumped against a light pole. He looked up, directly at Scott. His face seemed familiar. Where? When? Scott ran down the stairs and hurried outside. The man was still there. Scott stared at him. And then he knew. The man resembled Lewis Breedlove, a much younger Breedlove. Scott stepped toward him. The man moved rapidly away, vanishing in the darkness.

He slept badly. Several times he rose and looked out the window. The street was silent and dark. He lay tossing in the bed, haunted by visions of Breedlove.

In the morning two Mexicans in straw sun hats were waiting for him outside the hotel. "Please come with us," one said to Scott.

Arthur Rodriguez had once helped to build a rural wooden cross near a grape field close to Bakersfield, California. It had been constructed in memory of Sylvia, his sister, dedicated to her in the name of the patron saint La Virgen de Guadalupe. Saints had no meaning to him, much to the disappointment of his mother, but Sylvia had been real and had meant much to him. She had told him he could be something beyond a picker, and she had brought him books to read, books in English. He was the lazy one, his father said, lying in the sun to read, but his father, too, allowed it. So he came to know, very young, writers such as Dos Passos and Steinbeck and the poets Robert Frost and Carl Sandburg. He read the philosopher Plato and, secretly, Socrates became his saint. He learned why men died for what they believed in.

The family had lived in Delano, seven people in a modest house, cool in summer and filled with cooking smells. Their income came from following California crops, supplemented in a minor way by profit from his father's off-season junk business. They had a Model A pickup that seemed to go forever on a tank of gas. One day, following the spraying of pesticides, Sylvia had become sick, vomiting and foaming at the mouth, and had fallen down the stairs, striking her head. She had never regained consciousness. They had raced from doctor to doctor in the town, but no one would take their case without prepayment. So Sylvia had died, and Arthur Rodriguez had helped his sisters construct the cross. It had become more than a shrine. When it had been written about in a pamphlet that circulated throughout the valley, it had become a rallying point for agitators over the pesticide issue, a discussion point for union organizers, an inspiration for picketers and boycotters.

One night it had been burned down. He did not know who burned it. But, he thought now, if it had not been burned, he would have continued as a picker, following the crops with his family. Instead, he went to the union. They had burned not a cross but his sister Sylvia, who had shown him the wonder of books and had told him he could become somebody.

Later, other crosses in the valley had been constructed and burned. But none had significance to Arthur Rodriguez. He had only one cross in his memory.

"Were you with Chavez?" Scott asked.

He was seated on the grass near the labor camp outside of Olen, consuming fat tacos for breakfast. Rodriguez was seated before him. They were alone, in the shade of an elm tree that provided only minimal protection from the rising heat—alone, that is, except for the coming and going of a cook, a grinning man in an apron constantly supplying fresh tacos and lurking around suspiciously to make sure Scott ate them.

"I was with him, yes, for a while," Rodriguez said. "During his fast, I was with him."

"Do you represent him now?"

"I represent no organization, Mr. Scott. I am what you call the lone wolf. I go where there is trouble."

"They say you go to make trouble."

Rodriguez frowned. "Perhaps trouble follows me. It is sad."

"What do you think of Chavez?"

"Cesar, that is an unfortunate name. It has the connotation of a dictator. They have used that against him. The totalitarian state. Dictator."

"So you do not agree with all he has done?"

"I agree absolutely. He is one of my saints."

"Along with Socrates?"

"With Socrates, yes. Socrates, no longer Guadalupe."

"How about Marx?"

"You are baiting me. The wolf will not take the bait."

"I'm only trying to find out," Scott said. "What else will you tell me about yourself?"

Rodriguez told a story well, an ability he'd no doubt acquired while relating passages from the books to his family. Scott could feel the itch and pain of the pesticide blisters on pickers' faces when Rodriguez described them. But he would not say much more about himself. He'd acquired a fair working knowledge of labor law—correspondence schools and Hard Knocks U, he said—and he professed to be twenty-nine. He looked barely twenty. He was a thin, angular man with thick forearms and clear dark eyes. The eyes of a fanatic? Perhaps. Yet also they were the eyes of a born leader. It was a strange bargaining table, this red cloth between them, stained with grease from soft beef tacos and attractive to bees and ants, yet, Scott realized, it was indeed a bargaining table.

"Did you organize the demonstration?" he asked.

"As a protest, yes, I organized it. We have come here to work. We want to work. But we want fair treatment. We are paid under the minimum wage, after fees are subtracted."

"What fees?"

"For the labor supplier."

"He is paid by deductions from salaries, not out of plant overhead?"

Rodriguez nodded. "And there are other matters, Mr. Scott. We are not paid overtime. There is no disability insurance. There are no benefits whatsoever. Social-security payments are deducted in advance, in a lump sum. There is corruption in that plant, Mr. Scott. That, however, is your company's problem. It is ours, too, of course, because from our pay comes the graft. We want only fair treatment. And, as you see, we are united."

"You charge corruption. Can you elaborate?"

"It is all through this town."

"How do you know?"

"It is known to me," Rodriguez said.

He would say no more. It is known. Scott sighed. How much was known generally that was not known at the top? A saying he'd heard long ago—perhaps even in college—flashed through his mind. The higher up you go in a company, the fewer your friends and the less you really know about the company. In the paneled offices above the rest, you planned the fates of those below. The workers were unknown quantities. They were computer numbers. Their methods, habits, and attitudes were blended into mass reports read at negotiating tables. The individual's identity had been subordinated to the group's identity. The person had become a horde—blue denims and lunch pails and time cards—a crowd mechanical and programmed. Scott, in three summers on a canning line, had known workers individually; their shoptalk and manners, temporarily, had become his. But, as he'd risen, he'd realized he would never really know them. It was too large, too diversified, too widespread geographically. He also realized that he did not want to know them. It reduced his effectiveness at collective bargaining. Already he had a reputation as a friend of the worker, one that earned him more respect with the unions than with the BII board. And if the worker wanted your blessing, he did not, in reality, want your close attention. He had his job to do. You had yours. Now, in this involvement, he'd spent too much time with the ranks. It was not a supercilious judgment; it was a practical one. Work was piling up at headquarters. But he would see this matter to its end.

"The woman's death," he said. "It has helped your cause?"

"We have had a collection here," Rodriguez said. "To pay the old man's way to Mexico with the body."

"But you did not answer. Has it aided your cause?"

Rodriguez drew a strand of grass from the ground. "I suppose that it has, Mr. Scott. Yet people forget easily. And some of these people are afraid now. Some have already left. So the tactics were effective. I will not say that I wish I had not come here. There is some blood on my hands, yes. But I am not guilty alone. There was a service here last night. We do not have a real priest, but we held what service we could."

"I will do what I can to see that her killer is brought to justice."

"Few murderers are punished," Rodriguez said slowly.

"What is your next step?"

"We will not work. Not under these terms."

"What if I authorize a temporary contract, meeting your demands?"

"Then we will stay—most of us—for the harvest." They stood up. They shook hands. "You could do so much, Mr. Scott, a man in your position. I think you are an honest man."

BII believed in divisional autonomy, with each division sending five-year goals to headquarters on a semiannual basis. If a division failed to meet its goal, its manager had some explaining to do, often to Breedlove himself, at quarterly group-division conferences held at headquarters. If trouble appeared at divisional level, headquarters sent in squads of experts in various fields—finance, labor relations, production. Divisions sent balance sheets and profit-loss statements to headquarters each month. Every unit, such as the Olen plant, a Food Division entity, sent reports to division, which relayed them to headquarters. Divisional accountants could make surprise audits of any plant at any time. When Scott got back to the Olen plant after the meeting with Rodriguez, he immediately pried the books from J. B. Toms and carried them under his arm during a plant tour. The plant was ancient and also very dirty. Cans moved around them, rising and turning on a system of overhead pulleys and steel-balled conveyor belts.

"We'll get the cannin' done this harvest whether them Mexicans come in or not," Toms said. "It'll take longer, but we'll get 'er done."

"How?"

"Wal, I don't min' sayin' it, Mr. Scott, that it won't be easy. We'll have some college kids comin' up from Madison soon, and that'll help some. Not that they're the best of workers. They read more'n they work. Them Mexicans, I'll admit it, they know how to work, despite what anybody else says. That retort there by the office ain't workin', but we'll have it goin'. That line's where the peas come on. We'll worry about it come June. See here. The 9/32nds slot for petits, and 10/32nds for extra fines, the 11/32nds for fines."

"You could use some modernization."

"I reckon that's so, Mr. Scott. But the old-fashioned ways, they work in cannin'. Fruits an' vegetables, they seem to have a way of knowin' things. Send 'em down a swirl tank, you'd see. You know that a good apple'll swim, a bad one'll sink? You can run pears an' apples together. because a pear'll sink, a apple'll float. Also, let the fruit roll and jump a gap. Good one'll make it, bad ones—them with only a little decay spot—they'll not make 'er."

"Shall we go back to the office?"

"It's sweaty here, I'll admit. These things was built before air conditioning. You build 'em with the sawtooth roof, straight sides turned to the north, inclined sides to the south. So the sun on the south that way, it heats the underneath and when that rises it creates a flow of cooler air in the factory. Ain't workin' too good right now."

Over Cokes in Toms's office, Scott spread the plant books out before him on a desk. They were kept in pen and ink. The entries were vague, almost illegible.

"These are the same reports you send to divisional headquarters?"

"Identical, sure. Except she types up the ones we send in."

"It's plain to see the losses haven't stopped."

"Mr. Scott, you saw this plant. Anybody could make a profit or even break even here, he'd be a A-graded genius, or a man from Mars. I know you realize what labor's costin' us—here an' elsewhere."

"How do you contract for temporary workers?"

"Wal, you see, Mr. Lathrop, over at Milwaukee, he delivers so many people at the right times at so much an hour. We give 'em grounds to camp on out over there by Silver Creek. When they're workin', we give 'em a meal allowance, too, although I wanna cut that out. I don't pay the Mexicans. I pay Lathrop and he pays 'em. He's a job contractor, don't you see? We jus' sign 'em up, individual, an' pay out to Lathrop what they worked."

"Doesn't that leave room for graft?"

Toms stuck out his lower lip. "Maybe we do have our ways of doin' things here irregular to the way it's done at other places. I don't know about other places. It's the way we do it here. You change things, they get more complicated. This plant's got enough troubles without pumpin' up the payroll any more."

"You're non-union here, is that right? For the full-time workers?"

"Yas. But there's been unions voted in here from time to time, like the tinsmith's."

"And employees get BII fringes."

"Yas. Unless they're union." Toms avoided Scott's eyes. He looked away. "Mr. Scott, I figure you for a practical man. Got to be, else you wouldn'ta got high as you are. What I want to say is that there's items in them books I don't like to explain too much. A payout here, a payout there. The county's paid tax, but there's a lotta people round here have the power to close up this plant for health reasons—round here and federal government, too—and they'll look elsewhere if they get jus' a little fee. It's the way business is done."

"Around here?"

"Wal, ever'where, ain't it?"

"So you've given bribes?"

"Wal, you don't call 'em bribes, them."

"Have you taken any?"

"The way the bonus system works, the bonus is given on profits. There ain't no profit at this plant. I don't take bribes, no. I don't want to say no more about it. I got a crop to get in, Mr. Scott. I'm a production man. You want to fire me, fire me now. Lemme tell you this, Mr. Scott. You do fire me, a lot of men will walk off with me. And the crops'll rot in the fields."

"I didn't say I'm going to fire you. But I do have some orders for you. I want you to bring in the Mexican workers. I want them paid ten cents an hour over the minimum wage, if they'll work for that. And, if we run overtime on the harvest, I want them paid time and a half. I want you to call your Mr. Lathrop, the man from Milwaukee, and tell him we're breaking our contract with him. We'll settle with him later—in the courts, if necessary. The temporary workers will be paid from the plant's payroll. Our policy is to provide fringe benefits for temporary workers, and these workers will be given workmen's compensation protection, and, while on the job, accident insurance."

"If you say so, Mr. Scott. But get ready for double losses this month."

"I'll explain that to the division and to Breedlove himself if I must. Now. You and I are going to draw up a contract with those workers right now. On the back of an envelope, if we must. I'll dictate, you write."

"Me write?"

"If you can't write, bring in a secretary."

Toms's expression turned sour. "I think you're givin' in when you don't have to. I tell you that them Mexicans would come on under my terms, when it come right down to it. They always have. Jus' wait 'em out."

"Do you have a pen?" Scott said.

He got back to his hotel at dusk, driven by the secretary who had typed up the contract agreement. She was a pretty girl of about twenty-five who told him her father had known Scott's parents.

"Your father was a teacher, wasn't he?" she said.

"Yes."

"I went to normal school myself. But I didn't finish, you know. Got a job at the plant and never got away. I remember a movie with Bette Davis where she was in a small town and couldn't get away. It was called, I think it was called *Beyond the Hills*. Mr. Scott, would you like help on those books? I have experience on books, you know."

"No, I'll manage. Thanks for the ride."

"Okay," she said.

A Ford station wagon was parked in front of the hotel, boasting a bumper sticker that read, "AMERICA—LOVE IT OR LEAVE IT." Acting Mayor Cotton Meeks leapt spryly from it, advanced like a fox scenting prey, and claimed Scott with a firm clamp of his pudgy hand.

"We're gonna have supper together. Hotel's got it all set up. You like pheasant, dont'cha?"

Scott nodded weakly, feeling trapped.

Scott had to admit the pheasant was good. It was served with champagne from Meeks's private stock. They were attended by two waiters, including the ancient bellman, who had changed uniforms. Meeks was irrepressible. He chattered incessantly about the Wisconsin Badgers football team, the China menace, the Ruskie threat. Finally, between open-mouthed chomps on pheasant flesh, he got around to discussion of the Olen cannery.

"Mark, our plant, how much is it losin'?"

"*Our* plant? It is BII's plant."

"That's a fact, sure, Mark. But there's a lotta Breedlove stockholders hereabouts. Annual meetin's here next year."

Scott put down his napkin. "May I thank you for the meal? It was excellent. But I really must go now."

"Tell me, Mark. You a accountant?"

"Not quite. Almost."

"Help you read them books, you want."

"That's the second offer I've had tonight," Scott said.

*   *   *

He had just started on the books when a tap came on his door. It was the bellman-waiter, now reconverted to a bellman's regalia. "Somethin' I'd like to show ya," he said, his tongue flapping, one eye swimming crookedly in a bloodshot socket.

"I'm afraid I'm busy now," Scott said.

"You know Breedlove hisself was born hereabouts, dont'cha?"

"I had heard that, yes."

"I got pitchers. Brung 'em. Wanna see 'em?"

Scott let him in. The bellman flopped down in a chair, primed himself with a pull from a bottle of Old Grand-Dad secreted in his tunic, and began to talk. He told of a family that had settled nearby almost eighty years ago, a bad-luck family that everybody avoided, thinking it cursed and diseased. They had no money. The children were sickly. Harsh winters swept them to their graves. The bellman produced two old photographs. One showed a man and a woman posing beside a mule in the fields. The woman wore a long dress and a bonnet. The man wore overalls.

"Tysons," the bellman said. "His paw and maw."

The second photo was of a girl-child in a coffin. The coffin had been tipped up on its end. There was a bunch of wild flowers in the girl's hands. A small boy stood beside the coffin. Lewis Breedlove?

The old man nodded, as if he anticipated Scott's question.

"He was a real scrapper, him," he said. "Sometimes I'd meet 'im on the road, comin' home from school. We tangled more'n once. I'll admit it, he got the best of me in the end. He'd fight wit' anythin'. Sticks an' stones an' dirt clods. Then them Tysons was gone. The old man hung hisself in the barn after he'd split the woman's skull wit' a axe. The boy, he run off."

"When was this?"

"Oh, maybe nineteen an' seventeen, eighteen."

"How do you know the boy didn't die?"

"Seen 'im later, right here. Years an' years later. Seen his pitcher in the paper, when he come to build this plant. I don't forget a face."

"I want to ask you something else. This may sound strange to you."

"Nothin's strange you hear in this town."

"Have you seen him, or someone who resembles him, here in Olen recently?"

"Nope. Can't say I have. Nope."

"I thank you for telling me this."

"You keep them pitchers."

"I'd like to pay you for them."

"Naw. That's awright about that."

"Thank you."

"Watch out for that Cotton Meeks," the bellman said.

He returned to the books. They were carelessly kept and confusing. Numerous outgo entries were marked "Payment," with no additional explanation. The June "Payment" was $2,140. The books made one matter obvious—the financial condition of the plant was indeed precarious. It had been losing money for years. Its equipment had been amortized long ago.

Scott put the books down, realizing it would take several days to decipher them accurately. He found he could think only of Breedlove; again it seemed as if Breedlove's force had crept into the room. He recalled Anne's phrase—opportunity of a lifetime. He wanted it. That much he knew. He wanted it badly. Breedlove crouched beside him, chuckling and puffing a Lucky. Just like the man he'd seen last night, leaning on a streetlight. He walked to the window. The street was empty. Olen lay before him, swept in a pale light, already devoid of life. A small dog scampered across the street, paused to sniff around, and darted away. Scott glanced at the photographs the old man had brought. The presence of Lewis Breedlove filled the room, an encroaching, possessive, disembodied force, a chill that hovered and then left, drifting out over the town and the land and seeming to say, "This I own, created, and can destroy."

The phone startled him. "Yes," he said.

"Oh, Mr. Scott, this is Norma. Mr. Toms's secretary?"

"Yes, Norma."

"Well, I called because I was just wondering, there's nothing to do here at home, you know, so I was just wondering if you're sure you wouldn't like me to come up tonight?"

"Did Toms ask you to call?"

"Well, he didn't *ask* me, no."

"I think I understand."

"It's just that I find you an attractive man, Mr. Scott. You know?"

"Thank you. But I advise you to stay home."

"All right, I'll do that if that's what you think." She paused. "Mr. Scott, I hate to say this, you know, but you're from the cities and all where you must see a lot of girls all the time."

"Yes?"

"Well, here goes, then. Do you think I'm . . . well, attractive? I mean, by comparison. You know?"

"You'd match up with the best of them, Norma."

"I appreciate that, you saying that, Mr. Scott. I know you wouldn't say anything you didn't think was true. I guess you think I'm nervy. Well, I'll say good night now."

Scott lay back on the bed, his hands under his head. It was obvious that Toms had ordered Norma to call, either to start tongues wagging about the BII executive's moral fiber or to discover what he was doing with the plant's books. Innocent Norma—or perhaps not-so-innocent Norma—was bait in a trap so obvious that Scott found himself repressing laughter.

He tried to call Anne, but there was no answer. He left a message for her and then began to stalk about, thinking. He could not quite articulate his dilemma to himself, yet he knew he could explain it to Anne, and, between them, they could find an answer. Breedlove had dispatched him to kill a town; he was a soldier on a mission that could lead to another step up the ranks, perhaps the biggest step of his career. Apparently Olen was not without its own form of corruption, yet it was also the sanctuary of home for many committed families; within its sustaining fabric there existed a core of goodness, pride, Yankee independence. Scott felt the peace of the town in himself, heightened by his memories of a happy childhood. Olen, in fact, held him frozen in indecision. But yet his course was clear. To please Breedlove, to impress the BII board, he would have to recommend the execution of Olen. Its very existence now seemed a roadblock to the progress of Mark Scott.

He searched his mind for alternatives. There seemed none. If he did not kill Olen, would not someone else? Lancaster would do it with pleasure, a conquering king showing his power. Lancaster thought of Scott as idealistic, naïve, inno-cent, and almost boyish. Was he? Scott did not know. He saw Breedlove before him, telling him he was the select, the chosen. Surely, then, Breedlove, who could slash instinctively to the truth of a man's makeup, didn't think of him as naïve or indecisive. It was tempting. It was more than tempting. It was overwhelming, head-swimming. Two days ago he had thought of himself as locked in a position that in itself he considered on occasion to be too big for him. Now he could take it all, rise to the top desk of one of the world's largest international conglomerates. The cost? Certainly there would be no more periods of tranquillity. In its place would be more pressures, longer hours, and much disorder.

But he wanted it.

Anne was behind him. She wanted it for him.

Breedlove wanted him.

Perhaps he was on a path to it. Perhaps he could do nothing about it.

He wouldn't think about Olen and the plant right now. He had time. BII had scheduled its annual meeting in Olen next May. No announcement concerning the plant's fate would be made until after the stockholders met.

Anne called at ten. "I'm absolutely out of my mind, chasing kids all day," she said. "I'm so beat up now that I can't sleep. Then tomorrow—no, today—Orlando at six A.M. Is it going well for you there?"

"Honest answer?"

"Honest answer."

"No. It's not going too well."

"Mark? Do you want us to come there?"

"It would spoil the vacation for the kids."

"Well, maybe they should see their father's homeland."

"Ouch. I'm reminded again. The name Scott may not be very popular around here after the next few months."

"Why?"

"I'd rather not talk about it on the phone."

"Then we'll talk about it in person. I'm coming there."

"It's not easy to find."

"It's on the map, isn't it?"

"Barely."

"If it's on the map, I'll find it."

"I love you. Very much."
"I love you. And miss you."
"Don't hurry."
"I'll hurry," Anne said.

14

ONE OF THE FEW BOOKS HENRY LANCASTER HAD READ COVER
to cover during college had been C. Wright Mills's *Power
Elite*. Mills maintained that power groups—society celebri-
ties, corporate leaders, politicians, the military—were born to
their authority and seldom were self-molded from underprivi-
leged backgrounds. Their opportunities sprang from kinship
with position, power, and wealth. Lancaster saw truth in
Mills's theme, but it also discouraged him, so in the end he
rejected it. It was incomplete, because it did not concern itself
with an important factor—the power of will. Nor did Lancaster accept the simpleminded Horatio Alger syndrome, which
rewarded the hardworking, honest sycophant with success. In
the competitive jungle, he'd discovered very early, you rose in
one of two ways—through the gift of birth or the power of
will. For the disadvantaged, the will was all; if you were not
crippled, stupid, or black, the will could bring you power. It
was a strength the advantaged could not develop, for they
had achieved weakly. It was a philosophy, Lancaster knew,
that Lewis Breedlove shared with him. He called it achieve-
ment-by-will, and, with Lancaster, a central, driving point to it
was his readiness to take a chance. Chance-taking tough-
ened him, strengthened him, and instilled in him a confidence
that he not only was better than the rest, but also, if needed,
was almost superhuman. The bigger the challenge, the greater
the accomplishment. A single test was insufficient. Tests had
to come regularly. He'd categorized his attributes in junior
high. He was bigger and stronger than most others. He was
smarter than any of them. He was better-looking than most.
And he'd take a dare. The tests had begun when he'd been
eleven. He'd walked to the top span of the Brooklyn Bridge at

midnight on a four-dollar bet mustered up among his fellow inmates at the orphanage. That test had rewarded him with undisputed leadership at his school. There had been many more tests, lesser and greater. Conquering women, even teachers and social workers, had been one. He went on to more, like baiting cops or breaking into warehouses with no intent to burglarize but just to do it, like alley leaping from rooftop to rooftop of Brooklyn flats (a feat that killed one young competitor), or like playing high school football without pads or a helmet, an act his coach exploited for publicity and which attracted college and even pro scouts to the games. He was not the school bully but the leader of school bullies. No one dared challenge his position.

Football was not a game for him but another test. In high school, he played with reckless abandon, quarterbacking on offense, linebacking on defense. He enjoyed the crunch of contact, the adulation of the crowd, the responsibility of leadership. Long ago he'd learned that if you think of yourself as a superior person, you become a superior person. He could miss practice sessions to carouse at night with his dropout cronies and yet play and win; he could call Coach Anderson Flat Nose to his face and still play every game. Flat Nose had major college ambitions and could make it, too, at least as an assistant coach, if he took Lancaster with him. But Lancaster didn't need Flat Nose. He was a deal maker on his own. With great pleasure, he skipped his last game as a prep player and began a hitchhiking trek to Pennsylvania, an athletic scholarship in his bag.

He played only two seasons with the Nitney Lions, without particular distinction. The long, sweaty practice sessions and his stupid teammates bored him. He quit college abruptly when the Korean War broke out and joined the Army, another test. He earned a field commission, the Bronze Star for Valor, and the Silver Star. Both Harvard and Yale turned down his application for enrollment after he mustered out. He was not disappointed. He'd expected it. Coldly, the man who had killed in Korea, enjoying it, calculated his future. He needed a stake, he needed connections, he needed a reputation. He set aside two years to achieve them. He enrolled at a small eastern college that was building up its athletic program; in his senior year he set league passing and scoring records and was a second-round draft choice of the Bears. Coach Halas didn't like to play rookies, especially a brash hotdog scrambler, but what he didn't know was that Lancaster was much better than even his extraordinary junior-senior record indicated. In seven of his ten senior games, he'd shaved points for gamblers. He had over $100,000 in a New York bank. His goal was not to quarterback the Bears but to prove to himself that he could. His chance came in the fourth league game, when a Detroit Lion rush ruined the knee of the starting quarterback. Lancaster started the next five games, hitting six touchdown passes, one for eighty-four yards against the New York Giants. Then his injury came. A Viking linebacker broke a blood vessel in Lancaster's thigh.

It was enough. He'd met the test. He had a marketing degree, a tenth of a million, a minor reputation as a professional athlete that, exaggerated skillfully, could prove valuable, and some influential acquaintances from his college days, especially an Ivy League athlete-admirer named Colin Masters. He returned to New York, intent upon conquering Madison Avenue. His youth in the slums of Brooklyn was far behind him. He did not think about it. He was not a man of the past. He was a man of now, and of the future.

BII kept a suite of rooms at the Plaza Hotel in Manhattan, but when Lancaster arrived after his Vegas side trip, he took a suite in the Waldorf Towers. He landed at Kennedy at 10 A.M. and was showering forty-one stories above Park Avenue by 11:15. He changed into a gray pin-striped suit. He hadn't slept all night, or on the flight from Vegas, yet he was alert and ready. The phone rang. It was Colin Masters, whose agency handled Food Division advertising.

"When can we meet?" Masters said. "I've got a whole new program to show you. We worked in more animation this time, especially for pet-food commercials."

"Do you know Joe's Joint on Lexington?" Lancaster said.

Colin Masters was a veteran of the two-hour, four-martini expense-account lunch, and he seldom got to his point before the third martini. Over coffee at Joe's Joint, he could not be dissuaded from preliminary chitchat.

"This greasy spoon deli is CIA cover?" he said.

"Breedlove says they have good pie here," Lancaster said.

"How is Dottie?"

"Dorothy is Dorothy."

Masters droned on, his bloodshot eyes darting. He looked for another Dodgers-Yankees World Series. He dropped names—Rockefeller, "Duke" Wayne, Cronkite, and Reston. Did Lancaster think Carter could stay in office? Did Breedlove have any clout with the administration? Lancaster felt contempt for the talking machine across from him. Clearly Masters had lost his touch. He seemed to age a year every month. Twenty years on Madavenue had left him grossly overweight, puffy-eyed, and nervously twitching. He had no iron in him; he'd been given status, not earned it. Yet he retained that air of superiority and snobbery that came with money. Once he'd been Lancaster's partner in the Lancaster-Masters Group, a Bronxville blue blood and a creative war-football hero linked to set Madavenue on its ear. Masters's contacts with the eastern business establishment had brought in the accounts; Lancaster's acumen and daring innovations had kept the accounts. Masters's current agency —Masters & Ludwick & Burtleson—had handled BII's Food Division for almost a decade. It was considered one of the few solid, long-lasting accounts on Madavenue.

"Colin, you won't be working with me any more," Lancaster said, cutting off Masters in the middle of a sentence.

"Won't be working with you?" Masters twirled the ends of his mustache. He grinned. "Oh. Understand. Since your promotion, you mean. Who's your new marketing exec? I'll want to meet him. I'll fly out to the Coast, first chance."

Lancaster found he was enjoying this. He'd always resented Masters, although they'd been compatible partners. But Masters was too blue blood. Wasp success pattern. Rich family. Presbyterian. Prepped at St. Mark's. Zeta Psi at Yale. Member of the Knickerbocker Club. Lancaster grinned.

"Hank, you really should have brought Dottie," Masters said. "We could have made some of the old rounds."

"I see that you must be still making them."

"By the way, I ran into Cosell at ABC last week. Does he ever drop in to see you on the Coast?"

"No."

"I wish you'd drop in at the agency to look over the new layouts. We have a good chance to get Doris Day for frozen foods. I talked to her—"

"You're off the account, Colin."

"I'm *what?*"

"I'm switching agencies."

The color had drained from Masters's face. "B-b-but you can't. Not now. Listen, I've put my *blood* into this new campaign." Masters was rubbing his stomach. "Hank," he said.

"I've decided it's too big for a single agency," Lancaster said. "We're going to split it up by product line."

"You can't do this to me, Hank."

"Why?"

"There are reasons why."

"Reasons. Do you keep all your business with reasons?"

"Hank, I don't *have* any more business. I've passed up opportunities to concentrate on the Food Division. I've built the agency around that account. Jesus, we have a staff of almost sixty people, for Christ's sake. I just hired a new creative director. We've been working our *asses* off on a new approach. Now you say I'm out. Bang, bang, we're out."

"He wants a change."

"Who wants a change?"

"Breedlove."

"Well, can't I talk to him first?"

"You can try."

"Oh, good God, I don't know," Masters said, his bulky chin falling to his chest. His head snapped up. "We've been doing a *job* for you, Hank. We know the division, we know the company. We've given you good clean advertising, print and TV."

Lancaster sighed. "I know you've been with us a long time. For most of that time, you've done a fair job. But times are tougher now. I need a tougher agency, a tougher man. I need a creativity that will give us sudden new notice. I think you've lost something. I think you've grown too complacent with this account. There are new creative agencies here that are running rings around you. We need a new push, a totally different push."

"But we've been *working* on that."

"So have others."

"You've talked to others?"

"They've approached us."

"That's not ethical."

Lancaster suppressed a laugh. He was in a very good

mood, almost ebullient. "There isn't any more I have to say. Except that this has been a difficult decision for me."

"Will you ask me to beg?"

"Beg? Colin, if you want, sure, come and beg."

"Is there a chance you can leave me with something? One or two product lines?"

"No. It has to be a clean cut. You'll be all right, Colin. Fall back on the basic million."

"The basic million isn't there any more."

"Then add ten percent when you send in your final billing. I'll give you that, for old times."

Masters stood up. He drew in his stomach. "I won't say no hard feelings, Hank, because I've got them, right up to my neck. But I'm not going to make a scene. I think you're making a mistake. But I'm not going to argue with you, or try to change your mind. I know you too well for that."

"You have something up your sleeve," Lancaster said.

"No."

"Go have a drink."

"I will."

"Don't do anything stupid."

"My best to Dottie," Masters said, and hurried away.

Madison Avenue has its quick-flash information underground, so by the time Lancaster got back to the Waldorf, walking briskly along Lexington in the heavy humidity of midday, seven calls from agency principals had piled up for him, including BBDO, J. Walter, and McCann. He did not answer them. Instead, he had a leisurely lunch at the International Club—red snapper and a stein of beer.

The dining room was half filled. Most of the customers were elderly men in suits with gold or silver watch chains looped on their belts. Some had brought their ladies, matronly women in dark dresses adorned with pearl or diamond brooches. The atmosphere was bright, but no one stood out. Everyone seemed to Lancaster to be remarkably similar— men with patterned pasts and dull futures eschewing dessert and after-lunch cigars and women devoid of passion and perhaps even spirit with nothing on their minds but vacation plans and fashion shows. When the pudgy waiter brought the dessert tray, Lancaster selected a chocolate éclair and ate it with sensual slowness. He also took a cigar from the box, although he seldom smoked, and lit it over coffee. He heard his name and looked up with surprise to see George Powell standing by his table.

"Well," Lancaster said, extending his hand. "Welcome to Fun City. We are fortunate, this trip. No garbage strike, no policemen's strike, no firemen's strike. Have you had lunch?"

Powell nodded. He slipped into the booth. "I arrived last night," he said. "I checked for you at the Plaza but they said you weren't expected. So I assumed you would be here at the Waldorf."

"Are you at the Plaza?"

"No. The Americana. The Plaza suite is occupied by our Arab friend."

"I detest the Americana." Lancaster peered critically at Powell. "You don't look very chipper."

"It was a rough trip. We were in a holding pattern over Kennedy for well over an hour. And, speaking of airplanes, there is something I think we should discuss."

"The Taj Mahal? By the way, did you know the real Taj Mahal was built in memory of a woman?"

"In view of the recent—er—incident, I believe we should make it policy that no two BII executives fly together."

"Breedlove wouldn't like that. Breedlove is fond of holding conferences at fifty thousand feet."

"He has grounded the 727."

"Indeed? Well, not for long."

"This matter hasn't unnerved you?"

"No."

"It has unnerved me."

Lancaster leaned forward. He smiled. "George, there are hundreds of nuts free in the land. They've earned nothing, but they'd like to take our blood. What they fail to realize is that their era's past. So don't worry."

"I plan nevertheless to suggest policy for the plane."

"Insurance policy?"

"It is not the time for jokes, Henry."

"No time is joke time for you, my man."

"I am frankly quite surprised at your frivolousness. This company is facing a serious takeover threat."

"Mr. Mendenthal and his proxy fight?"

"So you do know of it." Powell's voice faded to a whisper.

"I'm having dinner with Mendenthal on Thursday. Do you think you can stay over and join us?"

"It's unwise to break bread with enemies."

"He has a side to tell. We may learn something."

"There is only one side. Ours."

"Don't underestimate Philip Mendenthal. Breedlove most certainly does not underestimate him."

"You wish to discuss Breedlove. Not Mendenthal."

"Why do you say that?"

"Do you think Breedlove is ill?"

"I have no reason to believe he is."

"I think he's dying," Lancaster said. "And I also think he knows it."

Powell began to fidget. It was a subject he obviously did not wish to discuss. "I assure you that I plan to do what I can to make this three-person arrangement work."

"You realize, however, that it will not work."

"We must try to make it work."

"What do you think of Scott?"

"Scott is a very good executive."

"And a moral man?"

"Of course."

Lancaster regarded the long, perfect ash on his cigar and then sought Powell's eyes. "There is no need for you and me to speak euphemistically. Breedlove's Troika race will come down to Scott and myself."

Powell blanched. "Why do you say that?"

"I think you know why."

"I most certainly do not."

"You would be wise to declare yourself ineligible now."

"I will not sit here and listen any longer to your Machiavellian ramblings, Henry."

"Very well. Then welcome to the shit corps. When it comes down to the nitty-gritty of it, we are all shits. It is shit versus shit. I will show you before this is over that even Mark Scott can become a shit."

Powell clasped and unclasped his hands. "Obviously you're unwilling to discuss anything serious today."

"Shall we enter into a conspiracy to defame Mr. Scott?"

"Most certainly not. We have the responsibility for this corporation."

"We are the three little pigs. In danger, we will gather ourselves alone in our houses. And two of the houses will go down to the huff and the puff of the big bad wolf."

"Your humor does not amuse me, Henry."

"There is another possibility." Lancaster paused for effect. "Breedlove could bring in an outsider to run it."

"I consider that unlikely."

"And I agree with you. A new man would have too much to learn about this company. Or, shall we say, too much to discover? Unless, of course, Breedlove recruits his man from the Mob."

Powell glanced at his watch, looked at Lancaster, and glanced at the watch again.

"My gods rage for bastards," Lancaster said. "And the gods of Lewis Breedlove also rage for bastards."

"I'm afraid that I will never understand you, Henry. Your language escapes me. I really must go."

"I think I have upset you."

"You have most certainly tried to upset me."

"Give my best to Susan," Lancaster said.

Powell pushed past him and rapidly walked away. Lancaster called the waiter and ordered a brandy.

Back in his tower suite, he found a message from Masters. He answered it out of curiosity.

"Hank, thanks for ringing back," Masters said. "Look. It's a social call. Little party at our place tomorrow night. You're invited."

"Why?"

"Why? Hank, look, I said I had hard feelings, but I don't. It just hit me hard then, that's all. You're right. I have the basic million for a cushion. How about seven? I'm still on Park."

"I'll try to make it."

Lancaster hung up and then phoned *Fortnightly Comment*, asking for David Kahn. "Not here," said a voice that sounded queer.

"You find him," Lancaster said. "This is Henry Lancaster. You have his ass over at the Waldorf by four this afternoon. Do you have that straight?"

A pause. "Right on, my man," the fairy said.

*   *   *

Fortnightly Comment was considered in the *New Yorker* class in wit and sophistication by eastern academic and social circles. It had published the early Cather and the early Hemingway. In some right places, the magazine was rated without a peer in criticism of art, literature, drama, and music. A 1976 study commissioned by David Kahn, its editor–general manager, showed the average income of its subscribers at $46,720. Yet, despite its elite acceptance, the magazine hadn't had a profitable year since 1948. Jules Mayer, the Philadelphia drug king, rescued it time and time again with his "grants," totaling $4 million. After BII acquired Mayer Drugs through an exchange of stock, cash infusions to the magazine stopped. It would have been folded immediately except that Jules Mayer, then a director and a substantial stockholder in BII, wanted to keep it alive, despite its losses; just as Mayer Drugs was his contribution to science, and to himself, *Fortnightly Comment* was his contribution to the arts. He was listed as its publisher on the masthead but he'd never been to the magazine's office. When he'd hired Kahn in 1972, Mayer admitted he'd never read the magazine and pledged he never would. Kahn was ideal for the job. He was a Columbia humanities graduate, an intellectual who didn't antagonize, a liberal who didn't make conservatives look too grotesque, and a practical man who refused to allow his hatred of Germans and Arabs to dominate editorial comment. He was a tireless worker and a social gadabout, all for the magazine. He'd slept with women he disliked, he'd drunk with Jimmy Breslin, he'd been insulted by Norman Mailer. Under Kahn's editorial guidance, *Fortnightly Comment* had become more modern and less sophisticated. It added cartoons and a race-track column. It became more satirical and gossipy. The result was a doubling of its circulation but also of its net loss. Kahn continued to publish, waiting for the inevitable axe.

"How much time do we have?" he asked Lancaster over cocktails at the Waldorf's Bull & Bear.

"You make it easy for me."

"Well, I'm not personally worried. *Harper's* was on the horn yesterday, asking for my services."

"When does your next issue come out?"

"August thirty-first. We have Buckley on Jimmy Carter

and Buchwald on Billy. We're leading with a blockbuster on Arab takeovers."

"Cheers," Lancaster said, raising his glass.

"Cheers."

"The magazine is folded, effective now. There will be no August thirty-first issue."

Kahn took it without blinking. "Whose decision is that?"

"Mine."

"We operate, actually, under the Drug Division."

"And I operate the Drug Division."

"Will there be severance pay for the staff?"

"A month's pay. Across the board."

"I'll make the announcement today, then."

"If you'd like, I'll go over and make it tomorrow. It will take the heat off you. Since this was my decision, perhaps it's my job to deliver the bad news."

"I see that you enjoy your job."

"I do not enjoy this aspect of it. No."

"I hear you're going to Masters's affair tomorrow."

"New York is a small town."

"All towns are. I think he's going to put on an act for you. I want you to know I had nothing to do with it."

"What act?"

Kahn waved his hand. "I'll handle the announcement at the magazine," he said. "I'll refer the press calls to you."

"You're taking this with remarkable calm."

"I had expected it, of course. Our system, despite words to the contrary, does not underwrite culture."

"A corporation simply cannot sustain unnecessary losses indefinitely and with no hope of improvement. We're responsible to the families of our employees, and to our stockholders."

"I have a response to that."

"And that is?"

"Bullshit," Kahn said.

Lancaster shrugged. He laughed.

In 1972 Colin Masters had invested $175,000 in a four-bedroom, three-bath Park Avenue cooperative apartment on the thirty-eighth floor, and had paid an interior decorator another $85,000 to make it livable. Joan, who aspired to a smaller apartment on Fifth Avenue, merely put up with it. She disliked its purple room with a fireplace, its den with elephant tusks, and Colin's velvet-carpeted bedroom, where she submitted to a painful ritual of sex on a weekly basis. The apartment seemed so much his and so little hers. Her room, of course, had a dainty feminine flair, but all the others were solidly masculine. She often felt like a visitor. A French cook ruled the kitchen; Colin's advertising associates were always dropping in unexpectedly for drinks or dinner. Joan felt confined, trapped, a woman without identity. After the children had left, she'd had her affair, which led only to increased drinking and psychotherapy bills; now she contented herself with discussions of the heart or cancer fund over long martini lunches with peers or almost peers, with theatergoing, with her former hobby and now near business of making bead necklaces, and with her dream, her hope that a change to Fifth Avenue would solve her problems.

"So glad you could come," she said as the stern and undoubtedly rented butler admitted Lancaster. She pecked his cheek. "Colin said you were only a possibility, so I was going to call you and scold you into a positive. But you didn't bring Dorothy." She was pouting.

"No," he said. "Home afflicted with the curse."

Advertising types he recognized filled the living room. The men smelled of after-shave lotion and musky cologne. The women smelled of scented soaps and perfumes. They wore ankle-length dresses. Glass earrings and necklaces of cultured pearls ornamented them. Their lips were savage red, twisted in mechanical smiles; they lifted their chins and held out their hands like mannequins in Macy's window.

A BBDO vice-president expelled whiskey breath into Lancaster's face and said, "Henry, you have found the fountain of youth."

"Right now, I'm trying to find a drink."

"I hear you have some business loose."

"Shhh. No business discussions."

"Phone you on the Coast," the BBDO man said.

Masters escaped from a cluster of men in dark suits and sincere ties and put his hand on Lancaster's shoulder. "Glad you made it," he said. He drank from a gold-fringed glass. "Haven't told my staff the bad news yet. Suppose I'll make it

official to them tomorrow. So, behold the wake." He winked.
His eyes flashed a red twinkle. "Only they do not know it is a
wake."

"Oh, come now."

"Well, perhaps they do know. You see, your presence here
gives them hope. Both my people and my competitors. My
people are thinking you're reconsidering. My competitors are
prepared to convince you not to reconsider. You are, both
ways, the man of the hour."

"I'm afraid I can't stay long."

"Videri quam esse," Masters said, winking again.

"Which means?"

"It is the opposite of *Esse quam videri,* which means, 'To
be rather than to seem.' Or, at least, I think it is the
opposite." Masters raised his glass. "Oh, thank you, heaven,
for the basic million." He issued a confident chuckle. "My
future is all laid out. I told you that I have recovered from
your telling blow. I'm going to a big agency. They have
one-fifty VPs. They have sixteen exec VPs. They have an
honorary chairman, a founder-chairman, a vice-chairman, a
chairman, a president. I shall be VP–office boys. In charge
of piggy-backing thirty-second spots on *Batman* reruns."

"You need a drink."

"Good advice. Good advice."

"Dinner, dinner everybody," Joan said, her bell slippers
tinkling, her bead necklace rustling. "You're by me, Henry,
you handsome creature. Bring your drink."

The main dish was a bad soufflé, undoubtedly catered, with
bits of inadequately cooked bacon which Lancaster picked
out with his fork and systematically arranged in a pattern on
his napkin, causing the rental butler to sneer. Joan chattered
nonsense, all local. She oozed liquid sweetness into Lancaster's ear. Was it possible that this brainless wren of a woman,
finished at St. Timothy's and Finch Junior College, didn't
understand what everyone else in the room understood perfectly? Or perhaps she understood but would not admit it. Or
had a faint lingering hope. Or didn't care. The basic million?
No. It was fantasy. The stock market must have hit the
Masterses hard. Lancaster knew Masters had been clobbered
in glamour stocks such as Litton, Xerox, and Polaroid. And
Masters had dropped at least $100,000 on a real estate–oil
venture now the subject of an SEC investigation. Also, he

owned two expensive, non-winning racehorses. Lancaster sat
picking at the hopeless soufflé and sipping his wine. The
conversation droned on around him. They hated Neilsen, they
loved Neilsen. They mentioned Monty Hall and the new
daytime quiz shows. They talked about Johnny. They said the
FTC was out of its mind. Lancaster leaned back, utterly
bored. There was not one woman in the room he'd take to
bed, except the big-breasted career girl–sociologist who said it
was ironic that the lower Manhattan homes of the old
Knickerbocker aristocracy had become the narrow alleys of
the tenement slums. Joan was imperturbable, unstoppable.
She suggested after-dinner drinks at Sardi's and ran to the
intercom to alert the bellman of the need for taxis.

"No, not for me," Lancaster said. "I have a day of work
tomorrow."

"But it's *early*," Joan gushed.

"Join me for a brandy here," Masters said. "Then I'll let
you go." He looked serious. "All right, Hank?"

"Oh, we want him with *us*," Joan said, stomping her
heel.

"But the fact is I am no longer with you," Lancaster
said.

"You two, you just want to get rid of us so you can discuss
your business."

"That's just it, I'm afraid," Lancaster said.

The admen fumbled. Was Masters still in the picture? But
they were committed to the nightcap at Sardi's, so they left in
a stream, Joan at the head. The sociologist looked as if she'd
like to linger.

"My best to the neo-Knickerbockers," Lancaster said to
her at the door. "Tell me. Do you like to fuck?"

She blinked. "Goodbye, Mr. Lancaster."

"I'm at the Waldorf. You come see me. Tomorrow night?"

"I have a date tomorrow night."

"Break it. Come show me those boobs are for real."

"You're remarkably candid. And ostentatiously Neander-
thal."

"And you are ostentatiously career, selfish, and opportunis-
tic. Which is why you'll come. Waldorf Towers. About seven
tomorrow?"

He closed the door behind her. Masters brought brandies.
He'd excused the butler. His jaw trembled as he spoke.

"I apologize for Joan. Lately she hasn't been herself. She seems always to be . . . well, running ahead of herself."

"I really don't want the brandy."

"Well, I need one. Two."

"You have a reason for detaining me."

"Yes." Masters was sweating. He gulped his brandy and pounced on the one he'd poured for Lancaster. "Yes, I want to show you something, Hank."

"Why are you frightened?"

"I'm not frightened."

"You're trembling."

"Well, it was quite a shock, yesterday."

"You shouldn't have put all your eggs in one basket."

"Well, I'm ruined now. But you know that."

They walked slowly down the carpeted hall to a rear bedroom. It was dark except for trickles of illumination from Manhattan's lights below. It contained a motion-picture projector and a rolled-up screen. Still nipping brandy, Masters moved across the carpet, glanced at Lancaster, and pulled down the screen. Then he flicked on the projector.

The movie's title came on. *She Didn't Cry Rape.*

It was in black and white. The camera panned across a giant bed. The door opened. A blond girl entered, wearing a sweater and a miniskirt. Her face was shrouded in shadows so that the viewer saw only close-ups of her breasts, her hips, her thighs. She sat down on the bed and began to remove her clothing. Slowly. One article at a time. The camera panned to the floor, where the clothing piled up. Then it moved across the room to the closet. The closet door sprang open and a huge black man leapt out, a pistol in his hand. He was wearing tight dark pants. The camera flashed back to the now naked girl on the bed. Her head snapped up, in full view.

It was Dorothy Lancaster.

Lancaster didn't move. Masters stood before him, breathing heavily, not looking at him. The black man shed his clothing, heaping it on top of the girl's. Then, naked, still holding the pistol, he advanced toward the bed. A close-up showed him on top of her, moving inside her. Lancaster snapped the projector's hold button. The still played on the screen.

He felt calm. He was in full control.

"Where did you get it?" he said. He reached out for

Masters. He gripped his shoulders, shoving him into the light of the projector. The sex scene now played grotesquely on Masters's face and arms. "I asked you a question," Lancaster said. "Where?"

Masters cringed back. "From Wright, from Wright."

"Has he any more?"

"No. No more. I swear. No more."

Now Lancaster had him by the throat. He squeezed, gently at first, then tighter. With his free hand, he jerked the film from the projector. He twirled it around Masters's head and neck. He tightened it like a noose.

"Open your mouth," he said. "Eat it, eat it, you son of a bitch, you stinking bastard. You're out. Nothing is going to get you back. I kept you alive. What you have I've given you. You haven't got the guts or the brains to get yourself. You're jelly, soft as jelly. I'm going to squeeze some of it out of you, squeeze until it comes out your fucking ears."

"Oh, Jesus. Christ, Hank."

"Destroy this print. Destroy the rest."

"Y-yes," Masters gasped. His eyes bulged. His throat was slippery, "I—I—"

Lancaster heard footsteps in the hallway. "Forgot my wrap, forgot my wrap," tinkled Joan's voice.

She opened the door.

"Oh dear," she said, peering in.

15

A JOKE AMONG LOWER-ECHELON BII EXECUTIVES HELD THAT when the company staged its annual barbecue for European managers in Zurich—an event personally hosted by Lewis Breedlove—top management from Los Angeles attended not to enjoy the festivities but to visit their money. This was in reality a gross exaggeration, but not for George Powell. He had exactly $942,421.07 on deposit in a numbered account in a Swiss bank. It did not draw interest; Powell, in fact, paid a fee to keep the money there. He felt that it was perfectly safe. A Swiss account could not be tampered with by anyone unless it could be proved that the money had been obtained by theft or fraud. Powell's fund had been built up over a twenty-year period. Part of it, perhaps a third, had been honestly earned—corn futures profits, bonuses he shielded from Susan's knowledge, a net gain of some $50,000 from the sale of a business he'd once operated on the side. The remainder had been acquired by outright embezzlement and betrayal of trust. When he'd told Carol about it, he had not been completely honest. Perhaps he would tell her later, when he had more time to explain. Or perhaps he would never tell her.

The bulk of the fund had been accumulated within the past seven years. He'd personally delivered much of it to the bank's manager in cash, principally U.S. dollars. Why had he done it? He couldn't fully explain it to himself. There were many reasons, there was no reason. He used to tell himself that someday he'd restore the money to the company. Now, after his talk with Carol, he'd abandoned any plans to restore it. They were both now different people than they had been alone. She'd brought out a man who had been hidden within him, one with an interest in art and music and poetry and not dominated by business ambitions. He'd brought out a woman no longer obsessed with the call of success and one who could love and share. It was one reason for the fund. Another was that, besides the Swiss fund, he really didn't have too much money, owing primarily to severe stock-market reversals. And he was insecure. An impersonal corporate structure could quickly turn its back on a man. Suddenly all your accomplishments could be forgotten and only your mistakes remembered. Powell had seen it happen to many others, at BII and elsewhere. Your responsibilities are reduced. You have difficulty reaching your boss. You're out. Weak recommendations. Then pounding the pavements in increasing desperation. The Swiss fund gave him security. It also gave him a sense of power. He could gloat over it secretly—something that in fact he often did. He felt it was justified. He'd worked many years at BII before recognition, moving up slowly despite Susan's constant prodding, and, even after achieving a long overdue vice-presidency, he'd suffered indignities and seemingly deliberate public embarrassments from an irascible Lewis Breedlove.

It was his fund. He'd earned it.

It had started mildly. For years he'd been in charge of corporation insurance outlays. It hadn't been difficult to devise a way to underinsure certain of the company's assets, particularly overseas, and draw down the differences to himself. Breedlove had overinsured ever since he'd been caught short on co-insurance after a 1950 fire had destroyed a plant in Akron. Powell kept the books personally in those days, subordinating very little responsibility. It had been a slow, careful embezzlement that years ago had been hidden in computer tapes no one would ever dig out.

The "insurance" portion of his fund was a very small part of its total. The bulk of the fund had been amassed in an entirely different way.

BII had begun its serious international thrust right after World War II, building up rapidly through merger and *de novo* expansion in the 1950s and 1960s. Powell had become treasurer in 1955 and chief financial officer in 1961. But he'd traveled overseas on business very little until 1968, when the international capital market entered a new phase with the imposition of U.S. balance-of-payments controls. Suddenly multinational companies had to look to foreign financial markets for funds. BII floated two Euro-Bond issues in 1968 and several more in 1969 and 1970. Powell found himself crossing to Switzerland and Germany several times a year. International finance had been one of his weaknesses, in fact, before BII's overseas explosion; now he considered himself an expert in it, a judgment backed by officers of many international banks and currency traders. He had saved BII perhaps $5 million in the past decade through intelligent analysis of the foreign money market.

His overseas acquaintance opened a golden door for him. It was stunningly simple. He'd built up trust. He violated that trust. At first, to his disgust, he became what Breedlove sometimes called BII's bagman. He carried cash, sometimes in suitcases and sacks, to representatives of foreign nations where BII operated, to businessmen and politicians and dictators in Africa, South America, and Asia. Occasionally it was in foreign-exchange instruments such as cable transfers or bills of exchange; more often, however, it was in U.S. dollars. It appeared on BII books as a charge against headquarters operations. Powell had become an expert at the various techniques; some of them even amused him. He'd dropped wallets on the floor following a meeting. He'd left paper sacks filled with money in a person's office. He'd slowly counted out hundred-dollar bills into the outstretched hands of foreign political leaders. He'd written personal checks, for reimbursement later by the company; he'd ordered certified corporate checks. Once he'd delivered gold. The leaders he paid assumed he was personally pocketing some of the money; they even joked about that. And soon he found himself doing it—a little at first, then more. Once, when an Argentine military dictator refused $100,000 offered by Powell, he'd banked the entire sum for himself and had told Breedlove that the dictator had taken it. Indeed, he'd asked for more. It had been a daring act on Powell's part, an irrational act. But he hadn't been questioned. He'd never been questioned. Sometimes he thought Breedlove suspected him; but, to his own amazement, he thought very little about that, or worried over it. Results in nations where he'd dropped cash were generally good. Labor problems lessened; in some cases, labor costs dropped. Difficulties in shipping and production disappeared. It was money well spent.

Powell's Swiss fund had risen very little in the past year or two. He had not delivered an overseas package since May of 1973, although he maintained a fund in case a sudden new delivery became necessary. Breedlove's pipelines to both houses of Congress and to federal agencies warned him of the possibility that foreign largess by multinational corporations would soon be a subject of investigation. So BII had cut its giving to a minimum. Packages went out only where it was absolutely necessary.

At first Powell had had qualms about the delivery of cash overseas. It seemed too blatant, too risky. He still suffered occasional nagging feelings that it was not right, but the qualms had lessened. They had been replaced by a sophisticated, worldly rationalization. It was a time-honored way of doing business in some foreign nations. It was necessary. Other companies did it. It produced results. Political contributions in the United States often did not produce results; the politicians promised, but few delivered. Overseas you got results. Business relations between nations were as necessary as political relations; there was, indeed, a strong tie-in between the two. It was not one world, despite proclamations by some political idealists to the contrary.

The BII board was responsible for approving outlays in excess of $50,000, but foreign payments needed only Breedlove's sanction. Breedlove discussed them only with Powell, and Powell discussed them only with foreign managers. They were called "sales agent" payments and, as such, were tax deductible.

Powell sincerely felt he deserved his fund, that he had earned it. When he faced the truth, he knew he was a bagman, a violator of trust, but he no longer faced the truth of himself. He still attended mass every Sunday, but he did not go to confession. He was proud of the fund. Secretly he feared a massive collapse in the world economy, with an absolutely debased U.S. dollar becoming valueless, replaced by what he termed Eurocurrency, a mix of Swiss francs, gold, and the German mark. The dollar already was losing its power as a reserve currency. Gold continued to soar. The White House's inflation program was naïve and asinine. It wouldn't take much to push the world into panic. Powell was secure, insulated against it. Much of the fund was in francs; a quarter was in gold bullion. He was safe. He was neither dull nor unimaginative. He was, in fact, a very clever man.

In the bright light of day, hailing a taxi outside the hotel, he found himself having second thoughts about his declarations to Carol the evening before. Perhaps the drinks and the wine had gone to his head. He considered himself a decision maker, not a man who vacillated from one alternative to the next. But now he simply did not know. Was he ready to give it all up? If he did, would he not regret it later? He did not think of himself as a ruthlessly competitive executive—like, for example, a Breedlove or a Henry Lancaster—but he had proved to himself in the past that he could compete. He could not have risen to his current position if he'd been unable to compete. Last night he'd spoken rapidly, without rehearsal, contrary to his nature. He was a careful man who always rehearsed. He rewrote memos several times, he drafted letters before putting them into final form, he never deviated from his prepared text when he spoke before a group. Yet last night he'd merely blurted it out.

"Where to?" the driver asked.

"Downtown."

"Where to downtown?"

"Wall Street."

"An' what?"

"Broadway. Wall Street and Broadway."

The taxi swung into the Seventh Avenue traffic. The driver crouched behind his protective shield. It reminded Powell of last night's attacker and of their mysterious rescuer, the man in the tweed jacket. He could not recall the color of the jacket. Had it been green? Carol had claimed it had been brown, but the light had been bad so she could not be sure. They could not describe the man to each other, except that he was youngish and tall. One thing was certain. He hadn't been merely a concerned onlooker. Powell was now certain he'd seen the man before the attempted robbery on this trip to New York. It remained an absolute mystery to him. He had deliberately avoided discussion of the matter with Carol at breakfast, but he'd found himself looking over his shoulder to see if he could catch sight of the man again. Now she was fighting the Fifth Avenue crowds on a shopping tour. He decided he would not bring up the subject again. He would try to forget it. Yet it still unnerved him; he found his hands unsteady and his knees weak. He'd slept badly last night, rising at 2 A.M. to smoke a full pipe while Carol lay on the adjoining bed, perhaps pretending to be asleep.

"Wall Street," said the driver. "Stock Exchange, Trinity Church, Oscar's, da Battery."

It had begun to rain, this time a certain downpour that caused instant rivers in the gutters and the quick snap of umbrellas over pedestrians' heads. Powell instructed the driver to take him down Wall to the exchange. He gave him a five, an overtip the driver did not acknowledge, and hurried through the door to the reception area off the trading floor. His target was a man named William Evert, a veteran New York Stock Exchange floor trader with whom Powell had done business in the past. His mission was to liquidate 200,000 or more shares of BII stock at the best price possible consistent with speed. He could arrange a secondary offering through an investment banking firm, but that would require the filing of a prospectus with the Securities & Exchange Commission and would take months. Perhaps he could sell the shares in hundred-unit round lots through a brokerage firm, but that could severely depress the price and would also take some time. A well-financed NYSE floor trader—exchange members who literally roamed around the floor buying and selling for their own accounts—would be the answer. BII stock had been active and higher in recent sessions, despite a generally declining market; it had closed yesterday at 23½, up ¾, so a 200,000-share transaction would involve some $4.6 million. It seemed too big for a single trader.

"No," Evert said five minutes after Powell had summoned him off the floor, "it's not too big for us. We can handle it. The way business has been around here, I'd welcome it. But I'm goddamn curious about it, I'll tell you that."

"Why?"

"I don't understand why Breedlove wants to unload."

"Because, I would think, he judges that this is a good time to sell."

"Do you agree?"

"Not really. I myself am not selling."

"The profit picture at BII is bright?"

"Yes. Very much so."

"Street says you'll earn two-fifty a share. Over. Is that in the ball park?"

Powell nodded.

"That means you're just over nine times earnings," Evert said. "Even in this market, I'd place your stock in the buy range, not sell."

They were meeting in what seemed to Powell a very strange place to conduct business, whether a one-dollar transaction or $4.6 million. Evert had directed him to the second-floor men's room in the exchange building, a vast high-ceilinged square with giant white marble urinals, spotless mirrors, and rows of polished silver taps over washbasins that jutted abruptly from walls perhaps thirty feet high. He said he couldn't conduct business with an outsider on the floor and added that the head was one place that was sure not to be bugged. Powell stuttered, flabbergasted, but followed him. Before Evert began to talk, he inspected the interiors of the toilet cubicles.

A little man in a gray suit came in, nodded at Evert, stood over a urinal for a few minutes, and then carefully washed his hands with soap and water before leaving.

Evert grinned. "That poor son of a bitch," he said. "He

hasn't said a word in two months. All he did was commit his firm to three hundred thousand IBM, short. Now Sec's closed him up. Liquidity rule."

Powell winced. He himself had shorted seven hundred shares of IBM right after the initial announcement of the antitrust suit. IBM hadn't reacted according to anticipated pattern. It had been rising. In the *Wall Street Journal*'s Abreast of the Market column recently, one broker had been quoted as calling the whole list "IBM's market." Powell had lost over $100,000 before he'd covered his short position.

"I'd think you Breedlovers would be buying in your stock, not disposing of it," Evert said, striding toward one of the urinals. "Especially now."

"Why especially now?"

"You have another proxy fight coming up, haven't you?"

"What makes you say that?"

Evert shrugged. "It's rumor, all over the Street."

Powell shrugged back at him.

Evert was a giant walrus of a man who was known as a hip shooter on Wall Street, and even as a slight eccentric. He made million-dollar decisions rapidly, and, some said, indiscriminately. When so accused, he merely shrugged and pointed out that bad decisions don't buy Rolls-Royces, and he had five of them on a farm in Connecticut.

"All right, George," he said, zipping up his fly. "I'll take your stock. Get Lewis to file a Sec report."

"Wait. You say you'll take it. At what price?"

"A point and a half under today's market."

"Well, I don't know."

"You go any way—secondary, third market, normal channels—you'll find it will cost you more than a point and a half. You know that."

"I'd like to tell Breedlove first."

"Ask him or tell him?"

"Well, ask."

"He has told you to dispose of the stock, has he not?"

"He wants to sell, yes."

"You're looking at the buyer. But I want your decision now. I don't like matters hanging over my head."

"You'll take it off the tape?"

"No. On the tape."

Evert stood above him, his hands on his hips. He hadn't

removed his floor badge. He seemed anxious to return to the floor. It was obvious to Powell why Evert wanted the transaction to appear on the exchange's tape. When a block of 200,000 shares of a stock that had been trading actively and higher on news of improving earnings hit the tape, traders would flood in with buy orders, attracted by the new action, and Evert would sell. In minutes he'd gain enough profit to buy another Rolls-Royce, or perhaps two or three.

"All right," Powell said. "I accept your offer."

"Done," Evert said. He hurried away.

Taxis were unavailable, so Powell suffered the indignity of a crowded subway ride back to the Americana. He'd intended to stay downtown to talk with some security analysts and to drop in at the Fed and Morgan, but he was feeling weary and could use a nap before Carol returned. As the BMT roared through the tunnel, he found himself looking for a man in a tweed jacket.

16

ANNE DID HURRY TO OLEN, BUT A GIANT NAMED CLARK Buzzey, the Milwaukee amusement king, beat her by a half hour. He came with four freight cars full of his wares, items marvelous to children—an elephant and a camel, a cage full of sweaty monkeys, a full-sized ape that grinned and spat at its teasers, a zebra that appeared terrified, parrots that could talk, two midget horses, and a droopy black bear sprawled out in its cage like an anesthetized patient. Buzzey was six-seven and had a booming voice. He wore a red jacket, a straw hat, and sported a cane. Children hung around the train in masses. In Olen you could see a mule or a horse or a bull any day of the week, but you didn't often see a grinning ape that spat. Out of the train next came the rides—the merry-go-round, the Ferris wheel, the tot roller coaster, the concession stands.

Scott, standing by the bus depot and watching the train, found himself drawn into the spirit of the event. A band had been deployed as an escort for the animal parade up Main Street, Olen's thoroughfare. The children skipped after it, zigzagging and hopping. The monkeys scrambled, the ape spat, the bear slept. The band blared inharmoniously, led by a loud drum lugged by Olen's barber, creating reverberant booms that startled the zebra and enraged the camel. A hairy pawlike hand clamped on Scott's shoulder.

"Mark, meet my missis," said Cotton Meeks.

She was dressed in a yellow skirt and a white blouse and she wore gloves and a hat. She towered over Meeks. She smiled and shook Scott's hand. "If he's been terrorizing you, don't pay him no mind," she said, and Scott decided he liked her.

Meeks had mustered a delegation for Anne's arrival, including *Record* editor Ted Dylan, a politician from Madison named Skibbs, an undertaker from Indian Falls named Ramsey Caton, a grocer called Red, and a Baptist known as Preacher Jim. Except for the undertaker, who wore a red jacket that matched the hue of his nose, the men wore suits and ties. Scott, in a green sports shirt, felt underdressed for the first time since he'd arrived in Olen.

The delegation, perspiring freely in the blaze of noon sun, was nervously quiet. The bus, as usual, was late. Skibbs mumbled something about an appeal he'd make to the governor concerning the unreliable service. Red paced. The undertaker examined his shoes. The editor put a flashbulb into his old-fashioned Speed Graphic camera. Preacher Jim searched for the bus in the sky. That seemed to work. A vehicle came into view over a distant hill. Scott had not felt so totally foolish since he'd been afflicted with hiccups during his high school valedictorian address.

"That was quite a greeting," Anne said as she unpacked in the hotel room. "I see you've acquired some subjects."

"Yes. But I'm going to abdicate."

"I guess we shouldn't make fun of them. They're just being sincerely respectful."

He drew her to him. "Thank you for coming here."

"Do you want to see the chigger marks?"

"I want to mess around."

"It's a little early in the day."

"No. The sun is over the yardarm. Do you think that Mrs.

Meeks will keep the kids at the amusement park for a while?"

"I think she will. Deliberately. So we can have some time alone."

"Then I'll nominate her for court social director."

"I think this has gone to your head."

"Let's not talk," he said. "Not for a while."

They were undressing slowly on the bed when a loud rap sounded on the door. Anne ran bare-breasted to the bathroom. Scott zipped up his pants. The door opened and the old bellman limped in, bearing champagne in an ice bucket.

"Compliments of Mr. Meeks," he said, brushing sweat from his forehead into the ice.

The harvest festival exploded the next day, under Buzzey's control. He was ubiquitous, tireless, and vividly conspicuous in his red jacket. He handled the camel ride, helped kids down the water slide, and gave direction to the Olen band, improving its tone.

"Pop, I think it beats Disney," Liz said. "There's a sky here even he can't build."

"Pop? Where did you come up with that designation?"

"Maryanne, she calls hers that. Pop."

"Who's Maryanne?"

"My new friend. She says the ape spits, but darned if I can make him spit. Can we get a camel at home someday?"

"The ape'll spit for me," Tod said.

They raced away, surrounded by whooping kids democratically unaware that their newfound playmates were offspring of on-high royalty.

Scott drove the Corvair to the plant after lunch, leaving Anne with Mrs. Meeks and other Olen ladies who were making final preparations for a massive outdoor supper scheduled to start promptly at 6 P.M. The plant was alive with activity and ripe with brine smell. He found Norma alone in the office, clanking an old L. C. Smith typewriter.

"Oh, hi, Mr. Scott. Coming to the supper tonight?"

"I wouldn't miss it. Where is Toms?"

"Oh, you know, this time of year he would be anywhere out there in the plant. How does it feel to be a genuine hero?"

"I'm a genuine hero?"

"The temporary workers have drawn up a resolution, commending you to high heaven. It's posted on the line. I think they've found a new saint."

As he passed through the line, the workers seemed to gaze respectfully at him. He nodded at some and smiled. J. B. Toms lay flat on his back under a husking machine, a wrench in his hand, swearing expertly. Finally he emerged. He looked at Scott, startled, and rubbed his cheek with his thumb, working in grease.

"Fourth breakdown t'day," he said.

"How long will it take?"

"Fixed, for now. Balin' wire. This whole plant's held up with balin' wire."

The line began to move. Toms got up and began to explain.

"It's jus' a big kitchen, what you got here, you see. Corn comes outta the huskin' machines, then we wash it in cold water, there, an' them inspectors pick out the overripes and underripes, then the chain feeds it to cullin' machines, there. Then, over here, the brine an' syrup mix, made with water an' salt or sugar, down next over there to the cooker-filler, steam-heated an' old as sin, then, in the can, sixty minutes, it's cooked at two-forty to two-fifty degrees."

"How long have you been doing it like this?"

"Ages," Toms said, and maneuvered the big executive from the cities toward the can-manufacturing section so he could display more of his knowledge.

"We roll the steel ourselves here, you see, thirty-two layers together. Them girls is the separators. Then the sheets is annealed to make 'em bendable, then we pickle 'em in acid and shoot 'em to trimmin'. We'll coat the molten tin with palm oil—that's palm oil—and draw the steel through it. Oil acts as a flux, makes the tin an' steel stick. That's the slitter at work. We can cut tops an' bottoms thirty thousand a hour."

"It's all very educational. But may we go into the office?"

"Suppose you brought them books back."

"No."

"Wall, I ain't had lunch."

"This will take only a minute or two."

"Doc says skip lunch, get a ulcer."

In the office Scott asked Norma to get them Cokes, and to

take her time doing it. Toms sat down in his squeaky roller chair. Scott stood up and faced him.

"I'm going to keep the books for a while," he said. "I'm going to take them back to Los Angeles."

"To L.A.? Jesus, Mr. Scott, I need them books here for reference."

"You'll have them back in a week. I want them to support whatever recommendation I make concerning this plant."

Toms swabbed at his brow with an enormous red handkerchief. "Oh," he said. He looked subdued and worried.

"I want your personnel lists, too, for the past three years," Scott said. "I realize you're busy now, so I'll ask you to send them to me. They're on computer at division, so make sure you send the right ones. I don't have anything else to say to you now, but you will hear from me."

Outside he passed Norma, who lingered by the Coke machine with a young man who had a pencil stuck behind his ear.

"See you tonight, Norma," he said.

The young man looked terribly impressed, realizing that Norma knew the big wheel from the cities. No doubt, she would have a date for the supper tonight.

The sheriff's car was parked by the Corvair. The sheriff leaned against its fender, chewing a toothpick.

"Is this an official or social call?" Scott said.

"Neither one. Jus' snoopin' around, jus' in case."

"I think our trouble is over here."

"Hope so, Mr. Scott. By the way, we picked up the feller shot the woman. Says he disremembered to unload his rifle. I guess he'll be held over for manslaughter at the inquest. J. B., he'll be lucky he ain't held accessory. Something else. I scattered that Colonel's bunch. Colonel Stetson's?"

"Sheriff, I think I have a new view of you."

"It's Johnny."

"Johnny," Scott said, shaking his hand.

He believed, indeed, that the tension and violence was over as he drove the sputtering Corvair across the bridge toward the labor camp. The sky was bright blue, filled with giant white clouds. Again Scott felt the serenity of the area. He also felt a full measure of nostalgia. He wanted to visit his old schoolhouse. He wanted to walk in the meadow to see if the old swimming hole existed. But he must not allow sentiment to impair his mission. He had new roads to travel. The Olen of his youth was a forever lost landscape of golden suns, frozen snowfields, and spring-swollen lakes that was best forgotten by the mature and rising Scott.

Except for a few women and small children, the camp was almost empty. A child of about two peered at Scott through the open window of a shack. There were tents all around and black remains of fires. Rodriguez was packing a duffel bag.

"You're leaving?" Scott said.

Rodriguez turned. "There is no need for me here any longer, Mr. Scott. At least for this year, my work is done."

"You'll return this spring?"

"If the plant is still here."

"It will be here."

Rodriguez gazed steadily into Scott's eyes. "I am glad to be able to see you before you go. I thank you for what you have done. You are a man who has much understanding and compassion, perhaps too much compassion to succeed fully in what you do. But I hope it will be your face I see when we discuss the worker next, and not the face of another from your company." He paused. He sighed. "It has been a victory here, but a hollow one, an expensive one. Perhaps, for some, death is necessary to accomplish what is only fair. It is a sad thing to contemplate."

"Adiós por ahora," Scott said.

"Vaya usted con Dios," Rodriguez said.

He and Anne held the bench of honor at the outdoor supper. The bench groaned under bowls of fried chicken, barbecued beef and pork ribs, potato salad, green salads, and warm homemade bread. There was lemonade, coffee, Cokes, nuts, candy, oranges, crab apples, and fat plums. The pies were apple, rhubarb, and pumpkin. Children turned ice-cream-maker handles. Mrs. Meeks, whacking out at encroaching flies with a giant swatter, sat between Anne and Scott. Toms was at the far end of the table, aiding his crippled wife. "Hear, hear," said Cotton Meeks when the politician, Skibbs, launched into a speech defending the deposed president. Undertaker Caton, gray and taciturn, amused his potential customers with card tricks. Red, the grocer, frowned morbidly and mumbled about inflation. Ted

Dylan captured the event for the Olen *Record* through the lens of his Speed Graphic camera.

"I was wondering," Scott said when Dylan returned to the bench. "I saw nothing in the paper about the trouble at the plant."

Dylan glanced at Meeks and Toms. "Well, we're a weekly," he said. "That edition's not out yet."

"Was there any reaction elsewhere?"

"Hardly any. Well, AP called from Milwaukee. But they didn't do much with it. After I had a talk with them."

Cotton Meeks sprang up. "We got a real preacher here, our Preacher Jim, that could give thanks, but we got to listen to him preach every Sunday. Mark, here, he's a part-time preacher, according to what I hear. So I suggest he give thanks for us before we tackle this food."

"Appreciate it," Preacher Jim said.

"Well, I don't know," Scott said. "I'm out of practice."

But they all had already bowed their heads, and he was trapped. He bowed his head and said a few words of thanks —for the good harvest, for children, for families, for peace.

"Amen," Preacher Jim said, and launched into rapid and prodigious eating.

"Mark, you got a way with words," Cotton Meeks said, gnawing at a chicken leg. "I suspect you could deliver a sermon that'd make even an old sinner like me fess up."

"The good Lord Himself couldn't do that," his wife commented.

Scott's duties weren't over yet. Meeks and Skibbs inveigled him into making a speech after they had all had their fill. They sent children scurrying to notify other benches, and before Scott could effectively protest he found he had the attention of half the town. He stood up. Anne smiled at him. It was now deep twilight and dragonflies filled the air. The sky to the west was a deep red. The air was warm and clean, filled with the scents of his childhood—geraniums, dandelions, chimney smoke, and newly mown grass and leaves heaped for lawn burning. He knew what his audience wanted to hear. They wanted to know about the future of the plant.

"I want to thank you for your hospitality and particularly thank the women of Olen for this overwhelming meal," he said. "I haven't had a feed like that since childhood, when I used to horn in occasionally on the meals for the threshing crews at the farms around here. I was at least partly raised here, as many of you know, and I still think of this area as home. It is a good place to have as home. To the workers and foremen at the plant, I would like to extend my appreciation for a job well done." He paused. His hands fumbled at his sides. The people stood hushed. He said, "When I was going to school, I used to come up to the plant and work on the canning line in the summer. I must say the line hasn't improved or gotten any newer since those days. What the company will do about this plant has not yet been decided. As you all may know, our annual meeting will be held here in the spring, and perhaps by then the decision will have been made." Again he paused. His audience looked at him. He saw Norma in the group, holding hands with a young man. "I think I can say this with fair certainty, however," he said. "If it is within my power, and I believe that it is, the plant will remain open and perhaps even be expanded."

"Hear, *hear!*" chanted Cotton Meeks, leaping up.

The people were applauding. Some were cheering.

"Have you lied to your subjects?" Anne said in bed.

"My subjects?"

"Yes. I think I'm married to the king of Olen."

"If I'm to believe my press clippings, I'm king of much more than Olen. And if I'm to believe Breedlove, I'll soon be the king of kings."

"All you have to do is step on his little plant here."

"Maybe I did get carried away before those people. This place is so peaceful most of the time it addles your senses. I've been sniffing too much nostalgia around here. I rather suspect Breedlove didn't send me on this mission to recapture my boyhood days."

"What do you think of him? Breedlove. Really, now."

"Oh, he's a riddle, I guess, a puzzle. Maybe he stays an enigma to keep us alert. You never know what he'll throw at you next, so you're ready for almost anything. I suppose he's a genius of sorts. He started this, clawed it out. What we have, we owe to him. Totally."

She touched his forehead. "I feel ridges. Ah, yes. BII. Burned right in."

"All right. Tell you what. I'll quit."

"Then they won't have a Scott to kick around any more."

"You're joking. I'm serious."

"No you're not."

"If I walk away, at least I can do one thing I've been avoiding. Drive up to Eagle Lake and see the folks. I could look them in the eye."

"Why do you say that? You know they're very proud of you."

"Not if they knew I was running around stomping on towns." He turned to her. "What do *you* think of Breedlove?"

"He can be charming. I really don't understand him at all, but I sort of like him."

"How about the others? Hank and George?"

"Hank? Cunning, terribly ambitious. George, down deep, is gentle and sweet, I think. It's Susan who's the cunning and ambitious one."

"Do you know her well enough to say that?"

"Maybe not. The only time we really ever talked was about a year ago, when she called me for lunch. It lasted three hours. I told her a lot about myself but she said very little about herself. When she left, I realized it was almost as if she'd planned the lunch to find out as much as she could."

He lay back. "You're right about one thing. I wasn't serious when I said I might quit. We're in the rat race."

"I don't see much peace in our lives ahead."

"I see Breedlove ahead. That's a storm warning."

"I think your Mr. Breedlove is getting to you."

"When I tell you something else, you're going to be certain of that. The other night from that window I saw a man who resembled Breedlove. A younger Breedlove."

"Now I'm just slightly scared."

"Good. I'll hold you."

"Do more than hold me. Get sexy."

She came into his arms and soon he was touching her in places, feeling her warmth, breathing in the scent of her body. Anne stroked his back, her parted lips on his, her small hips moving. A wall had grown between them, but now it was falling down, opening. It was all right now.

The next day, walking in the woods with Liz and Tod scampering ahead of her, Anne felt the same tranquillity about Olen that Mark had described to her. Except for Mike, who had been drooping and incommunicative, the kids seemed to be having the time of their lives. The weather was hot and humid and showers erupted without warning, but it was stimulating to her. She found she could think clearly. The past years had been too much of a whirl to allow her time to think. Mark's promotions, the moving, and the kids had filled her life. Filled, but not fulfilled. After all, she did have a master's degree in political science and, before meeting Mark, definite plans for a career in government. They had been sidetracked by the moves, the babies, Mark's rise in the company. What he still really wanted, she suspected, was a loyal corporate wife, one to watch the kids and organize the household, to laugh at customers' jokes, to entertain graciously, and to understand his pressures and comfort him in stress. The company wanted it that way, too. Could she live that way? Very possibly not. Not any more.

"Oh, hell," she said. "You worry too much, Mrs. Scott. And waffle. Waffle all over the place."

She stopped. Birds shrilled around her. She shied back. Silly Anne. Scared by a harmless bird. Talking to yourself out loud. That was a new habit. Also, she'd been growing more ambivalent. But she wasn't the ambivalent one in the Scott family. Mark complained about a lack of contentment, but he enjoyed his success. Once she had thought him too docile and unaggressive to achieve absolute success, but she no longer did. He had a strong inner drive, despite his almost diffident manner—a drive Breedlove undoubtedly recognized.

Anne stood still. The atmosphere of the place had changed. The birds were quiet. A wind had arisen. The sky was darker. She heard rustling in the leaves behind her. She thought she could hear labored breathing and faint, deep-throated chuckling.

"Tod?" she said. "Is that you? Tod?"

No response, only ominous silence. Her heartbeat accelerated. A tingling apprehension swept through her, and she began to back away, aware of dryness in her mouth and a quick numbness in her fingertips. Liz skipped toward her, holding a cardboard box.

"Mom, got a present for you. I think it's flowers. A whole shoe box full of yellow flowers."

"Flowers? Did you pick them?"

"Nope." Liz showed her mischief smile. "A dwarf did."

"Oh, come on now. A dwarf?"

"No. Not a dwarf. An elf picked them. An elf with big ears and a green suit. He had a pointed hat on."

Anne took the box. It was warm and moist. She pried off the string and removed the cover. She glanced inside. Her head snapped up. Treetops whirled above her. The ground seemed to move in tiny contractions.

"Mom, what's wrong?" Liz said.

"N-nothing," Anne said. She covered the box. She felt numb and shaky, but she must remain calm. "Who gave this to you? The truth now."

"A man in the woods."

"When?"

"Just a minute or two ago."

"Liz, we're leaving. Where is Tod?"

"Right here," Tod said, springing up from under a pile of leaves.

They were on the outskirts of Olen, in view of the cannery, when she heard the noise. It sounded like a sharp report of a cannon. White smoke shot up through the roof of the plant, scattering corrugated metal. Anne began to run, clutching the box. The sky to the east was dark, almost black, and a misty rain had begun. Liz and Tod pranced ahead, thinking it was a game. The rain descended harder. Heavy smoke poured from the plant's roof, surrounded by licks of flame. The bright, tranquil day had disappeared, fading quickly into deep, ominous darkness. Anne tripped and fell sprawling. The box came open, scattering its contents. Anne clamped her hand over her mouth to suppress a scream. Her stomach turned. About two dozen blood-spattered dead birds, sparrows and chickadees, lay strewn around her, limp and headless, soaking in the rain. Anne rose to her knees and watched Liz and Tod running back toward her. In the valley below, smoke rose from the plant in a tall spiraling column.

Scott had been in the west wing of the cannery when the explosion occurred. It was several hundred yards away, yet its force buckled the roof over Scott's head. He ran past the inoperative canning line, his shoes clanking on the cement floor. A jagged black hole had been blown in the wall separating the plant from the office space. Thick smoke poured through it. J. B. Toms limped up to Scott, his shirt tattered and bloody, his face dark with soot.

"Christ, Mr. Scott, it was a *bomb*! Under that busted retort. It flung 'er right into the office."

"Is there anyone in there?"

"Sure. They was some office workers in there."

Scott stepped toward the broken wall. Smoke forced him back. Shielding his face with his arm, he turned back to Toms. "Get some men," he said. "Bring up a hose. Shovels, Crowbars. Anything."

"I ain't doin' that, Mr. Scott. I'm gettin' out. I tell you that was a bomb an' there might be another one around here set to go off."

Scott seized Toms's injured arm. He squeezed. "If you run off now, I'm going to have you scalped and nailed to a wall. If you don't believe that, you try me. You try me. Now do as I say. Now! Move!"

Toms backed away, his face blank, and turned and hurried off. The smoke had lessened. Scott wet a cloth in a fire pail and put it over his mouth. He crawled through the hole into the office. The retort lay on its side, torn and scarred with black streaks. Rain poured in through a hole in the roof, diluting the smoke and extinguishing some of the firebrands on the floor. Scott heard a moan and turned to see Norma lying on the floor, trapped under a large, splintered beam. Blood stained her face. Her eyes were open and wide with terror. A man crouched beside an overturned desk, bent over in choking spasms, his arm twisted unnaturally, his shirt torn off his back. The smell was thick and acrid, penetrating deep into Scott's throat and lungs. He crawled to Norma's side.

"Mr. Scott?" she said. "I feel wet, Mr. Scott, all wet."

"Just lie still. It's only the rain."

He couldn't budge the beam. "Toms!" he shouted. Two men appeared, holding a fire hose. "Never mind the hose," Scott said. "Help me with this beam."

He knelt beside Norma, taking her hand, as the men freed her. Norma screamed, filling her mouth with blood. "Hold me," she said. "Hold me!" Scott held her, lightly and then tighter, his arms trembling, his throat dry.

"I'll carry her out," one of the men said.

"No. I'll carry her," Scott said.

The rain poured in from a black sky.

"TNT, a fair-sized charge, tamped with sandbags so the force of the explosion's controlled, sort of concentrated," the sheriff, Johnny, said in the hotel lobby. "Who done it knew what they was doin'."

Four of them stood in a semicircle—Scott, the sheriff, Cotton Meeks, and the editor, Dylan. It was time for calm appraisal. Even the weather had calmed. The rain had stopped and a soft, clear twilight bathed the town. Olen again seemed at peace. The blast had caused more fright than damage and had killed no one, but Norma was in serious condition with internal injuries and facial burns at a hospital in Elk Falls, and six others had been injured to a lesser degree. Scott's nerves crawled. He had placed a call to Breedlove, telling Miss Tompkins what had happened, and she had assured him that Mr. Breedlove would return the call. Anne and the kids were upstairs, packing to leave. She had told him the bizarre story of the mutilated birds, strain and repressed hysteria showing beneath her outward calm. They both realized something they didn't discuss. Whoever had done this knew a lot about Anne, for she seldom discussed her bird phobia. Scott did not think it mere coincidence. The person in the woods had known.

"Mark, you suppose it was them Mexicans planted that bomb?" Cotton Meeks said.

"It wasn't them, I don't think," the sheriff said. "That timer we found, it was foreign-made. Europe." He glanced at Scott. "Elsewhere in the company has there been anythin' like this recently?"

"No," Scott said. He was thinking of the airplane, and of Lawrence Breedlove's warning. "No," he said again.

The bellman shuffled up. "Call for you, Mr. Scott." He raised himself to his tiptoes and whispered a whiskey-breath message into Scott's ear. "It's him wants you. Breedlove hisself."

"Scottie?" Breedlove bellowed. "You finished up there yet?"

"No. Definitely not."

"I want you to get over to Kansas City. See Welles at the

Farm Machinery Division. He's sent in a report so insane it makes me think there's dust in his brain. You go straighten him out."

"Lewis, didn't she tell you what happened here?"

"Sure she told me. I have security people on the way there now. You get over to Kansas City."

"No. I'm going to stay here and see this out."

"Like hell you are, Scottie. You're a business executive. You are not a cop. You get out now. You'll fuck it up even worse there. Security will fuck it up, too, but not as much as you would. Besides, I don't want you to risk your skin."

"It's my skin. Let me risk it."

"It's mine, too, Scottie. Get out."

"Wait."

But Breedlove had already hung up.

17

LANCASTER STROLLED ON LEXINGTON AVENUE, SNIFFING FOR a strange piece of tail that would be clean, grateful, and not talk about it when it was ended. The evening was full of thick, moist heat that magnified and held the scents of Manhattan. Whiffs of exhaust and animal feces and garbage swirled piquantly in an atmosphere so heavy it smacked of rain. It was more than an odor; it was a taste, heady and arousing, stirring restlessness in his loins. He craved action, a search for exotic adventure, and to test himself.

It was early, just after seven. The whores were out, in singles and in pairs, strutting around as if they had something to sell beyond wide pussies and sagging tits. Lancaster stopped one, a black in tight slacks.

"Pardon me, ma'am, but I'm just in town from Akron—Akron, Ohio, the rubber capital?—and I just *gotta* find your Green Witch Village I hear so much about back home."

"Mister, you mean Greenwich?" She eyed him, the hillbilly from the sticks, maybe a quick trick to start off her night. "Just grab a cab."

"Is it safe there?"

"A big boy like you can handle himself okay."

"I'd sure like it if you'd consider going with."

Her jaws moved on a wad of gum. "That ain't exactly my territory. You got a bill in your jeans and a room, I'll show you a good time right here. I got a garden you can play in."

He gasped. "Lady, you mean to tell me you're a . . . a *painted woman* of the night?"

"Christ, mister, what farm you off of?"

"My mama, she told me ladies like you got *disease.*"

"Well, go fuck your mama then."

She strutted off. Lancaster continued on, feeling amused. He thought of Masters. The pornographic film didn't bother him. Dorothy had made several sex flicks years ago, and Lancaster had personally negotiated with R. W. Wright, a former vice king who now made television documentaries for children, for the great majority of the prints. It had cost him an arm and a leg, outright blackmail, but it wouldn't do to have evidence around that the wife of an up-and-coming executive like himself had once starred in porno films. It could ruin him, in fact. Wright now lived in Masters's building; undoubtedly, Masters had inveigled or stolen one of the prints from Wright to hold as insurance against losing the BII Food Division account. It was such a simpleminded approach that it amused Lancaster. It was a small mind in panic. David Kahn apparently knew about it, too, but Kahn was too smart and had too much of a future elsewhere to use it against Lancaster.

Another whore brushed by him—white, nice ass, fair tits. He skipped away before she could make her approach, remembering something. The sociologist with the boobs probably would be knocking at his door pretty soon, he was sure. He didn't regard her as easy meat; she'd be a little bit of a challenge. Briefly he considered inviting a hooker up, too, to do a double, but he discarded that idea. He didn't like paying for it.

Dorothy had made the films for Wright when she'd been eighteen, a runaway from the sultry brick apartment near elevated tracks in central Pittsburgh to a sultry brick apartment near elevated tracks in Queens. A developing beauty who combed her hair and talked like Marilyn Monroe, she'd wandered from agent to agent for a year with no offers beyond the couch. Then Wright had made his proposal.

Lancaster didn't blame her; it was—what the hell—fast pocket money. She'd been married to a drunken cop at the time; after the cop, she'd hooked an Ayer exec, who'd still had her when Masters had introduced her to Lancaster. She'd been dumb, but trainable. He was married, too, to tall, thin-faced Lorraine, the daughter of a pet-food client. He'd dropped both Lorraine and the client to chase Dorothy.

He didn't mind when men clustered around her at parties. He encouraged it. He was totally confident, secure in his possessiveness. He knew most of the men in her admiring circle would sell their souls for the pleasure of removing her panties. Regarding them with his knowing smile, Lancaster radiated superiority, because they knew he could strip her panties any time the mood struck him. Yet that was not all. There was something else, something he could not tell her. He had to have her. Possession of her ranked with any other wanting in his world. It wasn't sex. It wasn't love, a concept he did not understand. He couldn't explain it to himself, but he knew if he lost her he'd go to hell, completely.

The sociologist rang his suite at the Waldorf Towers from the house phone in the lobby. He told her to come up. Soon she was standing in his doorway, clutching her purse, avoiding his gaze.

"What do you drink?" he asked, closing the door.

"Well, right now, nothing."

He touched her shoulder. He lifted her chin and kissed her, exploring her tongue with his. Her breasts heaved. She held him awkwardly, her legs tightly together. She smelled of cheap perfume.

"I've never done this before," she said, moving away.

"You should, more. You go around only once in this life."

"I feel just slightly whorish."

"You can pay me. I'll be the whore."

"Do you like me?"

"Of course I like you."

"You don't even know my name."

"What's wrong with Boobs? I'll call you Boobs."

"I think I will have a drink."

"Pour me a gin-rocks. I have to make one last phone call and then we'll play." He dialed Dorothy, his eyes on the sociologist's breasts. "Look, I'll be home Friday," he said when Dorothy answered. "You sound half asleep. You been drinking?"

"I was taking a nap."

"Something came up yesterday. One of your old films."

"Oh, good Christ."

"I handled it. Did you look at the Greer house yet?"

"No."

"Do it tomorrow. Anything else?"

"No."

The sociologist handed him the gin-rocks. "Who was that?"

"Just my old mother."

"No. It was not your mother. It was your wife."

"Shall we get at the matter at hand?"

"No. No, I don't think we will."

Their eyes met. She was about thirty, he guessed, and not very pretty. Probably Jewish. The Jews became sociologists or journalists like the Irish became cops and the Swedes became farmers. What she lacked in face she made up for in body. He wanted her. He would have her. Slowly he walked to the window and opened it. Warm air rushed in. The city's lights danced for miles below.

"Tell me," he said, motioning to her. "What do you see out there?"

"I don't understand."

"I'll tell you what I see. I see millions of people. Crammed people. Some are in air-conditioned apartments with doormen, screwing, jacking off, watching television, getting drunk. Beyond, over there, they're sitting on porch stoops or lying outside on fire escapes or on hot, piss-stained mattresses inside, plotting how they can con somebody out of a dollar tomorrow. Have you been there?"

"I've done fieldwork, yes."

"Then you understand why they're there."

"They haven't had opportunities. There is a concept we call relative deprivation—"

"A bullshit concept, like all other semi-scientific ones." Lancaster put his hands on her shoulders. He squeezed. Her eyes flashed fear. "It is fake, just as you are fake."

"I think I will leave now, Mr. Lancaster."

"First let me tell you who you are. You are independent, total career. Down deep, you hate men because of their his-

tory of exploiting women. It is the same reason blacks hate
whites. Yet you use the fact you're a woman to gain your
ends. Part of the reason why you're here is because you think
I may do something for you someday. You came here not
really knowing if you'd go all the way, however, for you are
not a first-date fuck. You prefer preliminaries. Lunches.
Dinner dates. Then you'd drop your pants. That makes you
something close to a whore."

"You are a crude and abusive man."

"I am the only honest man I've met."

"Then you must travel in a shitty world."

He laughed. He touched her. "Take off your dress," he
said.

"I think that I will," she said.

Lancaster had traveled to all parts of the world for BII, on
stays ranging from a day to two months, but he'd never
checked luggage on an airliner. He had a fold-over four-suit
bag and a briefcase into which he could cram almost anything
he needed, regardless of length of stay. It enabled him to
leave late for airports, arriving just before takeoff, and it
eliminated the risk of losing luggage. Powell was always a
ludicrous sight to him, sweating with three or four bags even
if the flight were an overnight hop from Los Angeles to San
Francisco. Powell also had a mania for arriving at airports
fully a half hour before takeoff. Before hijacks had become
common, Lancaster had carried a snub-nosed .38 pistol in his
bag; now he carried a six-inch switchblade knife in a sheath
with a leg strap, hidden in his shaving kit.

The sociologist had proved to be all real, and even better in
bed than he'd anticipated. She'd been a writhing, moaning
fountain of passion, with an insatiable sexual appetite and
experienced and willing in all postures and techniques. Yet,
when he'd left her, after two massive releases on his part and
perhaps a half-dozen by her, the restlessness still stirred in
him. It was a restlessness he felt often, usually before an
important test or task, and he'd never been able to stifle it
completely. Gambling helped. Sex, especially with younger
women known as difficult lays, also helped. But neither could
quell as strong a stirring in his blood as he now felt. He
needed something else. He needed to take a risk. A big,
unnecessary risk.

In the taxi to the Madison Square Garden complex, where Amtrak trains ran from the old Penn Station, he catalogued his attributes. He had brains. He was a leader. He had experience. His appearance was excellent. His health was very good, his energy extraordinary, his drive all-consuming. The BII board respected him and Breedlove respected him.

It was a three-ring circus, with Breedlove the ringmaster. Lancaster, Scott, Powell. One of them would emerge to full power at BII, the other two would go down. He did not fear Powell very much. The era of the financial man in American corporations was over for a while. You couldn't snap up other companies with stock trades any more. The market was too weak. Scott would be Lancaster's principal competitor. He feared Scott, although he could not quite articulate to himself why he did. Perhaps it was because Scott had been such a fast comer. And Breedlove certainly had his eye on Scott. Yet this was the era of the marketing executive in business. The seller. The mover of goods. BII was principally a consumer-oriented company. Its salesmen were its key to success. Why then could not its top salesman take it all?

Lancaster felt his blood rise. He felt his strength.

What drove him? He didn't know. But of course he knew.

Just after he'd mustered out of the Army, he'd gone for a walk in the Holmby Hills area of Los Angeles. He'd gone up the hill on foot to the houses of the rich, the richest of the rich, living in mansions behind iron fences protected by mirrored alarms and private bodyguards. The houses had called to him. Come to me, own me, possess me, because you can. You can. He walked past the tall, stately magnolia trees and peered at the vast lawns and the giant roofs. Behind the iron fences lived people no smarter and no less aggressive than he. You can. You can. A guard had stopped him, ordering him out. "I'll be back," he'd said.

He wasn't quite there yet. He was a few steps away.

But he would be there.

It was worth any risk.

At the station he bought a ticket on the 11:15 P.M. train to Philadelphia and then tore it up and bought one for the 1:30 A.M. train. He was not leaving New York. Not yet. It was alive in him, the deep, inexplicable stirring that drove him, calling stridently for another test, another proving of himself to himself. He put his bag into a locker and took his briefcase to the men's room. He drew dark slacks and a blue T-shirt from the case. His pulse rate had increased. He took the switchblade from his kit. He snapped it open. Then he closed it, put it into its sheath, and rolled up his trousers and strapped the sheath to his calf. He changed clothing. In the mirror he did not see Lancaster but a man twenty years younger. He returned to the locker, hung up his suit, put the briefcase in. He took six dollar bills, two fives, and a ten and a twenty from his wallet. Outside he caugh the uptown IND train to Forty-second Street. Emerging into the freak parade, he stood in the light of moving neon, feeling sweat on his back, the knife against his leg, and the jostling movement of the crowd around him. He was not Henry Lancaster. He was a young hunter in tight pants, out to do his thing, his shtick action and excitement and risk, his demeanor cocky and superior. His senses were heightened. The sounds and scents and tastes of the city bathed him in a sensual glow. A taxi driver screamed at a customer. A fat cop languished in his curbside patrol car, reading the funnies from the Sunday *News*. Whores in mink-fringed skirts and tight sweaters strutted by, twirling their purses and chewing gum. A legless vendor hawked papers from his perch on a skateboard. Queers in lavenders strolled blatantly, holding hands, their little fingers intertwined. Rhythmic blacks lilted by, playing hard rock on transistor radios. Hippies and potheads and drunks joined the parade. Lancaster joined it. An area overrun with perverts, subway sleepers, muggers, petty gamblers, and con artists crawling from night to night in repeated routines practiced and perfected, a rote similar in pattern and hopelessness to the meanderings of the insect world. Dime-a-dance joints, bars, pool halls, burlesque, sex-book stores, pornographic movie houses. It was a world gone mad. It had no order. Lancaster moved in it, a part of it.

At Broadway, he darted back down in the subway. This station had become such a notorious hangout for queens and whores and dope dealers, intermixed with innocent soft-ice-cream stands and Popsicle vending machines, that part of it had once been sealed off. It stank with wet heat. The sign read, "No Spitting." The train roared in. Lancaster took a back seat in an empty car. He did not know where he was going. He'd like to easy-ride the New Lots express to Brooklyn, maybe out all the way to Bedford, but he didn't have the time.

He got off at Fourteenth Street. He walked west. The streets became narrow. Lights were fainter. Flies feasted on dented garbage cans. Faces peered from windows of brick tenements where animal-people sweated and festered trapped in closet compartments to mate in agony like cockroach matings, smelling inrooted cabbage odors and gag stenches of rotted wallpaper. A dog followed him, snapping at his heels. He hit it squarely in the neck with a sharp rock; it retreated, yelping. Ahead was activity, adventure. Faint headlights from creeping cars. Sparks of cat eyes in alleys. Neon of whore bars, dope bars. A red FUCK painted on the Coca-Cola sign on the door of a closed-up Mom and Pop grocery store. Furtive blacks in bright shirts darting in pairs from corners. Lancaster strolled with his shoulders back, his chin high, his arms at his sides. He slipped lithely from light to light, penetrating deeper. Noises from an alley stopped him. He peered in. Three blacks and two whites were throwing dice in the oblique back-door light of a bar. He went in. He stood watching them, unnoticed. Two of the blacks were just kids, perhaps preteens. One of the whites was an old man with a scraggy beard. The other was a punk of about twenty. The third black was a bad s.o.b. He was tank-shirted and barrel-chested, undoubtedly a wide-brim-hatter and calf-length-coater when he went out to swing, strutting in the alleys and streets he owned, the bad nigger who ruled his roost not with bloodline but with developed power. A wide-hipped black woman in blue stockings and a miniskirt came out of the bar. She was the first to see Lancaster. Then the others saw him. The game stopped.

Lancaster advanced. He smiled. "A closed game, dis here, or can any cat get in?" he said. His voice startled him.

The rollers looked at him. The two boys sneered. The white punk looked at the bad nigger. The bad nigger was looking at Lancaster's shoes, which he hadn't changed. He was sizing up. A cop? No, not in hundred-dollar 'gators. A white swinger looking for black action? Could be. Maybe a sucker.

"Naw, closed game here," he said, finally.

"He got money, why can't he come in?" said the old man, scratching his beard. "You got money?"

"I got money," Lancaster said.

"Naw, closed game," said Tank Shirt.

"Other says it ain't," Lancaster said. "Dint'cha?"

"Wal, I didn't say for sure," the old man said.

"I say it's closed game," said Tank Shirt.

"Who're you?" Lancaster said.

"Da guy says what things is, that's who."

"Whadda you say?" Lancaster asked the old man.

"It's up to him," the old man said.

Tank Shirt considered. He eyed Lancaster up and down, squatted on his haunches, scowling. He said, "Shit, man, you want in, shit, then you got money, shit, man, c'mon in, you want. You got money, shit."

The white punk shrugged. The two boys hadn't entered into it. The old man scratched his beard. They all squatted over a small pile of money, change and dollar bills.

"Is it all faded?" Lancaster asked.

"Five ain't," said the punk.

"I'm in, da five," Lancaster said.

The old man shook the dice in his hand beside his ear. His eyes sparkled. "Eight, eight, *eight!*" he cackled, letting out a rush of air through his broken teeth. The dice flew. They came up seven.

Lancaster withdrew his five and five one-dollar bills. "Whose roll?" he said.

"You want the dice?" Tank Shirt asked him.

Lancaster put out fifteen dollars. "Fade me," he said.

Dollar bills came out. Three from the two boys. Two from the old man. Four from the white punk. Six from Tank Shirt. Lancaster rolled. A natural.

"*Shit!*" said Tank Shirt, glaring at him.

"Play it," Lancaster said.

"Shit, man, can't cover *dat.*"

"Play five then."

Lancaster did. He crapped out. But it was the last play he lost in an hour-long game. When he got the dice back, he rolled two sevens followed by an eleven. They were good dice. They were honest dice. He was hot. He wanted to play. Finally the game came down to Tank Shirt and him. An audience had formed. The broad-beamed whore was still there. Tank Shirt was getting mad. His animal was coming out. His lips curled. Lancaster crouched before him. Animal eyed animal over the pile of dirty bills in the faint back-alley light.

Lancaster rolled a seven. He reached for the money. A black hand clamped over his.

"You cheatin'," Tank Shirt said.

"They're yer fuckin' dice, man."

"You switchin'. I seen that b'fore, switchin'."

"I'll roll you the works."

"Can't cover dat."

"Take up a collection."

Their eyes were two inches apart. Tank Shirt still had his hand over Lancaster's. The crowd moved back. Tank Shirt snarled. His jagged, yellow teeth snapped.

"Sure, man," Lancaster said.

He let go of the money. He looked down the alley and saw that a group of blacks guarded the exit. He turned. The other exit was also blocked. Lancaster smiled. Tank Shirt was smirking, his wolf eyes alive.

"Hey," Lancaster said. "Hey, man."

He reached for his leg. He felt the switchblade. Still crouching, still smiling, he unsnapped the sheath. The knife slipped into his hand. The alley was silent. Lancaster clicked open the blade. Tank Shirt knew the sound. His eyes narrowed. His mouth opened.

Lancaster waved the knife. "Pick up my money."

Tank Shirt began to scoop it up, slowly. His primitive beast's face was wet with sweat. The young blacks fled. The white punk and the old man shuffled silently into the darkness. The black whore remained, an amused smile on her lips.

"You ain't gonna git out, man," Tank Shirt said, handing the money to Lancaster.

They stood facing each other, hate like a visible wave between them. Lancaster pocketed the money, filthy bills crumpled and torn like trampled confetti. The lines at the exits moved toward him. He whirled, the knife blade flashing. He felt overextended for the first time since he'd been making test excursions into other worlds. He'd gone too far. Yet he waited calmly. In the silence it seemed to him that he was not there; he was one with the darkness, hidden by it, a part of it, and unafraid. He looked at the woman. Their eyes met. She knew him. She knew his past, the tough wanting and seeking and daring that had led to his escape, and he knew in her, beyond the carefree defiance of her eyes, the wantings and seekings but lack of daring that kept her imprisoned. She would lead him out. He knew it.

"Over here," she said. She pushed open the door to the bar. Lancaster bluffed back Tank Shirt with a flash of the switchblade and followed her. Inside, he snapped the bolt lock home. The stench of stale beer smote him. A clamor arose outside—scuffling shoes, loud raps on the door, a babble of voices. Lancaster followed the woman down a narrow backroom corridor with a sticky floor and high walls scrawled with pornographic graffiti and into a bar where an ancient round-domed jukebox blared soul music to a disinterested audience of blacks. His shoes slipped on the sawdust. The woman hurried. She opened the swinging front doors and pointed to an alley. "Hurry on," she said.

"Thank you. You saved my hide."

"Sheet, it ain't for you I done it, asshole." She sneered. "I'm savin' my man back there from another rap. Sheet, he'da cut off your balls. He never learn when you stick a white man you get the pol-ice."

"You want to go with me?"

"Sheet, you *crazy*, man? You jus' *scat!*"

He was gone, running into the alley, his legs tingling with hot blood, his armpits drenched with sweat.

On Amtrak to Philly, he counted his winnings. Fifty-three dollars. He leaned back. He slept soundly until the conductor aroused him. He tipped the conductor with five of the filthy dollar bills.

18

EVER SINCE HIS 1965 DEFEAT IN HIS ATTEMPT TO TAKE OVER BII, Philip Mendenthal had been planning to launch another proxy fight. He'd begun to accumulate a personal staff for the new onslaught in 1974, a group of carefully selected accountants, security analysts, lawyers, and public-opinion specialists who headquartered at Mendenthal's fifty-ninth-floor office in the Pan Am Building. Mendenthal was chairman of Dimension Corporation, a holding company that controlled several firms, but his chief function over the past two decades had been head of Dimension's investment committee. He seldom went to the company's headquarters on Fifth Avenue, preferring to work in private on merger and acquisition proposals at his own office, where the doors were unmarked and the telephones unlisted. For the past six months he'd spent nearly all of his time on the upcoming BII proxy fight. He'd hired a proxy-solicitation firm, a law firm, a public-relations firm, and taken additional offices on the fifty-eighth floor to house his expanded staff. Operational funds were drawn from Dimension's treasury, supplemented by bank loans personally guaranteed by Mendenthal.

An office on fifty-nine was filled with files on BII and on Lewis Breedlove. It contained all BII annual reports, both the 10-K form sent to the Securities & Exchange Commission and the pamphlet report sent to shareholders, plus every scrap of information that had appeared on BII in the public prints for the past thirty years. It also contained reports on BII and its executives that Mendenthal's staff had drawn up.

To his associates at Dimension, Mendenthal sometimes referred to his twenties, which he'd spent in California, as "the dead years." He knew himself, however, that they were among his most important formative years, for from the experience with Breedlove had come his understanding of the power of absolute hatred. The hatred had given him the drive to amass his own fortune. It was for a man who, ironically, embodied the business principles Mendenthal himself fervently supported—the self-made capitalist, the owner-manager, the entrepreneur who gained reward only after risk. Mendenthal thought of Breedlove as unethical and ruthlessly dictatorial, but he did not condemn him for that. He'd learned long ago that the always-gentleman and fair player does not prosper or even long survive in the jungle world of competitive business. He thought Breedlove crude and ill-mannered—but, again, that could be understood. To Mendenthal, Breedlove was a modern Mephistopheles with a yet formidable intellect and uncanny instincts. He could still cut quickly to what he wanted. They were attributes Mendenthal admired. His hatred of Breedlove was strictly personal.

In recent years he'd often regretted the lingering hatred, for it interrupted the pleasures of his private dreams. Often— too often—he dreamed, awake dreams that were really visions. In the visions he saw frozen ponds and infinite stretches of snow leading to country estates; he heard the bell chimes of St. Petersburg; he smelled musk odors of the great white horses that pulled the fragile sleighs. Mendenthal's visions were seldom of the future, and therefore unlike the visions that he knew still came to Breedlove. They were of time past. He was a Russian Jew with the blood of genuine aristocracy in his veins, yet when he'd come to America in 1910 with his sister, Anna, and her two-year-old daughter, Rebecca, he had only a single trunk of clothing, about five hundred dollars in gold, and mementos of his school days. They had been dispatched from Russia by their father, a true visionary who foresaw blood in city streets, prancing horses and flashing sabers, torture prisons, and death by revolution. Yet the father would not leave. He said he preferred to die in the land where his wife had died. Anna's husband also refused to leave, for a motive perhaps unpure—to guard what he stubbornly believed would remain the family's fortune. He could not be convinced that the fortune really no longer existed. It cost him his life. He died in the battle for the Petrograd garrison, exactly three months before Nicholas II was killed. It was not known when the father had died. The embassy could not trace the records. The date of Anna's death was carved on a stone in a cemetery in Queens, New York. June 16, 1910. Consumptive and spent on the boat across the Atlantic, she had seen little besides tenements and garbage-strewn alleys in the Land of Promise. Mendenthal stayed in New York for several years, caring for Rebecca and tending a cousin's fruit stand. Then, taking Rebecca, he'd gone west. He'd returned a wiser man.

George Powell knew very little about Mendenthal's years in California, for Breedlove never discussed them. He knew much, however, about Mendenthal's progress after he had returned to New York. Mendenthal had been in his thirties then, in 1923, and Wall Street had been in the early stage of a head-spinning bull market. Mendenthal had established an off-floor stock trading company in partnership with a man who had a seat on the New York Stock Exchange. He put $50,000 in cash into the company and borrowed another $100,000. By 1928 he had over $4 million and the seat was in his own name. It wasn't clear to Powell when Mendenthal had met Robert R. Young, the railroad proxy fighter, but he had worked briefly for Young at one point and he still expressed admiration for him. Indeed, Mendenthal's home in Connecticut was named the Towers, after the estate Young had once owned in Palm Beach. Young had left General Motors to form a New York brokerage firm himself. Powell assumed he'd helped Mendenthal by introducing him to some of Wall Street's elite. Also, it might have been Young's influence that had caused Mendenthal to dispose of his stock in the summer of 1929, before the crash.

The crash and ensuing depression, for a still young Mendenthal, had been a blessing. He had something few others possessed—several million in cash. He'd begun his corporate maneuvering in the early 1930s. A research file compiled by BII during Mendenthal's first proxy fight for control in 1965 described him as a man with an extraordinary, almost intuitive grasp of corporate finance. The dossier also said that Mendenthal read and spoke fluent Hebrew, Russian, English, and French. He had earned a law degree through night classes and correspondence schools.

In 1932 he'd acquired a company named Amax Industries, at the time merely a corporate shell. It had no real assets, stunted sales, heavy debt, and no profit. It was ready for bankruptcy. Mendenthal got control for $3,000. Then he began to look for a larger, cash-heavy company to merge into his shell. He decided upon a Newark-based building-supply corporation named Baylor Enterprises, which was ideal for Mendenthal's plan. Baylor had been weathering the depression by conserving its cash. Its stock was listed on the curb. Two of its directors owned the controlling blocks. Mendenthal offered to buy their shares at 10 percent above Baylor's market price; the controlling directors agreed to sell out and resign. Then Mendenthal went to a bank, offered its loan officers options on Baylor stock in return for a loan, and used the borrowed funds to buy the directors' stock. Next, Baylor was merged into Amax. Baylor thus assumed Amax's debts and Mendenthal could use some of the merged company's liquid assets to pay off his bank loan. He was on his way. All he had to do was keep merging. This he did, absorbing several companies during the corporate merger frenzy of the 1950s and 1960s. Now he controlled almost $1 billion in assets, a leveraged pyramid based on the $3,000 outlay.

Powell did not believe everything in the Mendenthal report, since he realized Breedlove investigators had slanted it against Mendenthal, but he believed enough of it to realize that their foe was not to be taken lightly. Mendenthal had fallen short by almost two million votes in the first proxy contest, but Powell was aware that Mendenthal really hadn't pushed too hard then. This time he would; he was far too old for another chance. And now he was much stronger, richer, and better connected. How much stronger? Powell really didn't know. One reason for his meeting with Mendenthal was to find out.

They met at Mendenthal's sea-oriented house in Mystic—a man's home, obviously, judging from the four fireplaces heaped with ship models, the seascapes and hunting scenes that dominated the walls, and the mounted sailfish curled and battling like a force undefeated and indomitable, even in death. To Powell, the house was in many ways similar to Breedlove's. The Breedlove house also was a man's house, especially the den, where elk heads, antlers, and a stuffed eagle with outstretched wings and dark, piercing eyes held sway. Both men were hunters, but hunters in arenas unlike those of stalking outdoorsmen. They also were old hunters, wary and wise ones now again pitted against not other game but each other. Powell had a drink. He had another. He felt relaxed. He'd met Mendenthal during the 1965 proxy contest, but he'd never spoken to him at length. They sat at opposite ends of the large dining-room table. Two butlers in formal dress served them.

"I will consider you Breedlove's ambassador, Mr. Powell," Mendenthal said. "And, at least for now, I will propose a pact. We will be civil to each other."

"Of course."

Mendenthal smiled. Lines crinkled around his eyes. "We are about to embark on warfare, but let it be said we began our war, at least, as gentlemen. I fear there will be few gentlemanly acts between us in the future."

"Warfare. That is an interesting way to phrase it."

"Business is not unlike war, at least the way it is waged by Breedlove. He would have made an excellent military man."

"It is my opinion that Lewis Breedlove would succeed remarkably at almost anything he undertook."

"Do you know him, Mr. Powell, or do you merely work for him?"

"He is not a man given to personal revelation."

"I have studied him, both personally and at a distance, for almost a half century. I'll admit to you that he is somewhat of an obsession to me. But he is not an enigma to me. You see, already my obsession shows. We are not five minutes into our meal and he is the topic. There he is, Mr. Powell, crouched at our elbow, smirking at us." Mendenthal seemed amused by the thought. His eyes flashed. "Forgive me as I ramble," he said. "It is really little else but an elderly personage you see before you, and I have, in my old age, become a minor student of the philosophers and the historians. I am now convinced that there are few figures of power in the past or present who could withstand an absolute delineation of their lives before the public. Tell me. Have you brought the list of your shareholders?"

"Yes."

"He has placed three of you at the top. I will assume, however, that he still rules."

"Your assumption is quite correct. He rules indeed."

"From his high perch he will fall very hard."

"You seem remarkably confident."

"I am confident, Mr. Powell, but not overconfident. My appeal, as you no doubt realize, will be made to the forgotten person in BII—indeed, in most large companies today. That is the small shareholder."

"We most certainly do not ignore our shareholders."

Mendenthal dismissed the butlers. "I had planned to propose that we refrain from business discussion during our meal, but it may well be there is little else we can discuss with authority. I have paid for my success, for it finds me a lonely old man in a castle. I am sure you also have paid, Mr. Powell. I suspect we are men with only one side."

"Perhaps that is so."

Mendenthal's eyes softened. He looked away, as if lost in memory. Powell realized he'd been eating without tasting the food, a crab cocktail and a sea bass fillet. He wanted the meeting to end. He wanted to return to Carol. Looking at Mendenthal, he saw little to support the man's expression of confidence in his ability to sweep out BII directors and replace them with his own slate. Mendenthal looked old and weary. He appeared on the edge of sleep.

His head snapped up. "Contemplation is self-defeating, Mr. Powell, a phrase Mr. Breedlove might well use. I will contemplate no more. Shall we have our coffee—or brandy— outdoors on the patio?"

"Coffee, yes, thank you. But no brandy."

The patio was beyond large glass-paneled sliding doors in the living room. The living room was almost dark, lighted by a far-corner floor lamp shaped like a ship's wheel. On the eastern side, toward the sea, there was a wide staircase. A beam of light from above played on the stair rails. As he followed Mendenthal toward the patio, Powell stopped abruptly. A hand had appeared on the rail, full in the beam of light. It was a woman's hand, old and gnarled. Then a face jutted into the light. It was the face of an elderly woman, wrinkled and white. A tangled disarray of long flowing hair fell over her cheeks and neck. The face held Powell. He stared, dumbfounded. He could see only the face and the hand, bright in the overhead light. The face lifted. The eyes peered down into Powell's. They were dark and deep-set, swimming in blood-red sockets, eyes at once piteously yearning and starkly insane. The woman's mouth opened. She uttered a low moan.

Mendenthal whirled. He pushed past Powell and darted toward the stairs, moving with extraordinary ease for one who earlier had appeared ready to nod off in an old-age after-dinner nap. A white-uniformed nurse appeared on the staircase. She and Mendenthal helped the woman up the stairs. The moan had risen to a deep animal-like howl. Mendenthal reappeared, opened the patio windows, and beckoned Powell outside. Sea smells wafted from the Sound.

"I believe I will have a brandy, after all," Powell said.

Mendenthal motioned Powell to a wicker chair beside a metal table. "It was Rebecca, my niece," he said. "She has not been well."

"I'm sorry."

"Many persons Lewis Breedlove touched came to some

form of grief." Mendenthal's hand trembled as he poured brandy from a decanter into snifters. He handed one of the snifters to Powell. "Perhaps you, too, will find grief from Breedlove."

"I don't understand."

"Breedlove once touched Rebecca. From that came our grief, hers and mine."

"Your proxy-solicitation plans then are personal."

"They are based on my desire to perform a public service."

"I suspect they are entirely personal."

"We have filed our intent with the SEC to engage in proxy solicitation for control of BII. I am in my rights in demanding your shareholder list. I now make such a demand."

"I do not have it," Powell said.

"Earlier you said you brought it."

"That was a misstatement. It is in my hotel room."

Mendenthal gestured. "I agreed to meet tonight only to obtain the list. We are wasting our time, Mr. Powell."

"You are wasting your time, trying to seek Breedlove."

"I do not seek him. I seek his company."

"It is the same thing."

"Ah, I see you do know him. A side of him, at least. Perhaps I should tell you about him. Then you will know the man for whom you work. Breedlove has not one but two sons. The woman you saw on the staircase just now is the mother of his first son."

"Why do you tell me this?"

Mendenthal became extremely agitated. He paced, flinging his hands into the air. "His first son has his strain, his seed. I tried to raise him, for in the past I have wanted a son, but as he grew I saw a person who each day resembled his father more and more, both in appearance and in temperament. It was not easy for me, seeing an image of a man I hated in my house. He had Breedlove's glint in his eyes. He left twenty years ago, after robbing my safe, took the name of Clinton St. John, and has lived a rootless life. He has been to prison for murder."

"You blame what you call the Breedlove seed?"

"I also blame myself. A man who strives for success should not try to assume the responsibilities of parenthood."

Powell avoided Mendenthal's gaze. "One can be an attentive

parent and also a success in business," he said after a pause.

"You have managed both?"

"I believe so, yes."

"Then you are an unusual and fortunate man."

Powell began to feel unease and restlessness. He stood up, tapped his pipe on his heel, and sat back down.

"I will tell you something of importance," Mendenthal said. "You may not believe me, but I do think what I have to say will interest you. It may even save your life."

"Save my life? What on earth are you talking about?"

"Ours is not the only group that seeks Breedlove. His sons—the one by Theresa Sanderson, whom he married, perhaps bigamously, for social status and banking relationships, and the one by Rebecca, whom he seduced as a mere child and married to gain a foothold in California—are allied with others in a plan to destroy him, and also to inflict damage upon his company and persons associated with it. Perhaps you, Mr. Powell."

Powell chewed on the stem of his empty pipe. His hand was unsteady, but he said calmly, "You were quite correct when you said I might not believe you. You are merely trying to frighten me. Your tactics are not only reprehensible but also ineffectual. I really must go now."

"I will win this proxy contest. My life to now has pointed to it. I have not used tactics to frighten you. On the contrary, I have given you this information because, by withholding it, by covering it up, I become a party to it. I tried to warn Breedlove, but he hears only what he wants to hear."

"If what you say is true, how do you know about it?"

"Clinton came to me and told me about it three weeks ago. I hadn't seen him for almost fifteen years. I had disowned him when he went to prison, although I financed his defense. He gave me no more details than what I have told you."

"But why did he come to you?"

"I don't know. Except perhaps to boast. He said he'd do in months that which I had spent decades trying to do."

"Have you informed the authorities?"

"No. I am informing you. You may do as you wish with my information. I have also warned Lewis Breedlove."

"It is irresponsible of you, if you have this information, not to inform the authorities."

"I believe Mr. Breedlove has more effective ways of dealing with adversity of this nature than all of the law-enforcement agencies of the world."

"I don't understand."

"Perhaps he will unleash his friends from the netherworld upon his foes."

"Netherworld? What do you mean?"

"He has been allied with organized crime for years."

"That is sheer nonsense. Preposterous."

"Very well, Mr. Powell, it is preposterous."

"If this man plans to attack him, what is his motive?"

"Perhaps Clinton wants to claim his birthright."

"Did you tell him he is Breedlove's son?"

"He discovered that fact by himself."

"I suspect, however, you transferred to him your hatred of Breedlove."

"No. I did not. My hatred is my own burden."

"Does Breedlove know of his first son?"

"Mr. Powell, our Mr. Breedlove knows everything."

"That seems an exaggeration."

"I think you're beginning to believe me."

"What I have come to believe is that you're a man consumed by obsession and hatred."

"I do not deny it. I have termed it a burden."

"Why do you hate him?"

Mendenthal spoke in a low monotone, his eyes far off. He said he'd taken Rebecca west in the early 1920s, primarily for her health. She'd been a sickly child since birth. He settled in the San Fernando Valley, where land was plentiful and cheap and where a new aqueduct across the Owens Valley assured growers of water. Mendenthal acquired some land and a part interest in a food-processing plant. Rebecca's health improved. One day a ragged boy of about fifteen came to Mendenthal and offered to sharecrop some of his land.

"Breedlove had made his way from Wisconsin to California alone, a boy who was really a man. He seemed piteous and ignorant, a gypsylike wanderer without kin or roots. I took him in. I gave him books to read and quarters at the plant. He learned quickly. Soon he had some land of his own and was making a small profit. It was easy times, free times, and opportunities abounded. All his profits went into down payments to acquire more land. He had discovered, early in life, that there was magic in a system called pyramiding. He borrowed on his land and used the funds to acquire additional land. Then he borrowed more, acquired more land. Just as you have bought companies, seizing your prey and then borrowing funds to pay stockholders, using their very stock for collateral."

"And you," Powell said.

Mendenthal folded his arms over his chest and gazed at Powell, gazed beyond him, through him. He was in the past again. "I should have seen deception in those dark eyes of his. But I had never met a soulless man before. I did not recognize a factor that could be termed the Breedlove edge. He has no remorse, no conscience, no sense of gratitude. His every action is a part of a coldly calculated scheme with his benefit, and only his, in mind. He took my shelter and began immediately to scheme against me. He was a good worker and had a way with the Mexican laborers. Some of their women no doubt sated his sexual drive. The land to him was a god and he worked literally twenty hours a day to acquire it. It wasn't long before he made his move against me. He did it through Rebecca. She was barely sixteen then, and somewhat free-spirited. I became alarmed when she began to show an interest in him. In return for his vow to leave her alone, I offered him an interest in the plant at par. But vows meant nothing to Breedlove. He repaid me by seducing Rebecca and bringing her to me pregnant, as trade merchandise."

"Trade merchandise?"

"He offered me a simple proposal. He would return Rebecca to me if I would sell my land to him. He had arranged bank financing. People, especially Rebecca, meant something to me, so I sold. It was Lewis Breedlove's real start."

"You could have aborted the pregnancy."

"Abortion is not in my nature, and he knew that." Mendenthal paced. "When the boy was born, I telegraphed Breedlove, saying it was a stillbirth. Rebecca went to Europe, and when she returned she was irrational, already aged."

"And you blame Breedlove?"

Mendenthal's voice rose. "I have said I also blame myself. I seek Breedlove not as a vendetta but as a benefit to humanity. You have been living high. You are thin. Your balance sheet is, in effect, false. The wonder is that your accountant approves it. You're borrowing from the future and trimming liquid assets to make your profit look good. You deceive your shareholders. When this is shown in the public prints, I think you will admit you are ripe for takeover."

Powell stuffed his pipe with defiant, exaggerated movements. Much of what Mendenthal said was true. Powell had, in fact, discussed most of it with Breedlove.

Mendenthal continued. "Also, you have not been wise in your political donations and foreign payoffs. With his connections, Breedlove might avoid punishment, but in reality Breedlove is finished. His childish mind regards me as a fool. He believes he can sell two hundred thousand BII shares to tell me he does not consider my threat real or substantial."

"So you know about the trade?"

"Of course I know. Four different persons called me about it yesterday."

Powell lit his pipe. He drew in smoke. "You do realize, of course, that you have eight hundred and thirty thousand shares against you from the start."

The stock, about 5.6 percent of BII's outstanding common shares, was owned by a Los Angeles company named Brighton Manufacturing. It had been sold to Brighton by Breedlove during the war, when money was tight and Breedlove desperately needed funds to expand. In the 1965 proxy fight, the stock had been voted for Breedlove's management slate and had been an important factor in Mendenthal's defeat. It had subsequently been pledged to Merchants Bank of San Francisco as collateral against a loan. Its voting rights were vested in trustees.

Mendenthal didn't seem disturbed about it. "I will have that vote," he said. "There is a way to acquire that stock for nothing."

"How?"

"I am surprised that you do not know how. Put on your thinking cap and perhaps you will see how. Sometimes the simple way is the best. If you will excuse me now, Mr. Powell, I believe we should terminate this meeting. We will meet again in the spring."

"I remain convinced that you do not have a chance."

"I forecast that you will change you mind before the end of the year."

"I really must go now."

"My driver will take you back to New York."

"The train station will be sufficient."

"Very well."

"I have been asked to see whether you would listen to a compromise proposal, one that could save us both time and money."

"He is not a man who compromises, Mr. Powell."

"There are people behind you, aren't there?"

"Yes. There is an investment syndicate that will put up to a hundred million dollars into BII if our proxy fight is successful. I tell you this because I am sure you will discover it anyway."

"If I told you that my feelings toward Lewis Breedlove are similar to yours, would you believe me?"

"No."

"On your side, I could be a strong help to you. It is something for you to consider."

"You are not serious."

"But I am serious."

"Perhaps it is true, Mr. Powell, that there is indeed no honor among thieves."

"Have I aroused your interest?"

"You have lowered my opinion of you. When I inform Lewis Breedlove of your offer, his spleen will swell."

"I believe that he would accept my denial."

"What if I tell you it is on tape?"

"Then I would explain it was merely a ploy to gain information."

"You are indeed capable of unprincipled duplicity, Mr. Powell. I see why you have made gains at BII."

"Tell me. *Is* this on tape?"

Mendenthal shrugged. "Everything is on tape these days," he said.

The face of the woman on the staircase haunted Powell all the way back to New York. It seemed to appear before him in the dark mist outside the rail-car window. The train was nearly empty. A man in a dark raincoat had boarded at Mystic with him. Now Powell found himself periodically looking behind him and to his right and left. The man was nowhere to be seen. Powell went to the smoking car and lit his pipe. But it was a bad bowl; the tobacco tasted bitter and strong. The door flew open, filling the car with a rush of wind and the sound of steel wheels clicking on the rails. The man in the raincoat entered, hurried past Powell without looking at him, and took a seat in the rear. Powell's hands felt chilled. The woman's face again appeared before him, wavering in the wisps of yellow fog that clung to the window like foam.

An urgent message to call Breedlove awaited him when he returned to his room at the Americana. He dialed the Pasadena residence immediately. Breedlove himself answered on the second ring.

"George?"

"Yes."

"I understand you moved the stock."

"Yes. It cleared the tape this morning. I tried to phone you yesterday—"

"We were off almost two points today."

"They had to take it down somewhat to facilitate this sale. I thought about various ways of doing this and decided the best and quickest would be to wholesale it to a floor trader. Your net will be a point and a half under yesterday's close."

"You moved it *all* at that price?" Breedlove sounded very pleased. "Good," he said. "Very, very good."

Powell's spirits picked up. "I've met with Mendenthal. I have some strong thoughts on him, and much new information."

"Tell me."

"You were right, Lewis. He's going to throw everything he has at us."

Breedlove issued a low chuckle. "Well, he can be a smooth old villain. I think he learned some of his tricks from me. What he hasn't learned yet, however, is that I am a wiser, more cunning, and much more villainous bastard than he ever could be."

"He's not exactly your biggest fan."

"George, understatement is not your forte."

"He told me some wild stories. He said your sons—sons, plural—were out to get you."

Breedlove spoke rapidly. "Don't let his amateur scare tactics and machinations bother you, George. But give me a full written report—confidential—on what he said."

"He seems given to exaggeration. For example, he claimed he could get the BII Brighton-owned stock for nothing."

"That may not be such an inane statement. Look at it this way. It's a seventeen-million-dollar deal, less if it's margined. Mendenthal finds a buyer for the stock. Dimension and a bank lend the buyer enough to swing the deal and the buyer gets a put option protecting him from a market decline. The buyer risks nothing, doesn't put up a cent. I could fly to Chicago without an airplane for a deal like that. If the stock rises, it's a windfall for the buyer. He goes on Mendenthal's slate and becomes Mendenthal's puppet voting against us. I'll bet my boots he learned that trick from Bob Young. Get our lawyers on it. Mendenthal is not going to get that stock without a court fight."

Powell was stunned. Breedlove had cut straight to the answer. Powell said slowly, "Something else. I have reason to believe Mendenthal has taped everything that goes on in his office or home. If we could get our hands on some of those tapes, perhaps—"

"You surprise me, George." Breedlove paused. "That may not be a bad idea, come to think of it. I want to emphasize to you now that I am not taking Mendenthal lightly. It's going to be one helluva battle. I want you and Lancaster to mobilize. Get a proxy fight law firm. Get a high-powered, dirty-fighting PR firm. Keep Scott out of it. He hasn't learned toughness. You've done a good job so far. Keep ahead of them. This is your baby, George."

Breedlove hung up. Powell began to fill his pipe. He was tingling with elation. Compliments from Lewis Breedlove were rare and meaningful. Powell lit his pipe. His attitude had completely reversed. Breedlove had put him in charge of what was now considered the company's top priority item. It was a strong vote of confidence. Powell felt he was equal to the task. He was not, after all, an old man. He had many good working years left. It was not a time to give up. It was a time for aggression.

Usually he was asleep by eleven. Now it was past midnight, but he was wide awake. He decided to get some work finished. His telephone jangled.

"You've been chatting for an *hour*," Carol said.

"Hardly that long."

"I bought a new dress tonight."

"You went out shopping by yourself?"

"Sure. Do you want to see the dress?"

"Now?"

"Of course. I'll be tapping on your door in a second."

"If you really don't mind, Carol, I'd rather not. I'm frightfully tired right now."

There was a pause. Then she said, "All right."

On the roof of the Pan Am Building, Powell watched the approach of the big helicopter. Carol had already left, taking a 10 A.M. flight to Los Angeles. Powell, after an afternoon meeting with investment bankers, was booked on the 7 P.M. TWA flight. He often took the helicopter to Kennedy; it saved over an hour. A hot wind whipped his face. Cabs streamed on Park Avenue below. The helicopter now hovered four feet above the roof. There were only five boarding passengers, all men. Powell stared at the huge hissing blade. Something about it held him almost in a trance. He did not want to think about Carol, Susan, the twins, or BII. He looked forward to a pleasant flight in the first-class section of the jet liner, to a few drinks, a meal, and perhaps a nap. A sharp sound, like metal hitting metal, jarred his head up. He flinched. The helicopter began to tremble and gyrate unnaturally. It veered sharply to its left. The pilot's hands came into sudden view. The landing gear, touching the roof, collapsed with a loud cracking sound. The helicopter whirled wildly, out of control.

"Look out!" a man shouted.

Powell felt strong hands on his shoulders. He was pushed down. Someone was on top of him. The helicopter spun crazily on the roof, its blades hacking deep holes. One of the rotors tore loose and streaked through the air, missing Powell by six feet. The helicopter smashed into a wall thirty feet from its landing pad and came to rest, its tail rotor clanking slowly. Powell tasted bile in his throat. The man was still holding him down.

PART THREE

THE INVISIBLE ENEMY

19

LAWRENCE BREEDLOVE THOUGHT, *I'm the son of big Breedlove of Breedlove International, which has a big building all its own. I am not a cod or a smelt or herring bait. It's almost like I'm a household word or name like Hershey or Sears or J. P. Morgan or B. F. Goodrich. Goodrich. So what am I doing here in rags walking on this beach with a Nazi named Horst?* Horst was a husky blond, about forty, who talked a lot and smiled often. He liked girls but he did not fool with girls on a job He could walk as quietly as a cat and sometimes be in a room with you but somehow seem not there.

"I like the American beer," he said. His English was perfect. "I like it better even than German beer. American beer is the best just as Russian pistols are the best."

"Do you want to stop for a beer?"

"I never drink when I'm on a job. Not even beer."

"I don't like this. What we're doing, that is."

"It is not wise of you to talk in that manner."

"Why do you do it?"

"I do it because it is a job I do well. It is a way to earn money doing something I'm good at and enjoy."

"Why do you enjoy it?"

Horst walked tall, his shoulders square "It's high adventure. It's a testing of oneself. I'm pitted against an enemy. I am not a revolutionary. Once I had politics, but I no longer

239

do. We were trying to destroy our affluent elders, but, as the money came in to us, we found we enjoyed it. I liked driving a Mercedes. Now I do not wish to change the world. I fit well into the world as it is. I live for two things—excitement and gold. And for challenge. Life is not worth living if you exist from day to day with no challenges, no excitement."

"I have no excitement."

"Of course not. You take drugs. There is no *Walpurgisnacht* for you."

"What's that?"

"A celebration. A dance of witches and a feast. You are not in the world. The world is too much for you."

"I detest the world."

"Faust was a man who had learned everything, and he was bored. He wanted to find the ultimate, to go beyond boredom to excitement and challenge. That is what I seek. Boredom is a form of death."

"What do you think of Clinton?"

"Your brother is a strong man."

"Stop calling him my brother."

"Also, he is dangerous. He is insane, therefore dangerous. He is cunning but insane. Such a man, in the right country at the right time, could become a ruler."

"Do you think the plan will work?"

Horst paused. He thought a minute. Then he laughed. He had even, white teeth. "Somehow, you have managed to employ the best planning brain in Europe, mine, and perhaps the best technical man in the world, Mario. Yet we do not guarantee success. I think we will be successful, yes, but we do not guarantee it. We are not washing machines or television sets, with warranties."

"I don't understand you. What sort of life do you live?"

"I live several lives. I could visit you tomorrow and you would not know who I am. I can even become a woman."

"Are you married?"

"You are an asker of questions. It is not smart for a man in my profession to reveal too much of himself. But I will tell you that I am not married. A man in my profession does not marry until he retires. Only foolish men marry early in life."

"I would like to be married."

"Because you need someone? Strong men need only themselves."

"How long will the attacks go on?"

"We have just begun."

"How long will they go on?"

"Until we are finished."

"I want to get away."

"You cannot get away. Just accept that."

"I'd like to find a good woman."

"Go to a whore. The best women are whores, for they do not pretend."

"I'm afraid. I don't mind admitting that I'm afraid."

"A man who is afraid is no man at all. You are better off dead." Horst paused. Their eyes met. "If you wish, I will dispose of you. Painlessly. Right now, you are nothing but a walking corpse. You are a weakling, but I find that I like you and will do this for you as a favor."

"Maybe you're right. Maybe I am better off dead."

"You decide. Let me know."

"My mother was better off dead, I guess."

"Well, you decide. Let me know."

"All right."

"It is a good world, good to be alive in, but only if a person is strongly willed. It has been ever so and will be ever so."

Horst hurled a stone at a gull, missing. Larry thought, *Do I want to die? I'm son to Breedlove, big Breedlove, with his own building. I'm a household word. Do I want to die?* On the next toss, Horst hit the gull.

A series of attacks began to disrupt BII plants and offices. A bomb scare in Cleveland sent office workers scurrying to the street, an explosion at a San Diego bottling plant injured three workers, and freak accidents occurred to company vehicles on the road. It all happened within a two-week period. There was quiet for another week. Then a natural-gas depot exploded at a major BII plant near Columbus, Ohio, setting off a fire that killed four, injured twenty, and caused over a million dollars in damages. There were no extortion notes. The attackers remained invisible and anonymous. Police speculated publicly that the Columbus explosion was probably the work of a terrorist group. BII security investigated each incident and sent reports directly to Breedlove. Security had always been a headquarters function. Now it reported directly to the top, although sometimes to Breedlove through Henry Lancaster.

"It's insane, these attacks," Joe Hopkins, BII's domestic personnel manager, told Scott. "We're at a point where employee morale is deeply affected. And I'm powerless as long as Mr. Breedlove keeps all the information to himself."

"Well, I'll try to reach him. And I'm going to Columbus."

"You're quite calm about it."

"Not inside."

"There's actually a fear syndrome around this company."

"Well, let's not make it seem worse than it is."

"I hear rumors that our insurers are getting anxious." Hopkins's face was strained with concern. His hands moved and his eyes flashed. "The FBI's in on the act, but they haven't got clue one. This is—well—almost professional. Organized."

"Joe, I'm not taking it lightly, believe me," Scott said. "It's affected me personally. But I'm afraid I feel just slightly helpless about it."

"You're not the only one," Hopkins said.

He'd tried to drive it from his mind, but found he could not—not completely. Sometimes pictures flashed in his mind—Lawrence Breedlove's anxious eyes, the BII 727, Powell's report of a close call in the New York helicopter accident, Norma's frightened face after the explosion in Olen. She had recovered, but her face was badly scarred, according to reports Scott received. The matter had been turned over to security, whose agents had interviewed Scott without expressing an opinion or answering his questions. He really didn't want to see security's report on the bombing, or to think about Olen and its plant. He didn't have the time. His new work load consumed him day and night. Yet Olen continued to nag him, and the pictures fled before his consciousness, sometimes interrupting his concentration in meetings.

His duties had changed radically, almost overnight. When he'd moved up from a line position as a plant manager to corporate status, he'd found his work load easier at first. A welter of experts, legal and finance and production, back-stopped him. He'd become a report reader and recommender, except for direct fieldwork in labor relations, which he still did and enjoyed. But now he no longer recommended; he approved or disapproved recommendations of others. Executives he'd once appealed to for decisions now appealed to him. Office seekers phoned or wrote him, citing rumors of posh new positions on his staff. Budgets, research and development proposals, and capital expenditure appeals crammed his briefcase, waiting for his comments before they went before the board.

Scott seldom saw or even spoke to Lancaster or Powell and wondered privately if they were duplicating some of his work. Breedlove, who now seemed completely out of touch, had never really delineated what the separate duties and responsibilities of his Troika would be, and the result led to some indecision and consternation at headquarters. But Scott did not think too much about it; he merely plunged ahead. Meetings dominated him. Time no longer was his own. Anne seldom complained. Her manner was supportive, helpful. They now had a full-time maid and the kids had been transferred to private schools. His pay was over $250,000 a year, a sudden tripling, and he found himself studying tax-hedge plans in what spare time he had. The perks had multiplied. A chauffeured Cadillac took him to airports, line executives called him mister, and employees before unaware of him greeted him by name in elevators. BII bought a million-dollar Key Man insurance policy in his name. He was invited to join the Jonathan Club and the Los Angeles Country Club. A house in Malibu and a lodge at Big Bear were available for his use, as well as a suite at the Plaza in New York. Except for the crush on his time, he found he enjoyed it. He enjoyed it very much.

Also, he made discoveries. One came to him about two weeks after his return from Olen, when Richard Saltzman, one of the Food Division's leading salesmen, insisted upon a private meeting with Scott, bypassing the division's head.

"I'll take only ten minutes," Saltzman said, fitting his bulky frame into a chair in front of Scott's desk. He was a bearded, red-faced man clad in a rumpled green suit. "I'd take this up at division, except—like you no doubt know—the wheels, they're in Europe," he said. He stroked his beard. He scratched. "I grew the rug on my chin when the rug on my skull fell out. Well, really though, I grew it after my brother-in-law died of a heart attack while shavin' before a mirror. Now I don't have to shave."

"Are you a superstitious man?"

"All salesmen are superstitious."

"What's on your mind?"

Saltzman hesitated. He stared around the office, rubbing one of his bushy eyebrows with his thumb. Looking at him, Scott wondered how such an untidy, inarticulate person kept any business, much less Liberty Markets, a supermarket chain that was a major buyer of BII canned vegetables. He wished now that he'd refused to see Saltzman. He made a mental note never again to see a subordinate who reported to someone else, no matter what the urgency.

Saltzman turned. "I'm afraid we're losing the Liberty account," he said. Before Scott could respond, he added, "They got a new exec vee-pee over there that's into astrology or something. I don't know what it is. He says he can't keep up his profit margin on our line. Besides, it's not moving."

"Well, tell him we have a new ad campaign in the works."

"I have a better way." Saltzman leaned closer to Scott. "What Liberty buys from us, most of it we don't produce but get through B & T, the wholesaler. I think B & T will cut their price to us if we up their ante a little bit."

"I don't follow you."

Saltzman's eyes narrowed. He grinned, showing crooked teeth. "Mr. Scott, you're new to the Food Division, so maybe you don't understand fully how it works."

"Then enlighten me."

"We buy from the wholesaler for part of our business, and we grow it ourselves and can it for another part of it. It's about fifty-fifty now. There's a series of commissions all the way down the line. We pay such and such a price for a lot of goods from the wholesaler, but we discount it, say five percent."

"Is it a discount or a kickback?"

"Discount."

"Who gets the discount? The wholesale company or individuals in the company?"

Saltzman scratched his beard. "It don't matter. What

counts, on the bottom line, is that it works. Now, I got some people over at B & T by the short hairs, if you know what I mean. I know about their discounts, IRS don't. You okay a little more discount, they'll cut prices for us. Then we can sell to the markets cheaper and keep our business."

Scott stood up. "Who do you report to?"

"Well, to Ted Mann, the sales manager, supposedly, but actually I report direct to Sampson."

"And Sampson knows of these discounts?"

"It's the way things work."

"Maybe the way they did work. But not in the future. Not in this company."

"I can't stop the way things are done, Mr. Scott."

"I can."

"You do, you might lose me."

"That might well be a net gain for the company."

"You lose me, you lose two, three big accounts in that division. I keep a lot of business there."

"I think your ten minutes are up," Scott said.

After Saltzman had left, Scott stalked around his office, seething. The man obviously had tried to play him for a fool, to get him to condone an action, skipping his chain of command, because Scott was new to headquarters management of the division. It was Olen all over again, except at a much higher level. Did the division encourage kickbacks? Obviously it did, or at least turned its back on them, for Saltzman had discussed the practice as if it were justified and honorable. Scott sat behind his desk, his fingers drumming the phone. He wondered if he should call Carl Sampson, the division's head, find him on the phone regardless of where he might be in the world, but he decided he would not. Breedlove, after all, had not specifically granted him authority over the division. Perhaps if he got involved now he would be overreaching. He did not know. He sighed. Joan Leeky buzzed him.

"The county supervisor is here," she said. "And don't forget the Compensation Committee meeting at four."

His briefcase was crammed with work for the night. He was scheduled to catch a plane for Columbus tomorrow. Already it was too much. And he knew it would get worse. Much worse.

*   *   *

A red Volkswagen followed Scott on the freeway the next morning. Scott slowed. The Volks didn't gain. The face of its driver was partially hidden under a sun visor. Scott went to the right lane and cut his speed. Still the Volks didn't gain. He had seen the car before; that much he knew. He peered into his mirror, trying to make out the license number. The first number was seven. The second appeared to be a four. The letters were LGN. Scott turned off on Century. The Volks stayed on the freeway. Now Scott got a glimpse of the driver. He was on Century before he realized fully that the man behind the wheel was the one he'd seen in Olen, leaning against a lamppost—the man who looked like a younger Lewis Breedlove.

Scott pulled up to the curb, his heart hammering, his palms wet with perspiration.

The 727 was operational again, but Scott had not flown in it since the Chicago trip. Somehow he'd managed to avoid it, taking commercial flights instead. The plane's home base was a leased hangar on the southwest side of Los Angeles International Airport. Late in the afternoon, his flight to Columbus delayed, Scott decided to drop by the hangar. He was greeted by a giant black guard, armed with a .45 in an unstrapped holster.

"I'm looking for Harold Long," Scott said.

The guard eyed him squarely. "Sorry. Nobody's allowed."

"I'm Mark Scott of Breedlove International."

"You can't hang around here, no matter who you are. I got my orders."

"I understand that. And I'm relieved to see that you're following your orders. You just tell Long that it's Mr. Scott."

The guard's hand brushed his .45. He stared at Scott, his brow furrowed, trying to make up his mind. Then he turned abruptly and went into the hangar. He was back in a minute, standing at the doorway, nodding at Scott and motioning to him.

Scott went in. He stared at the plane. The corners of the hangar were dark. A slight chill crept up his spine. Long arose from a bed strewn with magazines and newspapers, an alarm clock, rumpled covers, and cards spread out in solitaire positions. He was dressed in coveralls with bib straps.

"You have a Berlin Wall here," Scott said.

Long was pulling on his shoes. "Well, I can tell you this, Mr. Scott, for sure. Nobody'll *ever* sneak on this bird again."

"Who ordered this security?"

"Mr. Lancaster ordered it."

"*Lan*caster?"

"I have a note from Mr. Breedlove himself. It said Mr. Lancaster was the sole authorizer of future flights."

"Since Chicago, have you had it up much?"

"Three, four times."

"No more . . . problems?"

"Nothing. Although I'll admit to you I sometimes feel my nerves crawl when I'm up in her. I shouldn't admit it, being her pilot."

"What do you make of it? Chicago, I mean?"

"Frankly, Mr. Scott, I'm embarrassed red about that. I don't know how in hell anybody could have gotten aboard. I remember a catering truck that came in, though."

"A catering truck? Did you tell security?"

"I mentioned it to Mr. Lancaster."

"I'm not about to second-guess security, or Lancaster, but may I ask you to do something for me?"

"Sure. Shoot."

"If you spot anything irregular in the future, will you tell me first?"

"Awright. I can do that, I guess."

They shook hands on it.

Security at BII was a mystery to Scott—and, he surmised, to almost all BII executives. It was headed by a man named Nathan Bowler, who gave lectures occasionally on executive extortion. Scott didn't know exactly what Bowler did, but he had the uneasy feeling that Bowler knew much about him. Bowler's department operated out of a big house on Shatto Place, just off Wilshire. To satisfy his curiosity, Scott had driven by it once, but he'd been unable to discern anything. A lawn sign said, "Beware, Dog." The blinds were drawn. Security could be reached through a direct buzzer on Scott's desk. He'd used the department once, when Anne's car had been stolen from a parking lot two years ago. Someone named Forrest Ackerson had responded, and the car had been returned within forty-eight hours.

Security at BII also was a mystery to McKeen, primarily because he didn't want to know anything about the department. He was proceeding on his own. He had recruited five men from the Hudson organization to help him, picking brains, not muscle, especially in his assistant, who was working on his law degree. He had a fat file already, consisting of details on each attack. The only pattern he could detect was that they were all bombings or bomb threats, and they seemed to be building in intensity. He'd come to the conclusion that he was up against skilled professionals. He reported regularly to Hudson, who seemed to be holding his own—not getting any worse, not getting any better. Hudson told him to keep digging and not to worry about the bills. McKeen was getting caught up in the job. He sniffed the trail like a bloodhound. Whenever he got involved deeply in a caper, he suffered for it, developing massive psychosomatic toothaches that set his head on fire and robbed him of sleep.

"Why don't you see the dentist?" asked his wife, who had no idea that Hudson employed him, thinking him an investigator for an insurance company. "I'll call."

"A dentist wouldn't do me a damn bit of good."

"Please don't swear," she said, knitting.

"I think this is all planned in advance and that it's leading to a big hit. And I think I know where."

"Where?"

"The bird," he said. "The airplane."

She stopped knitting. "Mother is coming Sunday. You'll be home, won't you?"

"Naw, I gotta go to Columbus," he said, chewing aspirin.

To his surprise, Scott ran into Lancaster at the bombed depot in Columbus.

"Stop, that's far enough, sport," Lancaster told him.

"What do you mean, far enough?"

"Plant bombings belong to me."

Scott sighed. "All right, Hank. I grant you plant-bombing responsibility."

"I suggest you return to L.A."

"Hank, why don't you take the chip off your shoulder?"

"I'm just following orders, like a good soldier. He asked me to keep an eye on security, and I'm doing just that. I don't want any interference."

Scott stared at the burned-out rubble, which still gave off an acrid odor. Then he turned and faced Lancaster. "I'm not here to look for bombing clues. I have some union members to placate. I'm not sure we're going to muster up too many workers to return here."

"Then furlough or transfer them. This plant was losing money anyway. Whoever bombed it did us a favor."

"Whoever bombed it killed four persons."

"I'm aware of that. But there's precious little we can do for them now. You take the burdens of the bereaved on your shoulders, like a good parson, and I'll try to see what can be done to prevent another attack."

"I'm not looking for a fight, Hank."

"Just go home, my man."

He did, concerned and worried. Arriving at the office the next day, he didn't respond to Tim Hooten's hearty hello, although he usually did. He pushed hurriedly past Hooten, got into the elevator, ascended alone to thirty, and then pushed the lobby button and rode immediately back down. He found Hooten behind his desk, surrounded by intercom television monitors.

"Oh, Mr. Scott. Forget somethin'?"

"Yes. I have to go back to the car. My head is not on today, I'm afraid."

"I read about you bein' promoted. Durocher said nice guys finish last, a statement I don't believe, readin' about you bein' promoted."

"Thank you."

"Durocher, he was wrong about a lot of things."

"Tell me. You keep an eye out on who goes up, don't you?"

Hooten's eyes narrowed. He adjusted his cap. "I try my best, Mr. Scott."

"Lately—in the past two or three weeks—anything you would call unusual?"

"Nothin' I can think of. Kids, they come in a lot. We shoo 'em out. Salesmen, the type we don't like, I can spot right off."

"I'm referring specifically to a man—about forty—with a beard and green coat."

"Oh, sure. I remember. A hippie. He was tryin' to get up. I turned 'im around, sent 'im out."

"When was that?"

"I can tell you exactly. It was July the eleventh. We lose to the Reds, four to two. Sutton goes eight."

"You have a remarkable memory."

"Association. Associate somethin', you remember. Quick. Who won the National League home-run title in '73? Quick."

"I have no idea."

"Associate. Think three star. Seventy-three, Stargell. Three star. How many?"

"How many did he hit? Fifty?"

"Forty-four. Think Jerry West, number forty-four."

"I'd rather you didn't mention our talk just now to anyone."

"A ten spot? Mr. Scott, for you it's for nothin'."

"No. Please keep it."

"Awright, you insist."

"I do insist."

In his office Joan Leeky brought him his coffee, several phone messages, a white envelope with his name typed on it, and a clipping from the *Wall Street Journal*. The heading read:

DIMENSION CORP. PLANS
PROXY CONTEST TO CONTROL
BII ON WEST COAST

Scott put the clipping down and opened the envelope. He read:

Mr. Lancaster
Mr. Powell
Mr. Scott

Mr. Breedlove has telephoned to say he will not attend today's 11 A.M. meeting of the board of directors of Breedlove International, Incorporated. He has asked that you proceed with the meeting. He has also asked that I attend the meeting and send its minutes to him.

Henriette Tompkins

Henriette Tompkins

"Uptight day," Scott said to Joan.
"Yes, sir."
"I'm not in this morning."
"Yes, sir."

He closed the drapes and sat sealed in his office, his fingers drumming his desk. The coffee grew cold. He rose and paced briefly, his hands behind his back. Then he sat down, drew out the photos the old bellman of Olen had given him, and peered closely at them. Again the presence and spirit of Lewis Breedlove hovered around him, a powerful, haunting force that seemed to hold him frozen, impeding his actions and thoughts. Finally, with a decisive movement, he picked up the phone and pushed the security extension. A man's voice answered immediately.

"This is Mark Scott. Is Mr. Ackerson there?"

"Ackerson," a voice said a second or two later. When Scott hesitated, the voice said, "Mr. Scott? What can I do for you?"

"Well, you may remember the incident a while back with my wife's car."

"Yes, sir. I do."

"That was in the realm of a personal favor, and now I have another to ask of you."

"Anything I can do, Mr. Scott."

"It is very personal. Is this recorded?"

"I'll turn off the recorder."

"It's a license number," Scott said after a pause. "Can you trace license numbers?"

"Sure. That's easy."

"I have only a partial, I'm afraid."

"Was this an accident, sir? Hit and run?"

"Something like that. I have the letters. LGN. And the first two numbers. Seven and then four. I believe it was four."

"What make of car?"

"A Volkswagen."

"What year?"

"I'm afraid all Vokswagens look alike to me."

"Can't blame you for that, Mr. Scott. I can trace this through Motor Vehicles, but with a digit missing and another uncertain, it will take quite a bit of running down. Is it a high priority item, Mr. Scott?"

"It is personal, as I explained."

"I'll go to work on it and I'll be back to you on it. It may take several days, Mr. Scott."

"May I ask you to keep it confidential?"

"If I can, sir."

He hung up. Immediately he wished that he had not called. Ackerson's voice had seemed impersonal, far away, almost mechanical. He was as unknown a quantity to Scott as Nathan Bowler, his boss. He could not even recall Ackerson's face. A man who wore a hat. That much he recalled. His private line rang.

"Yes?"

"Oh, Mr. Scott. This is Ackerson. I'm sorry. I forgot to ask. Were they California plates?"

"California? Yes. Of course."

"You're certain?"

"Well, I—"

"Thank you, sir. We'll proceed on the assumption the plates were California."

He went to the meeting in a semi-daze. It was the first meeting of directors he could recall that Breedlove had not attended. Breedlove's chair had been removed; no one sat at the head of the table. Miss Tompkins sat at the stenographer's table, an assistant at her side. She did not look at Scott. Powell rose. He looked at Scott.

"Mr. Breedlove telephoned me and Mr. Lancaster this morning," he said. "He asked me to present a plan for calling the preferred and Mr. Lancaster to outline promotion plans for a new product in our Drug Division."

"Wait," Scott said. Heads turned. He felt slightly foolish. "Nothing. Go on. It's nothing, George."

"Thank you." Powell handed out blue folders. "The plan is not entirely self-explanatory, but, if you'll permit a minor speech, I believe I can fill in the blanks. Essentially, it proposes we call in the two-fifty convertible preferred stock, which, as you know, has voting rights. Each share we buy will be a plus vote for us in this proxy contest and remove a vote for the opponents." Powell paused. He drew out his pipe. To Scott, he seemed a vastly different George Powell—one more assured, poised, confident. He continued, "In addition, I propose we begin buying our shares on the exchange and retire them. This action, combined with the calling of the preferred, will result in an increase of approximately twenty-four percent in per share profits and perhaps forty percent in cash flow per share."

Scott's head snapped up. "It is my opinion that cash flow per share is a misleading figure. It is also the SEC's opinion."

"Scottie, who are you today?" Powell said. "The devil's advocate?" He didn't wait for a response. He went on, "We need all the leverage we can get in this matter. The income statement must look as good as we possibly can make it look for the next quarter."

"Not pumped up," Scott said.

"It will not be pumped up."

"We can fool the small shareholder, perhaps, but not the institutions and security analysts."

"Scottie, we're not trying to fool anyone."

Lancaster leaned back and smiled. "I'll buy George's plan without reading it," he said. "Will a voice vote do?"

It passed unanimously, with Scott abstaining. Powell discussed financial matters for a few more minutes. He said that in his opinion Philip Mendenthal was not open to compromise, and the proxy contest would go forward. He asked for suggestions on a law firm conversant with proxy contests; James Wright, the lawyer, said he'd draw up a list. Wright asked about the voting rights to the 830,000 BII shares owned by Brighton Manufacturing, and Powell responded that, although the matter didn't overly worry him, he was looking into it. Then Lancaster had the floor.

He was a master of the boardroom floor. His outline was eloquent. The Drug Division had been experimenting for several years with a new product, BII-2000; Lancaster described it as a breakthrough in blood anticoagulants. He had mastered its every technical detail. He outlined a marketing plan—blitz advertising in medical journals, a sales force hitting doctors and hospitals, all-out publicity. The division, after board approval, planned to introduce BII-2000 at a medical convention in Philadelphia next week. Test results, Lancaster said, were 98 percent positive.

"Now wait," Scott said. He was on his feet. The directors gazed at him. A child's face had arisen in his mind, a boy playing in Hyde Park in London in 1972, a boy with stubbed flippers for arms. He had been a victim of the drug thalidomide, a nontoxic tranquilizer often prescribed for morning sickness in pregnancies. Thalidomide had been thoroughly tested by manufacturer and distributor alike. They had found out everything about it except that it could produce abnormal babies. And so the thalidomide children had been born, hundreds of them, learning to write with their toes and ride bikes with their hands. He said, "We should table this until test results are one hundred percent positive."

"No," Lancaster said. "We need a striking announcement. We must show, right now, that our feet are not in concrete. This drug is safe. Our tests show that. The fed has okayed it."

"I'm against it. It could backfire all over us."

Lancaster issued a tiny animal's snarl through his curved upper lip. He spoke slowly, addressing the board. "When they tested the A-bomb in New Mexico, were they one hundred percent sure? They were not. Perhaps ninety-nine percent sure. But they did it, taking a one percent chance of a nuclear reaction that would kill everybody." He paused. He had his audience. "We can't afford the time to be one hundred percent safe now. These seats are at stake. That bunch of hijackers from New York has already half-convinced our stockholders that they can run this company. Any tactic by us is permissible now. Only one thing is important. That we win. Now I want a hunting license from you people. I have the analysis of this product. Detailed. Written down. Every member of the board will have the analysis before we adjourn. I'm not suggesting we vote on this matter now. But we should reconvene and vote before the convention in Philly. Then I want to go to Philly and announce this drug. I want to go all out on it. For headlines. I'm not afraid of BII-2000. I'd take it myself if the doctor prescribed it. The Drug Division is our white light, gentlemen. Last year, thirty-one point six percent net on sales, better than any other division by a mile. I want to make that white light even more brilliant."

"Hear, hear," Carter Mannering said.

It was Breedlove's custom to host a luncheon for directors in the executive dining room following board meetings. Scott could not recall an occasion when any of the fifteen had not stayed. Today, however, all but six seemed to have plans, even Carter Mannering.

"Be seein' you on the Late Show," he told Scott. "Tonight we hit 'em with *Home in Indiana*. Nothin' moves a Chevy like that movie. Shown it twenty-eight times."

"I've been meaning to tell you that my son Tod wants your autograph. You rate with Steve Garvey and Joe Namath."

"C'mon down. I'll give him an elephant ride."

"I'll do that."

"Well, gonna run," Mannering said. "Hank and I are lunchin' at Perino's. Entrée is skewered Mendenthal."

The directors who stayed for lunch avoided business discussion, preferring to talk about the Dodgers or the weather. Among those staying was Clemson Hawley, the retired banker. He was Anne's favorite BII director and had been a friendly personal and business adviser to Scott for years. He was a lifelong bachelor, seventy-two years old, who divided his time between business consulting and horse breeding. Hawley had been with Breedlove for decades. His stomach was flat, his voice was strong, his hair was thick and white. He sat by Scott at lunch, lauding the merits of old Seabiscuit and undermining Seattle Slew.

"Sometimes I think I'm the oldest of living old stuff in the world," he told Scott as they left the dining room. "I'm still living in the '20s, which, by the way, is where I want to live. You didn't have to stock cannons to protect your business then. First Powell almost gets a haircut with a helicopter blade, then bombs go off all around."

"Well, the Powell incident was just an accident, Clem. Don't you think so?"

"I'm not sure." Hawley pulled himself up to his full five-five height. "You scared, Scottie?"

"Hell, yes, I am. First I go through it in Olen and then I saw it in Columbus. It was like a war zone there."

"How does Anne feel? Scared, too?"

"I've shielded most of it from her."

*   *   *

At 2 P.M. Miss Tompkins circulated a second memo to directors. They were invited to dinner at Mr. Breedlove's home on Saturday. Cocktails at 6 P.M., dinner at 7 P.M. An addition to the memo appeared an hour later. It was an apology from Miss Tompkins for failing to state that the dinner was formal. Scott could not recall a time in the past when Miss Tompkins had made an error, even of omission.

"Formal?" Anne said at dinner. "Any more surprises?"

"Not now. One at a time."

"I can tell you had a bad day. You're uptight."

"Clem Hawley says hello."

"We haven't seen him for quite a while. I'll have him over for dinner soon."

"You'll see him Saturday night."

"I've never seen him in a tux. Somehow, Clem isn't the tuxedo type."

"Remember that he's on the Nominating Committee."

"What's the Nominating Committee?"

"They nominate officers for various posts. They give recommendations to the board."

"Who else is on it?"

"Well, Breedlove, for one. Actually, it's a committee of Breedlove, Breedlove, and Breedlove. But the others do count. Some."

She touched his hand. "Let's not talk business."

"I'm really too tired to talk about anything."

"I noticed. I've also noticed that you're getting home later and later. Tod and Liz are in bed already. Mike got parboiled on the beach again today."

"He can't take the sun. Like me."

"Will you talk to him tonight?"

"Why tonight?"

"Because I think you've been ignoring him. He thinks so, too."

"He's the one who's been ignoring me."

"Oh," Anne said, pulling her hand away from his. "My two eldest boys. One is a man-boy, the other is a boy-man."

"All right. I'll talk to him."

"I wish you'd realize you've been disappointing him. He

needs you. He's defensive now because he's hurt. When did you last take him away? Just the two of you?"

"Don't lecture me, Anne. Not now."

"I'm not lecturing. I'm only trying to tell you that if you don't do something about it, and pretty damn soon, you're going to lose him."

"You're exaggerating."

"Talk to him."

"I will."

He rapped on Mike's bedroom door. No response. He opened the door slowly. Mike lay on his stomach on his bed in his pajama bottoms. Light from a lamp over his desk reflected on the bright red skin of his back.

"Visitors welcome?" Scott said.

"Oh. When'd you get home?"

"An hour ago. I see you had too much sun again."

"I went to sleep on the beach."

"You'd better start avoiding that beach."

"Where else can a guy go?"

"I seem to remember you went to Miami not too very long ago."

"Yeah," Mike said.

"What does that mean?"

"Yeah. It means yeah."

"Sit up."

"It hurts."

Scott felt a stab of hurt in himself. "Before you go back to school, I'll take some time off. That sound okay? We'll go up to Big Bear."

"Sure."

"We'll get in some fishing."

"Sure."

"Do you want to talk?"

"Talk about what?"

"About anything. Sports."

"I'm not so big on sports any more."

Scott sat down on the edge of the bed. Mike didn't move. Scott touched his back, lightly, and Mike winced. Scott felt a surge of despair, almost of helplessness. Anne was right. A distance had grown between him and Mike, that of a son with developing teen problems inconsequential in the stream of history but colossal to him now and a father too busy, with too many demands, and, at this time, too obsessed with and dominated by the race of the world, its ambitions and office politics and crazed, headlong rush to ulcerated intestines and premature coronary thrombosis. Once they had been very close, the boy who admired and emulated his dad, the dad puffed with pride as he watched the miracle of a being that emerged from crib imprisonment to crawling and walking and then to boyhood and, finally, to the questioning and frustration and limbo of not-manhood, not-boyhood. Scott remembered it in himself—the first burst of puberty, the first date, the first love rivalry, the pals, the gang, the belonging, and also the problems and disappointments so massive and overwhelming. He remembered it in his father's house. His father had always been there. Now he had a son to get back. How should he go about it? Slowly. In stages. The distance between them, he realized, had become too great to overtake in a single stride.

"We could go up to Big Bear on Thursday," he said.

"If you want."

"Do you want to?"

"It'd be okay."

"Just okay?"

"It'd be fine. If you want to go."

Looking at Mike, Scott felt a surge of love. He wanted to hold his son, to make promises about family outings, Disneyland, and vacation trips together. But he didn't. He couldn't. He spoke rapidly.

"I'll bust away from the office for a couple of days. We'll go alone, just the two of us."

"Well, maybe not this week," Mike said. "I'm supposed to stay over at Tommy's house."

"Who is Tommy?"

"Friend of mine."

"How old is he?"

"Seventeen."

"Isn't that a little old for you?"

"Dunno."

"Well, you think it over. Big Bear, I mean."

"All right," Mike said. He hadn't looked up.

*   *   *

They sat on the sofa, his arm around her, letting their coffee get cold. Anne had lit the fire, the first time they had used the fireplace in months. The drapes were open. Moonbeams danced across the ocean.

"We used to dream about this," she said.

"I remember."

"I think we're spoiled. We don't enjoy it enough."

"Maybe we are."

"Are you going to take Mike away for a while?"

"I hope to. This week. Apparently it's up to someone named Tommy."

"Tommy? Oh, that boy who was over here last week. You didn't see him. His hair is longer than mine. I'm going to try to discourage that relationship."

"Because the boy has long hair?"

"I can't explain it. But there's something about that boy I don't trust. Besides, he's too old for Mike."

"Are you being overprotective?"

"Yes. I'm overreacting and overprotective."

"Now you're overdoing."

"I think I'll go to bed," she said, stiffening.

"You just lit the fire."

"You can stay and look at it. I'm going to bed."

"All right. I'll read."

"There's something I have to tell you, too. You're not the only one who has news. I have news, too."

"What is it?"

"We're pregnant again," Anne said, touching her stomach.

"All right," he said.

"All right? So calmly?"

"Yes."

"Are you happy about it?"

"Of course. Aren't you?"

"I don't know. I really don't. I see little Anne sitting home again, watching her belly swell. Come to think of it, I wonder when it happened."

"What is that supposed to mean?"

"We haven't exactly been—well . . . together—too much lately. It seems you've been too busy, working late. I thought at first it might have been in Olen in July. But, no, it was

later. Mark?" She turned to him, reaching out, and he held
her gently. She was trembling. After a while she said, "I think
I'll try out some amateur psychology on you. I really think I
got knocked up by my own design."

"How so?"

"So I could protect myself from the world. Or so I could
keep you."

"You can keep me, pregnant or not."

"But maybe I can't. You're my security blanket."

"I want to be."

"Provider."

"I want to be."

"I'm calmer now. The fire is good."

"Come home," he said.

"I'm home," Anne said.

20

BUT HE DIDN'T TAKE MIKE TO BIG BEAR. ON TUESDAY THE
board voted 13 to 2 to announce the availability of BII-2000
at the medical convention. Scott and Hawley voted against it,
asking for more time; Breedlove, in absentia, voted "yea"
through Miss Tompkins. Scott found himself in a blue funk.
It was aggravated by a developing labor dispute at a plant in
Kansas. He found himself with plane tickets to Topeka. "Oh,
Topeka, high excitement there," Lancaster told him. "If you
have some free time at night, I recommend you go out and
watch the Safeway trucks unload. And if the labor negotiators walk out on you during the day, take a bus downtown
and watch the locals getting haircuts." Scott didn't respond.
He went to the airport. Alone. With his briefcase. He called
Anne on Thursday.

"I let Mike stay overnight with that Tommy," she said.
"Against my better judgment."

"I'll be home tomorrow night."

"I have my new formal for the party."

"It's not really a party."

"No. I suppose it's not."

"Will you meet me at the airport?"

"Of course."

"Take care of yourself."

"Mark?"

"Yes?"

"Oh, Christ," she said.

Each time he wore his tuxedo, it seemed to become a little tighter around the waist. Now, late Saturday afternoon in their bedroom, he found he had to squeeze in hard to get the trousers on. The jacket was tight, too. A tap came on the door. Liz bounced in, dressed in shoulder-strap overalls.

"It's for you," she said. "Phone."

"Oh. I'll take it in here."

"You missed the game."

"Little League? I'm afraid I did."

"I finally got into a game. I got in the third inning. I dropped a fly, I struck out, and we lost twenty-three to two. So you didn't miss much. Tod, he hit a triple but it went only to the pitcher. The pitcher threw it into right field and the right fielder threw it over second base and the shortstop got it to the pitcher who was at third base then but Tod was already there, stand-up triple off the pitcher's glove. Mike's got cigarettes in his room. But they're not his. I'm not tattling. They're that Tommy's. You look good in a black suit. The baby-sitter's here already. I hope Mom eats a lot tonight."

"Is that all you have to say?"

"I'm done."

"Why do you hope Mom eats a lot?"

"She's eating for two."

"Oh. She told you about that."

"I could use a sister. Why do they call it baby-sitter when we're not babies any more?"

"We'll just call her sitter," Scott said, reaching for the phone.

"He," Liz said. "He's cute, too."

The call was from Ackerson of BII security. "I'm sorry to bother you at home, and on a Saturday, Mr. Scott, but I did want you to know that we traced that license number."

"Thank you for calling. I'd almost forgotten about that."

Ackerson hesitated. "Look, Mr. Scott. I'm not quite sure I should give you this information."

"Why not?"

"Did you say you had an accident with a Volkswagen?"

"Never mind about that. Just tell me why you think I shouldn't have the information."

"This is one helluva coincidence. Was the driver of the Volks a black man?"

"No. White. Male. Middle-aged."

"I'm sorry, Mr. Scott, but I'd better discuss this with Mr. Lancaster before I—"

"Why Lancaster?"

"He's been placed in charge of security. Mr. Breedlove's orders."

"I want to make it clear to you that Lancaster has no more overall authority in this company than I. Now I want this information you have. I want it immediately. I don't care who you report to or what you tell Lancaster. Or even what you tell Breedlove. But I want the information."

"All right, Mr. Scott. If you'll take the responsibility."

"I will."

"The car is registered to Mr. Breedlove's chauffeur. A man named Morris."

"You're sure?"

"I ran this one twice, Mr. Scott. I spent two days personally verifying it."

"All right. Thank you."

"You asked me to keep this matter confidential. I'm afraid now I won't be able to do that, Mr. Scott. It's simply too much of a coincidence to dismiss out of hand."

"I would prefer that you do keep it confidential."

"I'm sorry, Mr. Scott. I'll have to make a report to my boss and to Mr. Lancaster."

Scott snapped the receiver down.

At twilight Arbor Road seemed darker than other streets, enclosed in a private and premature shroud that descended almost perceptibly from the blended shadows of houses and walls and palms and oaks. In late summer a chill came to the air with dusk, and absolute silence seemed to prevail until the darkness was complete. Tonight wisps of fog crept along the curbs, rising in thin yellow patches that obscured the houses and clung like dirty smoke to the tops of the streetlamps. Scott turned on the headlights as the Buick approached the outer brick wall fronting the Breedlove residence. He'd been there only twice. Anne had never been there.

"Hi," he said.

"Hi."

"Why the silent treatment?"

"I've been rehearsing my C.W.E."

"All right. I'll bite. What is C.W.E.?"

"Corporate wife etiquette. If someone asks my political preference, I say, 'Republican, front row.' 'What do you think of the welfare state, Mrs. Scott?' 'Worries me to death, sir. Why do you think I have these hives?' 'And what is your view on the encroachments of big government on free enterprise?' 'It renders me ill and weak-kneed.' 'And what about big labor, Mrs. Scott? Does big labor worry you?' 'Worry me? Oh, sir, it is the principal cause of my persistent insomnia.' I shall wander around this evening with programmed answers and a mechanical smile. Oh. You forgot to wind me up."

"I think I know what your real problem is. I think you're nervous about tonight."

"I am. If you want the truth. Very much."

"Well," Scott said. "Here's a mystery."

"What is a mystery?"

"There's a guard at the gate. That's new."

The guard wore an unmarked blue uniform. A .38 was strapped into his holster. "Yes, sir," he said. "Good evening." Scott handed him the invitation. The guard made a check on a list of names attached to a clipboard. "Just drive ahead, Mr. Scott, and the boy will take your car," he said.

The "boy" was an elderly black in a red jacket. Several cars were parked in the driveway, neatly arranged about two feet apart, their hoods turned toward Arbor. Scott recognized Lancaster's Cadillac. He took Anne's arm and guided her up the cement walk to the door.

Anne lifted her dress at the knee. "There are no dogs. No wolfhounds. And where is the moat?"

They paused at the door, looking for a bell or knocker, but it proved unnecessary; the door opened before them and a stiff, unsmiling Scoggins beckoned them in. Scott heard the tinkle of feminine laughter. The hall was brightly lit from an overhead chandelier. Scoggins moved slowly away.

"Do you suppose he'll announce us?" Anne whispered.

"Of course."

She made a stern face. " 'Mr. and Mrs. Mark Scott, the third of a president Scotts—' "

"Stop teasing."

Lewis Breedlove's guests were assembled in what was now called the art room. The room fascinated Scott. Its immense walls laden with artworks and high domed ceiling reminded him of a cathedral. It was sparsely furnished with a few high-backed chairs, a modern couch that didn't seem to fit in, and some highly polished walnut tables laden with flower vases and statuettes. The carpet was a simple green nylon. The upward-slanting walks that led to the paintings were lighted by pale fluorescent fixtures built into the wall. The rest of the area was lighted by two chandeliers dangling from long cords. The guests were grouped in threes and fours. Already the wives had separated from their husbands; it was the beginning of the mixing hour. Each group contained at least one man and one woman. The women had fresh hairdos and manicures and, undoubtedly, new formals. They all wore jewelry; none, however, wore anything ostentatious or pretentious. The light was pale. No spot was cruel to complexions. Grave waiters in maroon vests served cocktails and sedate elderly maids in uniforms with crisscross shoulder straps offered caviar-on-pumpernickel hors d'oeuvres from silver platters. A strolling accordionist moved amid the assemblage, as anonymous and inconspicuous as the furnishings. Scott helped Anne down the four carpeted steps into the room. It had rendered her speechless. Her eyes were wide and bright.

"I'll be go to hell," she whispered.

Lewis Breedlove disengaged himself from a circle of tuxedos and gowns and moved slowly toward them. He shook Scott's hand firmly. His cheeks were sunken and sallow, but there was a bright twinkle in his eyes.

"Anne, you outshine them all," he said.

"Thank you for that little white lie, Mr. Breedlove."

"I've told lies, white ones and very black ones, but I meant it when I said that. Scottie, get yourself a drink. You look tense as a tightrope. I'll take charge of Anne for you."

Heads turned as they advanced on the groupings, Breedlove holding Anne's arm. Carter Mannering stood a head taller than anyone, resplendent in a frilled silk shirt and a velvet jacket without lapels. Lancaster, sipping a Beefeater-rocks and nibbling caviar, held sway over his group. Susan

Powell stood by his arm. She was not drinking. She smiled and offered Scott her hand.

"Scottie, why so grim?" Lancaster said. "Is it the Topeka blues?"

"Something like that."

"How did it go there?"

"Fair. At least the workers didn't strike."

"You gave them the keep-'em-in contract. Like Olen."

Scott stirred uneasily. "I'm not sure I understand."

"The back-to-work, give-'em-everything settlement."

"Hank, you make sure the goods are sold. I'll make sure we have the workers."

"At what price?" Lancaster said. Then he smiled.

Susan Powell touched Scott's arm. "Anne looks lovely," she said.

Scott smiled at her, feeling grateful for her intervention. He did not know her well, perhaps less than any other wife of a BII officer or director (thinking now, *We know none of them well, the men or their women; we know them only by face and gesture and speech, only the surface of them*). He and Anne had been invited to the Powells' house only once, a dinner of couples who were all strangers to them, and the Powells had been to their Palos Verdes home also only once, a Saturday beach luncheon that had been spoiled by rain and shortened by a call to Susan from her daughter. Like George, Susan seemed reticent and withdrawn in groups—at least, in company-member groups. Perhaps expression was a form of exposure, a risk they had agreed not to take. Scott had never heard either of them disagree with anyone, or express an opinion on a subject of controversy. His image of Susan Powell was that of a proud lady, perhaps from a wealthy or at least well-to-do family, who managed her household efficiently and perhaps exercised a firm influence on her husband. Tonight she seemed somewhat thinner than when he'd last seen her, two months ago at a plant reception in Sacramento. Perhaps her dark gown made her appear trimmer. She wore a simple gold-chain necklace and a gold bracelet clustered with small rubies. Her wedding ring seemed embedded in the folds of her skin. It was not a modest diamond but neither was it what Anne would categorize as a horse-choker.

Lancaster drifted to another group. Scott hoped he wasn't

expected to take charge of the abandoned one. He flowed with it, chitchatting, after securing a vodka martini from one of the waiters. He searched for Anne but could not find her. George Powell stood on the edge of one group, a glass in his hand. When Scott tried to catch his eye, Powell turned away. Scott sipped his martini, feeling restless and ill at ease. He was thinking of Lawrence Breedlove. He was thinking of Morris, the chauffeur. He was thinking of Lewis Breedlove. He looked at the walls, at the artworks, at the banistered walks jutting out like scaffolding; he looked at the high domed ceiling, the glass chandeliers dangling from thin metal cords like huge godheads, at the massive gray drapes that shielded them from the outside world. Quite suddenly, he did not like this house of Lewis Breedlove. It seemed gloomy and depressing, almost chilling. What scenes had played to its walls? Scott wanted to know. The last scene, he realized, had yet to be played; when it did begin, he probably would have a part in it.

For a reason he could not articulate to himself, the prospect almost frightened him.

Then he was thinking of Theresa Breedlove. He'd never met her; he'd never even seen a photograph of her. Others at BII undoubtedly had known her, but, if so, few mentioned it. No one from the company except Breedlove had attended her funeral, not even Miss Tompkins. BII did not encourage personal relationships between the families of executives; besides, Theresa Breedlove had commanded a status impenetrable to the wife of any other executive. There was a rumble around the office of an open dispute, a confrontation, between Breedlove and an unidentified man at the grave site, but the rumble quickly disappeared. Lewis Breedlove's wife was soon forgotten; it was as if she had not existed. Breedlove never spoke of her to associates.

The waiter pressed a second vodka martini into Scott's hand. The first had been a strong one; it had gone rapidly to his head. He reminded himself that he was a three-drink man, and, since Breedlove undoubtedly would serve wine with dinner, he decided he'd have no more. No one, in fact, was drinking much. It was not a dinner party but a skirmish, a maneuvering for position and favor, and it would be unwise to fog the mind with too much liquor. Scott could not recall a time in the past when Breedlove had issued a summons for the simultaneous appearance of all BII directors and their wives. The dinner had a business purpose, to be sure. Breedlove seldom made a move without a business purpose in mind. Already, Scott noticed, a pattern had formed. Each member of the Nominating Committee stood in a different group. Clemson Hawley was in Powell's group. Breedlove was in Lancaster's. And now joining Scott's was Robert Menlo, the third member of the committee and BII's vice-president–production. Menlo's huge face was damp with perspiration. Breedlove many times in executive sessions—and once in a memo—had made it clear that he preferred his subordinates to stay trim, but somehow Menlo had managed to survive despite his obesity. He even joked about it. Once at a board meeting he'd shown Scott a cartoon of a stereotyped hog-faced capitalist squatted like a Buddha clutching locomotives and steamers and had claimed, without breaking into a smile, that he'd modeled for it. His suit size, he said, was "eighty-four, stubby."

"I can read your mind," he told Scott. "You're thinking you'd rather be home."

"That's pretty close. Where did you learn to read minds?"

"To survive in this outfit, it's necessary." Menlo glanced around. "This house hasn't seen so many people at once since Theresa died."

"Now I know you're a mind reader. I was thinking about her a little while ago."

"Theresa was quite a woman."

"Tell me about her."

"She was the daughter of a banker named Sanderson. About as high a society as you had here in those days. Before he married her, she was a sparkler. Bathtub gin. Cords. She ran around with a bootlegger. Breedlove met her, through her father, and broke her like a horse."

"She had a son. Lawrence."

"He was not her son."

"I don't understand."

"He was Breedlove's, at least in Lawrence's early years. Breedlove took him to mold. It is very likely that Lawrence was Breedlove's only failure."

"What happened?"

"You tell me what happened." Menlo shrugged. "Either Breedlove pressed the boy too much or wasn't around enough to watch him. I don't know the answer."

A glowing presence floated into their circle—Dorothy Lancaster in a light blue gown, a fair golden goddess embodied in their midst, scented of lilac and exuding woman. She stood breathing. The group hushed, a hush broken by a sharp handclap behind them.

"Let's eat," Lewis Breedlove said.

Dorothy took Menlo's arm.

It was said around the office that Breedlove had an enviable wine cellar, but the dinner showed no evidence of it. The red was a tart Burgundy; the white was a dry Riesling. They were dispensed from decanters by Scoggins and two assistants into crystal glasses each worth perhaps five times the cost of a bottle of the wine. Scott was no wine connoisseur, but he took his cue from Menlo, the only board member who probably was a true gourmet. Menlo refused the wine, saying he was on a diet. The food also was quite plain—lobster or steak, or, if desired, a sampling of both. The vegetables were zucchini and asparagus, served from a silver bowl.

No one sat at the head of the table. Breedlove sat at its center, his shrunken body almost lost in his chair, between Anne and Susan Powell. The place cards had been arranged in a man-woman sequence, and no director sat beside his wife. Scott found himself between the mellow glow of Dorothy Lancaster and the melancholy presence of Martha Welles, wife of S. Timothy Welles, head of Farm Machinery. Welles was the executive whose "insane" report had cut Scott's Olen trip short. The report had seemed sane enough to Scott, but to placate Breedlove he'd asked Welles to revise it.

The accordionist disappeared in favor of a stereo system that piped in strains of a dreary Mendelssohn opus. Mendelssohn was not a favorite of Scott's, although he loved classical music. He and Anne had season tickets to the Los Angeles Philharmonic, but in the past two years Scott had heard only one concert. Anne had taken a friend, or one of the kids, to the ones Scott had missed, owing to company demands or trips.

The dinner proceeded amid chitchat between small groups.

The size of the table made it difficult to talk across it, and impossible to talk from end to end. Breedlove ate silently; his guests ate obediently. In the middle of the meal, Breedlove paused to light a Lucky Strike. His sunken eyes glowed. Yellow blotches covered his hands. Anne huddled beside Breedlove, looking lost and uncomfortable. Breedlove snubbed out the cigarette in an ashtray Scoggins had brought. He coughed, stopping individual conversations, sipped water from a large crystal glass, and resumed eating. The conversations started again. Dorothy Lancaster began to chat quietly with Scott about the movies. She recommended *Last Tango in Paris,* calling it a work of art.

"If you do see it, promise yourself you'll see it at least twice," she said. "You don't get its impact the first time around. You can still catch it occasionally at an art theater."

The only movies Scott saw were those on airplanes, and he usually tuned them out, preferring to work. Once in a while, Liz and Tod trapped him into taking them to a Disney picture.

"I'll confess," Dorothy said. "I've seen *Tango* fourteen times."

"I understand there's a famous butter scene," Scott said.

Dorothy smiled. Her eyes were very bright and deep blue, reflecting mirthful innocence. "Oh, yes," she said. "The butter scene. When the movie opened in London, BBC interviewed people leaving the theater. 'A frightful waste of butter,' said one matronly type." She laughed, her head back. She looked at Scott seriously, almost conspiratorially. "Oh, I'll admit it. I do like the movies. So cool and dark in the theaters. You can be a child again. I guess I'm talking too much. Hank is frowning at me."

Scott detected a small snort issued by Martha Welles. The girlish quality filtering through Dorothy's outward sensuality put him at ease in her presence. Occasionally her eyes grew distant. Once she stopped in the middle of a sentence and looked away in a lonely contemplation that seemed almost sad. Scott wondered if she was role playing. It was possible. Perhaps all of them played roles. Scoggins moved about, his face somber, his assistants following like animated mannequins. Mrs. Lamson, the pale-faced cook, darted in and out as if she were inspecting the success of her production. Martha Welles, a large woman with impeccable manners and a haughty air, occasionally glanced behind her with an almost fearful look, as if she expected to see an assassin creeping up with a knife between his teeth. Menlo's round face was like a red balloon. Carter Mannering was serious. Lancaster, perhaps concerned because his position was so distant from Breedlove, appeared strained as he tried to converse with the women to his right and left. Powell tapped his pipe on the table—a small, tentative tap, as if to ask permission to light it. Hawley sat silently. It came to Scott that Hawley seldom spoke to Breedlove. Sometimes Breedlove singled Hawley out for teasing and intimidation at board meetings, and Hawley always took it without response. Finally it was over. The assemblage headed back to the art room.

"Mark, you've been sittin' with a grin on your face all evenin'," Mannering said. "It's time you let us in on the joke."

"It's our private one," Dorothy said, taking Scott's arm.

"Ma'm, if I'd been placed beside you, I'd be happy, too."

"But remember that her bills come with the package," Lancaster said.

Menlo opened a roll of Tums and drew Scott aside. "You try bouncing that lobster? I swear it would bounce if you tried it."

Scott glanced around, trying to locate Breedlove. He could not. The party apparently had lost its host. Were they now expected to gather their wives and head for their cars? He glanced at his watch. A quarter after nine. Small groups again had formed, this time man-man groups and woman-woman groups; they stood almost in huddle formation, as if they were discussing what to do next. When Anne returned, Clemson Hawley took her arm and guided her up the walk to view the paintings. Menlo slumped down on the couch, where Susan Powell joined him. Scoggins entered, followed by his assistants, who carried brandy and snifters on a tray. So it was not over. They were expected to stay. He looked up at Anne and Hawley, hoping she wouldn't discuss politics with him. Anne was gesturing. Hawley turned away from her. Had it started? Scott looked at the high ceiling. He glanced down the length of the vast gray drapes. He felt mild dizziness. He wanted to leave. Get Anne. Go home. Take a few days off. Take Mike away. But he didn't move. He accepted a brandy from Scoggins. Glancing at the paintings, he searched for one that might be a Rembrandt.

Powell came toward him. "He wants to see us," he said.

"Breedlove?"

"You, Hank, me," Powell said. "Right now."

Clem held Anne's arm. "Let's snoop around," he said. "There are ghosts here."

"Ghosts?"

"Well, one ghost, at least."

"Frankly, I'm looking for the john."

"That shouldn't be a problem. There must be a dozen of them in this ancient palace. Try any door."

Clem's eyes seemed distant. He turned his attention to a Homer seascape. They had traversed the length of the art walks and were on the upper-level balcony. The dinner guests milled below. A series of doors greeted Anne, extending down the hall equal distances apart. The doors were stained dark brown, identical with the color of the carpet, and had gold-plated knobs. She tried the first one, pushing inward, and found herself in a large bedroom bathed in a dull green hue, a reflection off the walls from the light in the hallway. Anne peered around, intrigued by the furnishings. There was a Louis XVI table of delicate tulipwood, a veneered mahogany commode, and side tables of lavish gilt brass. The bed was surmounted by a silk canopy. Anne stepped forward. The green light cast soft, irregular shadows on the furnishings and floor, forming patterns at once attractive and eerie. She felt a chill. Turning, she walked rapidly out.

"What's wrong?" Clem said.

"When you mentioned ghosts, I guess you weren't kidding. I felt cold in there, almost like there was a presence."

"It was the rain. The wind."

"I don't know. But that room seemed creepy."

"The first door?"

"Yes."

"Oh. The green room," Clem said. "Theresa's room."

"Breedlove's wife?"

He nodded. They were back on the art walk, Clem again

holding her arm. He changed the subject. "Anne, most of me wants to see somebody like Mark go to the top in this outfit, but some of me says that if I'm really his friend I'll try to keep him away from it."

"Why do you say that?"

"Because there's something sick about this company. It goes way back. That room you saw. I think I pointed you to it on purpose. It's part of the sickness."

"I'm beginning to think you knew her quite well. I'm beginning to think you have quite a past, Clem."

"The past is gone. It's best not to think about it."

"Now you've aroused my curiosity."

"Only to let you down," Clem said. "I get a couple drinks in me, I talk too much."

Breedlove sat in his den, slumped in a big leather-covered easy chair before the blazing fireplace. He'd taken off his jacket and shoes, replacing them with a robe and slippers. A stuffed eagle with outspread wings perched on the mantel. Its eyes seemed alive, glistening in the dancing firelight. Scott paused, startled by Breedlove's appearance. The old man looked like a withered gnome, wheezing and puffing, deep creases slashed across his face, his eyes buried in puffy sockets. An open package of Lucky Strikes and a water pitcher with glasses were on a small table by his side. Within his reach was a larger table with a red telephone and his hourglass. He glanced up, his eyes quickly flashing to life, his thin hands gesturing.

"I trust you three will apologize to your ladies for my display of bad manners in taking you away, but I think they're more comfortable when I'm not around anyway," he said. "These asses I've hired who pass as doctors have me on sixteen pills after meals, and it takes a while for me to recover from the poison. Scottie, take your jacket off. I like it hot, a preview of my afterlife, but you don't have to stand and sweat because of that. Hank? George? Make yourselves comfortable."

But no one removed his jacket. Outside, the wind had increased and Scott heard the tentative beginnings of rain. Powell took out his pipe. Lancaster secured a spot near the fireplace to Breedlove's left. He touched the antlers of a giant elk's head.

"I'd tell you I shot that elk, but I got enough of a reputation as a black liar already," Breedlove said. He turned to Scott. "Imagine you're alone in the woods and a bear gets after you. Do you pray for strength for yourself or for that bear to have a heart attack?"

"I think this is an old one," Scott said. "You pray to God like this: 'Please, God, I'm not asking for help because I'm in a tight spot, but I am asking You not to help that bear.'"

Breedlove lit a Lucky with a stick match. He seemed relaxed and loose. "Well, maybe we're all in a little bit of a tight spot now," he said. "George, you've been looking a little peaked. Are you still shook up from the helicopter accident in New York?"

"It was unnerving, yes," Powell said.

"Well, I want you to try and forget it. Accidents do happen."

"Then you think it was an accident?" Lancaster said.

"Of course," Breedlove said.

"I'll tell you this. If there are some assholes out there looking for us, I pity the poor bastard who comes after me."

"I don't think they'd try you, Hank," Breedlove said. "These people pick on the weak links."

"I welcome them to try me," Lancaster said.

Breedlove waved his hand. "I want to assure you all that I am working hard on this situation," he said. "It may take me a little more time, but I will end it. I don't want any of you meddling in it. You have important work to do for this company. I consider these attacks my business, my personal business, and I will handle the matter. And one other thing. If I assure you that our airplane is safe, it is safe. Scottie, do I talk too much?"

"No, of course not."

"Well, you tell me if I talk too much. I want to switch the subject to you now." Breedlove straightened his shoulders. He peered at Scott. "You have a fault," he said. "Now, I could tell you this when we're alone, but I think it's going to be more effective if I tell you in front of these other two. Your fault is that you're too nice. You're too good a person to be totally effective in the decision maker's chair. You may be starting to live, breathe, eat, and sleep the Breedlove company, but that's not enough. I have your report on Olen. You gave away too much to those workers there. It could set a precedent. Now, I know you had your back to the wall there, but, later on, in Topeka, you turned right around and did the same fucking thing."

"May I have a minute to explain?"

"Let me finish. I know your value. As I've told you before, I'm not going to try to explain to you now what I think that value is. I selected you for this job, along with the other two here, because I saw that value. As I see my own job now, I'm a picker. A picker of people. There are book pickers, stock pickers, pickers of artists, and I am a picker of people of executive ability and who's right for what jobs at various times."

"And you've never made a mistake?"

"A fair question, Scottie, and I respect you for having the guts to ask it. I'll answer. The answer is no."

"Never?"

"Not any more. I've been wrong in the past, but I've profited from the mistakes. Now I'm wrong no longer. What I'm telling you is that you're going to have to get tougher. If you don't, these two here are going to grind you up. Here's the way the world is, Scottie. It's a world of groups and units in the groups. Call the units a series of families. The mobsters are in families, highly organized. The hippies are in families. So are the unions, the politicians, the preachers. So are we, the companies. Our goal is to protect ourselves and to grow. All groups and families within them run almost constantly in antagonism with each other. So it's a fight, one bareknuckled and bloody. Some groups cheat, so others have to cheat. Some of that may be changing, but it won't change for long. The all-important to us is our family. When you give in, you cheat yourself and the family. You might save a few jobs in a place like Olen, Wisconsin, but by doing it you jeopardize other jobs in the company. Scottie, you've been around too long at the top for me to have to lecture you about these things. But your actions lately indicate you haven't learned it all hard enough. Recently I sent the three of you away. Lancaster comes back with a new agency and a new advertising program. Powell brings back important information about the proxy fight we're up against. You go to see about a plant closing. You come back without a recommendation and with only information that you gave the workers a fat employment contract."

Scott turned away, fighting anger. His jaw tightened.

He heard Breedlove say, "All right, Scottie. I'll tell you something. I've got you good and pissed off. You have a choice. You can march your ass out of here now or you can stay. Stay and show your stuff." Scott turned back. Breedlove was not looking at him. He was looking at Lancaster. "Hank," he said. "Did you like the dinner?"

"Is it my turn on the carpet?" Lancaster said.

Breedlove had become more animated. His hands waved. There was color in his cheeks. He shook his hourglass.

"I want to say something to you all," he said. "You will not see much of me in the future, but I am here. As long as I can open one eye, I'll be here. This thing was pass. I have never been sick and I will not be sick now. It is a matter of mind, sickness. When I say in my mind I am not sick, I will not be sick. There is time. The only difference is that I must now do in hours what once I could spend a month or two doing. It is possible to learn to control time. I realize that now. I wish I had realized it forty years ago. Too much time was wasted."

Now the rain was falling heavily, driven by the wind, causing the fire to sputter. The room was quiet. Breedlove stirred, deep in his chair. Powell sucked on his pipe, making a hollow sound exaggerated by the stillness. The eagle on the mantel stared fiercely from its perch, its searching eyes surveying its dominion.

Breedlove spoke again.

"Everything on the dinner table tonight was a product of BII. The lobster was from our frozen-foods department, the steak from our meat packer, the vegetables were our canned goods, the wine from my winery that we're now integrating into the company. I think the demonstration should lead to some discussion here. I believe that our quality control has gone down. Should we spend fifty million dollars on quality control or keep it like it is and increase the advertising budget so the consumer will continue to think she's getting something she's not?"

"Who prepared the food?" Powell asked.

"A cook who's average. Like the average housewife with her Betty Crocker cookbook. A cook that's as good as you can get these days with no one willing to be a servant. And one that probably will leave abruptly someday, like others I've had have left. Recently I had a chauffeur. Now he's run off. He doesn't even wait to get paid."

Scott's head snapped up.

"How did you arrive at the fifty million?" Powell said.

"In my head."

"I think it could be done for less than that."

"No," Breedlove said. "It is a conservative figure. Are you with us, Scott, or still too pissed off to talk?"

"I've been concerned about quality control for a long time," Scott said. "I'm on record in board meetings expressing that concern. I think we should spend the money."

"Hank?" Breedlove said.

"No," Lancaster said. "We shouldn't spend it. Not now. Not with a proxy fight on our hands. I want our profit-loss and balance sheet to look very good in the next six months or so."

Breedlove smiled, obviously pleased. "How is the sales outlook?"

"It is excellent," Lancaster said. "And it will get better. I have a new Food Division ad agency now, and believe me they will be humping. I think it's important to remember what kind of business we're in. Remember we're not in the gourmet business. We're mass feeders. We sell VWs, not Rolls-Royces. We sell what most of the others sell. Aspirin is aspirin. What is important is to make the buyer *think* she's getting a Rolls, and for the price of a VW."

"How?" Scott said. "With mirrors?"

Lancaster whirled. "Oh, good Christ, Scott! Tonight it's raining on Bel Air and San Marino but also on Central Avenue and El Monte and the great middle-class San Fernando Valley. How many out there can *tell* quality? Or want it? Most of them wouldn't know the difference between filet mignon with truffles and our TV dinners. For the most part, it's a mindless beast out there. We can *direct* their taste. Create it."

"You underestimate Mr. Average," Scott said.

"Well, you have a lot to learn."

"All right," Breedlove said, waving his hand. "I didn't call this session to referee a fight. If you two want to fight, take off your coats and go into the next room. But I don't think Scottie wants to fight. Do you, Scottie?"

"I think I'm being just slightly more than intimidated here," Scott said. "I'm not sure I like it, or deserve it."

"What is your view on quality control?"

"The Food Division isn't under me."

"It's all under you now."

"My view is simple. Our product is bad. Our quality stinks. We've fought the price battle and lost quality. Our advertising is nothing but exaggerated ballyhoo and is probably false and misleading besides."

Lancaster's eyes blazed. "All advertising is ballyhoo. You don't move goods by emphasizing the negative."

Breedlove reached for a Lucky, tapped it in his palm, and straightened his shoulders. He kept tapping the cigarette as he spoke. "I've heard enough. Here is what we will do. Forget the fifty million for now. Concentrate on the proxy fight. For the next few months, that will be the top priority item. George, it's your baby, but keep checking with me because I have a trick or two up my sleeve for old Mendenthal myself. Hank, you help George with an anti-Mendenthal advertising campaign. Get shareholder relations off their asses. Get PR to do something for a change. Scottie, you stay clear of it. I want you to move more actively in the Food Division." He ceased tapping the Lucky Strike. His head lowered. His eyes closed. "Meeting's over," he said. "I suggest you rejoin your wives."

The owner of Joe's Diner on Colorado Boulevard was surprised to see the couple in formal dress settle into a back booth about 11 P.M.

"Going and coming, the silent treatment," Scott said.

"I'll be all right," Anne said. "I'm just hungry, that's all."

"I noticed that you ate very little."

"Everyone did. Your Mr. Breedlove needs a new cook."

"I could tell it wasn't exactly your favorite party. You didn't have a fight with Clem, did you?"

"No. But he said some things that made me wonder about him. Wonder about a lot of things."

"What did he say?"

"I'll tell you later. After I sort it out in my own mind."

"Then why is your mood ring glaring bright red?"

"It was the questions they asked. Not Clem. The others. While you were having your meeting, I felt as if I was being looked over, like a slab of meat."

"Well, we buy the wives, too."

"This wife is not for sale."

Joe stood over them. "What'll it be, folks?"

"What's good?" Scott asked.

"I'll bring you the special," Joe said, squinting at them. "Where you folks been? All dressed up, I mean?"

"To a drama," Scott said. "A tango in Pasadena."

"I never get out no more," Joe said morosely. He went away.

"What happened in your meeting?" Anne asked.

"For one thing, we decided not to spend fifty million dollars. For another, I got into it with Hank. In front of Breedlove."

"Good for you."

"And Breedlove invited me to leave the company."

"I don't believe that."

"He said I'm too nice."

"Well, tell him that with his personality, a balance is struck in the company."

"I thought you liked Breedlove."

"Not after tonight."

"What changed your mind?"

"I wonder if he's insane. Stopping in the middle of a sentence, looking around wild-eyed, jabbing his fork into the table." She touched his hand. "Mark, you're not *bound* to Breedlove."

"Sometimes I think I am. He made me so damn angry tonight I could have strangled him."

"Did you stand up to him?"

"I used some words, yes. But I didn't walk out."

"Maybe you should have."

"No. Not in the middle of a fight."

"Are you a fighter?"

"I might be."

"Maybe you are."

Scott took her hand. He held it tightly, feeling a surge of

closeness to her. "It's all so mixed up. I'm in a dizzy circle. There's something almost *malevolent* about it."

"You've been talking about a job to the dean of SC's law school. I know, because he called for you at home. Did he offer you a teaching job?"

"Yes. Starting at twenty-nine five. I could be making that per month at BII in a year or so."

"I don't care."

"Not long ago you wanted me to clobber my way to the top. I told you before that this is not a three-man race. I can have it. If I do the right things."

"Or the wrong things."

"What is that supposed to mean?"

"Oh, I know I've waffled all over the place before. But not any more. I don't want you to go on. I'm not going to change that position. You used the word yourself just now. Malevolent. I believe it was your word."

"Well, I'm not going to get out. Not now. Not ever. I'm going to hang in there."

"Why?"

"Because I want it."

"You may lose us if you do. I see that now."

"Don't ever talk like that."

"Mark, I'm frightened. I'm actually scared."

"Special," Joe said, slapping a steamy plate down between them.

21

THE SHAPE OF PHILIP MENDENTHAL'S CAMPAIGN TO ACQUIRE control of BII appeared in several lightning strokes over the next several weeks. Scott got his first hint of it when Donald Ralston, president of Brighton Manufacturing and a BII director, came into his office and said he was resigning his directorship.

"Why do you come to me to announce this?" Scott said.

"Who else? Powell is in Washington. Lancaster is in Sacramento. And Breedlove—well, Breedlove is apparently out of the world."

"Will you tell me what this means?"

"I think you know, Scottie."

"Brighton is selling its BII stock."

"Yes."

"Why? Why now?"

"Because we can get a good price. Because there is an apparent buyer."

"An *apparent* buyer?"

"It's being handled through a brokerage firm. If they didn't have a buyer, the broker wouldn't handle it." Ralston gestured. "Scottie, we can use the money, quite frankly. We took in this stock when BII needed funds and we were flush. It's been a damn good investment for us. But now we can't afford to hold it any longer. We're getting a yield of about two percent on it. We can get eight to nine percent in CDs with no risk."

"If you look at your yield relative to what you paid for the stock, it's much higher than two percent."

"That's beside the point. What is to the point is how much investment income we can get if we cash in the stock. I can't go before my board and argue it any other way."

"Is the buyer Dimension? Or Philip Mendenthal?"

Ralston stood up. "No. Neither."

"An ally of Mendenthal's, no doubt. Tell me. Will you be on the Mendenthal slate for a directorship?"

"No. Of course not. I'm finished with BII."

"Your tone of voice indicates to me that you have a special reason for saying that you're finished."

"Our people have been looking into BII, it's true. And into Breedlove. Especially into Breedlove."

"What am I to take that to mean?"

"We had better not discuss it any more, Scottie. Suffice it to say this. That man has some bad connections."

"Tell me more. My ears are open."

"I'm sorry," Ralston said. He walked to the door. He turned. "Scottie?"

"Yes."

"I've always liked you. Even admired you. So a word of advice. Get out. Now. I think Mendenthal may win this thing. I think you might get hurt."

Scott began to pace, his hands behind his back. He glanced at the photos of Anne and the kids on his desk. Turning sharply, he jerked the phone from its cradle and dialed Breedlove's private number at the Pasadena residence. The phone rang a dozen times. No answer.

He hadn't seen or talked to Breedlove since the dinner, but he was sure both Powell and Lancaster had spoken to the old man. Clearly both were mobilizing against Mendenthal. Lancaster had announced BII-2000, sending the stock up six points. Powell was talking with private groups of security analysts and stockbrokers. Both had been busy addressing clubs and civic groups, especially Lancaster. A food industry trade magazine, *Institutions,* had forecast that he would become the next chief executive of BII. Routine work had bogged Scott down—budget reports, labor flare-ups, computer malfunctions. Letters from shareholders inquiring about the proxy fight had begun to stream in; he hadn't found the time yet to answer one. Besides, he wanted to confer with Powell and Lancaster before he did, to establish a uniform policy in answering the letters. But he'd been unable to reach either one on the telephone, much less talk to them face to face.

Joan Leeky tapped on his door and peeked in, a little pale-faced and timidly, he thought. "Mr. Zimmer is here, Mr. Scott."

"I'm not sure I know a Mr. Zimmer."

"From security."

"Oh. Well, him I will see. I'd like to determine for sure that those people have faces."

She ushered Zimmer in and escaped with diplomatic finesse. Apparently his irritation in recent days had shown more than he'd thought, and Joan no doubt was puzzled by his uncharacteristic abruptness. He made a mental note to invite her to lunch, wondering when he'd find the time. Zimmer, meanwhile, was already at work, hustling around the office and peering suspiciously in corners and behind pictures. He was a small dark man who wore huge horn-rimmed glasses, obscuring most of his face. Scott watched him work, speechless. Before Scott could regain his voice, Zimmer had disassembled and reassembled the telephone receiver, crouched under the desk on his hands and knees, inspected the closet and bathroom, and searched with his fingers along the carpeting by all four walls.

Scott stood, hands on hips. "Do you mind telling me what it's all about?"

"Bug sweep, Mr. Scott. Wiretap check."

"On whose orders?"

"Security, sir."

"Am I clean?"

"Seems clean's a whistle. Do you have a scrambler, Mr. Scott?"

"No. No scrambler. I don't have my decoder, either."

"Scrambler will be issued. About the decoder, I don't know about that. I'd advise using a pay phone on your most important calls. There'll be a memo issued."

Zimmer was gone.

He had a luncheon date with Clemson Hawley, and on his way to the executive dining room he stopped at Miss Tompkins's office. She often ate her lunch at her desk—usually, according to office talk, an apple and thin slices of Swiss cheese on Melba toast—and now he found her door closed. He tapped. He heard a stirring within. The door opened a crack and Miss Tompkins peered out.

"I'm sorry to interrupt, Miss Tompkins, but I've been attempting to reach Mr. Breedlove on a matter of considerable importance. Would you try to reach him for me after lunch?"

"He calls in every afternoon, Mr. Scott."

Scott fumbled. He felt hopelessly foolish, a top executive of one of America's major corporations having to filter a request to reach his boss through a cold-fleshed protective shield so automated and precise that major gossip would result if she arrived at work one morning without wearing her white gloves.

"When he calls today, tell him I'm looking for him," he said.

"I'll mention it to him, Mr. Scott."

She closed her door.

The dining room was almost empty. Hawley sat at a far-corner table, his nose buried in a newspaper. He already had his lunch before him, but he wasn't eating.

"Have you read about it?" he said, squinting at Scott over the top of his glasses.

"Read about what?"

"You should spend some time with your *Journal*."

"Tell me where to get the time. Especially lately."

The article, by a *Wall Street Journal* staff writer in Washington, said the Securities & Exchange Commission was investigating several large U.S. companies for alleged payments to foreign politicians and military leaders in return for promised favors, such as contracts and smooth labor relations. The SEC's concern was based on the fact that the companies under investigation apparently had not delineated the payments to their shareholders, instead hiding them in the maze of their balance sheets. That violated federal disclosure laws.

One of the companies under investigation was BII.

Scott whistled. "Suddenly I'm not hungry."

"Is there any truth to it?"

"Will you believe me if I say I do not know?"

"It is nice fuel for the Mendenthal forces."

"I agree that the timing is bad."

"Scottie, I'm too fucking old to believe in coincidences. And this is not a coincidence. I think Mendenthal went to the SEC and pointed a finger at us."

"You could be right."

"And next it could be the FTC, then the IRS. What are you going to do about it?"

"Clem, right now I'm going to order lunch. And I suggest you eat yours."

"You seem remarkably unconcerned."

"The fish," Scott told the waitress without looking at her. He turned. His words tumbled out. "I am *not* unconcerned. If you have the rest of the day, I'll tell you my concerns. You don't, so I'll tell you about the top concern. I'm concerned because we're dashing around like we're playing a child's game of tag instead of concentrating on running a company with responsibility to millions of consumers and thousands of employees and stockholders. I'm concerned because I can't even *reach* Breedlove, and, if I could, I'd probably get only irrationality from him. Powell and Lancaster are racing around like political contestants, trying to pick up votes. They act as if it's an imposition on them to talk to me. Meanwhile, I'm dealing with spies and icy bitches and—"

Hawley held up his hand. "Stop. Enough."

"Look. Can we talk?"

"Yes. We can talk. When you and I can't talk, the world has come to an end."

"What's going to happen with this crazy Troika idea? In your opinion?"

Hawley stuffed his mouth with fish. He peered into Scott's eyes as he chewed. "You know as well as I do. Two of you will go down. Something else. The man who goes to the top will have to do some wholesale dumping. Some of the old farts may have to go down." Hawley avoided Scott's gaze. His thumb jabbed the newspaper. "For this, somebody'll have to go down. That's an odds-on bet. You make sure it's not you. I'm not sure you're keeping your guard up."

"Don't worry about me."

"I do worry about you."

"He told me I could have it."

"What did he tell the other two?"

"I believe him. He said he has a reason, but he won't tell me what it is. All I have to do to get it is to ruin a few lives, stomp around a little more, and beat my wife and kids more often."

"How badly do you want it?"

"Sometimes it's like White House fever, Clem."

"I'd like to tell you I'm surprised. I won't. I've seen some changes in you already."

"Am I getting tougher?"

"This is good fish."

"All right. Change the subject. I want to talk to you about something else, anyway."

"I know. Breedlove."

"I thought he was the mind reader."

"What do you want to know about him?"

"You know him well. You've had forty years with him. More."

"No one knows Breedlove well."

"You knew his wife and son. What was it like between Breedlove and his wife?"

"I'd rather not talk about that."

"I thought we could talk."

Hawley's jaw tightened. "It was all right between them at

first, I guess. But it didn't stay that way. After the boy was born, it became growing hate. Hate you could cut with a knife." Hawley's eyes grew misty. He turned away. "She had some of the stock, collateral for a loan to Breedlove from her father's bank, and she held that over him. He doesn't like things held over him. I think he just wore her down."

"How?"

"By taking control of Lawrence, for one thing. Are you ready for a surprise? Lawrence was the apple of the old man's eye, at least for a while. It was Lawrence this, Lawrence that. He'd grow up, go to school, run the company."

"What happened?"

"Who am I to know?"

"You must have some thoughts on it."

Hawley stood up. "Time I took a leak," he said.

Breedlove called Scott about 3 P.M. He didn't seem surprised to learn of Ralston's resignation. "I think old Mendenthal lined up buyers for our Brighton stock long ago. He's probably got a bank lined up, too, to put up the money. Scottie, you take your input on the proxy fight to Powell. I thought I made it clear that he's handling it."

"All right. I will."

"Don't think of this as a setback. Mendenthal is going to play hell getting that stock to vote his side."

"Are we going to court over the sale?"

"Of course we're going to court over it. Why do you think I have Powell in Washington?"

"You're four steps ahead of me."

"I'll take another step. I'll predict that when Mendenthal announces his slate for directors it will include a woman, a Jew, a college professor, a ditchdigger, and a preacher."

"A preacher?" Anne said that evening.

"Well, Breedlove's point was that Mendenthal will oppose us with a cross section of jobs and income levels. An all-American board."

Anne was in a good mood. She put her hand on his. "Mark, I want to tell you something. I'm not scared any more. Maybe I'm just an old-fashioned girl. Pregnant in winter, barefoot in summer."

"Hardly barefoot."

"I'm not going to push you. But if you really want to win this thing, I'll try to help you. That is the world champion waffler's latest position."

"I know one thing," he said. "I can run it."

"I know you can."

"Maybe it *should* be me."

"All right. It should."

"A company need not be an ogre. It can be a force for good."

"I think I see stars twinkling in your eyes."

"Don't be the iceman. I can run it and not lose my soul to it. Breedlove might be ruthless, but his elect doesn't have to copy him."

"His elect? Is he a god who elects?"

Scott smiled. "Damn near."

"Oh, elect," she said.

Brighton got permission to sell its BII stock when a federal judge in Washington ruled the sale normal and justified. An appellate court upheld the decision. BII then asked the court to allow the stock to be placed in a non-voting trust until the proxy contest was decided, basing its appeal on the fact that the stock had been in a trust when owned by Brighton. Again BII lost. The judge pointed out that the trust had existed earlier because Brighton was a competitor of a BII subsidiary, and the original purchase of BII shares by Brighton had been allowed without Justice Department intervention only after agreement to establish the voting trust. Now, with the stock in private hands, there was no justification for a trust, and the owners had the clear right to vote the stock as they saw fit. BII didn't appeal. Clearly the decisions were victories for Mendenthal.

"Jesus H. Christ," Henry Lancaster mumbled to Dorothy when he read the names of Mendenthal's slate for BII directors. "Here's a surprise."

"What?"

"The list of dissidents who'll oppose us for board election at the annual meeting. David Kahn is on it."

"So? Who he?"

"A fellow who lost his job when I killed off a magazine we owned. *Fortnightly Comment*."

She filed her nails. "What's so surprising?"

"Well, I had a hint from him once that he knew something about certain films you once made."

"You're kidding."

"I thought I had handled him. It goes to show you."

Among other directors being proposed by Mendenthal in his fifteeen-person slate was a woman, a laborer, a professor of law at Columbia, a Methodist minister from Ohio, and a retired Swedish farmer. The woman, an executive in a New York garment-manufacturing firm, owed 350 shares of BII. The professor owned 500. The minister owned 152. The ex-farmer, Nels Olson, owned 42 shares. Mendenthal listed his holdings as 93,000 directly and 120,000 indirectly, the latter held through Dimension Corporation. The buyers of the BII stock sold by Brighton Manufacturing, now owners of 415,000 shares each, were disclosed—a New Jersey shopping center builder named Bert Patman and a Los Angeles savings and loan founder named Bert McNally. Ironically, McNally had once headed a home-construction concern that had bought large tracts of BII-owned land in the San Fernando Valley in the late 1940s.

Mendenthal's slate was clear-cut down the line. The wealthy. The common man. The educated and the uneducated. Law, ministry, finance. East Coast, West Coast, Midwest. Jewish, Protestant, Catholic.

The dissidents owned about 1.5 million shares of BII. Current BII directors owned about 1.2 million, including the 920,000 still owned by Breedlove.

It appeared to be almost an even match, one to be decided by the small shareholder.

"It's amateur night in Dixie," Lancaster said. "Yet—you know?—those bastards stand a chance."

"Why?"

"Because they're common. They're simple. So are a lot of our stockholders."

"Well, I don't understand it."

"Don't try."

"What will you do if you lose?"

"Winners do not lose," Lancaster said.

* * *

Full-page advertisement, Los Angles *Times,* November 23:

BULLETIN

BII SHAREHOLDERS
OFFERED A CHOICE

A stock certificate is a piece of paper that is evidence of part ownership in a company.

It says, in theory, to its owner: "You are a part of this enterprise. You own a part of its assets. You have the right to vote."

In practice, all too much, it is not so.

Seldom do you have a clear-cut opportunity to elect your directors and your officers, despite the fact that you, as a stockholder, are their real employers. Seldom, also, do you really participate in major corporate decisions that, by law, require shareholder approval.

You're confused with proxy statements. You're confused with prospectuses. You're confused by legal literature, fine-print masterpieces, that not even the lawyers understand.

So, invariably, you place your X for management. Or, if you don't like it, you sell your stock.

Next May, at a small town in Wisconsin named Olen, a rare form of corporate democracy will be put on display.

You will have the opportunity to vote out the current directors of Breedlove International, Inc., and vote in a new slate of directors.

You don't have to go to Olen. You can vote by mail. We don't even think BII directors *want* you to go. If they did, they would meet in a larger city. New York. Chicago. Los Angeles.

But they chose Olen.

We hope you will go. We're prepared to assist your going. We urge you to hold your proxies and turn out wholesale.

You'll see corporate democracy in action if you do.

You'll have a chance.

In coming weeks, we will clearly spell out why the current management of BII is indeed mis-management. We'll show you in facts and figures they have held back from you.

Meanwhile, May 26. Olen, Wisconsin.

> PHILIP MENDENTHAL
> *Stockholder*
> *Committee for Better*
> *Management of BII*

"So far, it's been almost a classical pattern," Powell told Breedlove by phone on a Sunday morning. "Almost predictable."

"Absolutely predictable, you mean. He's copying Bob Young's second go-around for control of the Central."

"What action do you want us to take?"

"George, when I hired you I had the impression you would be the one to give financial advice to me, not the other way around."

"Very well. I'll proceed with a plan I've drawn up."

"Just keep me informed," Breedlove said.

Scott now was invariably working on Sundays, or parts of Sundays, either at the office or at his desk at home. The family usually went to church on Sunday mornings and stopped for brunch at a restaurant in Palos Verdes. Then they would go home and Scott would either go the office or seal himself in his study. Anne had become accustomed to it; she seldom complained. Liz and Tod constantly lobbied for Sunday-afternoon trips to Disneyland or Knott's Berry Farm, but, if they got to go, Anne invariably took them alone. Mike, who always had plans of his own, continued to worry Anne.

"He's still family age, but just not family oriented," she said as Scott parked the car in the garage one Sunday.

"Well, hello, here's a funny thing," Scott said.

"What?"

"Did you leave the kitchen door open?"

"No. I remember locking all the doors."

Scott got out, leaving the car door open. He peered in through the open door of the kitchen. Then he came back.

"Liz and Tod, you run down to the beach and play," he said. "Your mother and I want to talk. Alone."

"I'll get my suit," Liz said.

"No. Just scoot. Both of you. Now."

They started down the steps to the beach, Liz in the lead. Scott said, "Anne, I don't want you to get hysterical now. But somebody has been here. The kitchen is a mess."

"We've been burglarized?" Her eyes widened. "Why, I turned on the alarm system. I know I did."

"I don't think you should go in. Not right now. Drive down to the corner and call the police."

"No. No, I'm going to go in. If you're going to go in, I'm going with you."

"They might still be here."

"I don't care. I'm going with you."

He moved slowly and quietly into the kitchen, Anne behind him. They stopped, looking around. Neither spoke. The kitchen had not only been ransacked and messed; it had been violated. Towels were scattered all about. Food from the refrigerator lay scattered in piles on the floor. The sink was filled with chips from broken wineglasses. And, most startling of all, the linoleum and walls were streaked with fresh scrawls of red paint. Anne tried to talk, but no words came out. Her face was ashen. Scott felt only one emotion. Anger. They didn't keep weapons in the house, for Anne feared guns; Scott now placed obtainment of a pistol on top of his list of things to do. He picked up the phone and dialed the police; the desk sergeant said a car would be there immediately. Scott explored the other rooms. Fireplace ashes had been scattered all over the living-room carpet. Broken records were strewn about. Anne's favorite seascape had been spattered with red paint. Lights bulbs had been removed from sockets and broken on the floor. Wet paint saturated the carpet. All the bathroom walls and mirrors had been streaked with paint. The mattresses in the kids' bedrooms had been slashed and the sheets were knotted. The king-size bed in the main bedroom had been disassembled, its parts scattered. The paintings had been slashed. Red scrawls streaked the walls.

"Mark, what *is* it? What's happening?"

He found himself amazingly calm. "Vandals, I suppose."

"In broad daylight? On Sunday? Vandals who knew enough to disconnect the alarm system? Vandals who haven't taken anything valuable? Mark, something is going on. I want to know. You've been keeping me out."

He didn't respond. Two uniformed policemen had entered through the front door. "Holy Christ," one said.

The attackers, striking swiftly but with a strange order in their havoc, had missed one room, a den Scott used as a home office. He took Anne's arm and led her into it. It was beginning to hit him. His calm was leaving, replaced by shakes he tried to control. His head ached; his legs were weak. Perspiration ran down his back. Anne slumped down on the carpet and put her head into her arms. Then she looked up. Her face was white. Tears streaked down her cheeks.

"Mark?"

He went to her, kneeling beside her, holding her tightly. He felt her tears on his neck. She sobbed quietly, trembling as she held him. The boots of the policemen trampled in the kitchen. Anne pushed away from him.

"You've been fooling me, tricking me," she said. "You told me it was nothing, that nothing was happening." She paused, rubbing her eyes, catching her breath. "But all the while you knew. You *knew*! You've been keeping me out of it."

He grasped her hand and held it tightly. He tried to speak calmly, quietly. "Anne, I don't know. I don't. I have some hints, yes, but I don't know the reason for this. But there is something I do know. I need you now. I need you so I can get some semblance of order in myself. Here is what I think we should do. After you calm down, you go and get the kids. Don't let them in here."

"What will you do?"

"Stay and handle it with the police."

"Where is Mike?"

"At the Weedons. You know that."

"What if he comes home?"

"I'll be here. You get Liz and Tod. Go to a hotel. Now. Will you do that?"

"I'm better now. Just a little numb, that's all. And starting to get angry."

"Good. Good." The phone was jangling. He reached for it,

watching her. His hand remained unsteady and the pain pounded in his head, blurring his vision. "Hello."

"Oh, Mr. Scott. It's Harold Long. Sorry to bother you at home. Got your number from security."

"What is it?"

"Well, that airplane has operational redundancy on top of operational redundancy, yet something's come up that could offset it all. You asked me to call if—"

"Yes. Go on."

"Fuel line," Long said. "There's four, one redundant to the other, so you get fuel even if three fail. But I've found a loose locknut here, so if you're up you could find your fuel cut off. Whoever did this, he's not only the invisible man but he knows something about airplanes, too."

He felt, again, that he was losing control. The only emotion he felt was fury, a blind fury that stormed in his brain like a force thunderous and unmanageable. His hands were numb. Huge spots ran before his eyes. He needed a drink. He needed to drive. He needed to walk. It had gone too far. He'd been guilty of inaction, risking the sanctuary of his family in trust of a man inaccessible and invisible who'd promised power and riches in return for loyalty and trust. It was too much. To hell with it. To hell with Lewis Breedlove and his guards, purchased servants, hedonistic airplane. To hell with BII and its asinine rules and regulations, its caste system, its impingements on freedom, its outrageous demands. He picked up the phone. His strength had returned. He dialed Miss Tompkins at home, a number he knew by heart, and she answered on the first ring.

"Miss Tompkins, I want to see Lewis Breedlove. Today. Now."

"I'm afraid that is impossible, Mr. Scott."

"You call him. You tell him I'm coming over. Right now."

He slammed the receiver down. He led Anne through the ruined house to the door.

The guard at Breedlove's gate refused to admit Scott. "I'm sorry, sir. Mr. Breedlove is sleeping."

"Wake him up."

"I can't do that, Mr. Scott." The guard's face hardened.

Scott's fists tightened. He hurried away, almost running. He felt a hammering in his chest. He stopped. Turning, he looked back at Breedlove's house.

He felt a drawing power, a force emananting from the place, changing his resolve to leave into an unaccountable necessity to stay. He lingered, smelling the pungent geraniums, listening to the shrill cry of a mockingbird. Night was falling, a slow creep of lengthening shadows. He felt a moist chill in the air. The mockingbird had fled. Nothing stirred. The spearlike shafts of the black iron inner gate jutted over the top of the outer wall like points of a crown. The yard and the house faded almost perceptibly into a darkening silence. Now crickets began to sing and moths hovered over a yellow light near the driveway. Scott heard a rustling behind him. He whirled. The narrow dark eyes of a Doberman pinscher glowed at him from behind the fence of a house across the street.

Finally he left, walking in semidarkness to his car. He felt eyes from the windows of the Breedlove house watching him. He thought, *Stop it. Go home.* He did not consider himself an impulsive man; he considered himself a careful and calculating man. Yet this rush to Breedlove had been impulsive. As he opened the car door, he saw a woman in a shawl hurrying down the sidewalk in his direction. A two-wheeled grocery cart ran ahead of her. She moved after it with quick, short strides, almost a run, as if the moving cart controlled her pace. The cart was filled with sacks. The woman stopped at Breedlove's wall.

"Mrs. Lamson?" Scott said, stepping forward.

She shrank back, a pale woman with sharp features and the darting eyes of a frightened bird. "Who're you?"

"I'm Mark Scott, Mrs. Lamson. Don't you remember me?"

She squinted. "Was you one of them at the dinner t'other week?"

"Yes."

"Some dinner."

"My wife and I enjoyed it."

"Judgin' from the leftovers, no one else did."

"May I ask you something?"

"He'll be wantin' his supper now."

"Mrs. Lamson, has Morris left Mr. Breedlove's employ?"

"Them things I don't keep track of. I keep my ears and mouth closed. Speak when spoke to. Min' my business."

"Did Morris own a car of his own?"

"Morris and me, we never talked."

"It was a small car. A Volkswagen. A red one."

"He had a red car, I guess. He sold it to Mr. Lawrence. Or lent it to him."

"Do you mean Mr. Breedlove's son, Lawrence?"

"I gotta go. He wants his supper."

"Please. This is important."

She lifted her bird's-claw hand and jabbed at the push button beside the gate. "Don't ask me if you want to ask about Mr. Breedlove. You go ask Mona Luce."

"Who is Mona Luce?"

"She worked here when I come. Mona Luce. She'd say, 'Call me *Mrs.* Luce. I'm *Mrs.* Luce.' Oh, her. It was right away Mrs. Lamson do this, Mrs. Lamson do that. She'd have everybody running around like a chicken with his head cut off. She'd run, too. She'd leave, then come back, then leave, then come back. You ask her, not me."

"Where is she?"

"Pasadena. Near here."

"Thank you."

"I gotta get his supper now," Mrs. Lamson said.

Mona Luce was listed in the Pasadena telephone book. When he reached her, she ordered him to come over right away, giving him detailed directions. She didn't even ask him the nature of his business, merely whom he worked for. It was a small house near York Street. She had coffee ready for him.

"I don't get many visitors, Mr. Scott, and when a man calls, I don't hesitate. I'm the original little old widow-lady from Pasadena, I suppose." She smiled, a warm smile that completely destroyed the impression of her he'd gathered from Mrs. Lamson. She was a tiny woman with white hair and a flawless complexion, the little matron of a spotless little house. "Do you mind if I leave the drapes open? It's not often my snoopy neighbors see a man in here."

"How long did you work for the Breedloves?"

"Over twenty years, off and on."

"You have me outranked."

"You are quite young to be where you are, Mr. Scott."

"I wish you'd call me Mark."

"I have three grown sons. The middle one is named Mark."

"How did you find time to work for the Breedloves?"

"I felt I had to."

"I don't understand, Mrs. Luce."

Her eyes narrowed. "I'm not sure I should say things to you, or to anyone. But I am going to say them. One of the reasons why I jumped at the chance to talk to you is that I'm concerned about something and I think it will help to get it off my chest. I saw something growing in that house over the years, and when I think back on it now I know there's only one word for it. Hate. A house of hate. Now you think I'm a melodramatic old woman."

"Not at all. Tell me."

"Do you have servants, Mr. Scott?"

"It's Mark. And, no, we don't really have servants. Only a maid. There are three kids that rule my roost and one on the way."

"I can sense that you are a good man."

"Why did you ask me about servants?"

"In a big house like the Breedloves', there are two cultures. The domestics and their masters. The masters seldom learn about the domestics because most of them do not have the time or do not care. But the servants usually learn about the masters. Often they get to know them very well. I think I did. I think they talk about personal matters to the servants because, to them, the servants are not really people but sort of non-human objects. At least it was that way with Mr. Breedlove. And, to a lesser extent, with Mrs. Breedlove. But not with Lawrence. He had a streak of real human feeling in him. Oh, she did, too, but later, she was sick so much and hated to be sick so desperately that I think it affected her mind. I'm talking too fast. I'm not making sense."

"You are. Please go on."

"Your coffee is cold. I'll warm it up."

"You said you were concerned. Why?"

"There is a lot I have to say. I don't know really where to begin."

"Just tell me about Mrs. Breedlove. And about Lawrence."

Mrs. Luce got up and closed the drapes. "He was here," she said, turning with a swiftness that surprised Scott. Her tone of voice had altered; it seemed higher pitched and more strained. "It was several weeks ago. I hadn't seen him for years. I thought he'd been away in Europe, studying there. He was always such a bright boy. I hardly recognized him, Mr. Scott. So *thin*. And he'd grown a beard. He kept looking away from me but it wasn't hard to see that his face was all cut up. Finally he admitted he'd been in a fight with some men who had attacked him on the street. He wouldn't let me touch him. Something was frightening him, terribly. He asked me for some money and when I gave him all I had in the house, about twenty dollars, he started to cry. I'd never seen him cry before, not even when he was a little boy. He told me once that his father told him that only girls cry, not boys or men."

"How long did he stay?"

"Only about an hour. I went to the kitchen to make him something to eat and when I returned he was gone."

"You've never heard from him since?"

She shook her head. "No. But he sent the money back."

"Was there an address on the envelope?"

"No address. It had a Venice postmark."

"You mean Venice in California?"

"Yes."

It was Scott's turn to get up. He paced briefly, looking around at the small, neat room. Then he sat down beside her. He touched her hand.

"Mrs. Luce, tell me about Lawrence. You said he was a bright boy."

"He was a sweet boy, too. A good boy."

"Did you look upon him as a sort of son? Is that why you kept going back into Mr. Breedlove's employ?"

"It was the way he was being brought up," she said, her chin firming, a small blaze showing in her eyes. "He wasn't allowed any freedom. Oh, he'd try to run away, but they'd find him, dragging him back like an escaped prisoner."

"Didn't he get out to attend school?"

"There were private tutors, picked by Mr. Breedlove. Little martinets in black suits with vests. His books were selected for him. Once I asked him if he'd ever read *David Copper-*

field and he said he'd never heard of it. I gave him my copy, but he never finished it. They took it away."

"What kind of books did he read?"

"Advanced books, Mr. Scott, at least advanced for his age. Engineering, mathematics, economics. Even law."

It was never presumed around BII that Breedlove's son would someday enter the business. Breedlove seldom spoke of Lawrence. When Scott had been manager of a BII plant in Omaha in the sixties, the personnel department had called excitedly one day to inform him that Lawrence had applied for a job on the canning line. Scott had called Lawrence to his office and they'd had a long talk. Lawrence, dressed in a suit and tie, had been soft-spoken and polite. He'd started work but one day he'd disappeared. Now Scott envisioned him as a boy in the large dreary house reading advanced tomes, a prisoner shackled in an iron-gray atmosphere broken only by the beam of a reading lamp. He was not forming by himself; he was being formed. Formed in the image of his father. What were his thoughts, his desires, his needs? What of love? Scott looked at Mrs. Luoo. There had been, he knew, some love.

"I want to know more," he said. "Tell me about Mrs. Breedlove."

"I was in and out of their service, Mr. Scott. I'm afraid I wasn't able to control my temper too well. After the *David Copperfield* incident, I stormed out."

"But you returned."

"Lawrence came to me, a week after I'd left. He was about thirteen then. He acted like a frightened little rabbit. He begged me to come back. So I did."

"What was Mrs. Breedlove like?"

"Oh, all live and vigor, at least at first, according to what I heard. She'd go on his trips with him and she'd hold big parties at the house for his customers. For his business, she was very good. It became that kind of relationship, at least on his part. It was a business agreement. It became very cold and formal between them and finally just a sort of—"

"Of what?"

"I don't know how to describe it, Mr. Scott. Just a kind of thick, horrible hatred. They simply did not speak to each other."

"Did she ever speak about a Mr. Hawley? Clémson Hawley?"

"Oh, yes, Mr. Scott, she did. He's in the company, isn't he?"

"He's a director."

"She spoke very fondly of Mr. Hawley. She said Mr. Hawley was the boy's spiritual godfather."

"Then she did care about Lawrence."

"She did. I'm certain she did. Yet she hardly knew him. Mr. Breedlove took him."

"Was she faithful to her husband?"

Mrs. Luce gestured, palms up. "I think it's better not to discuss certain things, Mr. Scott. She's dead now. In peace."

"I'm sorry. I'm prying. But it's important that I know. Perhaps it's important to Lawrence's safety."

"For his safety? He *is* in some kind of trouble, isn't he?"

"I'm afraid he is."

"There were other men in her life, yes. She told me about them. It was all very discreet."

"Did he know?"

"Oh, I think he knew. He is not a man who is fooled. I don't think he cared, as long as it remained discreet. He cared only about the business. And raising Lawrence in his image. Finally I couldn't stand it any longer. I left again, for good this time."

"When was that?"

"I can tell you exactly. It was in March of 1962. Mr. Breedlove had been in a huff all day about something and at dinner he threw a tantrum, flinging his food against the wall and cursing horribly. Mrs. Breedlove just sat there, staring at him. He wanted something from her, a signature on some papers, and she refused."

"A signature on what? Was it stock?"

"I never really knew. Something she had that he considered rightly his. He even threatened to ruin Lawrence if she didn't sign. I left that night, Mr. Scott. Mrs. Breedlove said she envied me. I was getting out. I've been receiving a stipend from the household ever since, and I'm sure it was her doing."

Scott walked briskly around the room. He was not really getting anywhere. He knew more about Lewis Breedlove, a side hidden in the past, but the knowledge led neither to understanding nor solution. It only suggested more questions. Who had influenced Lawrence after the break from his father's domination? What had Lawrence done? Was he part of a plan in motion that he could not control or escape from? It whirled in a succession of microsecond pictures flashing vividly before Scott's consciousness—Lawrence, the chauffeur Morris, a red Volkswagen, the Rembrandt, the BII 727, the bombings, the violation of his home. Mrs. Luce's voice brought him back.

"I saw Mrs. Breedlove once more after that. I'd heard she was very ill, so I went to see her. I think that was the most horrible day of my life. There was a stench in her room. She had shrunk to under a hundred pounds. She just lay there, looking at me, an old woman. I couldn't help thinking of the times when she had been all life and vigor and I took her hand and burst into tears. She tried to say something, but she simply couldn't speak. And—I'm melodramatic, but this is a fact—she was clutching a rag doll."

"Why wasn't she taken to a hospital?"

"I asked Scoggins about that. He told me that she wanted to go to a hospital but Mr. Breedlove wouldn't let her. She had two nurses, and a doctor came almost every day. Mr. Breedlove would not go into her room. It's strange, Mr. Scott. All those years ago, but I remember it like yesterday. It sort of pulls at you, like a magnet that won't let you go."

"I think I know exactly what you mean, Mrs. Luce."

A loud rap sounded at the door. Scott's head jerked up. Mrs. Luce went to the door. She turned back.

"Someone is here for you, Mr. Scott."

"For me?"

It was a tall man in a hat and a raincoat. "Mr. Scott, Mr. Breedlove wants you to call him," he said.

"Now?"

"Right now."

Breedlove was almost shouting.

"Scottie, goddamn it, what are you up to?"

"How did you know I was at Mrs. Luce's home?"

"I'll ask the questions. Just what in the fuck are you looking for?"

"You're having me followed. I want to know why."

"If you're being followed, it's for your own protection."

"Why?"

"I explained that to you."

"You're carrying it too far."

"I'll judge that. You have a company to worry about. I put you in charge and you spend half your time playing Dick Tracy."

"My house was broken into. Not just broken into, but a vile attack. It wasn't an isolated incident. It was a part of something that's happening in this company. I simply am not going to stand idly by and let it continue to happen."

Breedlove was silent. Finally he said, "I'm sorry to hear about the house, Scottie. Did you tell security?"

"No."

"I'll take care of the matter."

"Lewis, just what *is* happening?"

"I don't know yet. Not fully. But I will soon. I will handle this, Scottie. You leave my personal life to me."

"Your personal life apparently has run over into mine."

"You'll be protected."

"I received a sample of your protection today. Now I'm going to act on my own."

Breedlove heaved an exasperated sigh. "You have a simple choice, Scottie. You can stop playing detective and concentrate upon becoming the head of this company. Or you can resign and play detective as much as you want. Give me your choice now."

"You have me in an impossible position."

"Trust me." Breedlove's voice was low, almost a whisper. "Trust me."

"You ask too much, Lewis."

"I know I ask too much. Yet I'm sure you'll stay."

"*I'm* not sure. Not at all."

"You will," Breedlove said. "I'll make book on it."

The conversation was over.

Mrs. Luce called him late in the afternoon of the next day. "Mr. Scott, I wanted to tell you that a lawyer from the company came to see me this morning and—"

"A lawyer from BII?"

"Yes. He said the stipend I receive from the Breedlove household is a gratuity, not a legal pension, granted at Mr. Breedlove's discretion. He said it will be discontinued if I discuss the Breedlove household with anyone in the future."

Scott's hand became a tight fist. "Mrs. Luce, I simply do not know what to say to you."

"Mr. Scott, I called to tell you that I can get along without that money. I would be glad to discuss the Breedlove household in any kind of bloody detail you wish."

"No, I won't let you take that risk."

"I'm quite willing."

"And angry, too, I gather."

"Well, I'll say this. That lawyer has broom marks on his backside."

The Scotts spent the next full week at the Century Plaza Hotel, in a large suite reserved for them in Breedlove's name. Liz and Tod enjoyed it immensely, since it meant escape from classes and the rerun of *Star Wars* was playing nearby. They saw it eighteen times. Mike moped in his room. Long periods of silence passed between Anne and Scott.

When they returned to their house, it had been repainted inside and out, the furniture and artworks had been replaced, and a new security system had been installed.

"You go in first," Anne said.

She waited outside for a long time, looking at the ocean, and then quietly entered the house. They looked at each other. It was like entering the house of strangers, strangers to be feared.

22

Kevin A. Sheehan had covered everything from the fights to murder trials in his twenty-three years on newspapers, and now he held a record of sorts at BII. He'd been corporate manager of public relations for almost four years. No one in the past had held the job that long. Whenever unfavorable news about BII hit the press, the PR manager usually went down. Somebody had to be blamed. Sheehan's heart had sunk when he'd read the story about the SEC's filing against BII for overseas payoffs. A week passed. Nothing happened. But when Sheehan got a call to report to Mark Scott up on thirty on a Tuesday morning, he began immediately to compute how much severance pay he'd receive.

At least he'd go out with class. It appeared he was going to get the sack personally from one of the top four officers in the company. It was obvious now that he'd made a mistake, leaving the copy desk of the Los Angeles *Times* (before that, the Washington *Post*) for thirty grand and a private office, with secretary. He'd never jumped to PR before, despite the many offers and the promise of a cushy job. He'd heard in his newspaper days that big-company flacks did nothing but take people out to lunch, but he'd found that to be in error. BII already had a PR man who did nothing but take people out to lunch—Bill Hecky, *director* of public relations and Sheehan's immediate boss. As PR manager, Sheehan wrote all of the headquarters releases and hand-planted them with local media. He seldom took people to lunch. His life was a constant turmoil of having to do things without ever being told what was going on. *Last to know, first to go,* he thought as he left the elevator on thirty. *Motto of the PRSA.* Just last night he'd told his wife, "We should never have left the *Post.* Jesus, I coulda been a *Bernstein.*" Joan Leeky admitted him to Scott's presence with a smile and an offer of coffee.

"You want it regular?" she asked.

"You're a New Yorker," he said. "Bronx."

"Brooklyn."

"I'd never know."

Scott stepped forward and shook Sheehan's hand. He also smiled. It was something, really something. They were giving him his walking papers with big grins and offers of coffee in company-monogrammed cups. Class outfit. What had they found out about him? Jesus H on a crutch, had they finally caught on to his drinking problem? He'd often been asked to go to a newspaper and kill a story, and had always failed, getting drunk with the reporter instead. They probably held it against him; most companies no doubt thought a flack who couldn't kill a story hadn't the right connections. Or maybe they didn't go for his sense of humor. He'd written a report on one newspaper writer, considered a BII enemy because of a series on how the company tried to influence-peddle in Washington to tone down an antitrust charge, in police-beat style: "Subject lives in one-bedroom apartment, West Side. Yellow rugs, green phone, no paintings on wall. Frequents Last Chance Pub, drinks Scotch-soda. Has friend (female, black) on switchboard at City Hall. Seen frequently in Washington at Justice Department."

"Tell me," Scott said, looking into a copy of the *Information Please* almanac. "Have you ever heard of Mysterious Billy Smith?"

"No, sir. I can't say I have, Mr. Scott."

"He was a boxer. Welterweight. He held the title twice, according to this. First from 1892 to 1894. Again from 1896 to 1900."

Sheehan smiled tolerantly. If the brass wanted to talk about the fight game, that was fine. There wasn't much Sheehan didn't know about it, although Mysterious Billy Smith had stumped him.

"Who is the welterweight champion now?" Scott asked.

Jesus, did the big wheel have nothing to do except conduct a quiz show? "Well, that would be Pipino Cuevos," Sheehan said.

"Lightweight?"

"WBA or WBC?"

"WBA."

"Gonzalez. WBC is Jim Watt."

"How about middleweight?"

Sheehan snapped it out. "Hugo Carro."

"One more. Light-heavyweight."

"Cinch. It's Glandindez."

"You want to know what this all about."

"Are you a fight fan, Mr. Scott?"

"I've never seen a fight. Not in the ring, that is."

"I've seen like maybe two hundred."

"Yes. I understand you used to cover the fights for a newspaper."

"Well, that was quite a long time ago."

"Long time ago or not, you passed the test with an A plus.

I want to ask you to do a little job for me. Have you ever heard of a fighter named Morris?"

"Last name or first?"

"I hate to admit this. I don't know."

"I seem to remember somebody named Kid Morris. A welter. Good record. Until he got his skull broken at the Garden one night."

"I want to find out about him."

"What is it you want to know?"

"Anything you can discover. And this is in confidence. Between just you and me."

"You mean, like this kid's record? Things like that?"

"Anything," Scott said. "Everything, if you can get it."

"We going into sports cards or something?"

"No. This is personal. I've called Mr. Hecky and told him I'll need you for a few days. Let me how when you've found out something."

Sheehan left the office in a blue daze. He hadn't touched his coffee.

The man who knew more about fighters than any other living human being was a trainer at the Main Street Gym named Blackie Dawson. He wasn't a black; the name had something to do with his past reputation as a gambler and a fixer. Blackie was no bigger than a dwarf and he had a high-pitched feminine voice. He wasn't really a talker, but he owed Sheehan a favor. Something about a 502 back a few years. When 502s could be fixed.

"You ever heard of Mysterious Billy Smith?" Sheehan asked.

"Sure. Welter. Late 1800s. Held the title twice."

"Who did Walcott beat for the title?"

"How much says I don't know who the ref was?"

"Ten bucks."

"You're on. Walcott beat Charles. The ref was Buck McTiernan."

"Has there ever been a heavyweight title bout in L.A.?"

"Ten'll get'cha twenty I know the year and who both boys was."

"On."

"Burns and Hart. 1906. Burns won. Weighed in at one-eighty."

"Who was the ref?"

"The twenty'll get'cha forty."

"No dice."

"Ref was Jeffries, James J. KO, twenty rounds. Jeffries hisself took out Fitzsimmons in eleven at Coney Island in 1899, June 9. He come in at two-aught-six."

"*Vox angelica*," Sheehan said.

"Huh?"

"You have the voice of an angel."

"I could use a angel. Put up twenty, ask me anythin'."

"Who was Kid Morris?"

"That's a thirty-dollar question."

"I'll go forty for a straight answer."

"On," Blackie said. "The Morris you refer to won some fights on his own but he won a lot more because the other guy sat down. Most of his wins was set up. Sure, he had a few real fights, but most of them the other guys dove. He had a legit last fight, this Morris you refer to, and his brains were leakin' all over the mat when the ref finally stopped it. This Morris you refer to had a crooked contract, a crooked manager, and crooked owners. They built him up for a big killing. His killing, almost. I don't think he ever knew, the dumb s.o.b."

"Is this fact or hearsay?"

"Fact."

"What else?"

"No more."

"Who owned his contract?"

"Some boys. Some boys around. Then."

"Bad boys?"

"I don't know no more."

"Can I buy your lunch?"

"Naw, I don't drink no more," Blackie said.

At six each evening the BII security department telecopied a report to Breedlove. On December 2, the following message went out: "It now seems likely that there is a relationship between the various attacks on the company, and perhaps also on some of its executives. Security has been tightened at all plants and offices, as well as personal key man security.

Suspect resurgence of terrorist group, one perhaps well financed, well informed, and technically capable. As per your request, no additional research is being undertaken on possible attempts to infiltrate or sabotage the corporate aircraft. Conclusion reached that a member of a terrorist group gained access to the aircraft in Chicago July 8. Aircraft now under ground surveillance. Despite surveillance, evidence that a second infiltration occurred, approximately Nov. 12 (see prior report). Urge you rescind instructions not to continue investigation of this matter." On December 5, the following went to Breedlove: "Re memo Dec. 2, on aircraft. Are your instructions still the same?" This time, an answer was snapped back: "Handling matter personally, due to obvious incompetence of security. Continue key man security."

McKeen was making progress. His connection in intelligence on the force had wired Interpol for information on European terrorists who might be away from their native countries, not in sanctuary in Czechoslovakia or Bulgaria but out working somewhere. Finally he got a list of names, photographs, and M.O.s. One M.O. fitted the pattern, a wop bomber named Mario who was considered tops in his field. Also, very expensive. The wop usually worked with a kraut who had a lot of names and identities but was more often than not called Horst something-or-other. They disliked each other, yet worked well together. There was no photo of the kraut. McKeen gave the wop's photo to his helpers, now referred to in the organization as "McKeen's boys." He felt deep frustration. Even if they nabbed this wop bastard red-handed, they might not be able to stop him. Hudson was sticking with his original instructions—do not take action without his okay. McKeen sulked, grinding his painful teeth; his wife, who knew his moods, avoided him. This job sucked. The company's security department consisted of a bunch of tire kickers and jackoffs who couldn't make it as grade-school patrol officers, and somebody high up had handcuffed McKeen, impeding his action. It was almost as if the company wanted to get bombed off the map. There was family in it, that probably explained it.

He was getting closer. The toothaches were constant and intense. He lived on black coffee and aspirins. Now he had a lead on Breedlove's son, a pothead who staggered from flat to flat at the beach, and also a lead on a big, ugly, pit-faced creep who just might be the organizer of it all. One of McKeen's boys, a smart heavy with uncanny street sense that Hudson personally had sprung from Leavenworth, said he'd known this creep there several years ago. And there was something else. McKeen had a rundown on the personnel at the Breedlove estate. One member, the chauffeur, Morris, had split without waiting for his paycheck, strong evidence of guilt. McKeen got a go signal from headquarters and put a man on Morris's trail. But they wouldn't let him go any further. A couple of his boys were eager for action, telling him their guns were getting rusty. McKeen told them to cool it, go get laid. Yet he himself was eager. It could be his big score with Hudson, and it was bound to get out in the organization if he did it right and maybe, just maybe, it would give him a shot at the top chair when Hudson cashed in. He could score points he couldn't possibly have scored in his old role as number-one enforcer.

He had run into an intriguing sidelight in this caper, a new mystery that caused his jaw to ring with pain. It concerned the attack on the house of the BII executive named Mark Scott, which he'd been asked to look into carefully. He was certain that the attack had been carried out by a group unassociated with the one he was pursuing; he also was certain that someone was ripping off the main scheme, taking an action for which the bombers would get the blame. Scott had been hit on the same Sunday that the wop (and probably his kraut sidekick) had hit a BII drug warehouse in Nevada. Breedlove's kid had been smashed on the beach that day, under watch, and the other creep, the character with the pitted face and broken teeth, had spent the day at a spade whorehouse in Watts. The mystery caused McKeen no end of pain, exhausting several tins of aspirin. This caper was getting more exciting and intriguing every day. He'd save up the accumulated pain and inflict it in triplicate on his prey when he was given the green light.

Board meetings without Breedlove came and went. BII decided to hold off its main counteraction on the proxy fight until the first of the year. Powell said a major push now would be a waste of effort and money. The SEC charges were not discussed, pending a report from legal. BII-2000, now in test marketing, also was not discussed.

In his office one morning after a meeting, Scott had a surprise visitor. "Scottie, why are you being such a stranger?" said a smiling Henry Lancaster.

"I'm not the stranger. I'm looking at him."

"Well, I have been on the road. I understand your house got painted while I was away."

"I'd rather not be reminded."

"Vandals?"

"I tell myself that. And try to convince Anne. But I am having difficulty convincing myself that I'm not being followed by some shadowy character wherever I go."

Lancaster laughed. "It's crazy Breedlove and his security troops. I play games with them. I know how to spot and lose them, which frustrates them no end. How do you like Mr. Sterling, our new TV cartoon character?"

"My kids like Mr. Sterling."

"The new Food Division agency has a million ideas. Look, I'm having some people over New Year's Eve. You and Anne are invited."

"Well, I don't know, Hank."

"Stick close to me, my man. I'll protect you."

"What is that supposed to mean?"

"I think you know. When Powell nearly lost his head in that helicopter crash it was no more of an accident than the painting of your house. I expect more action perhaps aimed at me next time."

"Well, security is your department. Or so I'm told."

"Not any more. Security reports right to Breedlove."

"That is an interesting development."

"So we'll just have to trust old Breedlove. Or get out of the company."

"Yes. He has said something similar to that to me."

Lancaster leaned close to Scott. "I'll give you a tidbit of gossip, for free. A chick met old George when he was in New York last July. You could have floored me with a feather. I didn't know he could get it up any more."

"I don't want to hear about it, Hank."

"I had a man on him, from A-1 Detectives. That was

before Breedlove's flatfoots started tailing us. My man was too good. He saved George and his love from a mugger. Then he flattened George when that copter crashed."

"Why tell me this?"

"To let you know that I know a good agency if you want to hire some protection for yourself."

"Are we business executives or CIA operatives?"

"Well, give my love to Anne," Lancaster said.

Two cops from the San Diego Police Department—a veteran and a rookie in a prowl car—found a dead man in a car about midnight the following Sunday. The man had gone through the windshield of a red Volkswagen. The Volkswagen apparently had run off the road and had smashed into a tree at a high rate of speed. Its front was completely crushed. Both front wheels had come off. The man, a middle-aged black, was found twenty feet from the Volks. The accident had occurred on a seldom used side road about a mile from the Pacific Coast Highway, near Torrey Pines. Almost all of the pines and vegetation in the area had been destroyed by a fire in 1971 and the debris had never been cleaned up. It was a giant ash heap, gray and black, with scorched trees and bushes bending to the earth like huge grasping claws. There was no ID on the body. The license number of the Volks was 741 LGN.

"This John Doe musta hit that win'shield awful goddamn hard," the older cop said. "There ain't much left of his head."

"Jeeze," said the rookie, choking back vomit.

23

His wife's optimism was one reason why Powell still held hopes of becoming BII's chief executive. But when he faced the matter squarely, he admitted to himself that his chances were slight. He considered Scott the front-runner. Susan didn't agree.

"He's too young. On occasion, he's almost boyish."

"He has Breedlove's full respect," Powell said.

"That statement is somewhat difficult for me to accept, George. Breedlove doesn't respect weakness."

"Our Mr. Scott is no longer weak, if he ever was."

Lately Powell's drive had lessened. He was seeing Carol quite often, stolen hours that relieved his tensions and temporarily restored his lost hope for happiness. He was confident Mendenthal would be defeated. The attacks on the company, as Breedlove had predicted, had ceased. Powell had once feared the helicopter crash he'd witnessed had been a step in a well-planned terrorist campaign to undermine BII and its executives, but now he considered that premise absurd.

Susan tapped on his door late one evening. "George?"

"Yes?"

"May I come in?"

"I'll come out," he said.

The robe he drew on had been a Christmas present from Sophia two years ago, and it reminded him that Christmas would soon again be upon them. Lights had been strung over city streets; the stores were open in the evenings. Residents of Sherman Place had agreed again this year not to decorate their homes with bulbs, a gesture to energy conservation. The holidays didn't mean much to Powell, only a signal that another year was ending. He'd enjoyed Thanksgiving and Christmas when the twins had been young, but those days, like most of his days, were gone. He'd taken Susan out for Thanksgiving dinner this year, deciding finally upon Scandia on the Sunset Strip. He detested the Strip, now overrun with hordes of juveniles in Bohemian garb, but he liked Scandia, where the maître d' and the waiters called him Mr. Powell and mixed special sauces and dressings for him. But the evening had been a failure. It had failed not in the quality of the dinner; it had failed because they had been trapped for over an hour in the presence of each other. They'd discussed only trivialities. Long periods of silence had passed between them.

When he opened the door, Susan no longer was there. He saw a light in the living room at the foot of the stairs.

"I thought you would like a brandy," she said when he came down.

"No. Thank you."

"I heard you groan. Is something wrong?"

"Wrong is right. Right is wrong."

"Are you ill?"

"No. Not ill. I must have been dreaming."

"Sit down."

"May I smoke?"

"Of course you may smoke."

"You used to like this brand of tobacco."

"I still do like it."

She, too, wore a robe, a blue one from I. Magnin he had given her last year. He was very attentive about gifts, although he had difficulty remembering dates. His secretaries were aware of it; they usually checked the dates and made the purchases. He seldom attended to personal matters himself. Now he could not recall if the robe had been bought for Susan's birthday or for their anniversary.

"I think I'll have a brandy," she said.

"One? Or five?"

"That was unnecessary."

"I suppose it was."

"Then I will have a drink. With your permission."

"You have my permission, Susan."

"Thank you."

It seemed as if the big house echoed their voices. He wondered vaguely if she would try to lure him into a spat. Her temper had quickened in recent months, vented primarily on domestic help and gardeners; the outbursts seemed to accompany what he noticed to be a reduced intake of alcohol and a renewed interest in fashion and careful grooming. Her abuse had not settled on Powell. Years ago there had been the beginnings of altercations, usually when she had denied him sex, but sex simply was not a consideration in their lives any more. Yet as she now moved slowly across the room, he felt a slight stirring in his loins. Her hair was down, flowing over her back, and he could see the movements of her breasts under the robe. She poured a carefully measured shot of brandy into a snifter and returned to the couch, shaking the snifter. He sat deep in an armchair across from her. He lit his pipe.

"It will be our first Christmas without Sophia and Timothy," she said.

"That sounds faintly like an accusation."

"It wasn't meant to sound like one."

"No," he said.

"If you would really try, I think you can convince them that they should return home."

"What else? There are other matters on your mind."

"I want your opinion on the proxy-solicitation threat at the company."

"We will defeat Mr. Mendenthal by several million votes."

"Then our threats narrow down to two—Mr. Lancaster and Mr. Scott. George, we will no longer be foolish about this."

"What do you mean?"

"I want you to stop seeing that woman."

"I don't understand what you're talking about."

"Your work has turned you into an expert liar."

"Would you care to discuss your own relationship?" He leaned forward. "I believe that her name is Maxine."

She laughed. "You surprise me, George. I would have thought you considered hiring a private detective a somewhat sordid act."

"I hired no one. As it happened, I saw her with you in Beverly Hills one day. She got into her car. The name was on the license plate."

"You followed me?"

"I did not follow you. Is the reverse true?"

"George, I refuse to allow our talk to disintegrate into a pointless argument."

"As do I. I have no energy for dispute after a week of disputes at the office. I merely wish to point out to you that your accusations to me come from one with unclean hands."

"I accuse you of nothing. Your actions are justified. My point was to be that it is not a time to carry on an affair. It could hurt you at the company."

"What of you? That could not hurt me?"

"It was a foolishness I regret and will terminate."

"What will we do now, Susan? Tuck away our seamy pasts and resume a conspiratorial war for success?"

"That is what we will do," she said.

"I've advanced quite high enough at the company."

"You neither mean that nor do you believe it." Susan stood up. She spoke through tight lips, almost with a hissing sound. "I remind you, George, that I could have had my own career. I gave it up because of my confidence in you. I still have that confidence in you. We are both guilty of some vacillation, but we no longer will risk what we have the opportunity to achieve over puny matters of the heart or glandular pleasures."

He put his cold pipe down in an ashtray. "It's late," he said. "I'm going back to bed."

"You're welcome to share mine."

"No."

"Would you like to see me now?"

"Susan, for God's sake."

She laughed, her head back. "George, I'm afraid dramatics do not become us." Their eyes met. "I can't explain my aberrations to you because I do not understand them myself. I would like to tell you that I plan to begin psychiatric treatment tomorrow."

"It is long overdue."

"George, there is something about you I have never been able to understand. It is your lack of confidence. Occasionally you act as if you lived in an old-age home, when in fact you're at the prime of your business life. Now opportunity has been thrust at you. All you have to do is seize it, instead of surrender to men less qualified and less able. If you love that woman, tell her to go away."

"So you propose a pact. Maxine in trade for—"

"Carol," she said. "Carol Lynn Reynolds."

"You deal interestingly and coldly in lives."

"Will you see Sophia and Timothy?"

He hesitated. Then he said, "All right."

"Talk to them one at a time, not together."

"Shall I give them your love?"

"I do love them."

"Until they showed you they no longer can be molded. Molded like plastic matter."

Susan peered at him. "It is true. They have been molded, yes. That is why they will return."

* * *

The news of George's promotion to the Office of the President at BII had startled Susan almost as much as it had startled him. She had feared that he was stalled at the company and had in fact urged him to forward his résumé to an executive placement firm. When the appointment was announced, she had difficulty in admitting the error in judgment to herself, for she did not often make errors in judgment, not about people. She prided herself on her ability to cut quickly to the truth. She understood nuances and innuendos; she differentiated rapidly between the real and the unreal. Careful, cold analysis, afterwards, invariably proved her flash intuitions about people to be correct. Her immediate impression of the man who was to become her husband was that this dull-witted but brilliant young man from Harvard who had the respect of his far richer companions needed only to be stirred from an outward pretense of lethargy and lack of ambition to achieve an almost limitless potential. Her work for him had begun almost immediately. She made sure that it was a church marriage. She made sure that relatives attended. After the marriage, she saw to his dress, encouraged him to maintain the proper social contacts, and swelled his ego with talk of his inherent brilliance and glowing future. She planned his diet, schooled him in etiquette, and made his appointments with doctors, dentists, hair stylists, and manicurists. When she began to deny him sex, she did not consider it a retardation to his career, reminding him that discipline was a factor in success and also that gratification would come to him in promotion. In other respects, in the more important ones, she was superb. When they had moved to Los Angeles after his appointment as BII treasurer, she had searched out ways and means to join the best clubs—the Jonathan, the Los Angeles Country Club, the University. Often they conferred for weeks before deciding on the proper guest list for a party. She never drank at her parties, or at parties where other important BII executives were in attendance. Some of her closest acquaintances thought she was a teetotaler. She never failed to send thank-you notes or sympathy cards. The Powells' Christmas cards invariably were the first in the mail, about December 10, and the list was carefully prepared and revised each year. She knew he realized her worth to him, and that was part of the hold she had over him. She had, in effect, created him.

But in the past few years she had seen evidence that he was wavering. She had fully expected him to have a few affairs, but she had not anticipated a serious one like that which apparently had developed between George and Carol Reynolds, verified to her at great expense by a Los Angeles detective agency. It caused her deep concern, for it could affect George's future with the company.

She did not worry about herself. She admitted to lesbian drives but not to committed lesbianism. She could control her urges, just as she could control her drinking. They seemed related. When she drank, another person seemed to come out of her.

At the psychiatrist's office she waited impatiently for fifteen minutes and then went to the receptionist's window. "My appointment was for ten," she said. "It is now ten minutes after the hour."

"I'm sorry, Mrs. Powell. Doctor will be with you soon."

"In that case, I wish to cancel my appointment."

She stalked out, found a phone booth in the lobby of the building, and dialed a number.

"Well, look who's calling," Maxine said.

"I want to see you."

"You can't. Not now."

"I'm on my way over. You be there."

She slammed down the receiver, went outside, and hailed a taxi. The taxi moved slowly on Wilshire, under the Christmas decorations, heading toward West Los Angeles.

She did not really know when it had started. There had been some experiments in college, with other girls who were also unsure, and one affair had lasted almost three months. It had been a love affair, as close to love as Susan could come. Before that, despite her attempts, she had thought of homosexual activity with disgust. After her first complete experience, at a ski lodge in the Catskills with a woman in her forties, she had felt dirty and on the edge of panic. She had never seen the woman again; she had forgotten her name. But the woman had revisited Susan in her dreams, a haunting vision of her thin, tanned face and strong, athletic body that had, for a few quick moments, shown Susan a pleasure she'd never before known.

Maxine reminded her of the woman at the lodge. She'd first seen Maxine—a thin young woman in a black knit pants suit—at a restaurant in Westwood. The dreams had returned. She considered Maxine a test, like a little drink after long abstinence. She admitted now that she had failed the test. It was time to rectify that failure.

In the taxi she felt total contentment. Why confess to a psychiatrist? It was as useless as George's confessions to a priest. It was a sign of weakness, like taking Novocain at the dentist's or clinging to the false protection of a St. Christopher's medal. Her father had worn a St. Christopher's medal. So had George's father. In many ways they had been much alike—businessmen bound by codes, slaves to order, and ardent Catholics. They both had clung to miserable marriages perhaps held together by mutual hatred of Communists and Protestants; their litany had been mass, baptism, confirmation, confession, ordination, extreme unction, holy matrimony. Susan held back a laugh. St. Peter at the Golden Gate. Pius XI and Pius XII, endowed with infallibility *ex cathedra*. The ultimate succeeders. Susan's father had succeeded within limits, but he could have succeeded fully. His failure to succeed fully had forced Susan to eat cold lunches at college and had prevented her from going to Vassar, where many of her friends had gone. She had never forgiven her father for falling short of the height he could have attained. Nor had George's father gone far. He had ended a drunk, a financial failure, and a suicide. Religion had given him nothing. Yet religion had its uses. It could be used for control. Who had termed religion the opiate of the masses? Karl Marx? George's code of order had a religious base; holy matrimony was one of its creeds. She'd never lose him.

Now was his biggest test. Their biggest.

Mark Scott. Henry Lancaster. George Powell.

The three really had received a backhand promotion by Lewis Breedlove. It meant quite a lot more money and more prestige. But the man who emerged at the head would become king. The other two would fade into obscurity.

She understood Henry Lancaster. She feared Mark Scott,

because she did not understand him. She feared him much more than she would admit to George. Yet she considered it unwise for George to challenge Scott openly, so she let him believe she thought Lancaster to be George's principal competitor. Privately, however, she considered Scott the leading contender, primarily because of his apparent closeness to Breedlove.

Scott was deceptive, unpredictable, and Susan's enemy.

Maxine opened the door.

"Get a dress on," Susan said.

Maxine pouted. "But I was going to take a bath. For you."

"Then get into the tub."

Maxine smiled.

Susan sat on the edge of the tub while Maxine removed her bra and panties, revealing small, hard-nippled breasts and a thatch of black hair between her legs. She had firm, thin legs, strong and supple. She moved with calculated slowness, bending over to test the temperature of the water with her finger, standing on her tiptoes in a deliberate display of her body. Susan removed one of her gloves. Maxine got into the tub with a little splash.

"Would you like to kiss me now?" she said.

Susan leaned down and kissed her openmouthed. She felt Maxine's tongue on hers, and a twinge of wanting went through her. She touched Maxine's breast with her ungloved hand and Maxine took the hand and guided it between her legs. She waas breathing hard. Susan broke the kiss and grasped Maxine's chin.

"Ouch," Maxine said. "Meanie."

"There will be no more money," Susan said.

"Oh, don't be like that. When you're like that—"

Susan's hand slipped to Maxine's throat. "It's over. The money. The good times. All your teasing. Do you believe me when I say it's over?"

Maxine struggled to talk. Her eyes were wide with surprise and fear. Slowly Susan forced her head under the water and held her down. Maxine's head bobbed up, shaking.

"I want you to understand something," Susan said. "If you make trouble, I will destroy you."

"I won't make trouble, Suz."

"You're sure of that."

"You don't have to be like this."

"It is the only way to end it."

"Cruel."

"I am cruel. It's time you understand that."

"Can I have just a little? To get by the month?"

"No. I'm sure that you will manage."

"I thought I loved you."

"There is no love," Susan said.

Powell met Carol at a small restaurant in downtown Los Angeles, far from his office and far enough from hers. They had been there several times and felt safe in its dark interior.

"You really don't have to say it," she said.

"Thank you for making it easy."

"She will peck your insides out."

"I fear that you are right. She has a need to be dominant."

"I'm not sorry for me. I'm grateful that I have had you, or half had you, as long as I have. Now I revert to type. The original, aboriginal Carol. In the final analysis these days, it's really all job."

"I will miss the look your eyes once had."

"Perhaps that wasn't the real me. Oh, well. I suppose I couldn't sleep with one man the rest of my life, anyway. It's not the temper of our times."

"Carol, please stop it."

"What should I say? That I love you?"

"I will always love you," he said.

"Will your life be good?"

"I don't know. I don't know."

"I only wanted you to find peace."

"Peace may not be an earthly thing." He touched her hand. "Will you take your job offer in New York?"

"Yes. I think so. Onward and upward, you know."

"I've brought your Christmas gift. May I give it to you now?"

"I've brought yours," she said.

* * *

The blatant double designation—SOPHIA POWELL, JUSTIN CLIFFORD—greeted Powell over the mailbox at the apartment house in Santa Monica where his daughter had lived since July. He winced. He pushed the doorbell.

"I can tell you're relieved because Justin isn't here," Sophia said over coffee in the living room. "And I do think I can guess the nature of your mission."

"It is not a mission. I merely wanted to see you."

"You do not lie expertly."

"It is not a lie."

"How is Mother?"

"Your mother is fine."

"I'll tell you this, Father. It is a shitty world."

"I'll assume that was meant to shock."

"It's not working with Justin. When he gets his degree, he'll go off seeking money and perhaps I'll go to Mexico and find a beachboy. The way I've been gaining weight, I may have to pay for sex pretty soon."

"Sophia—"

"No. Don't try. You haven't got the answers."

"Come home."

"No."

"Where is Timothy?"

"You'll find him, no doubt, on some beach in Venice."

"I do want you to come home. Both of you."

"Will that help? I think not. I'm totally unhappy, but I was totally unhappy at home, too. I don't know what it is, but it gets worse every day. I don't love anybody and I don't hate anybody. I'm just dead inside."

"We do want you at home. Believe me."

"Why?"

"Because we love you."

"Are you up for another promotion at the company?"

"What has that to do with it?"

"She sent you. That much I know. Tell me. Have you had *any* happy days? In your entire life?"

"Yes," he said. He was thinking of Carol. He wanted to tell her about Carol. But he couldn't. "I have. Believe me when I say that."

"I'll tell you where Tim is," Sophia said.

*   *   *

He saw worn tires anchored in the wet mud of the Venice Canals as he walked down Twenty-sixth Street, headed toward the beach. A sign on the door of one of the small shops on Speedway read, "The King Is Coming." A middle-aged black man in a gray leather coat with thongs sat on the sidewalk, striking a small drum with his palms. Three dogs growled over a stick. Young tanned bodies stretched on the beach, absorbing sun. A group of boys in bathing suits were playing volleyball. Looking at the youths, Powell felt a heavy weight of age and depression. He also felt completely out of place, in his hat and business suit with a vest.

"Excuse me," he said to a pretty girl in a bikini who idled barefooted on the sidewalk. "I wonder if you can help me. I'm looking for a boy, a young man, named Tim Powell, who—"

"Mister, I don't know nobody here named that," she said.

"Is he bothering you?" said a boy in a blue bathing suit who had come up from the beach.

"He's looking for somebody," the girl said.

"Yeah, I'll bet he is," the boy said.

Four others—two boys and two girls—young and tanned, their bodies glistening with suntan lotion, had joined them. They stood eyeing Powell. He turned to leave, but one of the young men held him by the arm. The group formed a circle around him, joined hands, and began to move in a counterclockwise rotation. Powell felt helpless, almost panicked. He had stumbled into a culture of young slim bodies so foreign to his environment that it was as if he'd walked through a door into another world. The group chanted as it circled him. He closed his eyes. Then he felt a hand on his shoulder and he opened his eyes to see Timothy standing beside him, wearing sandals and shorts.

"Well, you see what happened is that like last week or so they had a fellow down here that was playing with the girls, a fellow about your age," Timothy explained over a Coke at a hot-dog stand on Speedway. "Well dressed, respectable-looking, had money. They can come down, look for free, but when they start feeling and roll out money wanting more than looking, then we get a little upset. You know?"

He had lost weight since Powell had last seen him. He covered his bloodshot eyes with dark sunglasses. There were tattoos on both his forearms, a naked girl on one, a coiled snake on the other. He'd grown a scruffy dark beard.

"Well, Pop, just how're you doing?" he said. "Long time no see, you gotta drop by more often."

"I'll ask you the same question. How are you doing?"

"Getting along. Four of us share a couple rooms."

"I've just seen Sophia."

"She still shacked up with that dude?"

"Your sister is a very unhappy person."

"I know. I get vibes. We're twins, remember?"

"Have you given any thought to returning to college?"

"No way. I get my schooling down here."

"Your mother and I would like you to return home."

"There it is. The message. Well, thanks but no thanks. I don't like prisons. Here I got the whole sky, I can ball all the chicks in creation, and at night when we build a fire on the beach and get a little high it's like I'm dead and gone to heaven. You ever get that feeling?"

"I'm afraid not."

"Hey, life goes by. You know? Unstiff, Pop. Live. You go around just once. Before we know it, we're six feet down, food for worms."

"A remarkable statement for a boy of twenty-four."

"I'm that old already? You gotta be kidding."

"You know quite well how old you are."

"Hey, you still with Breedlove?"

"Yes."

"Breedlove has a son. Older fellow named Larry."

"I believe so, yes."

"I know the dude. I mean, I've talked to him. Once in a while he'll wander around here in a dirty old green coat and tennis shoes, smashed out of his mind, creeping like a spook. He tells me something. He says some people he knows are going to blow up that airplane of yours."

Powell whirled. "Just exactly what are you talking about, Timothy?"

"All I know's what this Breedlove dude tells me. I just thought I'd pass it on, for what it's worth. Ask me, I think the dude is crazy. Well, here's Hunk, one of my roomies. Gotta go. Take care, Pop."

"Timothy?"

"Sure. What?"

"When did we lose you?"

"You didn't lose me, man."

"Do you need any money?"

Timothy shrugged. "Sure, Pop. Everybody always needs money."

"I'll write you a check."

"Don't do that. I need money, sure, but I'm not going to take any from you. Your money's got strings attached to it. I take it, you pull the string, I find myself all bound up again. I don't need that. I want to be free. Let me tell you about me, tell you the way it is. I've been spaced out since I was sixteen. I've been high half the time. I've done nothing but loaf, demonstrate against anything, or ball chicks in the commune. Even if I do grow out of these things, I'm not going to settle down to slavery. I'm happy. I've got a soul."

"You realize what a disappointment you are to me."

"Well, don't blame yourself, Pop."

"I don't blame myself."

"That's the spirit." Timothy smiled. "Well, take care, Pop. Watch out for number one, okay?"

He went away, his arm around the shoulder of the black man he called Hunk. Powell stood alone, watching them go. He did not feel any emotional reaction concerning Timothy's comments about Larry Breedlove, although he probably would turn the information over to security or to Breedlove. The sun burned the back of his neck. Finally he returned to his car, emptiness deep within him like a weight. He had failed as a lover. He had failed as a father. There was only his business life left to him.

24

THE SCOTT FAMILY HAD A GOOD CHRISTMAS HOLIDAY, DE-
spite two blots for Scott. The first was a full-page ad in the
Olen *Record,* sent to Scott by his father. It read:

TO BII SHAREHOLDERS
OF OLEN:

The Board of Directors of Breedlove International, Inc., wants you to die.

Rumors of plans to close the BII plant in Olen
have been substantiated by our Committee.

This is a crime. Olen will be stricken from the
map by an arbitrary decision made two thousand
miles away.

We have previously said we intend to oppose and
unseat the current Board of Directors of BII by solicitation of voting proxies for our slate of opposing directors. The matter will be decided at the BII
annual meeting, to be held in Olen in the Spring.

We now announce that if we are successful in un-
seating BII directors, we will keep the Olen plant
open. We will, in fact, modernize and expand the
plant.

It is our solemn promise to you.

> Philip Mendenthal
> Chairman
> Committee for Better
> Management of BII

Scott phoned Powell at home.

"Yes," Powell said. "I saw the ad."

"Why didn't you tell me?"

"I don't consider it significant."

"Well, I do."

"Scottie, less than two percent of our stockholders live in Olen. Less than eight percent live in Wisconsin."

"I think we should do something about it."

"What should we do? Say that we are not planning to close that plant?"

"Well, I—"

"I think it wise to ignore it," Powell said. "Merry Christmas, Scottie."

Kevin Sheehan, the PR manager, phoned him the next day. "Mr. Scott, do you remember the fighter I checked out for you? Morris?"

"Yes, of course."

"He's dead, sir."

"Dead? When?"

"They found him near San Diego. A car accident. A reporter down there checked it for me. Apparently, Morris had a snoot full." Sheehan paused. "Mr. Scott?"

"Yes."

"Did you know he was Mr. Breedlove's chauffeur?"

"I did know, yes."

"They're sending the body back here for burial."

"Do you know when the funeral is?"

"I'll find out," Sheehan said.

They opened their presents on Christmas Eve, after Liz and Tod did a version of the manger scene and Anne played the piano while they all sang Christmas songs. Carolers from the high school carrying lanterns and dressed in hats and shawls came up the street, raising their voices in the cool, crisp air. Scott's hand found Anne's. He sat in the warm glow of family; gone were thoughts of Lewis Breedlove, the Troika, the SEC, the proxy fight, even the attack on his home and the lingering, unresolved attacks on the company. Only once did a disturbing vision come to him. He saw in a quick mind flash Morris's stretched-out body on a cold slab, toe-tagged and embraced by the iron of rigor mortis, a man whose life had been a delusion of manipulated fraud now ignominiously ended, apparently without kin or mourners.

For a change, he got almost as much of a haul for Christmas as the kids. Anne gave him a compass for the sailboat they'd bought last month, plus a Cartier watch, reminding him that he'd occasionally mentioned Lancaster's Cartier to her. The compass obviously was a hint for him to stay home and use the new boat more often; they'd used it only once. Anne also gave him a six-volume Shakespeare set. Scott's formal education had been all business and professional, but he'd been interested in Shakespeare since grade school, an interest that heightened when he discovered the Bard had an extraordinary knowledge of law and court proceedings.

After conferring with Joan Leeky, Scott had bought Anne a gold bracelet with three diamonds, similar to one she'd admired once at Tiffany's. Tod and Liz got games, Elton John and The Tubes records, and camping equipment. A big surprise for Tod was a special gift from his brother, a squeaking mongrel puppy they immediately named Cindy. Mike, who seemed in a family mood again, got a metal tennis racket, stamps for his collection, and a chess set with ivory figures. He promptly beat Scott three games in a row.

"A fellow who can play chess like that shouldn't have trouble with number bases at school," Scott said.

"Aw, you threw the games."

"Like fun I did. You just beat a fellow three in a row who once beat the chess champ of Wisconsin."

"You beat him? Really?"

"Well, he was a little high on hot rum that day."

"So were you," Anne said.

They all laughed. It ended with more songs and talk, grouped before a blazing fireplace.

"I think Mike is back with us," Anne said later, in their bed. "You paid attention to him, and he responded."

"Are you sure he didn't just drop in for a while to collect his Christmas loot?"

"Oh, Mark!"

"Maybe I'm becoming a Christmas cynic."

"You might have the Christmas blues."

"On the contrary, I'm very happy. If we could have lured my parents here for the holiday, Dad would think I probably turned out all right after all."

"Shall I show off my new bracelet at the Lancasters' party?"

"Oh. You've decided. We're going."

"No, you decide. You decide the company things."

Mike wanted to try the new tennis racket, so Scott challenged him on Christmas day. Mike won, 6–4 and 6–2.

"Dad, I've been thinking something," he said.

"What?"

"That you're not a bad father."

"Not bad? Well, that's a rather limp endorsement."

"I mean, what I mean is, you're a very good one."

"Because I lose at chess and tennis?"

"Tommy, his father always staggers around with a glass in his hand. What a klutz."

"Does he get drunk?"

"He's an alcoholic," Mike said.

"Your mother thinks Tommy is a bad influence on you."

"I feel sorry for him," Mike said. "He needs a friend."

Scott stood on a green knoll, watching as Morris's casket was lowered into the ground. A wind had come up, whipping the grass and snapping at his clothing. The grave workers picked up their shovels. The dirt made a plumping sound as it hit the casket. Scott turned and discovered Scoggins standing behind him.

"No one else came," Scott said.

"Well, he didn't have many friends, Mr. Scott."

"Did you know him well?"

"He guarded his privacy, Mr. Scott. I respected that."

"I hate to ask you this. But was Morris a drinker?"

"Oh, no, sir. He was an abstainer. He prided himself on his body."

Scott glanced up. A figure was outlined on the top of a hill behind them. It was a man in dark clothing, standing slump-shouldered, gazing at the men with shovels. Electric recognition flooded Scott's brain. It was the Breedlove-like man he'd seen in Olen. He ran up the hill, but when he got there the man was gone.

The Lancasters' New Year's Eve party was in full swing when Anne and Scott arrived. The drapes over the living-room glass were open and stars peered down at the celebrators like searching eyes. The dress was a blend of formal and informal, but all the men wore ties and the women wore dresses. Some of the men, reaching the Lancasters as their second or third party of the evening, wore tuxedos and their women wore gowns. The party was not sedate, nor was it disorderly. No one got really drunk, at least not before midnight. It was not only fun time; it was also contact time. Business-card exchanges were encouraged, aspiring actresses were pushed into the regal presences of authentic producers, free financial advice was solicited from expensive advisers. The best brands of liquor flowed abundantly. Youth mixed with age, the ugly chatted with the beautiful, business antagonists embraced each other. The new year promised to be better than the old, which itself had been extraordinary. Lancaster wore a blue blazer and white slacks. Dorothy wore a skin-tight black dress. Men clustered around her, languid and enchanted in the glow of her perfumed body. Two bartenders in red coats feverishly mixed liberal drinks, while four women in white dresses with yellow aprons served catered food from behind a buffet line. The roof over the pool was open and gas braziers flickered over the lawn, glowing in the eyes of the women near them. A cowboy star of yesteryear, still recognizable despite his swollen face, held sway over one group, talking in an alcohol-slurred twang; a young senator with a large thatch of hair spilling over his forehead held another, praising the tenacity if not the wisdom of Barry Goldwater; a blonde now starring in a Shubert musical hit held her subjects spellbound, chattering about the Hollywood she'd come to know. Above them the hills were dark, interspersed with lights twinkling from other parties.

"Scottie, loosen up," Lancaster said.

"Six minutes," Dorothy said, brushing by. "Are we all synchronized? Synchronize, everybody."

Anne touched Scott's arm. "Don't leave me."

"I won't."

"Oh! Look there! The Lancasters know *her*?"

"No. She knows the Lancasters."

"Don't leave me. I'm in over my head."

It exploded at midnight. Women in party hats kissed strange men. Men kissed strange women. The famous kissed the unfamous, the reticent metamorphosed into bombastics, the over-forties became under-thirties in spirit. Strobe lights jittered, catching cigarette smoke in their flashes; rock music exploded from the stereo system. Men danced coatless. Women danced shoeless. In due time magnums of Mumm's were opened with exaggerated cork-popping ceremonies and glasses were dashed against the fireplace. A woman did a perfect swan dive into the pool, and when she failed to emerge immediately two men shed their coats and plunged in to rescue her. Resuscitated, she asked for champagne. It swirled around Scott, affected by a four-drink unsteadiness; it seemed a color-splashed writhing parade under the stars, a revel squirming with beautiful-people bodies, red laughing mouths, and false eyelids flickering shut-open and open-shut like camera lenses. He stood stunned and fascinated.

"Hadn't we better go?" Anne said.

"In a little while."

"You're drinking too much."

"Yes. Don't you do it."

"I had only one glass of champagne. And somebody spilled half of that on me. A woman is passed out in the john. In the bathtub. Covered by towels."

"Anybody famous?"

"Men go in there," Anne said.

About 1:30 A.M. he found himself alone with Lancaster, seated in wicker chairs beside the pool. The party had changed character; it had become sober-up time, coffee time to avoid the police nets set for drunks. The music had been toned down to light classical. Hanger-on guests grouped before the fireplace in the living room, seated in chairs or on the floor. Some were still drinking, but quietly.

"Scottie, Scottie, Scottie," Lancaster said.

"Hank, Hank, Hank."

"Are we drunk?"

"I think I am. Halfway, at least."

"Have another. Get smashed. Ruin your image."

"You're a bad influence."

"I'm bad, period. I'm as bad as you are good. But worry thee not, clean Scottie, for God will punish me in the end for my sins. Tell me. Is there anything at all we can dig up to pin on you?"

"Well, yes, as a matter of fact. I took a dime from my mother's purse when I was eight."

"Hell, I burned the orphanage when I was eight." Lancaster snapped his fingers. "I have it. You are finished *because* you are Mr. Clean. You can't hurt anybody, and to go to the top you'll have to hurt."

"I think you're getting serious."

"No. Only when I said I burned the orphanage."

"I'd better take Anne home. Or Anne take me home."

"Have a nightcap first. It will be fun to see if Dottie and Anne start swinging their purses at each other."

"Are Mark and Hank going to swing purses, too?"

"If we do, bet on Hank, not Mark, because Hank fights dirty." Lancaster leaned forward. "But my best advice to you, my man, is not to fight me."

"I won't."

"I'll give you some more advice, some that might save you. Go away. Get out of the company. Escape with Anne and the kids while you can."

"I seem to be getting that advice from all over. Coming from you, however, it sounds more like a threat than advice."

"You came up too fast. You're in over your head."

"Maybe we all are."

"You hate to fight, don't you? Passive resistance."

"Hank, what are you trying to tell me? That I should be frightened? All right. I'm frightened. Are you satisfied now?"

"Ah, Scottie. The Bible Scottie, Scottie of the innocent and primeval countryside. Scottie, the noble savage. Shall we see the ignoble savage come out in our Scottie? Shall we see the front peeled away?"

"That's enough, Hank."

"Say it to me true, good parson. Wilt thou prone thyself in the street and let me run my tractor over you?"

"Try it and see."

"I may. I just may. Your shtick is still water, my shtick is the raging flood."

"I think this party's over."

"If I must, parson, I'll stomp on you. I will shit all over your birthday cake. Would you stomp on me?"

"No."

"No, no, no. He chants no, no, no. I chant shit, shit, shit. Bullshit, full bullshit." Lancaster had Scott's wrist. He tightened his grip. "You're beginning to see me as I am. When will I see you as you are?"

"We're not kidding now, are we? Not at all."

"No. We're not kidding."

"Let go of my arm, Hank."

Lancaster released it. He stood up. "Stay out of my way, Scottie. Consider that a warning." He went away.

In the Buick, Anne driving, Scott said, "What went on between you and Dorothy? I've seen cool good nights before, but nothing like that."

"It was something she said. About you."

"What did she say about me?"

"I don't want to repeat it."

"The car is weaving. Shall I drive?"

"Hardly. I don't want to end up in jail tonight."

"What did she say that you don't want to repeat?"

Anne hit the brake. The Buick stopped. "She said you sleep around when you're out of town. She said most of the executives do it and that she encourages Hank to do it. She said there are kept company girls all over."

"Don't tell me that you believe her."

"Oh, I don't know what to believe. But, no, I don't believe her. Not about you." Anne slipped toward him and held him tightly, her face against his neck. "Well, we're in it. I know that now. And I also know that I can play their sick, childish games too. Mark, I want you to win. If that's what you want, to win it."

"I do. Even more so, after tonight."

"Why more so?"

"Because Hank acted like an animal. I actually think he's dangerous."

"What did he say?"

"Well, he was a little high."

"That's when the real feelings come out."

"Anne, I'm going all out to win this thing."

"Are we making a pact?"

"I guess we are."

"Mark, I love you. Very much. I've waffled and waffled, but now I've decided. Even though I risk losing you, I'm with you in this campaign."

"It's no longer merely a campaign. It's a fight, one that's going to get more bloody and dirty."

"Just don't change too much."

"I won't. Honest injun."

"A funny word, honest," Anne said.

25

BII LAUNCHED A MASSIVE COUNTERATTACK AGAINST THE MENdenthal forces early in January, spearheaded by George Powell. The company's profits were at a record level, with sales up 18.5 percent and net earnings up 16.4 percent, and unaudited figures were sent to shareholders on January 13, fully a month ahead of such a mailing in a normal year. The income report also contained a truncated balance sheet and a letter over Powell's signature noting that BII had had steadily increasing profits over the past six years, despite recessionary trends in the world economy during some of those years. It also outlined steps taken by BII in recent years to cut overhead costs without impairing production efficiency and listed specific actions taken to weed out unprofitable operations, such as the closing of *Fortnightly Comment*. The letter ended with Powell's optimistic appraisal for the company's future, both short and long term. It did not mention the upcoming proxy contest or Philip Mendenthal.

It was followed by a series of newspaper advertisements in key cities. Again, the advertisements did not mention the proxy fight or Philip Mendenthal. They merely pointed to the record of accomplishment of BII's current management. The ads were signed, "Board of Directors, Breedlove International, Inc., Los Angeles." It was obvious to Scott that Powell was conferring almost daily with Lancaster, who had hired a public-relations and an advertising firm specifically for proxy-fight counteraction, and Scott suspected that Powell was also conferring with Breedlove on a regular basis. Breedlove had not been to the office since the Troika had been formed. Powell had not once conferred with Scott on the proxy-fight strategy. Scott, pressed with developing labor troubles, let it go until one day when he discovered that Powell had installed a telephone line BII shareholders could use toll free to talk to a member of management about the proxy contest or any other matter. Scott stormed past Powell's secretary and into his office, interrupting a meeting with the corporate treasurer.

"Scottie," Powell said, standing up. "Can this wait?"

"No."

"Please excuse us for a few minutes," Powell told the treasurer.

"For more than a few minutes," Scott said.

Powell sat down behind his desk, fingertips together. "Please tell me what is so urgent," he said coolly.

"I don't mean to be abrupt, George. But it appears I have to knock down your door to get in."

"I've been quite busy. We have all been busy."

"I see you've been busy installing telephones. I was under the impression that shareholder relations is my area of responsibility."

Powell stood up. "It is, along with everything else you have, but it is not as it relates to this proxy-solicitation threat. Do you really want to take charge of these telephones? It is a management-trainee task. I was under the impression you had more important matters to consider."

"I only wanted to know in advance."

"Scott, please understand something. Breedlove has put me in charge of counteraction to this proxy contest. I intend to do my job. Do you wish to discuss the matter with him? If so, we'll call him immediately."

Scott turned away. "George, why are we bickering?" he said, turning back.

"Indeed. Why?"

"I'm sorry."

He left, feeling despair and slight foolishness. He'd been put in his place by a man not his corporate superior but by one who had just now displayed superiority in judgment and also in demeanor. Powell had been right. Scott did have more important matters to handle, at least matters more pressing for the moment. One was a strike at the Farm Machinery Division's main plant in Lennox, a suburb of Kansas City.

Half of the plant's 5,500 employees had walked off the job a week ago, those represented by Local 21 of the Machinists & Farm Workers Union. Welles had been telecopying daily reports on the matter to Scott; the reports had warned of increasing militancy by union members, whipped up by a new business manager, and had suggested that picketing violence was possible. A federal mediator was on the job, but no progress had been made. The union was demanding a 10 percent pay raise for the first year and 5 percent each year for the next three, plus substantial increases in fringe benefits. BII's offer of a 6 percent a year increase for the next three years had been turned down. The plant was still operating, with some workers crossing picket lines despite threats by strikers. Scott had delayed going to Lennox, hoping that Welles and the mediator could settle the matter. The hopes were dashed on Monday, January 16, when Welles called Scott.

"Three people were hurt today," Welles said. "Somebody tossed a stone at a car, and before you knew it, we had a fight on our hands."

"Are you any closer to settlement?"

"Not an inch. This Crawley is a rough customer."

"Crawley?"

"The local's business manager. He thinks he's John L. Lewis or Jimmy Hoffa come to life. He's fresh, tough, ambitious. And he has the strikers mesmerized."

"All right," Scott said. "I'll be up tonight."

"You may not be able to get in. We're snowbound."

"I'll get there. How many picketers are out?"

"Oh, maybe a hundred."

"Are they clustered?"

"You mean bunched up? Well, yes. Sort of frozen together."

"That stone-throwing incident may work to our favor. Do this right now. Go to court and get an order against harassment of picket-line crossers. Most judges will sign those in two minutes if you can show some violence. Ask the court for an order limiting the picketers to three or four at any one location around the plant."

"Well, it was only a minor scuffle."

"Create another one if you have to. But get that order."

"This one's going to be tough to break, Scottie."

"Well, we're not going to give in to them."

"Breedlove says that?"

"I do," Scott said. He hung up.

He did not get to Lennox until the following day, owing to an unexpected revelation brought to him by a youthful computer-minded chap named Norman Jinkens. One of Scott's corporate status symbols since his promotion to the Office of the President had been the acquisition of a personal aide, called staff assistant by the title creators in personnel. After interviewing several applicants, he had selected Jinkens on the basis of his I.Q. (160), his appearance (Brooks Brothers grays and blues), and his personality (a bit prissy and superior but inoffensive). Jinkens was a graduate of Princeton (French literature major) and of Harvard Business School. His father was high up in the Internal Revenue Service, which was considered around the office to be the real reason he'd been hired. It wasn't. It was, instead, simply because Scott liked Jinkens, and so did Anne. So did Joan Leeky. Jinkens was twenty-two and worked with the efficiency of a calculating machine and the dedication of a West Point cadet. Such phrases as "inverse ratio" and "statistical theorem" littered his everyday conversation, but his favorite seemed to be "competitive equilibrium." In a report on crop forecasts for the next twenty years, he had included this sentence: "An integral element of continued success is the obtainment of information pertinent to preventative or fast reaction be the disequilibrium an act-of-God manifestation or traceable to competitive refinements potentially injurious to the organization; tho you have been most successful in counteraction to competitive refinements and increasingly modernistic and scientific in re matters now considered inherently unpredictable, the possibilities that remain for improvement are not exiguous and well may be syncretistic; also, some projected predetermination based on past variables is essential, for the momentum of events makes it crucial to obtain information more quickly and more encompassing of the entire area of vulnerability." When Anne read the report, which was followed by two pages of statistics, she laughed and suggested they give Norman a dictionary for Christmas so he could improve his vocabulary. When Scott asked its author what it meant, Norman stared blankly at him and said, "Surely you are joking, Mr. Scott." For a while Scott thought he'd been the victim of a collegiate prank, but, after studying the statistics, he realized that Norman had come up with a new method of crop forecasts that could save the company several thousand a year on the commodities markets. Norman got full credit for it, and a bonus. He also got Scott's respect.

So this morning when Joan Leeky admitted him to Scott's office, Norman wasn't immediately excused. He entered armed with a sheaf of papers and printouts from a computer.

"Mr. Scott, this matter now seems manifestly self-evident, but I wanted to leave the statistical aspects with you for your study," he said.

"I'm afraid I can't get to it today."

"I feel confident that it will interest you."

"Can you tell me what it is?"

"As you will see in the appended notes, the company's outgo for insurance coverage has risen an average of six percent per year over the past twenty-year span. In the past decade, this is due to higher premiums and also to increased coverage. But in the prior decade the coverage and premiums remained constant. Yet our outgo for protection rose."

"Perhaps the reports are in error."

"At first I attributed it to statistical error myself, Mr. Scott, but I have checked it on the computer."

"Well, this is Mr. Powell's department."

"I realize that, sir. Yet I thought I would show it to you, Mr. Scott."

"Why?"

"Because I report to you, sir. Please take it home, Mr. Scott, and check it thoroughly. There are year-by-year discrepancies between billed premiums and our payments. Our payments are higher than the billings."

"I'll look at it."

"I'd be glad to help, Mr. Scott."

"You can help by not mentioning this."

"Yes, sir. I understand, sir."

He studied the printouts until late in the afternoon, skipping lunch. At about 5 P.M. he called Anne.

"I'll be late," he said. "And I'm afraid I have to go out of town tomorrow."

"Not again," Anne said. "You're absolutely worn out."

"Already you've forgotten our pact."

She paused. Then she said, "Whenever I do, remind me."

"I'll be gone only a day or so," Scott said.

He returned to the printout sheets. He couldn't believe it. There must be some logical explanation. It appeared that several hundred thousand was missing from the company's books, covered up by an elaborate series of double entries. Jinkens had carefully red-penciled all of the discrepancies. One, for the month of March in 1959, showed insurance premium billings of $2,421.22, but the payment had been $3,222.46, issued in two checks—one for $2,421.22 and the other for $801.24. Payees were listed as Ohio Casualty, then one of the company's insurers, and a firm named BL Enterprises, of Fresno, California. An insurance agency? Why Fresno? Payments for 1959 were some $8,000 over what insurers had billed. The difference apparently had gone to BL Enterprises.

Could BL be Powell's company?

The total for the decade 1956–66 was about $250,000. It seemed unlikely that Powell, who now earned $300,000 a year exclusive of fringe benefits, would embezzle a mere quarter million. Yet he hadn't always earned that much; many BII vice-presidents made under $40,000 in the '50s. Scott wondered if perhaps the fund could be part of the money used to pay agents to open doors for BII in foreign countries. But that didn't make sense. There were better ways to hide such payments in the balance sheet and charge them against income for tax purposes. Billing-payment discrepancies had stopped about a decade ago. Powell had been treasurer then, with a reputation of never subordinating responsibility. BII had completed full computerization at headquarters just about ten years ago. Older records had been placed in storage.

Scott's private line jangled. "Honey?" Anne said. "It's after ten."

"I'm on my way."

"I have your bags packed," she said.

In the morning, after four hours' sleep, he called Norman Jinkens from home. "I've studied your report," he said. "Where did you get complete week-by-week accounting sheets for ten years ago?"

"They're now on microfilm, so I—"

"Why did you do it?"

"I was merely going over them to compare past results with the current in connection with the efficiency report you asked me to do. I am sure there is some explanation, Mr. Scott."

"There is. I have found it. So you are not to concern yourself with it."

"Yes, sir."

"That's all. No. One more matter. Personnel told me yesterday that your raise has come through."

The phone rang a second after he'd hung up. It was Lancaster. "Welles just called, wondering where the hell you were," Lancaster said.

"I'm leaving for the airport now."

"Take the jet. I'll call Long."

"I wasn't aware that the jet is your property to offer."

"Oh, tart," Lancaster said. "I would hope you'll be as tart with the union in Lennox."

"I'll do what is best."

"The plane offer is open."

"No. I'll go commercial. There is no sense in wasting jet fuel for a single passenger."

"Long is headed for Pittsburgh. He can drop you off."

"No, I'll go commercial," Scott said.

He took the computer printouts with him on the plane, intending to study them some more. Perhaps he would double-check them on the IBM at the Farm Machinery Division. But that really was unnecessary. The information was there. Scott searched his brain for a logical explanation. When he returned, he would ask Powell about it. Powell would have an answer. Or would he ask Powell? Should he check further first? Find out about BL Enterprises? He knew that Jinkens suspected outright embezzlement on someone's part, that BL Enterprises was perhaps a dummy corporation once owned by the embezzler. If so, it had to be Powell. No one else had been authorized to issue and sign the checks.

Unanswered questions swam in Scott's head as the plane cut through a bank of clouds and leveled at its cruising altitude.

Now he more than suspected Powell. He believed it to be true. With slightly more proof, he would have information that could destroy Powell. Jinkens more than suspected; he, too, knew. By calling Jinkens off, Scott realized, he had in effect placed himself under the thumb of a subordinate. He was legally in conspiracy with Powell if he perpetuated a cover-up. He had several choices. He could confront Powell. He could take the matter to the BII board. He could hire an accountant to check it. Or he could do nothing. He decided on the latter course, at least for now. Leaning back in his seat, he let his mind go blank. The printouts were in his briefcase.

Welles, bundled in a fur-collared overcoat, met him at the Kansas City airport. "I got your court order," he said in the taxi to Lennox.

Scott glanced out the window. The hills were covered with frozen snow, a glittering landscape of sheeted whiteness that hurt his eyes. The road had been cleared, but the farmhouses were almost obscured by huge drifts. Some telephone lines were down. Sleety snow thumped on the taxi's roof. Scott's feet felt like blocks of ice. He hadn't wanted to come here, he didn't want to stay. He felt a private disgust toward Welles; obviously, the man was incapable of decisive action. He was like Scott himself at Olen only a few months ago. The realization caused his head to snap up. It had been a young Scott at Olen. This Scott at Lennox was older, wiser.

"We're going on the offensive," he said. "You arrange a private meeting between Crawley and me."

"I'll try."

"Do more than try. Do it. And make it seem as if he's the one who's requesting the meeting."

"How will I do that?"

"Find a way. I've had Crawley checked out. I don't think he's above lining his pockets. Has he ever hinted anything like that?"

"No."

"I want you to do two other things. Get me in touch with a

good security agency. I want to rent some taping equipment. And I'll need some cash from your safe."

Welles was a list keeper. He was writing notes to himself.

From his hotel window that night, Scott watched the picketers around the plant. They had lighted fires in barrels and grouped around them, joking and singing, like soldiers preparing for a long siege. The snowfall had stopped and the temperature had dropped. Giant icicles hung from the eaves of the adjoining buildings. A wind curled under the window, chilling him. He hadn't called Anne. He wanted nothing to interrupt him, his resolve being to whip this problem and return to new tests at headquarters. The workers below him, clamping their mittened hands together and prancing like animals to keep warm, were his current test. They were also right now his enemies.

Crawley agreed to a private meeting, held at 7 A.M. under an ice-clogged oak about a mile from the union hall. Huge flakes of soft snow fluttered down. Crawley shivered and stomped his feet to keep warm. Scott stood stone-still, staring at him.

"I'm glad it's you come personally," Crawley said, extending his hand. "Your rep's that of a good and fair man."

"Yours is as a pretty tough fellow."

"Well, it's a thankless job." Crawley blew his nose into a large handkerchief with a great, prolonged honking sound. "No matter what you do for the worker, he wants more. But how's he to buy your product if you don't pay him?"

"I'm ready to submit a new offer."

"I'm glad to hear that, Mr. Scott."

"A six-percent raise, right now. Another six percent next year."

"And for the third year?"

"Again, six percent."

"In other words, the offer's the same as the one we pissed on just last week."

"We can word the contract differently."

"We're wasting our time out here, Mr. Scott, freezing off our balls out here in the snow for nothing."

"Your position is not good. Your timing is terrible. We're

over-produced now on farm machinery and a cutback in production won't hurt us. You can't keep them out much more than a month. We can afford to go much longer than that. Mr. Crawley, when I think about you, I think of one of two alternatives. Either you are not a very bright person or you've called this strike for some purpose of your own."

"I don't understand you."

"I think you do."

Crawley twitched. Fluid trickled from his sharp hawk nose. Finally he said, "All right, look, Mr. Scott, here's what I say we do. These things can take months if you got a bunch of negotiators around a table, so it's best like this, just we two." He grinned. His teeth were yellow and irregular. "Like a couple generals, eh, Mr. Scott? If the generals alone fought out the wars, there probably wouldn't be wars. All right. You get the ballots out and I'll go to them, recommend settlement. See there's something in there on new fringes. Just a little something. They won't be all that happy, but I can soothe them down. There's one thing."

"Yes."

"The Lodge isn't doing too well. Run down. Could you see your way to authorizing a little something for the Lodge?"

"I think something could be arranged."

"Well, say ten gran'?"

"No."

"Make a offer then."

"What do you think is fair?"

"I dunno, Mr. Scott. Maybe seven. Eight?"

"Perhaps seven."

"How'd it be? Check?"

"I could make it cash." Scott drew a bound packet of hundred-dollar bills from his coat pocket. Crawley's eyes widened. "What do you see?"

"Looks like about five," Crawley said. "Do you need a receipt?"

"No."

Crawley extended his hand. Scott placed the money back in his pocket. He said, "I want you to know that our conversation has been taped."

"Aw, naw, Mr. Scott." Crawley's breath came out in a white frost. "Prove to me the tape."

Scott opened his coat. "It's no larger than a beetle, but it will send over a mile. There is a panel truck next to your union hall. It has a recorder in it. The tape would interest the federal mediator. Shall we adjourn this now?"

"You son of a bitch."

"That doesn't sound very nice. On tape."

"You bastard."

The machinists returned to work the following Monday, after voting by secret ballot to accept the 6 percent offer. As he was leaving the office that day, Scott was informed by Miss Tompkins that Breedlove wished to talk to him.

"I don't know how you did it, but you did one helluva job in Lennox," Breedlove said. "One day in town and they take an offer worse than the one they'd turned down."

"Not worse. The same."

"You did a great job. Keep it up."

"Their negotiator made a mistake. He underestimated me. It's an advantage I may not have in the future."

"I think you're beginning to learn," Breedlove said.

Scott had decided to keep the computer printout. He kept it in his office safe. A private detective in Fresno had determined that the sole proprietor of BL Enterprises was a man named Paul V. Ryerson. Ryerson had died in 1960. A check of his bank records through his estate attorney had shown numerous canceled drafts made out to George Powell.

Scott did not confront Powell.

Nor did he tell Anne about the matter.

Lately he'd developed a sort of race to see if he could get into the office before Jinkens arrived. No matter what time he left the house, however, it seemed that Jinkens beat him. Out of amusement more than anything else, he got up at five one morning, shaved in the car, and was in the Breedlove Building by 6 A.M. He lost. Jinkens had checked in at 5:45.

"What are you doing?" Scott asked. "Working on your first ulcer?"

Jinkens managed a smile. "I would hope not, Mr. Scott. I merely find I would rather be here at the office than any other place. And I'm an early riser."

"Well, in the future I don't want to see you here before nine."

"Yes, sir."

"Tell me. I'm going to Washington next week. Something about a Senate subcommittee hearing."

"Yes. The Subcommittee on Multinational Corporations."

"As you no doubt already know, we've been asked to testify. Mr. Powell, Mr. Lancaster, and myself. Would you like to go with me?"

"I would, Mr. Scott."

"You could see your father."

"Frankly, Mr. Scott, Father and I are not on the best of terms."

"I'm sorry to hear you say that."

"I fear government and the corporations will be at odds forever."

"What is your ultimate ambition, Norman?"

"To do as good a job as I can on whatever I undertake."

"Well, you most certainly have my recommendation."

"Thank you."

"Let's see if we can find some coffee to make around here."

"I've already made it, Mr. Scott," Jinkens said.

26

THE RACE BECAME SWIFTER. SCOTT MADE IMPORTANT DE-cisions faster, no longer fearing their consequences. He began to subordinate more responsibility to others of lower rank in BII. He concentrated more on forward planning than on day-to-day operations. His areas of authority increased. He began to act almost exclusively on his own, avoiding Powell and Lancaster. Now he timed phone calls and curtly dismissed meetings. Often he didn't leave the office until eight or nine.

Since the attacks on BII facilities had stopped, the matter receded to low priority in Scott's mind. Nor did he concern himself any longer with his once active curiosity about the life and past of Lewis Breedlove, or Breedlove's son. He'd concluded, after some agonizing, that Lawrence was deranged and perhaps suffering from delusions. He clung stubbornly to the conclusion. No vacillation. No inhibiting fears. Scott agreed immediately when Lancaster suggested they fly together on the 727 to the Senate hearings. Jinkens was already in Washington, gathering information. Powell was to join them in D.C. He now was in New York discussing the proxy fight with mutual funds and other institutional investors that held substantial blocks of BII stock.

"Have you read up on your fifth?" Lancaster said when they were airborne.

"The fifth amendment? I don't think we'll have to take the fifth. What do we have to hide?"

Lancaster laughed. "Well, they'll concentrate on Powell, anyway."

"Why Powell?"

"He's our financial man. Or was. Then."

The airplane shuddered. Scott found himself grasping his seat.

"It's all so goddamn unnecessary, these hearings," Lancaster said. "The politicians and the bureaucrats want to make a name for themselves by pointing their unclean hands at us. They want to shift sin. Take it off their back and put it on ours."

"I'm not in the mood for your philosophical views right now, Hank."

"I've noticed your moods lately."

"Have a drink."

"I think I will."

"We have three hours in the air together. Do you want to have it out with me?"

Lancaster whirled. He stared at Scott. "You've been under too much pressure, my man."

Scott paused. Lancaster was right. He had been running too fast. He was putting in twelve to fourteen hours a day and was constantly on the road. He was exhausted; he needed a week off. Since the Troika had been formed, Lancaster's role had not extended significantly beyond the Drug Division and corporate marketing, and Powell's remained essentially finance and counteraction on the proxy fight, but Scott's duties had increased sharply. Before, he spent almost all of his time on industrial relations and personnel; now production, forward planning, and international reported directly to him. Plant managers now brought their expansion plans to him, researchers plagued him with five-year and ten-year plans, and foreign executives bothered him with details down to problems with Basque workers in Guipúzcoa. There was always a new crisis, always a new report to get out, always a new time-consuming, unpredictable development, such as this Senate investigation. He was snapping at the kids and he couldn't recall the last time he'd made love to Anne. He found himself waking up at night to worry about a storm in Iowa or the grain market in Chicago. The new duties were thrust upon him in brief memos dictated by Breedlove to Miss Tompkins. Now he glanced at Lancaster.

"I've found I like the pressure," he said.

"I think it's affected your judgment."

"Hank, we could have worked together. But it's apparent you and Powell don't want it that way. All right. Fine. Now I'm going against you whenever I can."

"Oh. Feisty. Shall we take off our coats?"

"No cracks. No wise comments."

Lancaster's finger jabbed Scott's chest. "Understand something. What interests me is the bottom line of this company. Your do-gooding attitude is an impediment to our progress. So I may find it my duty to squash you. Go run a Scout troop or a church."

"Get away from me, Hank. I've had it up to here with your taunting. I don't like threats. Get away and stay away."

" 'I fear thee, ancient mariner.' "

"I think you do. I think you should."

Harold Long stood by the cockpit door, gazing at them.

The chairman of the Senate subcommittee rapped a gavel and said, "We are here to gather information on corporate bribes, kickbacks, and payoffs in foreign nations."

His opening set the tone. Powell was grilled for two hours. He termed the payments "normal business procedure" in some countries.

"Can you be clearer about that?" the chairman asked.

Powell paused. He tapped his fingers on the table. He glanced at a BII lawyer, one of six assigned to counsel testifying executives. The lawyer turned away. Powell looked at the press corps, which paused in its pencil scribbling to look at him.

"When a corporation sells a product or a service to a foreign nation or foreign company, often the sale is accomplished through a middleman," he said slowly. "That middleman is entitled to a fee. A normal business commission."

"How does a fee differ from a bribe?" the senator asked.

"I am not a semanticist, Senator."

"Nevertheless, please try to answer the question."

Perspiration began to form on Powell's forehead. "I will try to give you an answer. A kickback is a slang word used for a business procedure whereby a percentage of the selling price, or merely an agreed-upon sum, is given to a middleman who handles the transaction. On the other hand, a bribe is a sum of money given to someone in return for a service. These are the best definitions I can give you. I certainly am not an expert on these matters."

"I suggest you are indeed an expert, sir," the senator said, evoking laughter from the gallery and furious note-taking by reporters.

Lancaster, who had not yet testified, seemed to be enjoying it all. "Who alienated that lawmaker?" he said to Scott at recess. "I thought Breedlove knew him."

At the afternoon session, Powell estimated that BII had paid approximately $150 million to foreigners for sales assistance and help with labor relations for BII plants in foreign nations. The IRS man in the gallery perked up. So did the SEC man.

"Was anyone else in the company aware of these payments?" a subcommittee member asked.

"I'm not aware of anyone who knew about them."

"I would like to ask Mr. Scott if he knew about these payments," the senator said.

Scott said he did not know.

"Mr. Lancaster?"

"I can state that I did not know, Senator."

"Mr. Powell, I would like to ask you if to your knowledge Mr. Breedlove, the company's chief executive, knew of these payments."

"It was standard business procedure," Powell said. "He knew that certain fees were paid, of course."

"Where is Mr. Breedlove?"

An attorney stood up and said Mr. Breedlove was too ill to travel at this time. The attorney produced a certificate from Breedlove's physician.

The subcommittee's chairman said, "Mr. Powell, you have repeatedly termed these payoffs—"

"Senator, I have never used that word in these hearings."

"Very well. These fees. You have termed them standard business procedures. Does that mean to your knowledge that other corporations also make such payments?"

"I believe that they do, yes."

"Would you name some other companies that do?"

Powell conferred with a lawyer. "I think that I shall decline to do that, Senator."

Scott testified late in the afternoon, repeating that he had no direct knowledge of the payments.

"You are a BII director?" a senator asked.

"Yes."

"Are you then generally aware of all facets of the corporation's activities?"

"Of course. Generally aware, yes."

"I find it incredible that, as a director, you would not be aware of payments amounting to one hundred and fifty million dollars, a sum your fellow director has testified that your corporation expended."

"Senator, I reiterate. I have no knowledge of any BII kickbacks, bribes, or payoffs."

"I remind you that you are under oath."

"You need not remind me, Senator."

"Thank you."

"You're entirely welcome."

Later in the week the hearings were complicated further for BII by the introduction of an article in the financial section of the Washington *Post*. It contained an assertion by Philip Mendenthal that fully $15 million of BII's 1977 net profit came from a non-recurring tax credit used to inflate earnings artificially. The chief accountant of the SEC was also quoted, saying he had asked BII to revise its profit downward to reflect the artificial inflation. The article pointed out that without the tax credit BII's 1977 profits would have been substantially under the results for 1976, instead of the sharp gain that had been claimed. The BII treasurer, reached by the *Post* in Los Angeles, had no comment on the matter.

In addition, all the major newspapers carried front-page stories stating that BII's top officials had testified that the company had spent millions in foreign payments. One paper called them "payoffs."

"I think we should get PR in on this," Lancaster said.

"No, PR will only make it worse," Powell said. "I suggest we adopt a no-comment attitude on this matter with the press. It is now a legal matter."

At breakfast at the Hay Adams with Powell, Scott said, "Did you actually receive notice from Sec on the profit matter?"

"Yes."

"And nothing was done?"

"I'll bring it up at the next board meeting."

"Do you think we should wait that long?"

"I see no reason to rush into it."

"Well, apparently Sec does. We're in enough trouble with Sec now." Jinkens was across the room, eating breakfast by himself. Scott glanced over at him, nodded, and faced Powell. "Look, he told me last night that IRS is looking into these foreign payments. We charged them off as normal deductions."

"Who told you this?"

"Jinkens."

"My lord, Scottie."

"Jinkens is well connected at IRS."

"And so are we." Powell chewed calmly and took a sip of coffee. He wiped his mouth with his napkin. "Scottie, our statement is not false. It is in accordance with generally accepted accounting principles."

"I will vote for revising the figures downward."

"It is not a matter for voting."

"It may become one."

Powell looked up. "You were absolutely angelic before those senators, Scottie."

"What does that mean?"

"You knew about those payments."

"I did not know."

"You suspected strongly, I'm sure."

"They didn't ask me if I suspected."

"You didn't volunteer much."

"Would you have volunteered?"

"No."

"I do not condone them."

"Everybody does it."

"So we must, too?"

"Yes. I'm afraid so, yes."

"I don't quite go along with you on that."

"What you seem not to understand is that we've done nothing wrong."

"I'm not sure what wrong is."

"Wrong is something you know is wrong."

"That seems too simple."

"I no longer search for complexities," Powell said.

On the last day of the hearings, the phone woke Scott at 7 A.M. "Oh, Mr. Scott, this is Colin Masters. My agency used to handle advertising for BII's Food Division."

"Yes. What is it?"

"I'm here in D.C. on a business matter. It's family business, now that I don't have much of an agency to worry about. I read your name in the papers. What're they trying to do? Nail you to the cross without a trial?"

"What is it I can do for you?"

"Well, I was wondering if I could see you before you hop back to Smogsville."

"What about?"

"It's not business. It's private. And confidential. Very much so. I'm sure it's something that will interest you, however. Perhaps very, very much."

"I don't like mysteries."

"I'll give you a clue. It concerns Lancaster."

"Then contact him."

"I'll leave it up to you, Mr. Scott. I'll be at the Press Club bar at six this evening."

The hearings adjourned at noon, ending in an atmosphere of near cordiality between the senators and BII executives and lawyers. The chairman thanked Powell publicly and announced that hearings would be resumed in two weeks, with representatives from other multinational companies being called. Powell left immediately in a cab for National Airport, saying he had to attend to unfinished business in New York. Lancaster caught the 3 P.M. Metroliner to Philadelphia to attend a Drug Division meeting. Scott had an appointment with Brendon Casey, one of BII's lobbyists, who always liked to meet at a White Tower hamburger stand.

Now Casey ordered four burgers and wet them down with mustard and catsup.

"It's a new town," he said. "We call it Jimmylove."

"You're a very resilient man."

"Have to be. Brooms sweep clean here." He chewed openmouthed as he talked. "I know the people on that committee that's been grilling you, but they're all pretty straight. Still, there are ways."

"Ways of buying them off?"

"No. No, I don't mean that. I mean, talking to them."

"Don't talk to them. Don't do anything. Stay out of it."

"I'm only trying to do my job."

"In this case, do your job by doing nothing."

Casey was more than merely resilient. He was remarkably adept at playing both sides. Democrats thought he was a Democrat; Republicans thought he was Republican. He could shift logically in the middle of a discussion from anti-abortion to pro-abortion, from anti-capital punishment to pro-capital punishment. What was extraordinary about him was that he could reverse himself so expertly that only the most perceptive of observers labeled him insincere. This was because he always knew the views of the person he was talking with and he knew with whom that person talked. So he could take sides strongly. He was fond of saying that the middle of the road was where the horse dung fell.

Now, before Scott, he said expertly, "You're right, of course. Nothing good is going to come if we try to fight this one behind the scenes. Those senators believe they have an issue and they're going to push it hard." He wiped mustard from his chin.

Casey was heavyset, red-faced, and about fifty. He was one of seven sons of Irish immigrants. He'd never been to college, although he'd studied some law. He was hired on a consulting basis and called himself a public-relations man. Actually, he entertained, paid off, and distributed campaign contributions to lawmakers. He paid very little attention to the White House, considering all administrations temporary; his targets were the Hill, the agencies, and the courts. There was no doubt of one thing. He was solidly in. He knew who was sleeping with whom, who on the Hill was rolling logs for whom; he knew which senators had drinking problems, which ones had mistresses, and which ones had debts. He could fix a drunk-driving charge, get Redskin tickets despite sellouts, kill a newspaper story; he'd lunched with Bill Miller, flown with Goldwater, and spent $21,000 for hotel suites during the Carter inauguration. He was on a first-name basis with high-ups at the Pentagon, the FTC, the CAB, and even the CIA. Scott had heard Casey had fourteen children.

"Who do you know at IRS?" Scott asked.

"The works. Why?"

"I've heard rumbles they might be auditing us."

"I'll check it," Casey said, jotting in a notebook. "Look, I wanted this meeting for a single reason. I know we already have Sec and this overseas payoff committee on our backs, but I just got wind today of another thing. Over at Food and Drug, there's talk about a new product our drug people are pushing."

"BII-2000?"

"I guess that's it. Now, all this comes from pretty far down the line, understand, so it may not mean anything. The drug was certified—you know that—but there are some dissenters on it there. They say it might be dangerous."

"In what way?"

"I don't know that."

"I think you should discuss this with Henry Lancaster."

"Henry and me, we don't see eye to eye."

"I would think you'd see precisely eye to eye with him."

Casey let it pass. "I just wanted to tell you."

"I'm grateful that you did."

He was eager to depart, for Casey usually made him nervous. He survived because he knew things, had uncanny sources, and was an artist at creative blackmail. Scott granted audiences with him, even putting up with the neurotic absurdity of the bugproof White Tower, because Casey's information often was correct.

"Just drive around the city for a while," he told a cabby.

The cabby waited while Scott got out at the Lincoln Memorial. Scott stood with his hands in his coat pockets, feeling the chilly nip in the air, looking at the memorial. Then he returned to the cab.

"Do you know where the Press Club is?" he said.

"Sure," the cabby said.

Scott was back at Los Angeles International before he realized he hadn't spoken once to Anne during the trip. He went to a phone booth. But he didn't call Anne. He called Clem Hawley.

"Sure, c'mon over," Hawley said.

"Have a martini ready," Scott said.

An hour later, settled down in Hawley's apartment, he said, "Tell me, O Great White Father."

"Great White Father? I think I like that."

"What is morality, Clem?"

"Morality is your area."

"I'll have another martini."

"That's three."

"I'll have another martini, please."

"I don't care if you have seventeen, as long as you don't drive. You can call Anne. Tell her you're staying here tonight."

"You haven't answered my question."

"Well, morals change. Rapidly. What seems terribly wrong now may seem all right tomorrow. And what's all right today may become a dark sin tomorrow."

"Where do we stand now? Business morality, I mean."

"This company or industry in general?"

"This company."

"Asshole deep in horseshit, despite some progress out."

"We're in deep trouble because of people like Breedlove?"

"Don't drink so fast."

"Don't dodge questions."

"What's bothering you, Scottie? The overseas payments?"

"For starters. For in-betweeners, we're test-marketing a drug that may be dangerous, we have payoffs in our Food Division that might lead to Sec charges and which, for expediency, I've failed to investigate, and we have hotshots like Brendon Casey on the payroll."

"Casey is a good man. He's in the know." Hawley's face softened. "Look, Scottie. It's not smart of you to ask questions, of others or of yourself."

"Once you advised me to protect myself. Is that what it's all about, Clem? Protecting ourselves? Our interests?"

Hawley scowled. "Yes. In business, that's what it's all about. You know it. Don't quiz me. Don't quiz anybody. You didn't get where you are—and where you're going—without knowing it."

"Where am I going?"

"To the top. You're the chosen. The favored son. But let me tell you this. Lancaster and Powell have such giant egos they can't accept the fact you're the chosen. They would crush you like a bug if they thought they could get away with it. Even Powell. Powell, too. What does Anne think about all this at this point?"

"One day she wants me to quit, the next she wants me to tear them apart."

"I'll tell you this. I don't think these attacks on the company are over."

"And I'll tell you this. I won't risk my skin for Breedlove."

"Don't be too sure you won't. He may ask you to."

Scott stood up and stalked around, holding his glass high. "To the top," he said. "The top of the dung heap." He lurched, spilling his drink.

"The preacher's drunk," Hawley said.

"No. The preacher, the ex-preacher, is angry."

"Good. Good."

"Angry at convention, at ways of doing things, at turning out cheapness for volume—"

"So? Go to the top and stop it."

"I will."

"You want it, and you know damn well you do."

"Great White Father speaks great truth."

"Well, if he recommends you, it's yours." Hawley gave Scott another martini. "Now, *sip* now," he said. He sagged into a big overstuffed chair, looking frail and very old. "I don't know how you got as high as you have, knowing so little about how this company operates. Maybe Breedlove shielded you. I think he did. And I think I know why."

"Tell me."

"No. I'll let him tell you. But here's a hint. You see, in a way, this Philip Mendenthal is right. This company has a self-perpetuating management. We're logrollers and ass kissers. We're under one-man rule. If Breedlove says shit, we squat. We pay off and we doctor the balance sheet. Others do it too, but not like we do it. We love our perks. We think we're above the law because Breedlove is madly convinced it's for the greater good. It's not. It's only for our greater good, a handful of brownnosers at the very top. We need a cleaning. We need to get the cowshit out of the barn. I think even Breedlove realizes that." Hawley snapped up his head and pulled off his glasses. He peered intently at Scott. "I'll tell you a couple of things, then I'll put you to bed. The woman Breedlove married, Theresa, was the daughter of a banker here named Derick Sanderson. I ran the bank for Sanderson. I guess Theresa saw something in Breedlove—drive, potential, excitement, I don't know what. What he saw in her was a key to a bank vault. He got a loan that saved him, although he had to put up twenty percent of the company's stock in her name. I'll say this. I wasn't exactly best man at the wedding."

"I think at last I begin to understand something, Clem. You were in love with Theresa."

Hawley seemed to look beyond Scott, through him. "The bank saved Breedlove and later he saved the bank. It was mutual give-and-take. Times were hard then. I was doing some creative accounting to keep us going. Breedlove came up with a million dollars on the spot the day before the feds hit us with a surprise audit. Then, in the '60s, when the bank was doing business with arms manufacturers, the radicals hit a couple of our branches. He sent over some of his boys to scatter the radicals."

"What do you mean, boys?"

"I'm talking a lot. What I really want to say is that a lot of people around BII owe Breedlove. He has hooks in them."

"In you, too? Is that why you stay?"

"No. I stay because I need the money and the connections."

"You aren't exactly Breedlove's biggest fan."

"I don't hate him, if that's what you mean. Hate can destroy a man. I roll with his punches. I close my eyes. Maybe you do, too."

Scott's head buzzed. The gin burned in his throat. "If I do go up, will you stay with me?"

"Let's get that out of the way right now. You can't keep me. And I'll tell you this, too. Things haven't been going too well for me. I need this directorship because it gets me consulting work. But I'm not campaigning. I'm just telling you that you're going to can me when you go up."

"Never."

"You don't see a goddamn thing yet, do you? You're not quite there, not quite the Scott you'll be when he recommends you. That Scott will send me down."

"I repeat. Never."

"Well, we'll see."

Scott raised his glass. "I toast the top," he said. "I kiss the hand of the great god Breedlove."

"I'll call Anne," Hawley said.

"I have more than Breedlove's blessing. I have Powell pinned to the rack. Now, after a talk with a person named Colin Masters at the Press Club in Washington, I have dirt on Lancaster. We're facing an IRS audit, Sec charges, terrorist attacks, a proxy fight, charges of payoffs, and I run around looking for dirt on others. But I feel only dirt on myself."

"Great White Father doesn't judge, Scottie."

"I love you, Great Father. There. Been thinking it. Now I said it."

"Finish your booze," Hawley said. "I'll call Anne."

27

McKeen's job took a sudden twist. He was given a difficult assignment by Hudson, one that intensified the toothaches and made him wonder if Hudson had overrated him. He was asked to coordinate a break-in at a rich man's house in Mystic, Connecticut. It was suggested to him that Cubans were good at that sort of undertaking, but he was told he wasn't bound to Cubans, just as long as he got the job done. He was provided with a description of the house and was promised plans of it; the house, apparently, was not well guarded and its principal occupant was often gone. The burglars were to look for a set of tapes, which were probably in a safe near a cabinet in the dining room. Not all the tapes were to be taken, only those dated July of last year. If possible, the burglars were to substitute replacement tapes, so it would look as if nothing had been taken, as if the tape mechanism for that period had not worked. This wasn't McKeen's forte, break-ins, and the assignment caused him intense pain and worry. There had been a man in the organization known as the Cat who was an expert at such work. The Cat was retired, but it was said he kept in shape. McKeen found him in a bowling alley on Western Avenue.

"Sure," the Cat said. "Hudson wants it, I'll do it. Try my best. It sounds like a piece of cake."

"Do you need help?"

"Help? Shit, no. I work alone."

"It's five thou up front, ten more when done. Expenses, too."

"Fair enough."

"Appreciate it," McKeen said.

Deepening troubles beset the company, accompanied by ceaseless rains in the state. The rain was a blessing that cured a previous drought problem, but, for BII, a disaster. Carl

Sampson, head of the Food Division, came grim-faced to Scott's office.

"I hate to bother you with this, you got your pants so full with everything else," he said.

"Never mind that. Let's hear it."

"This rain isn't only here. It's much worse up north. It's a big flood up there. I'm afraid we're going to have to cut production, and what we do produce is going to cost a helluva lot more. Meanwhile, Lancaster has a big ad campaign going for the division. We're going to have strong demand and a sharply reduced supply."

"Have you discussed it with Hank?"

"Hank never was a reasonable man, but now he's totally unreasonable. His response is to tell me that production is my problem, selling is his."

"How much of a production cutback do you see?"

"Something like twenty percent, Mark. Maybe more. We can hedge some of the cost increases on the commodities market, but it's too late to get much benefit from that."

"Whose fault is that?"

"Mine. I'm not dodging it. But there was no way to anticipate this much rain. Not that I'm making an excuse. I will forecast this. I think the division might be in the red for the first quarter."

Scott groaned. The Food Division always had operated on a slim profit margin, about 2 percent of sales, and Breedlove lately had been sending Scott brief, heckling memos, with carbon copies to Sampson, demanding a program to fatten margins. Improvements could be made, but not without substantial outlays for plant modernization and research and development—outlays that the board, led by delaying tactics from Powell and Lancaster, refused to grant, at least for now.

Sampson stood up, walked to Scott's window, and looked out at the rain. He turned sharply. He was a thin, bald man of about sixty, recruited by Breedlove from General Mills five years ago, and so short he suffered from taunting, particularly from Lancaster, because of the irony of being named Sampson.

"I don't like it, Mark," he said. "There's something very wrong in this company."

Scott gazed at him. He'd never told Sampson he knew about Saltzman and his "discounts," principally because he'd half convinced himself there was nothing wrong with the practice, which Jinkens's investigation showed to be common in the food industry. Perhaps Sampson would bring up the subject now. But, no. Sampson had other matters on his mind.

"We have our feet in concrete," he said. "I run a division that's supposedly autonomous, but I have Lancaster dictating my marketing strategy, Powell monitoring my plant-expansion money, and now my foreign operations are under you. That's all right. What concerns me is that we seem to be going in opposite directions." Sampson returned Scott's gaze, his brow wrinkled. "This Troika idea of Breedlove's. It's not working, is it?"

Scott hesitated. Finally he said, "No. No, it's not."

"It's all over the company that you're the front-runner for the big job."

"I have no comment."

"Well, in many ways, I don't envy you."

"What is your labor outlook like, Carl?"

"Changing the subject, are we?"

"I'm doing a report for the board on minority employment and illegal aliens. Or, rather, Jinkens is doing it."

"The division's labor picture is good, thanks mostly to the hiring of illegal aliens."

"I'm going to recommend to the board that we lobby for the reestablishment of the Bracero program. Do I have your backing on that?"

"I'll back you, although it might increase costs."

"We had a Chicano protest march here last week, opposing Carter's illegal alien program. I'm sick of policies that encourage unrest. God knows, this company has had its share of unrest."

"Well, that's past. Our bombers have run."

"Knock on wood," Scott said.

"Haven't they?"

Scott spread reports out on his desk. "Not overseas, I'll tell you that. Terrorists in Italy are taking potshots at our people. In Soweto, South Africa, we have *children*, of all things, raging over U.S. assistance to white-owned concerns. And in

Pamplona, Spain, I have Basque laborers, now freed of Franco, ready to march on us unless we support their political freedom."

"I said it," Sampson said. "I don't envy you."

Nor did Scott envy himself. He was spending about two nights a week at the Century Plaza Hotel, too tired to drive home after meetings that often went past 9 P.M. Most of his requests to the board were tabled or rejected, often on the basis that they required an immediate outlay of funds, a factor antagonistic to the current priority item of defeating Mendenthal's proxy contest. The board was indecisive, almost apathetic. Breedlove was out of touch. The atmosphere on thirty was tense and cool. Scott noticed that second-level executives seemed to be taking sides. Some cozied up to him, others favored Lancaster or Powell. A few of the more adept played all three sides. Clearly Scott was the favorite of the Food Division, just as Lancaster was the favorite of the Drug Division. Another development also became obvious. Secretaries to the Troika members began to snub each other.

"Cold war," Joan Leeky explained.

"Don't you think it's somewhat foolish?"

"Well, I didn't start it, Mr. Scott. I'll tell you something else. The office boys have a pool. They're actually setting odds and I think some betting goes on."

"What are my odds?"

She smiled. "They won't tell me. But I found out Mr. Powell is ten to one."

"This borders on absurdity."

"I agree," she said.

Powell remained merely aloof, but Lancaster began to taunt Scott from a distance. He launched an advertising program for the Drug Division's consumer products—toothpastes, deodorants, shaving creams, hair oils—that had a blatantly sexual theme. The ads showed silhouettes of men and women in near-amorous positions. The product labels were changed to feature the same images. The slogan for the campaign, used on all billboards, was "Getting Together." Lancaster made sure advance proofs of the ads appeared on Scott's desk. Often he appended notes to them. One said, "Thinking of changing slogan to 'Living Together.'" Another: "How about using the theme, 'Keeping It Up'?" Scott ignored the taunts.

But he didn't ignore a letter that came to him from Dr. Allan Curry, a chemist for the Drug Division. It was actually a letter of resignation, and Scott couldn't figure out why he'd received it until Dr. Curry explained.

I have been in communication with Mr. Lancaster concerning my aprehensions about BII-2000, but he has systematically ignored such communications. That is why, as my last action for the company, I am bringing this to your attention.

Information in the attached tables is from my personal research, not sponsored by the company. In it you will see that, while BII-2000 appears from animal tests to be effective and perfectly safe, there is some evidence —enough evidence—uncovered in my research with primate animals, mainly tarsiers and lemurs, that the drug, instead of improving arterial flow, may have a longer-term effect of limiting arterial flow, especially in older patients. I cannot support test-marketing of this product at this time. Therefore, I am submitting my resignation

Scott saved it for the next board meeting.

Lancaster merely smiled.

"Tell me, Scottie, have you met old Curry?" he asked.

"No."

"Have you ever spoken to him?"

"No."

"So you're unfamiliar with his reputation."

"I've heard his reputation is excellent."

"You're misinformed. He's regarded as a semi-quack in academic circles and he has a very minor standing in his profession. Nor has he resigned. He was fired. The letter, no doubt, is a vindictive response to the firing."

Scott sat down. The board took up another matter, a report of a committee formed to look into foreign payoffs. Carl Sampson, chairman of the committee, said its research so far was inconclusive. At a break outside the boardroom, Lancaster ambled up to Scott. He was not smiling.

"I want you to know something, Scottie. Know it well. The Drug Division is mine. Completely and absolutely. I will not tolerate your meddling in it. Am I clear?"

Their eyes met. Lancaster's teeth gritted. Scott whirled and stalked away, feeling a sense of defeat and helplessness.

A one-two punch hit the following week. The Securities & Exchange Commission filed a suit against BII, accusing it of making kickbacks to its wholesale food customers. The complaint alleged that the kickbacks were a form of bribe to wholesalers and amounted to an unnecessary expenditure of funds. BII's public-relations department, in answer to press queries on the matter, said such payments were common industry practice.

Philip Mendenthal waited only two days to follow up. In behalf of Dimension Corporation, which owned some 100,000 BII shares, he filed a $50 million shareholder's derivative suit against all current BII directors and two former directors, charging fraud and breach of fiduciary obligations. The suit also named BII's principal accounting firm as a defendant. When he read the complaint, it became clear to Scott that Powell had been using some questionable tactics in fighting Mendenthal's move for control of BII. The suit alleged that BII directors used their positions of trust to maintain themselves in office. It claimed that BII had sold some 600,000 of its common shares, authorized but previously unissued, to "friends and acquaintances of defendant directors," including a block of 200,000 to a New York investment banker named Horace Wittenberg, who had served as a BII director for three months in 1971. In a separate action, the Dimension complaint repeated the SEC's charges. It asked for restitution and punitive damages and an injunction to prevent BII from participating in "further questionable practices and improper accounting procedures."

Scott put down the complaint and dialed Powell's office. To his surprise, Powell was in.

"The suit is without merit, Scottie, and you must know that. I'm surprised that, as a lawyer, you're upset about it. It's defensible on the basis that it's obvious harassment."

"You're going to tell me that you anticipated it?"

"After the SEC suit, yes."

"Tell me if I'm wrong. I was under the impression that our bylaws state that sale of authorized but unissued stock requires board approval."

"Your impression, as you call it, is correct."

"I don't recall this matter being brought before the board."

"It was brought before the Finance Committee."

"You're compromising the board, George. And you're compromising me, as a member of the board. I simply am not going to stand for it."

"I have someone in the office now. May I call you back?"

"No. You may not. Not on this. I regard this little act as downright unethical. More than unethical. It's grounds for action against you and your Finance Committee."

"That is exactly what we need right now, Scott. To sue each other." Powell paused. "Look—need I remind you?—we are right now at a crisis stage in this company. It is entirely possible, despite Breedlove's passive attitude toward it, that we could lose control of this company. Where do you go then? You, as Mark Scott?"

"Maybe to an honest outfit."

"I really must hang up now. May we discuss it later?"

Scott hung up. He had directed anger at Powell knowing in reality he'd been angry only at himself. The Food Division was Scott's headquarters responsibility; Breedlove, at first orally and then by memo, had placed him in charge. He'd known about the rebates but had taken no action. He had stalled indecisively, failing even to confront Carl Sampson with the matter. No longer could he fault others for indecision, for apparently he could not make up his own mind. He tapped a pencil on his desk, feeling drained and inadequate. Joan Leeky entered.

"You have a visitor," she said.

His son, Tod, looking bedraggled and frightened, hid behind Joan's skirt.

Tod had a story to tell, a story about Cindy. To Tod, Cindy was a member of the family.

"You lost her?" Scott said.

Tod nodded, choking back tears. Scott fumbled impatiently, but Joan listened with a sympathetic ear. She had an Irish setter named Spike who held a lofty status in her household, a rank almost equal to her husband and three children.

Finally Tod managed a form of explanation. Cindy had escaped from somebody's car at some street corner in Los Angeles (Tod *thought* it was in Los Angeles) several hours ago.

"What were you doing in a car in Los Angeles when you're supposed to be in school in Palos Verdes?" Scott asked. "And whose car? And why?"

That was the tough part for Tod to explain. There was something about a rift with his mother, who had spotted dog puddles on her new carpet; Cindy had been banished from the house to the backyard, which wasn't escapeproof. Then Mike's pal, Tommy, had come along, in his hot rod. Mike had already left for school. Tod, worried sick about Cindy's escaping, had decided to plead his case in person with Dad, even if it meant bribing Tommy with five dollars from Tod's allowance to take Tod and Cindy to Los Angeles.

"Skipping school, is that it?" Scott said.

Tod had a weak defense. Tuesdays, he said, were his pud days at school, pud meaning easy. His story continued. Cindy had begun to squirm on Wilshire, an action Tommy interpreted as a signal she needed to piddle. Tommy had stopped the hot rod; Tod and Cindy had got out.

"Then she ran away," Tod said miserably. "I chased after her, but she just got away."

"Did she have a license on?" Joan asked.

Tod shook his head. Scott began to pace slowly. He looked at Joan. "Who's on my schedule for the rest of the day?" he said.

"Everybody," she said.

"Well, cancel everybody then. Tell them I'm out on a dog hunt."

The hunt cost Scott several mornings, time he couldn't afford to lose at the office and which he made up by night work. It began with a search near the Wilshire-Robertson area, almost on a house-to-house basis. Suspicious residents, asked by the stranger and the boy if they'd seen a stray pup, shut doors in their faces. A mammoth German shepherd sent Scott and Tod scurrying to their car. Two policemen promised they'd keep an eye out for a stray. Cindy remained lost.

Returning to the office, Scott phoned the Los Angeles *Times* and the Santa Monica *Evening Outlook* and placed lost-dog ads. In the evening they visited dog pounds in the area. Again, no luck. They left their phone number and address with the pound clerks. Tod crouched by the phone at home at all waking hours. There were no calls about Cindy. Tod's mood drifted from discouraged to miserable.

"Dad, we're not going to give up, are we?" he asked—a plea, not a question.

"Your father doesn't give up," Anne said.

"We'll try the pounds again on Saturday," Scott said.

"The pounds keep lost dogs only a week," Tod reminded him. "Then they're . . . they're *gassed*."

"Well, a good family might claim Cindy," Anne said.

Finding Cindy had become very important to Scott. It was more than a hunt for a dog. In the past few days, watching Tod, he'd begun to realize how close he'd come to losing the boy. Crushed in the corporate race, he'd given only cursory attention to Anne and the kids; they had receded to second priority, obscured by the lure of the great god achievement. Now, chasing around on a search for an animal that had become a love object for Tod, perhaps a substitute for fatherly attention, he felt he was coming back. Anne felt it, too.

"You are a very good man, my Mark Scott," she said in bed, following a warm, gentle love session.

"Why, thank you, Mrs. Scott."

"Maybe even a great man."

"Just because I won't give up my dog hunt?"

"Cindy can stay in the house when she comes back," Anne said.

They held each other.

Liz went with Scott and Tod on the Saturday trek. The West Los Angeles pound, ripe with animal smells and writhing with captured strays, had nothing among its panting prisoners that even resembled Cindy.

"You lost your dog near Robinson?" said a woman volunteer worker. "A week ago. Well, there is one more chance. Try the Twelfth Avenue pound. Take the freeway, get off on Crenshaw. But hurry. They could be taking her out by now."

Tod had a horrified look. "Dad?" he said. "Dad?"

Scott got a speeding ticket on the Santa Monica Freeway, written out slowly as Liz tried to explain to the motorcycle cop that they were on an emergency. Scott made a wrong turn on Crenshaw and had to go back three blocks out of his way. Finally, after asking directions at a filling station, they found the Twelfth Avenue pound. Tod scooted in while Scott parked the car. Soon Tod was back, his eyes wide as quarters.

"She's *here*!" he shouted. "I found her!"

Scott heaved a sigh of relief. He and Liz followed Tod past the cages to the end. A yipping pup nibbled at Tod's fingers from behind her prison bars.

"I'll go outside, talk to the lady to bail her out," Scott said.

They all went. Scott walked with a spring in his step. He'd not felt quite so fulfilled in years. Tod stood by the door leading to the cages, guarding the pup from a distance, while Scott confronted the woman behind the counter.

"Male or female?" the woman asked, coolly.

"Female," Liz said.

"Well, fill out this form," said the woman. "Now, you're sure it's your dog?"

"We're sure," Liz said. "Tod, he's sure."

"Some people, when there's no identification, they think it's their dog when it really isn't. We get a lot of pups like yours. They are runaways, that kind of dog."

"They are not," Liz said.

"Liz," Scott said. "That's enough."

Tod was suddenly by their side, breathing unsteadily. "They're taking her away! Some man, he's put a leash on her and is taking her out."

"Maybe just for feeding," Scott said.

"No, they feed them in the cages," Liz said, with authority.

Scott, trailed by the kids, walked rapidly down the row of cages. He looked around. Dogs barked at him. At the end of the row, a man was leading four reluctant, leashed dogs toward a truck. Scott caught up to him. The dog handler was a swarthy man with a black mustache. He wore rubber boots.

"Where are you going?" Scott said. "We came to pick up our dog. Now you're taking her away."

"Eh?" said the man, talking loudly over the barks of dogs. "These all been here seven days. They're going out."

"But that's our dog," Scott said.

"Whyn't you pick it up then before seven days?" said the booted executioner. "Whyn't you come get it sooner?"

He was pushing the dogs into compartments in the back of the truck.

"Wait," Scott said.

The executioner turned sharply. "Awright, which one?"

"That one."

"Awright, I'll put it back, you get a release slip. Next time, don't wait seven days."

It was useless to try to explain to a disappointed executioner deprived of one of his prey. "All right," Scott said weakly.

"Dad?" Tod said as they headed back toward the counter.

"What now?"

"I hate to say this, Dad."

"What do you hate to say?"

"That's not Cindy."

"What?"

"I just noticed. Cindy, she didn't have a collar. That dog had a collar."

"Oh, good lord!" Scott felt a blend of disappointment and impatience. He also felt a form of defeat. He went to the executioner, who was returning the pup to her cage, and lamely tried to explain the mistake. "I'm sorry," he said.

The booted man shook his head from side to side. He retrieved his prey and tugged her toward the death truck. Scott turned to Liz and Tod, who were busy conferring with one another on some matter. Quickly Scott found out what it was. Liz, a finer diplomat than her brother, did the explaining. They had decided, in conference, to try to talk him into claiming the doomed pup as a stand-in for Cindy, who was now apparently irretrievably lost. Liz lobbied effectively, even as the engine of the death truck fired up and it began to pull away.

"All right," Scott said. He'd found a challenge. Stop the death truck, save the substitute Cindy. "We'll try."

The truck had left. They raced to their car. Scott fumbled as he tried to unlock the door. The keys fell to the curb. Finally he got the car open. They piled in. He streaked away, burning rubber, executing an illegal U-turn, and searched the area for the truck.

"There," Liz said, pointing. "Right ahead."

Scott cut around a Ford and squeezed in behind the truck. He tooted the horn. The truck sped up. Liz held the horn down. Tod bounced on the seat. The truck showed no indication of stopping. Scott flashed to the outside and drove alongside it, tapping his horn. The executioner was driving the truck, peeping at them with a disgusted frown.

"You're on fire!" Liz screamed at him.

The truck stopped. The executioner got out to examine it. Scott pulled up behind, slowly got out, and faced the big man in boots for the third time in the past fifteen minutes.

"I know this seems a little crazy," he said. "But we've decided we want that dog."

The man was stunned to silence. "Jeeze," he said. "You said b'fore it ain't your dog."

"It's not," Scott said. "But we want it." He held out a twenty-dollar bill. "For your trouble."

The man took the bill, looked at it, and tapped his heel. "Jeeze," he said, but he released the doomed animal.

"I think we have a father back," Anne said at dinner.

"Just because I got them a dog?"

"It's a sign," she said.

But he did not know. The dog hunt had cost him three mornings at the office, valuable time he could not afford to lose. In the midst of it he'd felt old stirrings of family values, but the office had also been on his mind. It was like a vicious tug-of-war within him, one that robbed him of sleep, increased his irritability, and occasionally brought on states close to nervous exhaustion. He didn't want to face it, yet he realized he might soon have to decide between the big chair and his family. Anne was gazing at him fondly, but he could not return her look.

"When you said we'd go slumming, you weren't kidding," Dorothy Lancaster said. "Hank, I'm actually scared here."

"Just don't show it," Lancaster said.

They had been to dinner at Chasen's and now were nightcapping at a Chicano bar deep in the East Side of Los Angeles. She had wanted to go home right after dinner, but Lancaster, feeling restless, hadn't listened to her. He'd driven across town in the Cadillac, top down, to Brooklyn Avenue and beyond into Boyle Heights. The population was largely Mexican, with some blacks, but it wasn't considered a dangerous neighborhood unless you were looking for trouble. Lancaster wondered if he'd look for trouble. They were far overdressed for the bar he'd selected, a tiny local dive with a sawdust floor, filled with the stench of beer and fried tacos; she wore a mink and an ankle-length red dress, he wore a dark suit with a sincere tie. They were drinking brandy-rocks. He was on his third. She was still sipping her first. Three languid Chicanos sat at a table across the floor, eyeing them. They were getting drunk on Saturday-night beer. The bartender polished glasses. He was a chubby Mexican with nervous eyes and a thick mustache. One of the Chicanos at the table got up to go to the john. A paperboy came in, a stack of *Herald Examiners* under his arm.

"You scram!" the bartender said.

"Maybe somebody wants a paper," Lancaster said.

"He's underage, shouldn't he in here," the bartender said.

"How many papers you got there?" Lancaster asked the boy.

"Dunno," the boy said, shrugging his shoulders.

"Here's three bucks. I'll take 'em all. You go buy yourself a hoop." Lancaster looked at the bartender. "If that's all right by you."

The bartender turned away. He polished his glasses. The Chicano returned from the john, sneaking glances at Dorothy, and sat down at the table with the other two.

"Jesus H. Christ on a crutch," Lancaster said, putting down the paper.

"What now?" Dorothy said.

"This little item back here. Somebody broke into old Mendenthal's house in Mystic. Doesn't say what's missing."

"What does that have to do with the price of rice in China?"

"I fear Breedlove has awakened the sleeping Jew and given him resolve," Lancaster said.

"Sometimes I think I'll never learn to understand you."

"Don't try."

"You're in another one of your moods. Let's go home."

"And fuck?"

"You know I'm having my period."

"There are other ways."

"You know I don't like your other ways."

"The last time I was out of town, this chick I met taught me something new."

"If she went to bed with you, I pity her."

"We nylon fucked. She wrapped her panty hose over my dick and sucked me off. I thought I'd never stop coming."

"All right. You're in a foul mood. But if you're trying to take it out on me, you're not succeeding."

"I'll have another brandy."

"Have fifty. I'll take a taxi home."

"I think I'm losing this Breedlove fight. On points. I think Scott is ahead."

"So? Go to another company. You're the big hotshot."

"You are a stupid broad."

"Hank, don't pick on me. Not any more."

"Let me explain something to you." He seized her arm. "I can go to another company, yes. It would take me exactly fifteen minutes to find another job. Even a better job. But that is not the point. If I lose, I'll have a black mark, not on the résumé but in my head. Is that something you think you can try to understand?"

"Can I have my arm back now?"

"No."

"Let go!"

"Get those greaseheads over there to help you."

"Let *go*!"

One of the Chicanos got up, shuffled to their table, and stood above them. He grinned. "Lady, he bother you?" he said. He was a big man with a hard brown face and huge, calloused hands.

"No, I'm all right," Dorothy said.

Lancaster released her. He looked up at the Chicano. "You come over to save her? To save this fat cow? You speak English? American?"

"I am American," the Chicano said.

Lancaster sipped his brandy. "Fuck off, Pancho," he said.

The bartender stirred. The two other Chicanos got up and moved toward the table. Dorothy's eyes were huge. Her face was pale. For a full, long moment, no one moved. The silence was absolute. Now the three Chicanos stood around the table.

Dorothy's hand trembled. She wet her lips. Lancaster stood up. He moved very slowly. He was smiling. He faced the Chicano who had came over first.

"I told you once, Pancho, fuck off," he said.

The Chicano's eyes flared. His companions stood behind him. Lancaster looked at them, sizing up. Two were giants, field or construction workers, no doubt, with great strength in their arms and torsos. The third man was smaller and younger; perhaps he'd just crossed the border. He wasn't much more than a boy. He was the trio's weak link.

The two big men flanked Lancaster.

Lancaster grinned.

He turned, as if to go quietly, and then whirled back. His arm snaked out and grabbed the young Chicano's wrist. He bent it back sharply. He heard a cracking sound. The young man shrieked and went limp. Lancaster's arm encircled his neck, holding him up. The man's broken wrist dangled at an unnatural angle. Already it had begun to swell and turn purple.

"Back up," Lancaster told the other two. He felt good. He felt just fine. Faint twinges of sexual excitement stirred in him. "Pancho, old horse, you're not backing," he said. "I thought you understood American. Do it. Do it, or I'll break his neck, too."

They backed away, their eyes flashing.

Lancaster motioned to Dorothy. She got up and went to the door. Lancaster backed up, holding the limp young man. The two Chicanos stood by the far wall. The bartender continued to polish glasses, as if nothing were happening. When he reached the door, Lancaster pushed the young Chicano forward onto the floor. He turned and fled, taking Dorothy's arm. The Cadillac was across the street.

He stopped in a dark residential district five minutes later. He switched off the Cadillac's lights. The sharp ring of a barking dog came from nearby.

"Hank, now what?" Dorothy said. Her voice was unsteady.

"Touch me," he said.

"Hank, for God's sake! They're still chasing us."

"Go down on me," he said.

"Hank? Please? Let's go home. I'll do anything for you at home."

"Go down on me," he said. "Now. Right now."

PART FOUR

THE
VICTORS

28

BREEDLOVE SAT IN HIS EASY CHAIR IN THE DEN AT HIS PASA-
dena home, writhing in pain. The fire in the hearth sputtered.
The stuffed eagle on the mantel gazed at him. His senses were
very alive. Birds cried shrilly outside, and the scent of
burning pine logs was thick in his nostrils. His vision was
sharp, homing in on the eyes of the eagle. He jabbed at his
fingernails with the point of a pocketknife, producing tiny
bubbles of blood. The pain shrieked deep within him. He now
took morphine injections daily, often administered by Henriette Tompkins, who brought his correspondence and messages to him every afternoon. The pain usually began about
noon. He endured it until she arrived, battling it with physical
contortions. Last year doctors at Mayo had told him he had
inoperable cancer and had given him six to eight months to
live. He did not believe them.

He was in a good mood, despite the pain. He chuckled. His
eyes darted. For long moments he stared at the eagle. He felt
almost contented, at peace. This morning a bonded messenger
had delivered a package to him that contained a thick
typewritten report, some tapes, and a few maps and sketches.
Breedlove rubbed his hands and chuckled as he read the
report. He played the tapes and, listening, found himself
suppressing something akin to childlike giggles. He now

knew. He now had proof. The information confirmed most of his suspicions.

The report was from the Hudson organization, a group Breedlove regarded as almost totally efficient and effective. Breedlove had first met Kenneth Hudson in the winter of 1925, at Hudson's speakeasy on the Strip. At the time Breedlove's company was under way and growing, about to issue its first public stock offering. That night in 1925, in the basement of the speakeasy where the liquor was distilled under naked overhead bulbs and surrounded by copper vats topped with extended coils, Breedlove had met a man almost identical to himself in makeup and design, in background and ambition. Both had experienced poverty of an intensity so severe it could have killed them if they hadn't had the cunning and the courage to escape. Instead of killing them, destitution had given them the toughness and daring to take risks that led to growth. They were about the same age. Both saw vast opportunities in the west. They'd talked that night until dawn, a long, conspiratorial discussion that led to an ever deepening cabalistic relationship now stretching over five decades. No one, not even the Justice Department's Organized Crime Strike Force, knew that a relationship existed between them. They had seen each other only twice over the past thirty years, yet on numerous occasions had been helpful to each other. Breedlove had arranged loans for Hudson in Hudson's early years of struggle; Hudson, through nominees, owned some $4 million in BII stock, much of it bought on Breedlove's advice in the mid-1930s. Dividends alone each year paid Hudson several times over his original investment. Hudson, like Breedlove, was not a man who forgot those who had helped him.

The report had been slow in coming, but Hudson, as always, had come through. Delays were now over. The end would come swiftly. It told Breedlove who had been attacking BII and how the plan had been developed and implemented. It gave him the answer to the riddle of the Rembrandt. It named names. It said the leader of the group was a man who called himself Clinton St. John, Lawrence's half brother and Breedlove's son by Rebecca, Philip Mendenthal's niece. Proof that his older son had lived, grown to manhood, and turned to criminal activity against him neither angered nor disturbed Breedlove. It amused him.

He sat very still, pondering. He felt just fine. The pain was gone, at least temporarily, and he was totally relaxed, his mind as alive and penetrating as it had been at any time in the past. He smirked, then laughed out loud. The servants surely thought him mad, a shriveled deathlike figure with dry skin and red eyes huddled under a shawl like a scheming old miser counting his pennies. But he was far from mad, just as he was far from dead. He'd found out what it was essential for him to know. He'd deliberately held back from taking action for reasons private to himself, reasons shielded even from Hudson. Now it was time to authorize steps that would lead to reprisal.

The report implicated the chauffeur, Morris. It said Morris had fled in fear. Hudson's agents had found him and killed him, the only action taken so far. A police stat sheet, attached, said the cause of death was a highway accident and noted that Morris's blood-alcohol level had been high enough to list him as intoxicated at death.

The report asked what action Breedlove wished taken concerning his sons. Breedlove uncapped a pen and wrote at the top of the page, "Find them. Kill them." He threw the page in the fire and watched it burn.

The information was worth much to him, and Hudson would be paid for it just as any other consultant was paid. The method of payment, however, was unusual. Breedlove transferred cash from his account in a Geneva bank to a Hudson-owned company named Interurban, based in Liechtenstein and incorporated in the Bahamas. There were no bills. Breedlove paid what he thought a particular service to be worth.

Scoggins entered, bearing a luncheon tray.

"How does the old fart look to you today?" Breedlove asked.

"You look just fine, Mr. Breedlove."

"Horseshit. He looks like he's been dead for a month. But he is far from dead. He can defeat death."

Breedlove closed his eyes. Vivid scenes flashed before him. He was a boy of fourteen, crouched in deep, protective milkweed, watching his father emerge from the barn, an axe in his hands. The boy could see their house—not really a house but a square hole in the ground, dug by hand and roofed with tar-papered pine slats. Animals had better. He watched as the father went to the mother, who lay on the lawn. He saw the axe flash down. There was no sound of its striking the mother's skull. He recalled that now. There was no sound. He recalled the soft buzz of flies around him, a rich patch of purple-flowered clover in the field, the smell of milkweed, and yellow foam trickling from the mouth of a horse that munched grass nearby. And he recalled an eagle that soared high in the sky. The boy thought of himself an an eagle, possessing the limitless reaches of the sky. He did not run. He was not afraid. There was a wild man who lived in the neighborhood who ate chickens raw and sometimes wailed at the moon anchored naked and knee-deep in a creek in spring; the wild man said Death was a real substance, although invisible, a force known by the men He sought but one that could be defeated by those who are unafraid of Him. The boy saw the father coming toward him. He did a strange thing. He stood up. They stood looking at each other, six feet apart, the father holding the axe. There was blood on his shirt and face. His eyes were red-veined and huge. In the sky a second eagle joined the first. They swooped lower in graceful dives.

The father lowered the axe. "Git on," he said.

In the future he would wonder why he'd been spared. It had been partly because he had refused to show fear. Perhaps it had also been because the father judged that the boy could not long last by himself anyway. Years later, after he'd become a man of wealth and power, he would form another theory—the father had allowed not a boy to escape, but himself. The boy who'd fled through the cornfield to the railroad tracks where freights ran east and west carried in his blood and flesh all that remained of the father.

Now he said, "Tell me, Scoggins. You have family, do you not?"

"Why, yes, I do, Mr. Breedlove."

"A daughter, am I correct?"

"Yes, sir."

"How is your daughter?"

"She is just fine, Mr. Breedlove."

"You said she was in Europe. An art student."

"No, sir. No more, sir. She has taken up, I'm afraid, with a band, sir. She is a singer."

"In Europe?"

"Yes, sir."

"Has she been in Venice recently?"

"I believe so, Mr. Breedlove. I'm afraid, sir, she doesn't write often these days."

"I was sorry to learn of Morris's accident."

"Yes, sir."

"You will have to arrange for a new driver."

"Yes, sir. I already have received references to check."

"I'm going to try to get some sleep. If I do nod off, wake me when Miss Tompkins arrives."

He did not quite go to sleep, nor were his dreams really dreams. Again visions filtered through his consciousness like shifting pages, at times so vivid they were full of smells, feelings, sound, and motion. His life to now had been a series of stages and cycles, all moving on a planned pattern. It had begun in a Los Angeles freight yard, when he'd first realized that the world was a three-part division, composed of workers, bosses of the workers, and owners of the plants where the work was done. The owners were the most prosperous. They wore spats, straw hats, and tailored suits. Their women were slim and frail and pretty, like cultured flowers. It was a world of the exploited and the exploiters, of doers and non-doers, of thinkers and non-thinkers, of planners and non-planners. The owners took, through money and position; the workers gave, with sweat and agony. It was a simple world; only by surviving and growing could a person hope to achieve, to obtain. The laborers were non-humans without vision or a plan. He left freight-yard work for the country after saving fifty dollars. The land of the valley was level and rockless. It was also obtainable. While sharecropping for a valley landowner named Philip Mendenthal, he lay awake in his tent at nght after long study hours, hearing bird sounds and thinking about the rich at their hotel parties, dancing in fine clothing while their coachmen waited for them outside, currying white horses. He hated and envied the rich, particularly those who had not earned their positions, but he wanted to be like them. One way to them, he realized, might be through their women.

Rebecca, Mendenthal's young, ripening niece, seemed a likely starting point. She had begun to show an interest in him. Mendenthal had warned him to stay away from her, but, foolishly, at the same time he'd allowed his niece to strut sensually about, humming her teasing singsong tunes and wriggling her plump behind. His matings with her, often at dusk in a field full of the smells of ripe strawberries on the vine, had been mechanical and purposeful. She was a passive receptacle, a girl-woman like a doll. It was not the need to expel his energy, as he'd previously done in the willing wombs of the Mexican field women or the fifty-cent whores in the city who had taught him sex. After Rebecca's pregnancy had been verified by a gypsy woman, he'd married her before a drunken justice of the peace in Ventura and had immediately confronted Mendenthal. Mendenthal raged helplessly and then gave in. A banker in the city, Derick Sanderson, handled the transfer of Mendenthal's land to Breedlove, and also the loan. Sanderson also had a daughter, a high-spirited woman named Theresa. She became Breedlove's next target. The women of status lived sheltered and protected like artificial plants, nourished by the blood and sweat of stooped field-workers and plant slaves writhing like hungry animals before hot fires. They had not worked. Position had been given to them, and therefore they were weak. They had white necks and pale skins and thin faces with bright red lips that sneered savagely at classes below them; they were inferior, yet they maintained superior airs, a training that came with money and status. To conquer them was not only a pleasure. It was also a revenge.

Breedlove came fully awake, in deep pain and streaked with sweat. He saw Henriette Tompkins's angular face above him.

"How long have you been there?" he asked.

"Not very long."

"I dozed off."

"You shouldn't have gone to sleep in your chair. You should have gone upstairs to bed."

"No. Once you let them put you in a bed in the day you never get out. Theresa spent two years in bed, raging at the servants and breathing hellfire. If I'm going to breathe hellfire, it's going to be in this chair or on my feet."

Henriette had first come to him in answer to an advertisement for a secretary's job after he'd moved the company's headquarters from the valley into the city. She had proved to be astonishingly efficient and willing to endure long hours and low pay. He'd also found he could talk to her. When he'd made sexual advances to her one night, she had submitted without hesitation. He was sure it was her first time.

"If you have a needle up your sleeve, hold it off," he said. "It's not too bad right now."

"How bad has it been?"

"Bad enough."

Her face softened. She did not talk. She had never been given to talk; she'd been the listener.

"Well, I'm not ready yet to be put out of my misery," he said. "I have a couple hurdles to jump yet. And here I've been sitting wasting time, dreaming about the past. Tell me this. When I told you years and years ago that I was going to marry Theresa Sanderson, why didn't you leave?"

"Because I knew she could help you more."

"I needed the Sanderson money."

"Yes."

"But that wasn't the main reason why I married her." A spate of coughing struck him. Spittle ran down his chin. She wiped it off. His eyes were wet; he felt disgustingly weak. He clenched his fists. Again he felt his blood surge. "Believe it or not, I married her to produce a son. Somebody to carry on. I made a mistake. There was no iron in the Sanderson line."

"I don't think you should talk. Not right now."

He squared his shoulders and reached for a Lucky Strike. "I'll tell you something, as if I have to tell you. I've never felt much in the way of emotion in my life because I've never had time for that. I try to reward those who help me, and are loyal to me, but I most certainly do not do it out of affection, or what people call love. Now, I suppose there are people who would say I missed something."

"Many people never love," she said.

"At least I know what I am. The total tyrant, the ultimate son of a bitch."

"No. You're not."

"Not to you, no. But I am to others. I'll tell you why. I've had too much to take care of to worry about any one person. I have a company of three hundred thousand employees. To create it, I've bent the rules, paid off, used whatever force I could. Is it wrong that I've given my life to the company instead of to one or two or three persons?"

"No. It isn't."

"So you understand."

"Of course."

"Well, I think I have the man to pass it on to now. Scott."

"Mr. Scott is an extremely capable executive."

"Yes. I think I see some iron in him now." Breedlove smiled. He was thinking back. "Sure, I've pulled some tricks, but I'm proud of most of them, not ashamed. Once when it was between us and a competitor to get an important military food contract, I got a gang to picket outside the competitor's plant when the buyer came to town. He thought they were on strike, so he came right to me and signed on the dotted line."

He winced. Henriette touched his shoulder. "I think you should have a nurse," she said.

"I don't need a nurse. You're my nurse."

"All right."

"You're taken care of, don't worry about that. You know I don't believe in counting my chips, but I've had a law firm do it now. There's something over four hundred and fifty million dollars in liquid assets. Most of it goes to the Breedlove Foundation, but some of it goes to you."

"You need not leave anything to me. Besides, you'll probably outlive me."

"You've earned it, you'll get it," Breedlove said. "I've earned it, too. Every red cent of it. You get paid by the hour in this life, and I think I've averaged fifteen hours a day for the past sixty years. The painters and the writers think they're the only ones who create. But I've created, too. I used to have a chamber pot under my desk because I didn't want to stop work long enough to go to the john and take a leak. I've heard that Beethoven did the same thing. I've created, too."

"And what you've created will last."

"Maybe you shouldn't have stayed with me. Maybe you should have married."

"I've never even considered marriage."

"I suppose that I should have married you."

"No. She was good for your business."

"At least we could have produced a reliable son." He looked into the fire. Again he thought of the past, the learning struggle, and of the eagle in the sky. "Well, soon this old bull goes to pasture. But not quite now."

"There is time," she said. "A lot of time."

He felt a flash of well-being, almost merriment. "Christ, how I wish I could get a hard on and stick it in you. Does that shock you?"

"I'm not so easily shocked as people think I am."

"It's the one thing I wish I had done more of in my life. Especially with you. I think I can put off dying but I can't raise a boner."

"I'll sit here beside you for a while."

"I think you'd better go home."

"I have nothing to do at home. I'll just stay here for a while."

"I'd like you to fly with me to the annual meeting when we go, but I think I'll have you stay here."

"Whatever you wish."

"There's a one percent chance of danger on the plane."

"Then why are you using it?"

"To prove something."

"To prove what?"

"Oh, nothing. Really nothing. If there's a one percent chance of danger on the plane, there's a two percent chance every time a man leaves his house in this day and age."

"I suppose you're right."

"I feel better now. I feel good."

"You look good."

"I'll say this. You were a damn fine-looking woman once. And you still are. With a brain in your head to boot."

"Well, thank you, Lewis."

"Get Scoggins in here. Scoggins will marry us."

"My, you *are* in a good mood, aren't you?"

"I see daylight. I also think Zeus himself could not strike me down. Him or any other god."

"I'm inclined to believe you, seeing you now."

"I might take a nap."

"Why don't you? You could use sleep."

"Don't let anybody in."

"No. I won't."

"Stay here a while."

"I will. I'll be right here."

The eagle stared down at him. Before he slept he felt her hand brush his.

29

THE GUARD AT A BII GRAIN STORAGE ELEVATOR NEAR AMES, Iowa, an ex-Marine who walked with a limp from a war wound, carefully made his rounds. It was dusk and insects hovered in the air. The sky was red. The air was moist with high humidity. The elevator rose into the sky like a sheer white tower, a monument that interrupted vast stretches of flatlands. The guard was thinking of the glories of war and the dullness of peace. His inspection was far from routine. Despite the fact that attacks on the company apparently had ceased, guards had detailed instructions from BII security to report anything unusual in their areas, especially the presence of strangers. The ex-Marine yearned to find something worth reporting. His world at night consisted of back issues of *Leatherneck* magazine and a shortwave radio in a shack beside the elevator. Last night he'd listened to Moscow. Now, finishing his rounds, he moved slowly toward his night home, again frustrated in his efforts to detect potential danger. Then he heard the first explosion. It came from within the elevator, high up, a dull sound like the low rumble of thunder. Another blast followed, a sharp crack from the ground floor. It lifted him off his feet, hurling him against the shack. He was out of himself, out and in; he seemed to be whirling in a strange hot fluidlike atmosphere. It was like the time he'd been hit on Iwo over thirty years ago, a sudden flash and then darkness. He was dimly conscious now in this darkness. Heat struck at him. He could not move. A giant sheet of flame curled toward him. He did not hear the main blast.

* * *

For Anne Scott, watching the grain elevator burn redly into the night sky on television, it seemed a fitting end to another nervous evening. The announcer said the cause of the explosions was unknown but pointed out that several BII facilities had been attacked last summer and speculated that this occurrence could signal a renewed aggressiveness by terrorists. Anne found herself biting her knuckles. She hadn't felt quite safe in the house since they had moved back after that horrible Sunday, although she wouldn't admit it to Mark. She always hesitated before answering the doorbell, particularly if company wasn't expected, and she tested window locks before going to bed. When Mark was out of town, like tonight, her sleep was often restless. The alarm system installed by the company was considered fail-safe, and prowl cars seemed more in evidence on the street. But it all made Anne feel only more uneasy. It seemed as if they lived in an enclosed, protected environment, watched and imprisoned.

She rose from the couch, turned off the television set, and went to the kids' bedrooms, walking heavily and flat-footed, conscious of her swollen stomach. Liz and Tod were sleeping soundly. Mike was out at a school play, and overdue. Mark was in Philadelphia. Returning to the living room, Anne looked at her watch. Ten. She glanced at the phone. Silent. A feeling of unease crept through her, a shivering, a tingling. No. It was stronger than unease. It was fear. Call Mark. But he'd be asleep. Why bother him with her childish fears? Were they childish? They were. No. They were not. They were justified. Perhaps it was the house. They should sell it, dispose of it, burying the memory of the Sunday shock that often revisited her in dreams, jarring her awake, Too often, Mark wasn't in the bed beside her. He'd been traveling more than ever before. Anne, reverting to the role of the stoic corporate wife after a brief, unsuccessful revolt, found herself all too often moping at home at night, playing cards with the maid or sipping wine. This was the maid's night off. Where was Mike? Why was the neighborhood so dark?

Silly, she thought.

Something was going wrong between her and Mark, and perhaps that bothered her more than anything else. He didn't have time for her. He seemed abrupt, less loving, less concerned about the family, obsessed by the madcap race at BII.

Anne felt trapped, lonely, and depressed. It was as if she were living with a man different from the one she'd married. Living with? She repressed a laugh. Living with half the time. But he had changed, a change she didn't want to think about and hesitated to discuss with him. In fact, lately they discussed very little. Maybe it was her fault; maybe she wasn't with it, as Mike would say, just an old-fashioned girl too lovesick, too dependent, too weak. No. She wasn't weak. Hadn't she herself almost challenged Mark to meet his competition head-on? Hadn't she felt triumph when he'd told her Breedlove wanted him to emerge on top? She wanted it for him. For them. She would simply have to pay the price. Looking down at her stomach, she felt slight resentment for the form that was taking shape inside her.

She thought she heard a noise behind her. She whirled. Nothing.

Watch TV. Read a book. Make some calls.

It was the house. That was what was really bothering her. No. Not that, either. Oh, she didn't know. She knew only that, quite suddenly, she was afraid.

She felt slight nausea. Pain danced in her forehead.

The phone rang. Her hands jerked up.

She tried to laugh. It was silly. It was so silly.

"Hello," she said.

It was a deep male voice. "Mrs. Scott, I have called to warn you about something. Do not talk. Listen."

"Who is this?"

"Do not talk. Listen." She heard breathing. She heard a low cough. "We have not left. Today we have struck again. You or your husband need not be among those affected. All he must do is sever his ties with Breedlove. Immediately. In a very short time we will strike again. But he need not be affected."

The phone went dead. Anne sat motionless. Her hands were cold. Slowly she replaced the receiver. Her head was swimming. She had no feeling in her body. *I'll have a drink*, she thought calmly. *Then I'll call Mark*. It was all right. It was just a crank, a horrible crank. But no. It wasn't a crank. Something was happening. It had been building, building slowly, and now it was about to come together, to explode. Mark knew about it. He was keeping it from her. Now she no longer felt frightened. She felt angered. She had a right to know. Whatever it was, she had a right.

Again the phone jangled.

Don't answer. It's the same man again, very possibly a sick person, trying to frighten you. She remembered the voice. There was something about it that seemed somehow familiar to her. Where? When? Had someone been watching her? She glanced around. The drapes were drawn. The phone continued to jangle. With sudden resolution, she picked up the receiver, feeling her heart thump.

"Mrs. Scott?" It was a man's voice, but not the one who'd called earlier. "This is Sergeant Bellerman, Redondo police."

"Yes, what is it?"

"Your son, Michael Scott, is here."

"Mike is there? What do you mean?"

"He's been in an auto accident, Mrs. Scott. Oh, he's okay. Just scratches, a few bruises. But you'd better get down here. We're holding him."

"Holding him? He's under arrest?"

"Yes."

"On what charge?"

"Driving under the influence." the sergeant said. His tone was flat. "There was another boy with him, a Thomas Weedon. We found marijuana in the car, Mrs. Scott. Both boys had been smoking."

Scott hurried home from Philadelphia, canceling several meetings, feeling cool anger. Anne had seemed deliberately incommunicative and vague on the phone; her tone and the sharp edge of her voice indicated that she blamed him for the incident involving Mike. Yet she had handled it effectively, getting their lawyer to arrange bail and hiring an emergency sitter while she drove to the station to get Mike. She hadn't called Scott until she'd returned home.

"It's not even absolutely necessary that you come home," she said. "If it's important to you that you stay there in Philadelphia, then stay. There isn't much you can do here. Not now."

"No. I'll come right home."

"Whatever you like."

"I'm grateful you're keeping your poise."

"I'm not. Not really. I'm all jumps inside."

"I'll be there as soon as I can."

He'd been in the house less than an hour when Miss Tompkins called. "Mr. Scott, Mr. Breedlove has heard about your problem, and he asked me to call and assure you that he will take care of it," she said.

"Take care of it? What does that mean?"

"He merely asked me to tell you that," she said.

Scott turned to Anne. She looked weary and pale. "I think I might have a drink," she said.

"I think I might join you."

"Will you talk to Mike now?"

Scott was pacing. "She said Breedlove would take care of it. I wonder what she meant by that."

"Who said that?"

"Tompkins. Well, I do think I know one thing he was trying to convey to me through her. He wants me to return to Philly."

"All right. Go. Go back to Philadelphia."

He sat down beside her on the couch. "Anne, are you *sure* Mike was driving that car?"

"The police said so."

"Did he tell you he was driving?"

"No. He simply will not talk about it."

"Well, I'll make him talk."

"Your tone of voice makes me wonder if you can ever make him do anything again."

"What does that mean?"

"I think you've lost him. That can happen pretty fast."

"I haven't lost him, Anne."

"If you approach him with anger, you most certainly will."

"It's about time I was firm with him."

"All right. Approach it like a business meeting then."

He stood up. He avoided her eyes. He found himself thinking not about Mike but about his canceled meetings, about Lancaster and Powell, and about Breedlove and the company. It swirled around him, in graphic mind's-eye scenes —the boardroom, the interplay of tactics at meetings, the unrelenting day-to-day struggle with employees, customers, production, the unions. It was totally demanding and at the same time totally irresistible.

"I don't expect you to understand, not fully, but I hope you'll try," he said. "At this stage I simply cannot be as giving and as attentive to you and the kids as I'd like to be."

"I was afraid this would happen. We've talked about it more than once. You've changed. A lot."

"I haven't, Anne. Not down deep."

But he knew one thing. BII had become the dominant factor in his life. The top chair beckoned to him, saying, You can do it, you can have it. He wanted it. It had become even more than a want. It had become a need. He told himself it was because he could be a force for reform in the company, but in his private moments he faced the truth of it. It was the lure of the top, the desire to direct, create, accomplish, to boss. It was the lure of power. The Breedlove Troika. They were at the near top, men with manicured fingernails, expensive suits, and posh offices, yet in reality they were in a jungle, a power jungle. It had affected him both mentally and physically. His intake of alcohol had increased, he'd gained weight, and he seemed constantly exhausted. Depression often gripped him. His temper was short. He'd found himself snapping at subordinates, even at his secretaries.

And, now, he wanted to return to Philadelphia.

He'd been sent there by Breedlove for talks with BII suppliers and eastern bankers. He'd discovered they were quite concerned about the company's financial condition, a concern intensified by Mendenthal's campaign. Suppliers were uncertain about extending credit. The bankers seemed nervous about their loans.

Anne gazed at him. Her eyes softened. "I love you," she said. "But I want you to know that I'm afraid. For the kids, for me, and for you."

"Afraid of being harmed?"

"Yes. I'll tell you now. I received a threatening phone call last night. A man said you might be killed if you didn't leave the company."

"A crank," he said, turning away from her.

"No." She touched his shoulder. "Mark, look at me." He did. Her eyes were wide, almost pleading. "You keep saying don't worry, it's all right. But it's not all right."

"Breedlove says he'll handle it," Scott said absently.

"Is there a relationship here?" Anne said. "Are the others

you're competing against in the company trying to frighten us?"

"No. No, I'm sure it's not that."

"A group is trying to take over the company. I've read about it in the papers. We used to talk about your business. We don't any more, but I still can read. Something is happening that I know is bad, dangerous. Is this takeover group responsible?"

"No. I'm certain they're not."

"Mark, whatever it is, it's not worth it. God knows I want things, money and security, but I will not stand by and allow you to risk our lives for it. I want you to quit."

"Is that what you really want?"

"Yes."

"But you know I won't. I'm not going to run away, and you know that."

"Do you realize that you *are* risking your life?"

"I don't think I am."

"All right. Then I'll tell you what I'm going to do. I'm going to pack up and go away for a while. Take the kids."

"If you think that's best."

"Well, one thing is certain. I'm not much needed, or listened to, around here."

"You are needed. And listened to."

"And loved?"

"Yes. Of course."

"Say it."

"Say it?"

"You know."

"That I love you? I do. You know I do."

But he was thinking about Philadelphia.

When Mike's hearing came up, after two postponements, the results were almost exactly what the lawyer Breedlove had sent in had forecast they would be. First of all, the lawyer got a change in judges, explaining that the one originally scheduled to hear the case was the toughest drug enforcer in the state. Then, at the hearing, he pointed out that Mike, at fourteen, couldn't even drive a car and obviously was covering up for Tommy. Neither boy appeared on the stand. Mike got three months' probation; Tommy was assigned to juvenile hall for six months. Leaving the courtroom, Scott avoided the eyes of Tommy's parents, who sat in the back row.

"Now I'd like the truth, once and for all," he said to Mike, driving home. "Who was behind the wheel?"

"Well, you heard the lawyer in there."

"It wasn't you?"

"You heard your lawyer."

"Then when you first said you were the driver you were covering up for Tommy?"

"You know I can't drive."

"But you were smoking?"

"A little. Just a little."

"Why?"

Mike turned away. "They all do it," he said.

"So you must, too?"

"I dunno."

"You're out of trouble now. Stay out."

"Sure," Mike said.

Scott's jaw firmed and his hands tightened on the wheel. He could no longer talk to Mike and he did not know why. There was little joy in their household. Gone were the family sessions of talking, joking, game-playing; gone, too, it seemed, were laughter and closeness and even love. He told himself he would get it back. But a second side of him, the whispers of another man who seemed to have formed stubbornly within him, wondered if he really wanted to get it back.

Consternation greeted Scott when he returned to the office after Mike's hearing. The area was alive with police cars, fire trucks, and milling people. Many were BII employees. Scott caught the arm of the security guard, Hooten.

"Bomb threat, Mr. Scott," Hooten said. "They're just about all out of the building now."

"When did you receive the threat?"

"About an hour ago."

"By phone?"

"It came by phone, but not to me. I was on lunch break. My backup got it. But there's something else, Mr. Scott."

"What?"

"That hippie type in the green coat we talked about."

"Yes."

"Well, he was here again t'day, askin' for you."

"What time was this?"

"Little b'fore noon. When I told him you ain't in, he left a note for you."

"He did? Where is it?"

"At the desk in the lobby. I'll get it soon as they let us back in."

Lancaster pushed his way through the crowd. He grinned at Scott. "Surrender," he said, putting his hands over his head.

"What is the hidden meaning of that, Hank?"

"If you're going around planting bombs to scare us out, then, well, I'm scared out."

"I'll assume that is Lancaster humor."

"Speaking of kidding, or kids, I hear yours got off."

"News travels fast."

"These kids nowadays. Something else."

"How would you know?"

"Powell looks so forlorn over there. I shall go speak to Powell, cheer him up."

"You do that. He'd appreciate it."

After searching for an hour, the police found two four-stick packets of dynamite taped to an elevator shaft in the subbasement. The timer had been set for 5 P.M., the height of the exiting rush hour. Scott tramped around, nervous and impatient. Perspiration dampened his shirt. He was approaching the truth. A scrap of paper, pigeonholed in the desk of a security guard, might well contain information that would lead him to that truth. His heart hammered. It had built in him for months, frustration and anger and fear that sometimes came to him in restless night stirrings or from shadows that crouched behind him when he walked alone in the dark. It had been carefully planned. It had been effective. And it had become personal to Scott. The attack on his home. Anne's intimidation in the woods near Olen. Now the phone threat. He would do it alone. He would not tell security. He would not tell Breedlove, at least until he knew much more. It was his, Mark Scott's, matter to settle.

30

At the intersection of Twenty-fifth Street and Santa Monica Boulevard a Mercury sedan bearing two ex-policemen now employed by BII security had a minor collision with a blue Chevrolet station wagon that also had two men in the front seat. It was just after dark. The Chevrolet blocked the Mercury's path. Horns sounded. One of the security men touched the telephone in the sedan. A hand reached in through the window and stopped him.

"Don't fiddle with the toys," a big man outside said.

Another man was already in the back seat of the Mercury. "Pull it around the corner," he said. He pressed a .45 to the driver's neck.

It had begun to rain, a light patter unusual for the late May evening. The Mercury moved slowly, its front fender scraping its tire. It stopped outside a funeral home on Twenty-fifth. There was a fire station across the street.

"Now we sit here a while, that's all," said the man in the back seat. "All I'd like to see is four hands up there that don't move. We sit here a while, then you boys go home, play with your dicks or something. Some friends of ours will take care of what you two were up to."

"Who sent you?" the driver asked. It was chilly, but he was sweating.

"Right today, we're workin' for the same company," the man in the back seat said.

"Breedlove?" said the other security man.

"Well, he sent us via a Hudson," the man in the back seat said. He chuckled. "You think a Chevy hit you, but it was a Hudson." He paused. "When you suppose this rain'll end?" he said. "I read where we got ten inches already this year."

The rain tapped the Buick's hood as Scott stopped by the apartment house in Venice. A few surfers remained in the ocean, paddling out to wait for their wave. On the freeway heading west, Scott had thought he was being followed by a red Mercury, but the Mercury was now nowhere in sight. He found a parking space a block away and got out and stood in the rain, hatless and coatless. Water ran along the curb, stirring up small mounds of debris. Scott walked rapidly to the apartment house, his shoulders hunched, his clenched fists jammed deeply in his pockets, his jaw set. This was the third place he'd been to since finding a note from Lawrence Breedlove in the guard's desk. He'd found new instructions on papers pinned to doors at two other places. It was beginning to get absurd and melodramatic, and he wondered vaguely if it could all be a runaround to satisfy someone's perverse sense of humor.

But no. It was real. The note giving him the first address had told him to come alone, and he'd obeyed, spurred to action by his insatiable desire to find answers to the riddles that had plagued him for many months. But now, as he entered the apartment house and hurried up the stairs, his adrenal flow high, his breath labored, he began to have second thoughts. He paused before a door marked 17. There were no further notes, no further instructions. He was here. It had come down to this. He hesitated, a stench of rotted carpet full in his nostrils, a cold sensation deep in his stomach. Slowly he walked to the end of the hall and looked out over the fire escape. The ocean was dark. Rain fell in heavy sheets. A bushy form darted between Scott's legs, startling him. It was a large gray cat, which bounded away, stopped, and lay eyeing him.

This was not his job. It was foolish. What danger lay behind the door marked 17?

Phone security. Go home.

But he knew that he wouldn't. He had come this far. He would finish it.

He walked down the hall and tapped on the door. No answer. He tried the knob. The door creaked open. Scott glanced inside. Darkness. "Larry?" he said. He heard only the rain. From inside came a pungent odor, a smell of uncleanliness, of decay. Scott hesitated. Then he entered.

A flashlight beam struck his face. He stepped backward, dodging, but the beam followed him. He blinked.

"You're late," a voice said.

"Larry?"

"Larry is a name. Am I Larry? No, I am not Larry. I am a cat. I am a little cat who sees in the dark. I eat mice. I lick myself to stay clean."

The light moved away, settling on an overstuffed chair that spilled dirty cotton from gaping holes in its fabric.

"Sit down," the voice said. "Watch the moths, or they'll eat you."

Scott sat down. The light went off.

"Don't be frightened."

"I'm not frightened," Scott said.

"Breedlovers do not scare."

"Oh, they scare, all right."

Scott saw a shadowy figure moving by the window. The unclean odor filled his nostrils. He could tell by the voice that it was Lawrence Breedlove. He tried to relax. For a fleeting moment he again wished he had not come, and he felt deep within him a sense of peril, a flooding anxiety that amounted almost to panic. His impetuosity and curiosity had addled his senses. He had not thought clearly. He was not a brave man, not a chance-taker. He wondered how Lancaster, the risker, would react in this situation. He thought about the red Mercury. Breedlove's security men? Were they now outside in the rain, watching this window?

"I have my wits," Larry said. "Don't worry about that. I do my job. I got you here, didn't I? Pretty soon the man will show his face."

"What man?"

"The main man. My main man. We're brothers, at least under the skin. We came from the same cock, although from different snatches. Do you think I have my wits?"

"Yes."

"I do. I'm all right. It's been a long time, too long, but we're closing in now. It's going to work. Once I thought it wouldn't work. That's when I came to warn you. I was trying to get out. I didn't really know the man then, but I do now. He can pull it off. He has a proposition for you, my main man has."

"Who is he?"

"A ghost," Larry said. "Now I hear him breathe."

"You're not making sense."

"I don't try. I'm hung up. Spaced out. There was a geek I knew in a circus where I worked once, someplace in Germany I guess it was, who ate mice and raw chickens. I'm like that geek. Crazy like him. But I'm not a zombie. Not any more. Do you know what a zombie is? Tell one to walk, it walks. Say turn, it turns, stop and it stops. Like at military school. Walk, turn, stop. Stand. Hold."

"Larry, how long have you lived here?"

"Well, I don't live here, you see. We use the place. I move a lot. Moving's easy around here. Just go to another pad, trade with the john or chick that's there."

"I think you need help."

"No. I have my wits."

"Your father would help you."

"Yes, yes, oh, yes!" Larry said, his voice animated. "In my father's house there are many mansions. We stake claim to one. From skunk hollow, we raise our voices to stake our claim."

The shadow shifted. Scott saw Larry's form outlined against the window. He thought of Anne. He thought of Mike. And he thought of himself, the anointed of Lewis Breedlove, speeding toward the top chair. He'd observed the change in himself, the metamorphosis of the idealistic, family-oriented Scott into the practical, ambitious Scott. What would be next? The ruthless Scott? An electric feeling surged in him. He saw a parallel. Breedlove and Larry, Mark Scott and Mike. His hands opened and closed rapidly. It was a trap, this power jungle, and, even now, fully aware of his potential loss, he knew he would not get out. It was like this chair, where he seemed caught and immobile, powerless to act, mesmerized in the dark and cold atmosphere that stank of filth, the words *Breedlove Breedlove Breedlove* burning in his brain.

"He is a murderer," Larry said. "But my main man, he is a match for the murderer."

"Who has he murdered?"

"Oh, many. Many. Start with my mother, murdered because he let her die. But you don't care to hear this."

"I do. Go on."

"She comes to me, very still and quiet, sometimes when I'm

sick, a lady in a hat and a fur coat. I saw her when she was dying." Larry paused, his voice breaking, and Scott saw that his cheeks were wet with tears. He turned his face away and spoke in a low, almost inaudible voice. "She told me something. She wanted to see her lawyer, something about her stock in the company, but he wouldn't let her. Then she gave me something. A bodkin."

"A what?"

"A bodkin. You know, a sharp stiletto. A bare bodkin. He would not come into her room so she could use it on him, even if she did have the strength, so she asked me to use it on him when he slept. Do you believe that? A slice of life among the upper crust. I kept that bodkin for a long time, wanting to do it. I really wanted to do it. I wanted to do it, but I couldn't decide. I've decided now. I've made up my mind. All my life I've been scared and unsure. But I'm sure now. I'll tell you something. I've drifted in and out of a hundred jobs. I haven't even succeeded in killing myself. I don't know what sex I am. Sometimes I even forget what my name is. But this cat I met, my main man, gave me confidence. I've waffled all over the lot, wondering who I am, but now I know. I've made up my mind. I *can* do something. I will."

"Where did you meet this man?"

"I'll tell you. Don't interrupt. If you do, I won't tell you."

"All right. I won't interrupt."

It had begun just a year ago in Paris, when Larry had become aware that a man was following him. The man made little pretense of it. Larry saw him trailing some hundred yards behind him on the streets by day and occasionally under a lamppost at night, eyeing him. He suspected that the man was a collector for his heroin connection, Jean, to whom he was deeply in debt, but there never was an attempt to stop him or accost him. He walked a lot in Paris that summer, through good districts and bad, sometimes asking for work at the shops but never getting it. His French was bad. He found it difficult, in fact, to speak at all. It was not mere depression; it was beyond depression. He slouched the streets, smelling his sweat and filth, often feeling on the edge of nausea, a slumped ghost in a green coat with a past so blurred that it blotted out his very identity. Walking helped, although he feared that someday he would walk too far, go out too far like a swimmer and be unable to make it back. Back to where? He really did not know. He had a small, dirty room on the Left Bank, near the Vaugirard in the Fifteenth, but he did not usually go there at night. He slept in alleys, in theaters, on the subway. He did not bathe; he did not shave. He kept five francs in his shoe as a last resort. A girl he'd known in Boston occasionally wired him some money. She thought he was an art student. He knew a place where he could order a glass of wine and sit for hours without the waiters bothering him. One afternoon the man who had been following him took a table next to his. Larry felt a twinge of fear. That was good. A man who wished to die did not feel fear. The man didn't speak for a long time. Then he said, "I have paid your bill."

Larry whirled. Pain streaked through his forehead. "What bill?"

"The man called Jean, who supplies you. He is paid in full. He promises more credit for you. But you will not need him again."

"Why are you following me? If what you want is a blow job in the alley, then say so."

"I know who you are," the man said.

"Then you're one up on me, because I don't know."

"I believe that you do. I believe that you know your name is Lawrence Breedlove." Carefully the man took out a package of cigarettes and lit one, an American Lucky Strike. "My name is Clinton St. John. I am a man who is very close to you. I also am your benefactor."

"Ask me, I think you're just another queer."

He was suddenly not feeling well at all. Dizziness began to overwhelm him. The pain burned in his head. A fly was crawling on his wineglass; reaching out to swat it, he upset the glass, spilling wine on his coat sleeve. The street was crushed with people and autos moving in a crazy pattern of shifting colors and blended noises, a circling maze that increased his vertigo and sent undulating, nauseous waves to the pit of his stomach. He tasted bitter bile in his throat. He was tired, so tired. Today he'd walked too far. Who was this man before him, swimming out of focus, trembling like a sinister wraith, claiming to be a benefactor? The man was rising. He was beckoning to Larry. He was coming toward him, his hand outstretched. Where will we go now? What will we do? The words were a singsong in Larry's head. He went with the man, dimly conscious of a taxi ride, apartment steps, the smell of garbage and fresh paint, and then, in a cool room, he was asleep. He came awake suddenly, jarred with fear. He was lying on a couch and it was night. A woman sat on a chair under a light, filing her nails. He shook his head. The pain seemed gone. The man who'd talked to him in the café was squatted on the floor beside him. Larry's throat was dry and his body cried for water. As if she knew, the woman got up and filled a glass from the tap over the kitchen sink. He drank it in huge gulps, asking for more. She gave him a half glass. He fell back, brushing his beard.

The man said, "You're better now?"

"I—I don't know."

"I am sure that you are better." The man leaned forward. "Tell me, Lawrence. Do you think your father would allow you to come home? Just for a few days?"

"I have no father."

"Does he ever send you money?"

"No."

"Then how do you live?"

"You see how I live. Slopping garbage or sucking cocks."

"You have a great desire to live. It is very dear to you, life."

Larry turned away. The couch smelled of mothballs. He tried to get up, but discovered he was still too weak.

"It is important that you return to your father's house, that you return within the next few days," the man said. "I have worked out a way to do it."

"Why is it so important?"

The woman spoke for the first time. Her voice was high-pitched, almost harsh. "Don't pussyfoot with him," she told the man. "Clean him up, get some food in him, and send him on his way. He'll do it."

"Her father works in the Breedlove house," the man said. "She is the daughter of Scoggins, the butler."

Larry's senses had returned fully. "Old Scoggins?" he said. "We used to call him the Undertaker." He felt somewhat amused. "I never saw him smile. Do you think he can smile?"

"Tell him what we want," the woman said, filing rapidly.

"Are you alert now?" the man asked.

"Yes. I'm okay."

"We want you to go to your father's house, the house in Pasadena. Your father has a Rembrandt painting. A man I know in Paris, an expert art forger, is already busy reproducing the painting. My plan is to switch the unauthentic for the authentic and to sell the Rembrandt in Europe. Victoria has already contacted a dealer in Venice who will handle the transaction without questions. It is a simple plan, and, with your help, an easy one."

Larry could not believe it. Again he felt amused. "I'm the guy you picked to do the switch?"

"I will be there to help," the man said.

"What's my split?"

"I have not told you the entire plan. The money from the painting will be invested. It will be invested in the hiring of expert extortionists who will make millions for us."

"It won't work. He's too strong a man."

"I, too, am a strong man. You could become a strong man. This could help you become a strong man."

Larry giggled. "Wild," he said. "Wild." The giggling continued. He was filled with mirth. "Wild, wild, wild."

The man rose. He put his hand on Larry's chin and stared deeply into his eyes. "Look, look deeply," he said. The eyes blazed in the dim light. Larry's mirth had quickly changed to fear. He heard the noise of the woman filing her fingernails, exaggerated and sharp in the silent room. He wanted to leave, to run, to escape, but the man's eyes held him powerless and motionless. He felt the need for a fix. His hands seemed cold. Then he knew. It came to him in an electric flash. The eyes blazing into his were identical with the eyes of his father.

Larry did it, joining with the man who claimed brotherhood to him, in a plan that seemed impossible yet clearly possible. He found himself caught up in the excitement of it. At times, it was all brilliantly clear to him; at other times, it was as if he lurched through events and time in a deep mistfog. Always, he had the sense that it was something fated for him, planned long ago, as if his part in it were not under his control but instead dictated and directed from the distant past. Within a week after meeting St. John in Paris, Larry was on a flight to Los Angeles, money in his pocket. St. John left the same day, on a later flight. He had planned well. He called it a military mission and said it must be precisely timed. Victoria Scoggins had learned from her father that Breedlove planned to spend several days at Mayo Clinic in May; that, said St. John, would be the time for the initial action. There were two watchdogs at the Breedlove house, Scoggins and the chauffeur, Morris. St. John figured Larry could worm past Scoggins, but he feared Morris could be a problem. Morris guarded the mansion carefully when Breedlove was out of town, and St. John maintained they could not take a chance that Morris would discover them. It was enough of a chance to risk arousing Scoggins's suspicions. So there was only one solution—enlist Morris as an aide or, at least, buy his silence. St. John had a scrap of evidence— something Breedlove had let slip before Scoggins and was relayed by Scoggins to his daughter in a letter—that Breedlove had once been instrumental in fixing Morris's fights, setting him up for a vicious kill one night at Madison Square Garden. St. John said he would work on that.

"When you offer a man money, you might insult him," he explained to Larry. "A chance for retribution for a man once proud is much more enticing bait. We will make our move on Tuesday."

"That doesn't give us much time. To work on Morris, I mean."

"I need only a little time," St. John said.

Morris's pattern was easy to follow, particularly for someone like St. John. The chauffeur always spent his day off—usually Sundays—at a gym on Colorado Boulevard, watching the fighters work out, but he was always home by dark, pacing in his loft, sometimes until midnight. St. John decided to approach him at the gym. Outside he turned to Larry.

"You may go in, but only if you say nothing and leave when I tell you."

"Don't worry, I'll stay outside."

"As you wish."

Larry hesitated. "Wait. I'll go in with you."

Morris was lounging in a chair, watching a black middle-weight pound the heavy bag. The gym smelled of sweat and thick heat. St. John walked directly to his target. Larry slouched behind him. St. John touched Morris's shoulder and Morris whirled.

"The reflexes haven't been damaged, I see," St. John said.

Morris stood up. He looked frightened, almost cringing. "Who are you?"

"My name is unimportant. But I do remember that I used to watch you fight. You had the best left in the game in those days."

"Well, I guess it wasn't bad," Morris said, turning away. The black fighter viciously banged the bag, grunting, his eyes narrow and white. "Not so bad," Morris said.

"Now you work for a rich man," St. John said. "That's not bad either."

Again, a flicker of fright appeared in Morris's eyes. "How do you know that?"

"I know what it is my business to know. Isn't it true that you drive a rich man?"

"I suppose he rich."

"How rich are you?"

"He give me a job. A job's all I want."

"And is he good to you?"

"He too busy to think about that."

"How good do you think you were?"

"What d'you mean?"

"I mean in the ring."

Morris looked down at his shoes. "I was okay. Maybe I was pretty good."

"But what did it get you? As I understand it, it got you a broken head."

Morris fumbled. He was a little punchy and sometimes he stammered. "I-I-I came up too fast. My manager, he—"

"Your manager was employed by the man who now employs you."

Morris turned away and watched the black middleweight hit the bag. "What you sayin'?" he said quietly. "Why you talkin' to me?"

"Your rich man you drive around the city now set you up for that broken head."

Morris couldn't quite understand. He turned and silently regarded St. John, his mouth partly open, his eyes rolling in his head.

St. John said, "He set you up. Now I want you to help me set him up."

"Man—you know?—I think you crazy, man."

"Then listen to a crazy man. I want only for you to shut your eyes one night this week. For one turning away, you will earn the pay of a month." St. John's eyes bore into Morris's. "That is not all. There is much more. Listen as this crazy man talks. Who is your employer? What do you know about him? You see only his face. You listen only to his orders. How many others of your race has he exploited? He is where he is now due to exploitation of the masses, thousands of people like you."

Again Morris regarded the fighter, who continued to strike the heavy bag. St. John turned sharply to Larry. "Leave us," he said. "I will meet you outside."

Larry lounged outside in the sun. He watched the cars rush by. The sun was warm and he felt good. He knew that everything would be all right. It was almost an hour before St. John came out.

"The man will cooperate," he said.

So the plan proceeded. Approaching the Pasadena estate on the following Tuesday evening, Larry felt an exhilaration and confidence he had not known for years, perhaps never. He picked up the gate phone. Scoggins answered immediately.

"It's the long-lost soul, the wicked prodigal son," Larry said. "Scoggins, it's Larry, returned to feast upon the fatted calf. Buzz me in."

"Mr. Lawrence?"

"In the flesh, and hungry. Buzz me in."

"Well, I don't know—"

"So you don't believe it's me, you really don't? Well, remember the time I pulled a temper tantrum and busted my hobbyhorse? Remember you got it fixed for me? Remember Mrs. Luce?" He felt total confidence in himself now. "Remember old Reamer, my math tutor? I think I was more afraid of him than of the old man. We used to talk about it. Remember? Now buzz me in through this prison gate. We'll talk old times. I'll show you my new hat."

After a hesitant moment, the buzzer sounded. Larry walked toward the house, stirred by memories, most of them unpleasant—black-suited Reamer with the tight lips and bad breath, the difficult books he hated, the food brought on trays under cloth-covered warmers, the green room where his mother had died, the old man's bellowing and belching and his hard, dark eyes. For a few seconds he hesitated and felt something that approached fear. Then, his chin high, he went in.

Scoggins wasn't sure. "Mr. Lawrence, I do fear I cannot allow you to stay even one night without Mr. Breedlove's permission."

"Aw, Scog, loosen up. I'm not exactly here to rob the joint. I'm here just to breathe a little nostalgia."

"What have you been doing?"

"Oh, walking around."

"You're looking well."

His coat and pants had been cleaned, and he'd bought a new shirt and tie. His beard was trimmed. "It'll be only one night, maybe two. I just want to get another look at the old place before I amble on."

"Very well. But I must telephone Mr. Breedlove in the morning and tell him."

"You're a good egg, Scog. Where'll I plop?"

"Mrs. Luce's former room is unoccupied."

"Superior," Larry said.

"This is somewhat irregular, but I suppose it's all right."

"I got a car on the street. Station-wagon type. Shall I pull it in?"

"Morris will do that. Is there anything I can get for you before I retire?"

"How about a blonde with big boobs?"

Scoggins gave him a horrified look and backed away. Larry found the room, fell on the bed, and congratulated himself. He'd done it. He was in. He was too exhilarated to sleep. He did not feel a need for drugs. Mrs. Lamson, after giving him a snoop's peek, retired to her room. Larry waited, and then, in his stocking feet, went out into the hall. He could hear

Mrs. Lamson's loud snores behind her door. The light under Scoggins's door went out. Slowly he moved down the hall, a flashlight in his hand. He paused by the door of the room where his mother had died, the green room, and carefully pushed on the knob. The door opened. The flashlight beamed on the bed and the furniture. The room seemed cold inside, and he thought he could hear a sound like breathing. He backed away and slowly went down the stairs, toward his father's den. If Scoggins should awaken and discover him, he'd explain that he got hungry. He could not recall a time when he'd been in his father's room. Now he approached the door cautiously, opened it, and flashed the light inside. He jumped back, startled. The light glistened on the eyes of the stuffed eagle. The eyes seemed to pierce into him, causing a small, sharp pain in his head. The flashlight moved around, illuminating the man in the Rembrandt painting.

St. John came the next night precisely at eleven, quietly pushing through the gate left open with an alarm neutralized by Morris's simple tampering with a screwdriver and knife. His demeanor was confident and almost cocky. He was dressed in a suit and hat and had a large package wrapped in white paper under his arm.

Larry, meeting him on the lawn, said quietly, "There's a hitch."

"What do you mean, a hitch?"

"Old Scoggins. He's still up. He's in the kitchen drinking milk, for Christ's sake. I think he suspects something. He watches me like a hawk."

"We have to do it tonight. There will be no more opportunities."

"Well, just how? You tell me, just how?"

"I'll wait."

"I don't think he's going to go to bed. It's like the old fart *knows*."

"I have to do it now. Even if I have to get rid of him, making it look like robbery."

"Get rid of him? Kill him? Not that. Oh, not that."

"Calm down. You're talking too loudly. Just do as I say. Go talk to Scoggins. Keep his attention. I need just five minutes."

"Why don't we try it tomorrow?"

"No. He might be back tomorrow."

"Scoggins suspects, I tell you."

"Go," St. John said. His jaw was set. "Go!"

Scoggins was standing up, his back turned, when Larry entered the kitchen. Larry cleared his throat and Scoggins whirled. His eyes were deep-set and bloodshot.

"Well, I couldn't sleep either," Larry said.

"Mr. Lawrence, I would feel much better if you were to leave. Leave immediately."

"That's not like my old Scoggins."

"I'm sorry."

"Did you reach the old man?"

"Yes, I did reach Mr. Breedlove. I told him you were here, but I am not sure he understood. He was rather ... well, incommunicative."

"Doped up? What's wrong with him, being at a clinic and all, I mean?"

"I don't know. I haven't the slightest idea. Mr. Breedlove does not discuss personal matters."

"Well, let's hope it's not serious. Shall we?"

"I think I'll try to get some sleep."

"Naw, stay up a while, talk to me."

"You seem nervous about something, Mr. Lawrence."

"Can't you cut out that 'Mr. Lawrence' crap? Call me Larry."

"That would hardly be proper."

Larry thought he could hear St. John's footsteps in the hallway. He thought he could hear the creak of a door opening. He paused, listening. He looked at Scoggins. Scoggins's expression was blank.

"I don't mind telling you something," Larry said. "You probably know it. I never exactly considered the old man my biggest hero. But you know all that. You keep your mouth shut, but you know a lot."

"I really must go."

Larry kept him. "Will you shake hands with me?"

"If you like."

"I'll be going in the morning and it may be early so I might not see you."

"Very well."

They shook hands. Scoggins's hand was cold. He pulled

away from Larry's grasp, turned quickly, and went into the hall. He paused outside Breedlove's den, opened the door, and peered in. Then he closed the door and went upstairs to his room.

"So St. John made it, despite old Scoggins's suspicions," Larry told Scott. "He got out of that house with the real Rembrandt and got it over to Italy—I don't know how, but he could do things—and then he hires on these two professional terrorists and we all go to work. Well, at least, the two pros go to work. I hang around waiting for the payoff. I guess you know most of the rest of it."

"There is something that is not clear to me at all. Just why did Morris agree to help?"

"I felt sorry for him, Morris."

"You didn't answer my question. Why did he help?"

"I think Clint frightened him as much as he tempted him. When you look back on it, I guess you'd say Morris was a sap, but he was a good guy. Maybe he was as good as anybody I've met. Listen. I'll tell you something. There was some dead time early in this and I'd put on my old coat, that I felt comfortable in, and take the bus out to the old man's house in Pasadena, sort of to look around, like I belonged there. Maybe it was that I was getting cold on Clint's idea. Morris spotted me once and he came out and we had a talk. He was a pretty easy guy to talk to. I don't know why, but I found myself even telling him about it, even about the Rembrandt and all. I said I was thinking of backing out, maybe even of going to tell someone about it. Somebody in the company, maybe. Somebody like you. Morris said, 'Do it, man. You ain't in so deep you can't get out.' Clint, he didn't want me to have a car. We'd turned back the station wagon we had rented. So what does Morris do? He loans me his car for a few days. I think Clint wanted me to be without a car so he could keep his eye on me. But, Morris, he was the type of guy who would give you the shirt off his back."

"Do you realize Morris was murdered?"

"He was killed in an accident."

"It was not an accident."

"I don't know anything about it. Only that his car crashed and he's dead. That's over. I liked Morris, but I don't think

about him much." Larry chuckled. "I'm not afraid any more.
I've been afraid of things all my life, but I'm not afraid any
more. Add Clint to me, we're a match for that old man."

"I don't think so."

"You'll see."

"What happens now, Larry?"

"Clint will tell you."

"He's coming here?"

"He is here," Larry said.

Scott's body ran cold. Again Larry chuckled. The flashlight
came on and beamed into the face of a man who stepped
from an adjoining room. Scott stared at the face. It was the
man he had seen in Olen, the man who had followed him in
the Volkswagen, the man on the hill at Morris's funeral. His
dark eyes peered at Scott. The eyes were like Breedlove's.
The man threw back his head and laughed. His laugh was like
Breedlove's.

31

CLINTON ST. JOHN HAS SEEN SO MUCH OF DEATH IN HIS TIME
that the word scarcely had meaning to him now. At sixteen,
then bearing the Mendenthal name, he'd enlisted in the U.S.
Army and had seen combat in the Pacific, where he'd killed
with such efficiency that he'd won the Bronze Star and two
Silver Stars. Despite his record, however, he'd been given a
dishonorable discharge, following a general court-martial in
Japan, accused of killing a military policeman with a knife. It
had been a bum rap, the first of a series that would continue
to plague him. He'd killed, it was true, but in self-defense, for
the M.P. had drawn his .45 and was advancing on him when
he'd dropped, rolled, and thrust the knife upward into the
man's stomach. He had fled, leaving the M.P. writhing on the
ground, only to be arrested a week later. They had thrown
the book at him, despite the fact that the M.P. had been a
black man and his plea that blacks were irrational and
dangerous. He was taken, a prisoner by the Army he'd served

so well, to the States and spent eighteen months in federal prison at Leavenworth. Then, stripped of his honors and still seething over injustice, he'd gone home to New York and Philip Mendenthal.

Before the war he'd known soft beds and clean sheets in the Mendenthal house in upstate New York, but he'd known little else there. His mother had never really acknowledged him and Mendenthal had always been too busy with business endeavors to pay much attention to him. Returning home after his release from Leavenworth, St. John found his mother showing strains of madness and Mendenthal even more unreceptive than before. He had violated a code of honor that Mendenthal thought important. Yet he was taken back.

"We will call you the prodigal son," Mendenthal said. "You may stay at least until you find what you want to do with your life."

"I have no idea what I want to do."

"You should go to school."

"No," he said. "The Army taught me all I need to know."

The house was comfortable, but he knew he was unwanted. Mendenthal was not his father and in addition seemed to harbor a private resentment toward him. He could not even look at his mother, who had sealed herself in an upstairs room and communicated only by written message. A young English maid named Mary showed an interest in him and often came to him in his bed at night.

"It's all a bore," he told her. "Even sex is a bore."

"You don't like sex with me?"

"I've had a hundred girls better than you."

"You're a rat. A bloody rat."

"Then why do you come in here?"

"I don't know why. Because I can't stay away from you."

"Japs are the best when it comes to girls. We killed the Japs so we had to make up for it by screwing their women. If the Russians take over here, would you screw them?"

"I suppose so," she said.

"That's what a woman is good for."

"I like to do it. Why not do what you like to do?"

"I did. For two years."

"What?"

"I killed," he said.

"Now you frighten me."

"I'm merely telling you the truth. Killing one another is what human beings do best. We'd stack up Japs like cordwood, pry the gold from their teeth with pliers, and bury them with bulldozers."

"You always talk about the war. Why can't you forget the war?"

He didn't want to forget it. He had found purpose and order in war. Each man knew his job, units depended upon each other, and the military strategy was a symphony of harmony and beauty. The music of combat resounded in his ears at night. He would have re-upped if it had not been for the black M.P. He could have become a colonel, or perhaps even a general. Now his life was rootless and dull, as it had been before the war.

One night Mary told him his father was a man named Lewis Breedlove. "She told me. Rebecca told me."

He had heard Mendenthal speak of the Breedlove company. He said, "Are you sure? How do you know?"

"I said she told me."

"That's not enough. She's wacko."

"She has a photo of him when he was about your age. It looks exactly like you."

"Show it to me."

"She won't let go of it."

Mary's information seemed worth investigating. He borrowed fifty dollars from her, promising to return soon, and caught a Greyhound bus to California. In Los Angeles he took a room in a flophouse near the bus depot and began his search for Lewis Breedlove. He appeared at the main office, then on Wilshire, lurking around until guards became suspicious. He visited several Breedlove plants. Finally he found Lewis Breedlove's home in Pasadena. He went there on a Sunday afternoon, taking the red-car rail line, and stood outside on the street for a half hour, looking at the house. It was a magnificent neighborhood, far exceeding Mendenthal's, and he imagined himself a part of it. The prospect delighted him. If he could prove his kinship to the rich man who lived here, he might be able to enter this realm, or certainly claim some payment.

His mind turned. He felt alive with excitement. He felt he had found his roots.

A black man in a patrol car stopped by him. "What you doin' around here?"

"Minding my business."

"Well, go mind it someplace else."

It would not do to lose his temper. Not now. He went away. When he returned to his room that evening, two men in suits and hats were waiting for him. They flashed badges.

"We hear you been snoopin' around," one said, a fat man who wore suspenders. "We don't want you snoopin' around no more, hear? Wherever you come from, get back on the bus and go there. We want you out tonight."

He always carried a knife, hidden in a sheath on his back. He reached for it. But the fat man was quick. He bounded across the room in one huge stride, his big fist slashing down. It hit with a heavy splashing sound. The other man was on him, too, slashing out with both fists. They beat him until he could not feel the blows, grunting and grinning as they struck.

The beating left no scars, except that it rendered one cheekbone slightly flatter than the other, even now causing him severe pain on occasion. He didn't mind the disarrangement of his face. He'd never been what could be called a handsome man. He had a rugged, pitted soldier's face, with a skin roughened by the elements. Some women found his ugliness attractive, but most of them fled from him in disgust or fear. He seldom looked into mirrors. In another sense the beating, which he knew had been administered by Breedlove's goons, lingered with him. He could no longer concentrate. He drifted, joining the tattered, hopeless winos on Main Street, learning their tricks, like a newspaper propped under your chin while you slept in an all-night movie, learning to panhandle, to shave without soap or water, and how to catch freights. Eventually he returned to Mendenthal.

"Do not disturb Mr. Breedlove," Mendenthal said. "He is mine to disturb."

"Is he my father?"

"No. Your father is dead."

"You're lying to me."

Mendenthal whirled. "I've given you a home despite your

dishonor, and you repay me with ingratitude and scheming behind my back. You have even stooped to seduce household help. You are like him."

"Oh. I see. You want Mary yourself. Is that it? Well, I give her to you."

"I want you to leave this house."

"Sure. I'll go." He grinned. Now he was quite certain of the truth. The truth sparked in Mendenthal's eyes. "I got a better house to go to."

He left at midnight, packing his belongings in a war-surplus duffel bag. He paused by his mother's door, put down the bag, and went in. A lamp beamed beside her bed. She would not sleep in the dark. She lay stiffly, her hair in tangled disarray, a shrunken, aging form already so hideous it made him shudder. Her eyes opened. She sat up. Her lips curved into a crooked smile.

"Oh, Lewis, you've come," she said.

He backed away. He'd entered the room hopeful of finding the photo Mary had mentioned, or any other material that might link him to Breedlove, but this unexpected occurrence had given him all he needed. The moaning madwoman had mistaken him for his father. It was final proof to him that he was the son of Lewis Anthony Breedlove. He hurried out.

He knew the combination of Mendenthal's safe. For all his fastidiousness, Mendenthal was careless about security. He took three thousand dollars in hundred-doillar bills. When he turned, he saw Mary behind him. She was fully dressed and had a suitcase.

"Think I'm stupid, do you?" she said. "Think you can sneak off without me, eh? Well, your little Mary, she ain't as stupid as you think. You take me with you."

"I can't. I'll meet you somewhere."

"You won't. I know you. I'm comin' now. You got your little Mary in the family way, you 'ave."

"Whose fault is that?"

"Don't care whose fault. You take me, or I'll tell 'im you robbed 'im."

"He'll know anyway. I was thinking of leaving an IOU."

"You take me."

He shrugged. "You sure you want to go?"

"Sure."

"Positive?"

"Positive."

The words assured her of an early death.

"I'll admit now that it wasn't too smart," Clinton St. John said to Scott. "But I still had a buzzing in my head from that beating in L.A. I wasn't thinking clearly. Before the sun came up that day, I'd used the knife on her. I left her hidden in a pile of wood by the railroad tracks."

Scott realized he'd been sitting in the same place for over a half hour, without speaking and hardly stirring, listening in stunned awe as St. John related his narrative. St. John spoke in an emotionless low monotone, seldom gesturing or raising his voice, seated in a stoic unmoving squat, his features illuminated by a low-watt naked bulb that dangled from a cord over his head. The face caught and held Scott. Up close, it seemed a face broiled in hell—pitted, scarred, eyes that swam crookedly, jagged teeth that snapped and hissed. Larry crouched in a far corner, occasionally issuing a low laugh. Scott felt as if he had been thrust into an alien world. Before him, gaping boldly like an actor onstage, was a man giving him answers to riddles that had confounded him. He'd sought the answers recklessly and compulsively but now, getting them, he realized he didn't want them. He wanted to leave, to flee, run out into the rain. Shivers went up his spine. It was not fear, but instead disgust and shock. The face transfixed him. St. John spoke.

"On the freight heading west, I got to thinking about it. Her body would be found and they'd trace it right to me. So I decided I'd lie low for a while. I had money and time. I went into Mexico and then deeper, down to South America. It was time to take a new name, a new identity." St. John grinned, and Scott saw Breedlove in his face, in the jaw, the dark eyes, the mouth. "But that was really impossible, a new identity. Do you know what identity is, Mr. Scott? It's what you remember. Your remembrances can't duplicate another's. So you can't really change your identity. You can only change your looks or your name. I had a lieutenant in the Army named St. John, and that seemed like a good name for me. He got his head blown off by the Japs, but he took out his share of them before he got his. I got identification cards and a work permit and even a job in one of the Breedlove plants down there. They had a strike there one week, and that's when I found out a lot more about the old man. Goon squads were sent in to work us over. I escaped it, but before I did I saw a lot of broken heads. It reminded me of a lot of things, but mostly of who I really was, a Breedlove out to get a bigger Breedlove. So I returned to the States. That was a mistake. I had made that mistake of identity, you see. I had convinced myself I was another person, could hide under another name, because I had cards that said I was Clinton St. John. They picked me up two weeks after I crossed the border. Mendenthal sent in a lawyer, but he only made sure I went to the can, not get off. I got the big casino. Murder one, twenty to life.

"Prison is a good place to think. I figured this out there. I decided, for one, that I wouldn't rush it when I got out, and, for two, I decided that I needed the right personnel. I found them in Europe. If you'd met them, I'm sure you'd be quite impressed with their capabilities. You have, of course, seen evidence of the capabilities. Call one Mario, call the other Horst. Between them, they're responsible for almost half of the recent acts of terrorism in Europe. They're thinkers. They work well together. They also are expensive, very expensive. I've paid them only a small amount of what they've asked. They have ten percent of the action, and they intend to collect it. So you see that I'm committed to this. They would be very angry if they do not receive their ten percent." St. John paused, a short pause. He remained in his squat, hardly moving. "There is not much else to say, Mr. Scott, except to present our business proposition to you."

Scott stirred. He heard the rain.

"We will negotiate," St. John said. "It's like an insurance transaction. I wish to sell you insurance. You need insurance, for you have had trouble lately. And since you have had so many claims, the premium will be high."

"How high?"

"I want three million dollars. In cash. Within the next twenty-four hours."

"And you want me to tell this to Breedlove?"

"Yes."

"He would laugh at you."

"Do not forget, Mr. Scott, that I also am a Breedlove. Tell him that, and I think he will understand." St. John's brow furrowed. His lip curled upward. "You will visit your master, Mr. Breedlove, and tell him that he will raise the money. You will have twelve hours, at which time you will be contacted and given additional instructions."

"He will say no."

"I think he will say yes."

"If you do not get the money, those who want their share will deal harshly with you."

"I quite realize that I am playing a dangerous game." St. John shifted on his haunches. His eyes glinted. "I do assure you of this, Mr. Scott. If I do not receive the money, that airplane will be bombed. Perhaps tomorrow. Perhaps another day. I am at the point where I do believe the airplane in flames would give me almost as much satisfaction as reclaiming part of a legacy that belongs to me."

"You are an obsessed man."

"I spend very little time in self-analysis, Mr. Scott. There is very little a person can do about himself, at least after time has passed." St. John paused. He looked at no one. His eyes were vacant. "If he had made only one small acknowledgment of me, even a simple nod, then perhaps this obsession could have been exorcised. He did not."

"Did he know?"

"Of course he knew."

"Then it is Breedlove you want. Only Breedlove. Yet you threaten others, innocent people."

"Innocent? Like yourself? Are you innocent, Mr. Scott? You work closely with him. Therefore, whether you admit it or not, you are somewhat like him. Thus, you are far from innocent. And you and the others have usurped rights that are mine." St. John's voice began to rise. Spittle ran from his mouth. "It is in motion. It cannot be stopped. Only the money can stop it. Arrest me now, Mr. Scott. I will trade the money for the flaming airplane."

He extended his hands toward Scott. The numbness in Scott's brain was gone, replaced by a flare of temper. St. John stood before him, a criminal who had related his tale of murder and extortion with pride and glee, like a naughty child. Looking into St. John's eyes, Scott saw the flickering dance of madness. Shifting, bright scenes rushed through his consciousness—the months of living on the edge of terror, the eruption of another expected yet unexpected attack, Norma's torn and burned face, Anne's frightened eyes. He stepped toward St. John.

"I do not think of myself as a brave man, yet I would match what small bravery I have with yours," he said slowly. "You think of yourself as strong, as cunning. You are neither. I think of you as a mad child. And as a coward. Hiding behind imported thugs, you attack my house, threaten my family—"

St. John looked squarely at Scott. "I did not threaten your family," he said.

"Then who attacked my house? Who threatened my wife?"

"It was not us. Perhaps, Mr. Scott, you have other enemies."

"I don't believe you. I saw you in Olen."

"I was in Olen, yes."

"It wasn't you who tried to frighten my wife?"

"Mario and I were much too busy with other matters there to waste time with minor threats."

"Then you did bomb the plant?"

St. John's eyes twinkled. He brought his hand up to his chin and stood pensively, watching Scott. "It was marvelous fun," he said. "Mischievous mischief."

"Did you kill Morris?"

"Morris's death was accidental."

"Do you really believe that?"

"Yes."

"I think you believe what it is convenient to believe."

"Mr. Scott, it is time to end our meeting. I leave you with this thought. I have my mother's mad, warm blood and I have my father's cold, thinking blood. You know him well—"

"I do not know him well."

"But you know him well enough so that you might agree that he is a man difficult to destroy. Destroying him is a formidable challenge. It is an operation similar to the military. Perhaps it is true that only another Breedlove could kill him. He is now old and vulnerable. His hour is past. It is now my hour."

From his corner Larry chuckled.

32

HE SUSPECTED HE WAS BEING WATCHED, BUT HE DID NOT care. His body fluids were running too high for him to care about anything except reaching a phone and contacting Breedlove. Hurrying in the rain, he saw two men in a station wagon parked in a red zone. One of the men got out and walked past Scott without looking at him. Scott squeezed into a phone booth at a gas station and dialed Breedlove's private number. His hand was cold and unsteady. Scoggins answered on the second ring.

"I'm sorry, Mr. Scott, but Mr. Breedlove has left orders not to be disturbed."

"I don't care about his orders. I'm going to be over there in one hour. You tell him that. Tell him that it is vitally important."

"I'm afraid I must not—"

"Scoggins, you have a daughter, do you not?"

"Yes, sir."

"If I tell you that this is important to her—perhaps even to her safety—then will you do as I say?"

"I—I don't understand, Mr. Scott."

"Don't understand. Just believe me. Don't talk. Listen. Wake Breedlove up. Get him ready for me. Tell him I'll be there. I've been put off too long. You tell him that. I don't want any locked gates, I don't want any guards stopping me. Now do I make myself clear enough?"

He clamped the receiver down. He was breathing hard. He felt his heart squeeze. A shiver went up his back, forcing him to hunch his shoulders. He walked in the rain to the car, his teeth chattering, his legs numb. He'd left the apartment in stunned astonishment, not sure of what he'd do. Now, blood rushing in his brain, awakening, he wondered if he'd overreacted, dashing through inclement weather at midnight to Breedlove's doorstep. He'd been intimidated and frightened; he'd reacted impetuously, not with calm appraisal. But this was not a time for appraisal. It was a time for action. How long was he to stand by, trusting Breedlove while he risked more attacks on his family, his home, himself, and the company? He drove the Pasadena Freeway resolutely through a lessened rain, his jaw set, his mind alive. The windshield wipers dashed before him. Now the rain was heavier and thin streaks of lightning darted across the sky to the west. California Street off the freeway was flooded, and he was forced to use side streets in a zigzag pattern until he reached Arbor Road. Rain thumped on the hood and glistened in the streetlights. He stopped before the brick wall surrounding the Breedlove house. Lightning flashed, bathing the area in a blue, sizzling glow. Scott pressed the buzzer and the gate opened. A porch light came on. Scoggins stood by the door, an umbrella crooked over his arm.

"Mr. Breedlove is in the library, Mr. Scott," he said when they were inside. "He will see you immediately."

"Thank you." Scott turned. Scoggins's face was austere, incurious. "How did he react, getting roused out of bed?"

"He wasn't asleep, sir."

"Are you wondering what's happening here?"

"I am sure I will be told if it concerns me, Mr. Scott."

Scott paused before the library door. Thunder rolled overhead and the wind and rain lashed the house with sharp whipping sounds. Inside, before a blazing fire, Breedlove sat in his customary chair, his thin hands folded, his fingers intermeshed. His back was to Scott, and he did not stir. A tray with cigarettes and brandy was by his side. Breedlove's mounted eagle stared down from the mantel, its eyes blazing in the dancing firelight. Also catching the firelight were the deep-set, piercing eyes of a man in a painting that stood on an easel to Breedlove's right. Scott approached carefully. The drapes were open. Rain thumped on the windows. Breedlove stirred.

"Scottie, goddamn it, don't tiptoe up behind me like you're some servant or something," he said.

His voice was strong. He looked up, opened his eyes, and turned his head. Scott could not hide a small gasp. He hadn't seen Breedlove since the dinner party. The old man seemed years older, a slumped relic with a sunken mouth, a pinched nose that oozed liquid, and blotched red skin stretching over his skull like dry tissue paper. He rubbed his cheek with a withered hand and peered at Scott with dark eyes embedded in sockets over black pouches. A tough layer of whiskers covered his chin.

"I think I know why you're here," he said, his voice labored. "Shall we spar around or come to the point?"

"I believe I'd like a drink."

"Take one. Take two. You need them. I know I look like a spook, but you look almost as bad." Breedlove's mouth twitched. Spittle ran down his chin. He wiped it off on the back of his hand. "I warn you that I don't feel my best tonight. I let you come over despite the fact you've disobeyed me to go adventuring again, but I'm not going to be the perfect host. Pour me a small one. And hand me those cigarettes."

Scott poured some brandy into a glass and gave it to Breedlove, who drank it in one gulp. He coughed. The glass slipped from his hand and shattered on the tile by the fireplace. Immediately Scoggins appeared. Breedlove snarled.

"Get out, damn it, get out!" he shouted. "When I want you, I'll call you." Scoggins left, closing the door. Renewed coughing struck Breedlove, bringing moisture to his eyes. He said slowly, "Son of a bitch lurks by the door waiting to carry the body out. Scottie, sit down. Talk."

"I've just seen Lawrence again."

Breedlove seemed not to hear. "You see there I got my Rembrandt back. I've had agents chasing all over Europe for it and finally that little fart Andre LaMont found it in Italy. It cost me an arm and a leg to buy it back, but I wanted it. It might be that my money to get it back was used as seed money by those pricks that are attacking us." Breedlove's thin jaw jutted out. His dry lips crinkled into a slight smile. "When it rains like this, you're grateful for a fire and a roof over your head. I had times when there was no roof and you'd go sleep with the cows to keep warm. Hell, I learned to *read,* for hell's sake, from old newspapers we used on that farm for wallpaper. But you're not interested."

"I am interested, but—"

"I like rain. I like thunder. I still can raise hell."

"You can indeed, Lewis."

Breedlove adjusted his shawl. He gazed into the fire. "I know all about it, Scottie. I know about Lawrence, about this asshole called St. John, what they've done, how they've done it, what they plan to do now."

"They want three million dollars."

"You're their messenger, are you?"

"They told me tonight."

"And I told you to stay out of it."

"But you knew I wouldn't. I couldn't."

Breedlove spoke softly, between gasps for breath. "Scottie, you're the philosopher, the thinker around the office. Those who are out to get you call you the dreamer. They say you're an idealist, a God-believer."

"A God-believer, yes, but an idealist—well, I don't know any more."

"If I believed in God, I'd ask only one thing. Another ten years. Then I'd see it. The green revolution, fully. Artificial foods." He looked up. His eyes twinkled. "You see, I dream, too. I saw it a long, long time ago."

"I believe that you did."

"It's not all hollow, I'll tell you that. Talk to me with your idealism about families and sons. I'll talk to you about this company. Families grow up, go away, disappoint and embarrass you. The company stays. Don't lecture to me about the way Lawrence turned out."

"I'm not lecturing you."

"But you want to lecture. He had his chance and he messed it up. Enough said."

"What will we do about the three million?"

Breedlove spat on the carpet. "Fuck them," he said.

"If we don't deliver, they say the bombings will continue. The airplane—"

"Well, we're not going to deliver." Breedlove faced Scott. He sucked his teeth. His eyes were cold. "You've snooped around, against my orders, and you've found out a few things. I don't like people knowing about me. My life is my business. I don't apologize for it. I've had good reasons for everything I've done. Not everything worked out perfectly, but enough did. I still am in control. I will handle this matter. It is already in the works."

"Through the security department?"

"I have other ways. Better ways." Again Breedlove grew agitated. He struggled to his feet, limped to the window, and stood with his back to Scott, looking at the storm. Then he whirled. Thunder rolled behind him. A bolt of lightning cast a blue glow over his face. He clenched his hands and repeatedly bashed his knuckles together as he spoke. "Lawrence had every opportunity. A chance to make something of himself. I wanted him to make it. I tried. It didn't work. He turned out bad. Should I cry over it? No. I do not cry. Should I blame myself? No. And I don't have to explain myself to you. I don't have to explain myself to anyone. You stand there and judge me, throw stones at me."

"I am not judging you."

"Don't. Don't question my attitudes or methods. I am me. I don't want your sanctimonious, holier-than-me judgments. Go preach to somebody else. Go look at yourself."

"What does that mean?"

"It means that, underneath, you're a pretty self-centered fellow. You may not see it, but I do."

"Whatever I am, I am not a drone, a yes-man. If you want a drone, go pick one. You have many from which to choose." Black spots swam before Scott's eyes. He stepped forward. "We're under *attack*, Lewis! Have you buried yourself so deeply that you do not understand that? It is something pernicious and sinister that endangers all of us. You say it is personal. I maintain that it no longer is. I don't care about your personal life, how you treated your son or your wife."

Breedlove's teeth snapped. "What d'you mean, my wife?"

"Larry told me you kept her imprisoned in her final months, refusing to allow her to see a lawyer about her stock."

"Oh, that," Breedlove said quietly.

"Then it's true."

"She would have given the stock away, signed it over to a church or a charity, just to spite me. If you had been in my shoes, would you have allowed it? No. I don't think so."

Scott spoke between clenched teeth. "I'll tell you this, Lewis. I will not board that airplane. Not until this matter is cleared up."

"I think you will. You'll fly with Lancaster, Powell, and me to the annual meeting in Olen on Thursday."

"No. Lewis, this man as much as *told* me there'll be a bomb."

"Lancaster'd fly. At the snap of my fingers. Powell would. Without hesitation." Breedlove's eyes softened. He gazed at Scott. His eyes seemed almost benign. He advanced slowly, pointing a thin, trembling finger. "We elect a president in Olen. This time, I'm really stepping down."

"The president well may be Philip Mendenthal."

Breedlove scoffed. "No. Mendenthal is defeated."

"How can you be sure?"

"Believe me. I am sure." Breedlove slumped into his chair and looked at the Rembrandt. The storm had abated to an almost gentle sound of heavy rain. The fire sputtered. Breedlove winced, sniffed the air, and when he spoke his voice was low and strained. "After we get to Olen, we'll talk again. Right now, I'll say only this. It still can be yours. I know you want it. You want it much more than you'll admit. You say the right things at that meeting in Olen, it's yours. I told you that nine months ago. Now I'm reconfirming."

"You're sure I want it."

"I'm more than sure. I'm positive. You're frightened right now, that's all. You'll come to your senses. I like the way you've been handling things. I used to think it was too big for you, but I no longer do." Breedlove leaned forward. His eyes narrowed and held Scott's in a glistening, almost conspiratorial gaze. "Of course, you'll have to send some of them down. Can you send them down?"

"Who?"

"Powell. Lancaster. Hawley."

"Why Hawley?"

"Because he's old, scared, and doesn't have balls." Breedlove paused. He grinned. "He tried to take a poke at me once, at Theresa's funeral. If he'd tried to do that a couple times later, maybe I'd have more respect for him."

"Then why do you keep him?"

"Because he knows a lot about things I don't want known. But when I go, his knowledge will have no value. And he realizes that."

Scott looked at the eagle, the painting, and back at Breedlove. It seemed extraordinary to him that any energy at all could emanate from the shriveled frame slumped before him like a fire-eyed dwarf. He felt repulsed, yet drawn. There was a spirit, a spark in the old man, something unique and innate to his being, a force that defied weariness, pain, and perhaps even death. Scott felt disarmed. He'd fled through the dark rain to the old man full of reserve, swearing to confront him with dangerous issues; now, like the lessening storm outside, he'd been calmed, lulled by talk of business and promotion. He saw Breedlove in a different light, a harsh light of truth—as a sinister, driven manipulator of people and events, a man totally devoid of feeling, his sole motivation Breedlove progress, Breedlove control, Breedlove domination—but he also saw that the old man could be excused. Breedlove was different from others. He'd never known human relationships. He'd sublimated everything to business drive. He was the last of something. The last American entrepreneur. The entity he'd formed now lived, Breedlove's creation, abounding with energy, blood flow, and brain waves. It was Breedlove; in a very real sense, it would always be Breedlove. And he was like his timeless eagle—dominant and protective, proud and preying, unconquered and immortal. Scott detested him. He also admired him. He thought, *We're totally different, despite our coming together, and that's why we attract each other.* He stood staring, his fists clenched. No longer could he hear the storm.

"Go home, Scottie," Breedlove said quietly. "Be on that airplane."

He closed his eyes. Scoggins waited by the outside door for Scott, holding an umbrella.

33

THE MAN WHO ACCEPTED THE ASSIGNMENT TO KILL VICTORIA Scoggins lived under the name of Frank Steener with his wife in a comfortable house in the suburbs of Miami. Once he'd been an enforcer in Hudson's organization; now, at sixty, he was semiretired. He didn't like taking assignments, especially hitting a woman, something he'd never done, but, what the hell, he did owe Hudson and he knew dues were always collected. He studied the information he'd received from Los

Angeles for two weeks and then made reservations on the SST to Paris. His wife drove him to the airport. He had a rose in his lapel.

"How long will you be gone?" she asked.

"No more than a week."

"You could look up Clara." Clara was her sister, married to a computer technician employed by an American company in Paris. "Shall I call and tell her?"

"No. I don't want anyone to know I'm there."

"All right."

She was a good wife. She never questioned him. She didn't know the rose had been his trademark when he'd been on a hit in his active days.

Life in an itinerant band had never really appealed to Victoria Scoggins, primarily because she always had difficulty in sleeping during the day. Once, before she'd given up her ambitions to become an artist (the instructor in Venice had blatantly declared her a no-talent in front of the class), travel had appealed to her. But now, it seemed, nothing appealed to her. In addition, she was frightened. She had allied herself with St. John for two reasons. One was her hatred of Lewis Breedlove, a man she'd never met but whose autocratic inhumanity had been vividly described to her in long letters from her father. The other reason was her desire to buy the cottage near Dover that had been an almost obsessive need in her for more years 'than she liked to remember. Yet, until she'd met St. John, she never seemed to get any closer to the cottage. She'd met him in Paris last year; he'd come every night to hear her sing. He said he was a retired U.S. Army major. At first his scheme, presented to her after a torrid sexual session that had left her drained and satisfied for the first time in many years, had seemed absurd to her, almost laughable. She was to receive a stolen Rembrandt masterwork and sell it through her art connections in Europe, return the proceeds to him minus a small commission, and then wait for what he described as her share of a big payoff. Something in his manner, his confidence, his way of speaking, made her believe him. Perhaps it had been his eyes, so clear and dark and deeply penetrating. Now she hadn't heard from him for several months, and she lived in almost constant fear. She

really didn't know why. But strangers   terrified her and she
found herself shrinking more and more into herself. She had
always been a loner; she had always been self-reliant. But
now she found herself deeply within a shell, without feeling,
without hope, and miserably depressed. Only the cottage and
its surrounding green, moist fields, she knew, would bring her
out of it. She had given up even hearing from St. John again.
She took large doses of sleeping pills only to awaken in the
bright day with a sharp headache and stinging, bloodshot
eyes. Time and time again she contemplated suicide and only
the vision of the cottage sustained her. Yesterday, from her
hotel room in Paris, she had written a letter to her father,
explaining in detail her role in the plot, and how it had begun.
It was a form of confessional. A confessional before death?
She did not know.

For three nights at the café a man with a rose in his lapel
had been at a front table at both the dinner and midnight
shows. He had sent her a note, complimenting her on her
voice, saying he was a talent agent from New York. He had
asked to see her. She did not know. But why be afraid? It
might be a break for her. She knew her voice was going, but
lessons perhaps could help, and certainly she no longer
wanted this kind of unsettled life. She decided she'd talk to
the man. He had a kind face.

Horst wasn't a student of poetry, but he did enjoy reading
it on occasion, and was fond of some lines in Eliot's "Prufrock."

> There will be time, there will be time
> To prepare a face to meet the faces that you meet;
> There will be time to murder and create.

He had just murdered, an act that often aroused him
sexually, and the lines buzzed in his head. BII security had
assigned a man to check luggage before all flights of the
company's airplane, and that man had become Horst's target
several weeks ago. He knew his habits, where he lived, even
his telephone number; he regarded the man as careful and
meticulous, one of the better operatives in a largely ineffec-
tive department. American companies seemed careless about

security, at least relative to European companies, but that did not mean Horst allowed himself to be careless or complacent. Something else bothered him, and Mario, too; there was another force operative here, one antagonistic to theirs, not a company force, but outside. He feared that force. Yet he could not allow his fears to hamper his progress. This morning he'd easily followed his target to the airport and had killed him in the garage with a throat wire, stuffing the body into the trunk of the man's car. Luck was an element in all of Horst's missions. There was always some tiny bit left to the gods. He liked that. It increased the chance-taking, which increased the excitement. This time the luck was that the dead man was about the same size and age as Horst. He even looked somewhat like Horst. In a compartment of the men's room at the airport lobby, Horst took out a mirror and his makeup kit. He had a color photograph of the man he had killed. He had the man's pistol and ID cards. He smiled as he became the dead man.

There will be time to murder and create.

Mario was a professional, trained initially under a Russian colonel in Cuba, and he feared only other professionals. More than instinct told him something was not right about this series of jobs in America. The black man, Morris, had been killed in a highly skilled manner, professionally. He agreed with Horst; an outside force was at work. Yet, despite the warnings, Mario continued on the job. After all, he, too, was a professional. He'd made a commitment, the money was good and promised to get better, and it was a challenge. It would be his last job. Soon he'd return to his family in Salerno, where he had a fifty-acre vineyard that he loved— the warm sun, the plump purple grapes ripe for picking, and the ceremonial wine-making dances.

This job—which, under St. John's hesitant direction, already had taken too long—was now ending. There was one more task, to infiltrate and place a bomb aboard the airplane. He had been watching the hangar since dawn, and now the doors had been opened by a black guard and the plane was being pulled out by a tractor. There were several armed guards around, including two rifle marksmen. Long ago Mario had learned that success was obtained by using the simplest and sometimes the most obvious ploys; trained security men looked for the unusual, the unexpected, and often overlooked the obvious. He was dressed as a skycap. Before him was a handcart with some cardboard boxes marked, "Confidential Files—BII Headquarters." They had been shipped by a messenger service for placement aboard the plane, and he had obtained temporary custody of them through a simple bribe. It was, perhaps, a stroke of luck; yes, as Horst sometimes said, luck often was a factor in their success or failure. Mario had been at the airport since midnight, arriving not quite sure of his course of action, then seizing his opportunity upon discovery of the files.

Among the files was a smaller box that contained a four-pound firebomb. The bomb was homemade, and simple. It would explode by chemical reaction. It consisted of a sealed iron tube filled with potassium chlorate and sugar. Mario had carefully inserted an inverted vial of sulfuric acid, stopped with a cork, at a hole in one end of the tube. The acid already had begun to eat through the cork. When it ate all the way through, in about two hours, it would combine with the potassium chlorate–sugar mixture and erupt in a sheet of hot flame.

St. John had ordered the action taken. Mario disliked the man intensely, but he had accepted the job—his last, he again reminded himself—and he would finish it. He stared at the plane. He really didn't like Horst, either, or any other German superman he'd met, but he respected Horst's efficiency. Horst still bragged about the helicopter accident he'd caused in New York, calling it a masterpiece of timing. He was extremely clever at impersonation and an expert at radio and wiretapping. He spoke four languages without accent, and he was capable of standing cat-still against a wall, barely breathing, for hours at a time—a feat he practiced almost daily. He scoffed at this company's security, an opinion Mario shared but would not discuss. But what of the unknown professional antagonists? They seldom discussed it. But they both knew a force was there.

He waited. The timing must be precise. Finally he left, pushing the cart toward the airplane, knowing that Horst would be there. He was thinking of his vineyard.

*   *   *

Scoggins rode beside the hired driver in the Cadillac to the airport. It was a fine, warm morning, and the traffic was light. Breedlove crouched in the back seat, studying legal-size papers. Scoggins had become a nurse as well as a butler, responsible for carrying Breedlove's drugs, both pills and injectable morphine. The drugs were in his satchel, along with plastic hypodermic needles. Also in the satchel was a letter from his daughter, her last letter, which he'd read several times. He read it without emotion. It confessed that she had had a part in the theft of the Rembrandt. Yesterday evening Scoggins had received a telegram from the Paris police. It said his daughter was dead. That was all. Dead. An apparent suicide. Even then Scoggins felt no emotion. He was aware of Breedlove's presence in the back seat. He did not believe his daughter had committed suicide. The morning sun warmed his neck.

Slightly ahead of them on the freeway, Lancaster drove with the top down. He was whistling.

Larry felt a flash of fear as he approached the door of the apartment house. He'd been dragging from joints all night at a beach party, but now he felt the need for heavier stuff and he knew where it was. He paused. He considered. The stuff inside, taped under the sink, won out. He entered the apartment. The shades were drawn.

"Clinton?" he said.

No answer. Lawrence walked slowly toward the kitchen. Sweat ran down his back. He paused by the bathroom. Slowly he pushed aside the dirty curtain that served as a door. He peered inside. A numbing chill ran through his body. His legs sagged. He fell to his knees, bile welling up in his throat.

St. John sat naked on the toilet, his head back, his eyes open, a small red hole in his forehead. Three of his fingernails had been torn off. Dried blood coated his hands.

Get up. Run.

But he didn't. He touched the mutilated hands. He felt deep sadness, total emptiness. He realized he'd loved St. John, his brother who'd given him confidence. He coughed out vomit. Anger and fear and indecision beat in his brain.

He rose and backed away. His heart thumped heavily. Calm yourself. Get it together. Find your wits. He knew what he must do. Find a telephone. Call the company. It was in motion, Mario and Horst with the bomb at the airport, a final reprisal by Clinton because the money hadn't arrived. Now someone was striking back with the suddenness and fury of their own strikes. He was probably next on the list. There had been times in the past when he had wanted to die, but now he knew only that he wanted to live. He glanced again at St. John's body and then went outside into the hall.

He stopped. Two men in suits stood at the end of the hall. He backed up. The men advanced. He began to whimper. *Now I lay me. Now I lay me.* It was a prayer Mrs. Luce had taught him when he'd been a child.

Four down, McKeen thought, *two to go.*

He'd struck quickly, yet he still felt anxiety. His face was hot and his jaw hurt. They weren't out of the woods yet. The last two were the toughest. He'd concentrate on the bird, which was flying today. He had a sick premonition that he just might fuck this one up. He seldom had premonitions.

Two to go. Maybe even three, if they wanted to do anything about that little matter of ripping off from the main scheme. But at least two. A big, big two.

Susan Powell waited for the company car that was to take her to the airport. She and the other Troika wives, plus lower-echelon headquarters management, were booked on a special charter flight taking them to the annual meeting. Susan felt calm, confident, and complacent. George had left by taxi, looking confident also. It had all pointed to this, the years of struggle, the molding of him, and she felt he was ready. He would win. He must win. She had risked much to help him win. She felt she was the best qualified by far of the Troika wives. It was a plus for George. The other wives were unqualified. Anne was a weak link in Mark Scott's chances, perhaps his only weak link. Dorothy was too artificial, stupid, and immature to be much help to Henry Lancaster. It would be George. It must be. She would not let herself think any other way.

The telephone rang. "You owe us more, sister," a man said.

"No," Susan said. "You've been paid."

"Not for all what we done, we ain't been paid. Not enough."

"I didn't ask you to do all you did. You exceeded my instructions. You will not get one penny more."

"Hey, society lady, don't bet on that, oke? Two thou more, for now, cash on the barrelhead."

Susan hung up. She wanted a drink. But it would not do to drink now. She raised her head and gazed at her handsome face in the mirror.

Scott went. He was the last to board the 727. Breedlove, reading legal briefs, crouched in a forward seat. Scoggins sat across from him. Lancaster was in the rear, reading a newspaper. Powell sat in the lounge, his open briefcase on an adjoining seat. Scott slumped down across from Lancaster and immediately buckled his seat belt. The action seemed to amuse Lancaster, who sat relaxed and unconcerned, his lips curved in a slight smile.

Scott stiffened. It was calm aboard the plane, too calm. He detected a tension under the quietness. Why had he come? He did not know why. He'd blindly followed Breedlove's orders, not discussing it with Anne, leaving the house before she and the kids had awakened. He'd gone to the kids' rooms, one at a time, adjusting their covers, kissing their cheeks as they slept. He'd lingered in Mike's room, feeling a love for his sleeping son that he could not express. Why? Why? Because love impeded his progress? He'd left, hurrying, trying to drive the questions from his mind. Now, waiting for takeoff, struggling to keep his hands from trembling, thoughts crowded his mind. Larry. St. John. Breedlove and his Troika. Lancaster saying, "He may ask you to take the risk." Powell quoting the poet Wallace Stevens. And old chaos of the sun. The emperor of ice-cream. The fading emperor of BII—perhaps himself, like Stevens's emperor, a ruler over what was upon analysis a realm inconsequential and artificial relative to family and love and certainly life itself—had captured them all, forcing them aboard his kingly aircraft, asking them to trust, to risk, and to obey.

"Scottie, you look a little peaked," Lancaster said.

"I'll make you a deal," Scott said.

"What's the deal, sport?"

"You get off this crate and I'll get off."

Lancaster grinned. "You scared? Scottie scared? An army of guards and Scottie's scared?"

"You're scared, too. You know it."

Lancaster didn't respond. He turned away. Scott searched forward to catch a glimpse of Breedlove. He could see only Scoggins's shiny bald head.

It must be safe. Breedlove would not have come if he were not certain it was safe. Lancaster and Powell somehow also knew it was safe. It was a test of him, Mark Scott, or a joke on him. The others were in conspiracy, leaving him out. He was with enemies. They had plotted behind his back. They were serene and complacently secure because they knew something he did not know. He had been tricked, duped. He told himself to stop it. He told himself he was being neurotic. His fists opened and closed and perspiration was heavy on his palms.

Harold Long emerged from the cockpit, looked around, glanced at Scott, and returned to the controls.

Then the 727 was moving.

Scott thought, *Get up. Stop it.*

But he did nothing. He sat stiffly as the plane rushed down the runway. His throat was dry and there was a hollow ringing in his ears.

They were airborne, streaking through clouds that hit the wings with sharp cracking sounds.

Walking down the corridor toward the exit, Mario felt certain elation but was not yet congratulating himself. He would not do that until he was free of the airport and having a glass of wine at a quiet bar in the marina that he liked because it reminded him of the bars at home. Under the eyes of the guards and despite the presence of the unseen-yet-there professional force, they had done their job. The firebomb was in the luggage hold of the airplane, placed so that much of its force would concentrate upon the pilot's cabin. So now Mario would go home. He yearned for home. The last job was over.

"Redcap!" shouted a man close behind him.

He did not turn. He walked only slightly faster.

"You!" the voice said, nearer.

Mario reached into his coat pocket. He was unarmed but he carried a pill, a death pill, for use in situations such as this. His instincts told him the end was near, but he was calm. Only twice before in his career had he reached for the death pill, and both had proved to be false alarms. But this, he knew, was no false alarm. Three men blocked the path ahead. They were reaching for pistols. Footfalls sounded behind him. He began to run, pushing aside startled passengers hurrying to catch their flights. He had the pill in his hand. Still he was calm, very calm. As he raised his hand to his mouth, strong arms grasped his neck from behind, stopping him, forcing him back. The men in front of him bounded up, driving him down with the force of their pistol butts and barrels.

He heard a voice. "For Christ's sake, you dumb bastards, don't kill him for Christ's sake!" Looking up, his vision blurred by blood, Mario saw a big red-faced man in a suit, and he knew he was gazing into the eyes of the other professional.

"Oh, good Christ, we *did* fuck it up!" McKeen screamed to himself. "They got heat aboard that flight." It was a half hour after takeoff and McKeen had been sure the bird had left clean, despite what he termed deliberate attempts by BII security to fuck things up. He couldn't do anything about BII security, but he figured now that if he'd been able to wipe them out, send them home to play with their telephones and books and reports, he could have had this caper cleared up a month ago. But maybe thinking like that was a rationalization for his own fuck-up; and, shit, man, shit, he *had* fucked up. Unless he unfucked it quick, Hudson would be on his ass like a wolf on raw meat. He was furious with himself and as jumpy as he'd been before his wife delivered their first baby. His premonition had been right. He'd set up a network at the airport, including two men at the plane, yet the wop had outfoxed him, using the oldest trick in the book, a redcap's uniform. And the kraut had moved in like he owned the place, wasting a BII security man and, like magic, taking the man's place. Now the plane was up there, a lethal dose somewhere aboard, despite the fact that they'd been, for Christ's sake, almost *told* it would happen. McKeen felt total despair. Not even the FBI or the CIA could have fucked it worse. He'd been given the go signal, and an hour or two ago he'd considered this one in the bag—St. John down, the old man's pothead kid down, the Scoggins dame hit, long ago the chickening-out spade, Morris, eliminated. St. John had turned into a real pussycat under persuasion, cracking and confessing it all on tape before they'd put him out of his misery. It had moved like clockwork until now. Dumb. Dumb! He'd bagged the amateurs but had let the professionals play tricks under his nose. McKeen's lower jaw throbbed with pain, shooting up to his ears and pulsating on the back of his head. He shook aspirins from a tin into his hand, flipped them into his mouth, and chewed them like candy. He blamed only himself. Shit! His men had been watching all of them, including the two foreigners, for weeks, planning a coordinated strike. He'd been pointing to this for long months. Both the German and the wop had eluded their tails this morning, an unpardonable fuck-up, and apparently they had done their job. The tails were as good as dead. Or maybe they were dead, and that might explain it. Shit. It didn't matter now. The fuck-up had occurred; he'd been outfoxed and he was pissed, pissed to the gills. They had the wop in the van on the airport parking lot, itself a lucky hit. Tyler, McKeen's assistant, had recognized him. It had been as lucky as that. *Christ*, McKeen thought, *I'm getting old*. This was one tough wop, a professional's professional, and he sure as hell wasn't going to crack under routine questioning or any amount of persuasion. McKeen would have to find his vulnerability, and he thought he knew. Tyler agreed: "This is a tough wop and I don't think he'll crack." McKeen said, "He'll crack. He'll crack or we're all up shit creek. I'll make him crack if I have to crush his balls."

He was in the cab of the truck, trying to contact the airplane by shortwave radio, but the signal seemed jammed. Christ, that's all he needed. Jesus, it had been going smoothly until now, especially after the information on the wop and the kraut had come in from overseas. He'd loved the cat-and-mouse game he'd been playing with him, experts he respected; they moved like ghosts, striking swiftly and unexpectedly, eluding traps, almost taunting him with their skill and daring. Hudson seemed patient. Breedlove didn't pressure him. Breedlove's faith in Hudson must have been absolute. Maybe Breedlove lived in the past, remembering when Hudson had been more effective than now, when he had more clout and muscle.

He said to Tyler, "You keep working this fucking short-wave, try to reach them. I'm gonna give it about five minutes and then try to reach them through the tower. I don't want to put this out on the public airwaves, but I'll do it if I have to. Not that it'd do much good. I'm certain there's heat on that bird, but I don't know where the package is or when it goes off."

He went inside the van. Mario's face was a bloody mess; the men had been using knuckles on him. McKeen pushed them away. He squatted beside the bleeding wop.

"Your name is Mario," he said. "I know you."

The wop said nothing. He knew it was over.

"I respect you," McKeen said. "I've been playing tag with you for like nine months now and you won a lot of the rounds. But it's over now. Where on the plane was the bomb put? When does it go off?"

The wop lay bleeding. He didn't look so fucking tough now.

"Everybody who worked with you is dead," Mckeen said. "You took one fucking job too many. The kraut has managed to get away, for now, but we're on his ass and I promise you he won't get out of the country. Even if he does, he's had it. You guys took on a little too much this time. How much time do we have before the bomb goes off?"

The wop spoke. "There is no bomb."

"You will die whether you talk or not. You know that. But there are pleasant ways to die and there are ways that are not so pleasant."

"I know of no bomb."

"I have no more time. You have a family, a son and a daughter. Foolish a man in your profession should have a family. I know where they are. Unless you tell me what you know, they will be dead within a week."

For the first time, a flicker of emotion showed in the wop's face, and McKeen knew he had won. If they had enough time, he had won. The pain had left McKeen's jaw.

*   *   *

Scott wandered into the 727's salon and noticed that the red light on the shortwave set was lit. He didn't know how to operate the set—had never, in fact, seen it in operation—so he buzzed Harold Long on the intercom system. Long left the controls to Russ Chambers and hurried back to the salon.

"Sure, it's simple to operate," he said. "Tune in the frequency, like this, and put on the headphones." They looked at each other. Scott put on the headphones and Long switched the set to receive.

"Hello, BII 727?" a man's voice said clearly.

Scott swtiched to send. "Yes. This is BII 727."

Receiving: "Who do I have?"

Sending: "This is Mark Scott."

The voice was very calm, controlled. "Mr. Scott, my name is unimportant, but you must listen carefully. This is going to hit you, so brace yourself. I'm going to relay a message to you, and when I am finished I want only that you switch back to sending and acknowledge it. In the forward hold, the forward luggage hold, there is a small package. It is marked 'Rush' in blue crayon. It is a bomb, Mr. Scott, and it is timed to explode approximately twenty minutes from now. Acknowledge, please. Acknowledge."

"Mr. Scott?" said Long. "What is it?"

"Acknowledge please. Will you acknowledge?"

"Mr. Scott?" Long said.

He felt the blood return to his brain. He switched to sending and said, "Yes, I acknowledge." The headphones slipped from his hands as he removed them. Long seemed to sway in front of him. He could feel his body functions—heart and pulse and little waves rippling in his brain—exaggerated and almost painful. His mouth was dry. He thought, *Anne*. He became conscious of Lancaster by his side.

"Scott?" Lancaster said.

Scott said, "That message. There's a bomb in the hold. Set to go off in twenty minutes." He could not hear his words. He wondered if he had stammered.

"All right, calm down," Lancaster said.

"I'm calm."

Lancaster glanced at his watch. "Long, how soon can you get us down?"

"Not in twenty minutes, that's for sure."

"But you can try."

"I can try, yes, but we're over some terrain that's pretty hilly. If I go in wheels up, we'll break up."

They were speaking too quietly, too calmly. Scott said, "Where is Breedlove?"

"He's deep under, sedated," Lancaster said. He wasn't smiling. He wasn't joking. "Powell is asleep. We'll let him sleep."

Long said, "I'm not going to risk an emergency landing, not here."

"You will pretty well do what I order you to do," Lancaster said.

"No, sir. I will not. This airplane is mine. You will pretty well do as I order. Sir."

"And what is that?"

"The forward hold can be reached. Normally it can't in these birds, but this one is made with hatches. Someone's got to go down there and find that bomb."

"And then what?" Lancaster said. "Break a hole, toss it out?"

"No. I'll slow her to near stall speed and lower the gear. If we have time, the bomb can be dumped through the nose-wheel opening. It's a long shot, but if there's a bomb down there like Mr. Scott says, it's our only chance."

"How do we get down there?" Scott said. He was coming out of it. He felt his body functioning normally again. His brain was clear. His hands were steady.

"I'll show you," Long said.

"I'll go, Scott," Lancaster said. "You stay up."

"No. Two people searching for that package are better than one. Now I'm all right, Hank. I'm all right."

Now Lancaster grinned, the familiar grin. "Sure, parson. And if you have an extra prayer, use it up now. Let's go."

Lancaster went first, dropping into the luggage compartment through a circular trapdoor opened by Long in the midsection of the plane. Scott followed, holding a flashlight Long had furnished. They made their way toward the front, hurrying on their hands and knees, Lancaster leading, Scott shining the flashlight beam ahead. He found that he was not afraid. He felt he was totally in control of himself. He admitted that Lancaster's presence helped; somehow, with

Hank there, he knew it would be all right. They had fought, schemed against each other, and clashed repeatedly over corporate policy matters and were locked in a winner-take-all battle for the top chair at BII, but that seemed distant and unimportant now. The plane had slowed and Scott felt a rush of cold air as Long lowered the gear. There was a bulkhead between the cargo hold and the landing-gear compartment, but it had a hole large enough for a man to squeeze through, at least to extend his body outward so that an object could be dropped. Scott looked at his watch. How much time had passed? How much time did they have left? Had the caller been accurate when he'd said they had twenty minutes? Scott struggled against the stream of chilly air, his hair tossed, his clothing pinned to his body. He gasped for breath.

"All right," Lancaster said. "Here."

They had reached the forward luggage hold behind the nosewheel opening. Scott squatted beside a row of boxes. The boxes seemed identical. Lancaster fell to his knees. He seemed calm, in command. He began a methodic search, pushing the boxes aside. He removed his coat, almost slowly, and crouched on his hands and knees, looking. The airstream caught the coat and flung it against a bulwark, where it clung as if pinned. Scott was momentarily frozen to inactivity. He kept looking at his watch. A box. A small box marked "Rush." In blue crayon. How much time now? But why think of the time? What was going on inside Lancaster? Fear he would not betray? Lancaster's lips were set tightly and his jaw was square. His eyes were like a cat's, alert and preying. He'd been in the war. Perhaps he'd been in spots like this before. Don't think about Lancaster. Don't look at him. Search. Search. Don't panic. Be calm. There was time. A little time. If the man on the radio had been right, they might have ten minutes, maybe even more.

"Shit, there's nothing here," Lancaster said. He looked at Scott; they squatted before each other, their faces inches apart. "Now *think*, for Christ's sake. What exactly did the man say?"

"I told you. Exactly."

"The forward hold?"

"Yes."

"I think we've been had."

"Hank, you're giving *up*?"

Again the Lancaster grin. "Shake, sport. Two buddies. War buddies."

"We're wasting time."

"It could be inside this luggage."

They attacked the luggage, tearing into it with frenzied grunts and cries, scattering its contents. Lancaster, with an incredible display of strength, literally ripped open a locked suitcase. Nothing. Scott's hopes fell. Time? Six minutes? Five minutes? His eyes were heavy. His arms were tired. A sudden headache struck him, sending sharp waves of pain to his brain and reminding him that he lived, had the power to think and the energy to take action. It was under five minutes. He knew that now. The plane was steady. What thoughts were going through Harold Long's mind, watching his instruments, his hand steady on the yoke, perhaps radioing Mayday? Lancaster was tearing open the final suitcase, Breedlove's battered case that accompanied him on all his trips. Only shirts, some ties, papers. Scott whirled on his haunches, a trapped animal desperate to survive, a sense of hopelessness ringing in his mind, feeling the pain alive and throbbing. Four minutes? Three? Two? The airstream caught him. He tripped, sprawling backward. He fell sharply, awkwardly, striking the back of his head, and for seconds he was not aware of his surroundings, flapping helplessly on his back, thinking, *How much time is passing?* and trying to rise, gritting his teeth to summon strength to sit up. His hand had struck a hard object. That much he knew. Turning his head, he saw it, the package marked "Rush," hidden in a corner under a canvas flap.

"Hank," he said.

"I see it," Lancaster said.

Scott's brain was moving. He was calm. He calculated there were seconds, perhaps quite a few seconds. It would be all right. But, looking at the object, knowing what it was, he froze. What if it exploded with the slightest jar? No. That couldn't be. He had already jarred it. He reached out for it. When he touched it, he winced, as if it were very hot or very cold. He was conscious of Lancaster above him. His body was cold, especially his hands. He put both hands on the box and squeezed, slowly lifting it up. He rose in sections, first on his knees, then on his feet. His eyes met Lancaster's. Lancaster behind him, holding him, helping him forward, he moved against the airstream toward the nosewheel opening. His mind was blank. He was unaware of the wind, the creak of the plane, and the coldness. He saw land below. The package was light. They moved slowly, interlocked, not two men but one. It seemed to Scott as if he were not there, as if instead he were an interested observer standing above them, watching this strange pantomime dance with an amused smile. He leaned forward into the opening and flipped the parcel out. Had he thrown it or had it just fallen? Scott was aware of a hot blast of air, tossing him backward, and then everything seemed dark and whirling like a surrealistic dream where natural forces, gravity and equilibration and continuity, had surrendered their powers to chaos.

34

THE ADVANCE MAN FOR BII's ANNUAL MEETING WAS KEVIN Sheehan, the public-relations manager. He drew the assignment when Bill Hecky, the PR director, was hospitalized with bleeding ulcers. It was Sheehan's biggest job since he'd been with the company, such a massive logistical headache that he wondered if it would give him an ulcer. He reached town three weeks before the event, finding light snow on the ground. But the weather turned shortly after he arrived, and the snow became running streams that swelled the river. The townsfolk, notably Cotton Meeks, told Sheehan that the annual meeting would be the biggest event to hit Olen since the '32 tornado. The Meeks forecast proved to be somewhat correct, for what struck Olen the week before the meeting seemed quite tornado-like to Sheehan. The hotel filled, except for the rooms reserved by BII's top execs and the Mendenthal forces. The bars did turnaway business. Kiddie rides appeared. Noisy hawkers set up shop on the streets, offering balloons, popcorn, soft drinks, and portraits of Lewis Breedlove. A parade was organized by a Chamber of Commerce, itself organized to stage the parade. There were 4-H calf-judging contests and Boy Scout camp-outs. Rumors flew that bookies from Madison were taking wagers on the outcome of the proxy fight, with BII favored 3 to 2. The weather warmed even more, showers descended daily, and the nights were filled with stars. To Sheehan, a city boy, it was marvelous. The town smelled of spring, a ripe renewing essence from blossoming flowers and trees that seemed to turn from gnarled winter brown to green budding overnight.

"We had a problem," he told Hecky by phone the day before the meeting.

"What problem?" Hecky was still in the hospital, and his mood was sour.

"Space. The town hall here burned a decade ago and was never rebuilt. There's an auditorium in the plant, but it stinks like garbage. So I came up with an answer. I shipped in the biggest circus tent I could rent. We're holding the meeting in a tent. I got two thousand fold-up chairs. Box lunches."

"A circus tent for a circus," Hecky said dryly.

"Well, it was the best I could do."

"It's genius," Hecky said.

Sheehan beamed. "We got press from all over, even network. I set up a press tent. We bought half the booze in town. Something else. Our security people are all over this town. What's that all about?"

"Don't bother worrying about that."

"When do the big wheels arrive?"

"Tomorrow," Hecky said. "They left today for Madison on the Taj Mahal, will stay overnight there, and go to Olen by car tomorrow. The lesser wheels and the big wives are scheduled to get in there today."

"The hotel is something else. It's like a century old."

"Well, so is Breedlove."

"Rumor's all over we get a new pres and c.e.o. tomorrow."

"We may get a whole new board."

"Rumor's also all over we're going to close this old plant here. Do I say anything to the press about the rumors?"

"Sure," Hecky said. "Say no comment. In a nice way."

The Troika wives spent almost three hours together on the chartered jet without saying a word to each other. Anne sat quietly, pretending to read a magazine, wondering if she should have come. Mark had wanted her to stay home, using her pregnancy as an excuse, but she'd known as she had debated the matter with herself that she'd end up going, pushed by her curiosity if nothing else. In truth, she felt more than curiosity. She felt concern. Clem Hawley slipped into the seat beside her.

"What magazine?" he said. "*Modern Bride?*"

"Oh, funny, Clem. Very funny."

"Sorry. I was sitting back there wishing you'd stayed away from this grotesque sideshow."

"Well, I'm in it. And this is the main event, isn't it?"

Clem nodded. "The feature race," he said. "I hear the horns blowing, I see the horses in the gate." He smiled. "Why the steady frown? You'll get wrinkles."

"Oh, I don't know. Nervous, I guess."

"About Mark?"

"He left this morning without saying a word. In fact, he hasn't said but two words for a week."

"Well, we're all uptight."

"Because of Philip Mendenthal?"

"That's one reason."

She put her hand over his. "Clem, I have a terrible feeling. If I can't tell you, who can I tell? I'm worried. Worried sick. I wish I could stop it all. Stop this airplane, stop Mark's airplane. Am I being silly?"

"Yes," he said. "You're being silly."

Susan Powell, who'd said only a curt hello to Anne since boarding, looked up from her book and smiled thinly, a private smile. Dorothy Lancaster filed her fingernails. Her eyes looked vacant, almost dreamy.

Sheehan found himself pacing nervously outside the tent a half hour before the meeting was scheduled to start. The wives had arrived, but there was no word from Breedlove or his Troika. Cars filled the town. Business students had arrived from the university in Madison. The governor of Wisconsin was expected. A group of ample-bodied housewives from Milwaukee, concerned about high food prices, picketed morosely, displaying homemade signs. No one paid much attention to them. The shareholder turnout was greater than

Sheehan had anticipated, and he wished he'd arranged for outside chairs and a loudspeaker. The Troika wives sat near the front of the tent, where Sheehan had placed a podium, a head table for directors, and a microphone. He hoped the microphone would work. The day was already quite warm, and shareholders used their proxy statements as fans. Sheehan tried not to ogle Dorothy Lancaster. He'd heard she was a stunning beauty, but he hadn't expected to see a graceful sexpot animal with frontal structure and posterior symmetry who looked like a *Playboy* centerfold in clothes. Powell's wife moved with the self-important air of a queenly bitch. Anne Scott looked as if she'd drop a baby on the ground any minute. They sat in a row, the big wives as Hecky had called them, trying to avoid looking at each other. Around headquarters Sheehan had become known as Scott's boy, which had given him new status. And he did like Scott. He tolerated Powell, he detested Lancaster.

There was a stir. Philip Mendenthal strolled into the tent, his eyes piercing, flanked by inquisitive reporters. His slate of directors followed him. They went to the front.

"Old Mendenthal's as closemouthed as your old Breedlove," a UPI man told Sheehan. "By the way, where is your old Breedlove?"

Sheehan shrugged. "He'll be here."

But he wasn't sure. He wasn't sure of anything. He knew only that Breedlove and the Troika had left LAX on the corporate jet yesterday morning.

The shareholders grew quiet. Guards with holstered pistols patrolled the aisles. Prissy Norman Jinkens, whom Sheehan regarded with the affection he would bestow on a toad, wandered around silently, a large briefcase attached to his hand like a permanent growth.

It was five minutes to eleven.

Sheehan needed a drink. Instead, he went to the press section and took a seat. He bit his knuckles.

It was eleven.

"I think we have some no-shows," the UPI man said.

Sheehan heard the noise of a car outside. Heads turned. A murmur went through the group.

Lewis Breedlove, trailed by his Troika, strolled in, puffing a cigarette.

35

SEATED AT THE HEAD TABLE BEFORE THE BII STOCKHOLDERS, flanked by Lancaster and Powell, Scott thought, *Zero hour.* He was stumbling in a deep fog, a dreamlike wandering; he was in Breedlove's spell, Breedlove's web, and he could not break out. They had landed in Madison yesterday, had spent the evening without holding the strategy session they'd expected Breedlove to call, and this morning had been chauffeured to Olen in a Food Division limousine. Breedlove refused to discuss BII, Philip Mendenthal, or the incident on the airplane. It was as if he did not know of it, or, knowing, had chosen imperiously to ignore it. The explosion had left some slight burn scars on the bottom of the 727, but had done no serious damage. Scott's hands were singed and his back still hurt from the jolt, more of an instinctive reason by him and Lancaster than from the force of the explosion. But he was all right—physically if not mentally. After Scott and Lancaster had returned from the luggage compartment, the flight resumed, Lancaster had sipped a martini and taken a nap. Scott had sat speechless, numb, not even speaking to a visibly shaken Harold Long until the plane had landed. He was still numb.

He looked at Anne, seated between Dorothy Lancaster and Susan Powell in the fourth row, and she smiled. He glanced at Breedlove, who'd spurned the head table to seat himself inconspicuously at the far end of the second row, and again he felt the force of the man. Breedlove, reading legal documents, seemed almost uninterested in the proceedings. His appearance had improved remarkably since Scott's confrontation with him at the Pasadena home. His eyes were bright and there was color in his cheeks. Mendenthal stared steadily at him, but Breedlove did not look up. Behind him sat Scoggins, stiffly, like a guard.

Powell called the meeting to order. He hadn't finished three sentences before Ellis Culvert, a New Yorker who owned shares in many companies and attended stockholder meetings to crusade for shareowners' rights, was on his feet, demanding recognition.

"Mr. Chairman," Culvert said loudly. "A point of order."

Powell recognized him, and Culvert began to talk. "I most certainly excuse you for being late to our meeting, considering the difficulties of reaching this place. I found my way, but only after much frustration and agony. After the flight to Madison, I found a bus to Lincoln, and from there, being extremely fortunate, I managed to catch a wagon to Olen." Boos rose from the background. Culvert ignored them. He waved his proxy statement at Powell. "Your excuse for hiding this meeting away is of course that BII has a plant here, but that is merely a shroud, for in reality you wish to discourage stockholder attendance."

"It seems to me, Mr. Culvert, that attendance today is pretty good," Powell said.

"It is remarkable, considering your hideaway," came the retort. "If you had held the meeting in New York or Los Angeles, however, your attendance would have doubled. In truth, you do not want a high attendance, for you do not want high exposure."

Powell tried to respond, but Culvert cut him off.

"I hold proxies for several thousand shares of BII, many of which have been sent to me by independent shareholders sympathetic to my cause. How I will vote these shares will be decided only after I hear statements from both sides in this matter. Mr. Chairman, I am *concerned* about this company, a concern that has deepened with my reading of material Mr. Mendenthal has published to enlighten the public." Culvert stepped out into the aisle and waved tear sheets of Mendenthal's newspaper advertisements. "We read here of pumped-up, perhaps false and misleading earnings reports. We read of investigations into overseas payoffs and political contributions. We read about the perhaps indiscriminate use of the corporate aircraft. What else is there, we think, in this pattern of questionable operations that may well border on corruption? Who gives this company such free rein? I am not saying to you, Mr. Chairman, that because of Mr. Mendenthal's campaign I will vote my shares for his candidates. What I am saying is that we, as shareholders, as the owners of this company and the real employers of its management, have the right to know the truth."

Powell said weakly, "There will be a question-and-answer period later in the meeting."

"Before the election of directors, I would hope."

"Yes."

"Very well, sir," Culvert said. "I assure you that I will be asking questions. And I warn you that I will not accept evasive answers."

Reporters at the press table scribbled furiously. Culvert sat down amid a ripple of applause. Breedlove hadn't moved; he sat as if he had not heard. Again Scott looked at Anne, and then at Breedlove. He felt that the spell was lessening. The shareholders waved before him like a massive, accusatory jury. Culvert was right. Mendenthal, also, as Clem Hawley said, was very probably right. They had lived high at BII. The perks, the salaries, the expense accounts, the bonuses. BII was vulnerable, under attack, and its defenses were weak. Was he, Mark Scott, guiltless? He had tried repeatedly to warn directors about these matters in board meetings, without success, but that did not excuse him. He had used and even enjoyed the excesses. He had put his family second, changed his outlook and personality, to join in a race for the top, lured by Breedlove, knowing about but really doing nothing to stop practices he considered unethical and even dishonest. His rationalization was that the others do it, so you must do it to remain competitive. Mike's phrase, excusing his use of marijuana, rang in Scott's ears: "They all do it." He felt rising anger, and he also felt shame. He wanted Anne, he wanted the kids, he wanted to get away. He could do it. He could escape. Yet he did not know. The web of Breedlove had weakened, but it still held him. How many times had he debated with himself about this in the past few months? How many times had he made up his mind to break away, to speak out and break away, only to end up again in Breedlove's spell, Breedlove's lure? It came to him, looking down at Mendenthal and Culvert, that BII very possibly could lose this proxy fight, that they could all be swept from their seats by the end of the day. Mendenthal had influence with the institutional investors who controlled vast blocks of BII stock, and also with the "street name" stock kept by brokerage firms. This much Scott knew. It was close. It was so close that it could well be decided right here, by the vote of shareholders in attendance, although it might take several days to get a final count of the ballots.

"Ho, ho, look here," Lancaster whispered in Scott's ear.

A murmur arose from the group. Breedlove had stood up and was walking slowly toward the podium, the slumped, shuffling walk of a man who bore pain in his legs and back. He paused to snuff out a cigarette under his heel. Powell made way for him at the microphone. Breedlove stood before the shareholders, his drawn face searching out Mendenthal, and waited for absolute silence. When he had his silence, so complete that the rustling of the trees in the slight wind outside could be heard, he said, "Mr. Mendenthal, I suggest you and I have a meeting."

Mendenthal didn't respond. He stared silently at Breedlove.

"I will hold a meeting with you before this group, if you wish it that way," Breedlove said. "But I prefer to discuss some matters with you privately."

"I have nothing to say to you," Mendenthal said.

"But I have much to say to you," Breedlove said.

"This is highly irregular."

"Nevertheless, it is to our mutual advantage. And to the advantage of the shareholders. As I have said, I will make my statements publicly, if you so prefer."

"Very well," Mendenthal said. "I will meet with you."

Again a murmur arose. Breedlove spoke to his shareholders. "I will be brief. Very likely here, later today, you will hear more nonsense, exaggeration, and well-constructed lies concerning this company. They are not worth comment from your management, because comment gives them a dignity they do not deserve. We stand on our record. We stand on steadily advancing capital appreciation in your shares, rising dividends, and rising profits. Our structure is stable, our outlook is extremely bright. I have no more to say, except that I will not be with you in the future, yet this company, I assure you, will continue to grow and prosper with an excellent managerial team. Thank you. I suggest we adjourn for the lunch and reconvene at one P.M."

He stepped down. He had made his move.

*   *   *

"Scottie, you stay," Breedlove said. "I want you in on this Mendenthal meeting. Then we'll all meet."

"All meet? You mean directors?"

"I want to hold the board meeting before we go back to the annual meeting. I want to have a new president before we reconvene."

"I'm not sure I can take many more of your twists."

"There are only a few more."

Breedlove's manner was firm, unsmiling, businesslike. He paced in the small hotel room where Mendenthal had agreed to meet him, seeming extremely anxious to get this over. Again Scott felt his power, a radiation invisible and magnetic, and he wondered what intricate web the old spider had spun to snare his ancient enemy. He knew very soon.

"Mr. Scott is a lawyer, but he's not here as my lawyer," Breedlove said as Mendenthal entered. "If you wish, Philip, you may bring in a lawyer."

"That will not be necessary," Mendenthal said.

"Sit down."

"I prefer to stand."

Breedlove also stood. The room's narrow width separated them. Scott detected an invisible tension that seemed to sizzle between them. Breedlove cleared his throat, spat phlegm into a handkerchief, and stuffed the handkerchief into his back pocket.

"Philip, I want to do this as quickly and as unemotionally as possible. No fanfare. No outbursts. I want you to announce this afternoon that you are withdrawing from your proxy fight."

Mendenthal remained silent, his jaw set, his manner distinguished and, to Scott, quite imposing. He stared piercingly at Breedlove. A breeze wafted in through the window, and indistinct voices came from the unusually heavy pedestrian traffic on the street. Scott could see the slumped old cannery by the river.

Breedlove cut to his point. "Philip, as you know, BII has been subject in recent months to repeated attacks, a series of criminal acts, including one that occurred here in Olen. You, sir, are indirectly responsible for this."

"And you, sir, are desperate. And very possibly insane."

Breedlove reached for a Lucky Strike, lit it with a large

stick match, and flipped ashes on the carpet. "Shall we conduct this meeting without insult, without discussion of personalities, as two businessmen? It has come down to the generals, Philip. You and I. Are you sure you do not want a lawyer?"

"No. Continue your bluff."

"You will not win this fight anyway. You may come close but you have lost."

"I may not win, but you have lost," Mendenthal said.

"What sense does that statement make?"

"To me, much."

Breedlove sighed. He drew in smoke, coughed, and regarded Mendenthal with a gaze at once contemptuous and pitying. "Philip, this hasn't been a fair fight. You have been foolish. You have made mistakes. It has been a desperate fight for you, and as a result you've ignored the obvious and made terrible blunders. You want my hide. You don't want this company. You wouldn't know what to do with it. You've foolishly devoted much of your life to trying to skin me alive under the rationalization that my type is bad for American industry and must be deposed for the good of humanity, when in reality your motivation is to gain personal revenge because you think I have wronged you. You continue blindly on when your chances of succeeding have grown slimmer and slimmer over the years. I will say only this, and we will end this matter. BII has been attacked under the leadership of a man named Clinton St. John. I know all about him. He grew up in your household. No doubt you told him more than once of your lifetime passion to destroy me. Shall we say that you programmed him against me?"

"I told him nothing."

"All right. You told him nothing. But he told you something. He told you of his plan to raise hell with us before he set that plan in motion. That makes you, I believe, an accessory to criminal acts, for you told no one about him. Had you told the proper authorities, it would have ruined your chances to win this proxy fight, because you, not I, are the one linked with St. John. Am I correct?"

"You are not correct."

"There is a confession by St. John—including his statement that you knew of his plans—on tape."

Still Mendenthal betrayed no emotional reaction. "I did warn you about him," he said. "I warned your man Powell."

"Prove it. You have no proof."

"I need not prove it. I tried to warn you also, at your house. This is merely another Breedlove ploy."

"It is hardly a ploy, Philip, and you damn well know that. The burden of proof of your non-complicity falls upon you. I could have stopped these attacks earlier, but I waited for my proof, and I knew each attack further implicated you, because you knew the force behind them and refused to come forward. You did tell Powell. I know that. It was on tape, but I, not you, now have that tape."

"Now I am certain that you are mad."

"Try me," Breedlove said. "Test me. Take me to court. But don't tell me you can win this company if I delineate to shareholders and the press my evidence that you knew who was behind these attacks and sat on your hands. My risk is low compared to yours. And I will risk showing my unclean hands if by so doing I keep this company from the clutches of amateurs." He turned his back to Mendenthal. "You call me insane. Try me. Test me. You will see that insanity in full power. Go now. Decide wisely."

Mendenthal whirled and left. Breedlove slumped down on the bed. A coughing fit seized him. "No, I'm all right," he said.

Scott realized that the old man was consumed with pain. "Shall I get Scoggins?" he asked.

"No, shit, not Scoggins. Get the board in here."

Scott gazed at him with amazement. Breedlove had summoned energy from somewhere for his confrontation with Mendenthal, calling upon an uncanny force deep in his system, and now, despite almost total exhaustion and racked with pain, he was pushing for the immediate start of the board meeting. His face was ashen; his eyes were red and sunken. Loose skin flapped under his chin. He stood up. His eyes met Scott's.

"It's my last board meeting and I'm going to fucking well open it on my feet," he said. "Get 'em in here, Scottie."

"Wait. You owe me some answers first."

Breedlove sighed. "All right, what's on your mind?"

"Was that true what you told Mendenthal just now?"

"Some of it. Most of it."

"Then you could have stopped the bombings but you deliberately delayed to further implicate him?"

"Partly true, yes."

"Do you realize that by not taking action you also implicated yourself?"

"I realize that, yes. You do, too, with your lawyers's head. But who's to prove it? Mendenthal doesn't even believe it. You saw his face. Sure, he thinks I might try to use it on him, but he really doesn't believe it. So we're all right on that score. Besides, the plants were insured."

"What about the people who died?"

Breedlove's dark eyes blazed. "Scottie, I had something more important to stop. Do you realize how close Mendenthal was to winning this time around?"

Scott stared at him in disbelief. Larry had said, "He is a murderer." Now Scott was beginning to make up his mind about something. He wanted out. He wanted no more to do with this sick-minded old man who had promised him the world. It was a world of filth, bribes, and corner-cutting, and even one of murder.

Breedlove's dry lips crooked into a grin. "You showed mettle on that plane yesterday, Scottie. Lancaster, too."

"So you admit knowing about that."

"There was a fuck-up. But it's all right now. It's all over, taken care of."

"Why—for God's sake, *why?*—did you have us take such a chance?"

"What was I to do? Call the cops?"

"All right. You didn't call the cops. Who did you call?"

"Some people I know."

"What people?"

"I know some people. Let it go at that. In the final analysis, since it came out all right, thanks in part to you and Lancaster, they did their job. When you have a force against you, it's necessary to fight back with an equal force, a better force."

"What force did you use? Organized crime?"

"Your expression amuses me, Scottie."

"I'm not believing what I hear."

"Then don't. And don't worry about it. When I leave this company, those people leave, too. And certainly don't worry any more about those amateur extortionists. St. John has been handled. Lawrence, too. All of them."

Scott felt a rising horror. "What do you mean, handled?"

"Exterminated," Breedlove said.

Scott's lips moved. No words came out. He stared at Breedlove, a figure wraithlike and haggard, diminutive, aged, senile if not demented, wondering how this shriveled old fox could have so captivated and blinded him. He had saved his life, yet Breedlove would not even acknowledge it. Breedlove had made a mistake, risking all their lives, yet he would not admit it. Now Scott saw. Breedlove could not be excused. He was without conscience, corrupt, an influence buyer and manipulator who placed himself above the law, joining with underworld figures to serve as judge, jury, and avenger. Scott felt free of him. He felt total relief, a physical surge through his body. He knew what he would do. He knew it clearly and resolutely.

He found his voice and spoke between clenched teeth. "You stand there telling me two sons of yours are dead, perhaps the result of orders you gave, you stand there without emotion, without feeling—"

"Lawrence was not my son. You're more of a son to me than Lawrence."

Scott drove his fist into his palm. "Goddamn it, Lewis, I am not your son! I'm *nothing* like you. I say in blood that I am nothing like you."

"I know that," Breedlove said quietly.

"I'll stay for the board meeting. I might even make a speech. Then I'm leaving. I'm going to a place where I can find a human being."

"Give a speech, sure."

"I will."

Breedlove's eyes flashed. Energy again radiated from him. "I'd love to hear your speech, Scottie. I'd love to hear a good old-fashioned sermon on morality here in the Bible Belt of America. You tell us how bad we are. You tell us how good you are. Show some righteous indignation. Rave. Rage. Use biblical allusions."

"I might. I just might."

"I'll tell you what you do. Strip Powell first. Tell the board he's been in the books."

"Oh. You know about that."

Breedlove grinned. A dry cackle came from his throat. "I also know his wife's a les. And I know she's been ripping off from St. John's act."

"What do you mean by that?"

"The woman is sick. She set up some nasty phone calls to your wife, working with a sleazy private detective. She had a man spook Anne here in Olen. She set up the raid on your house, which went further than she'd wanted. You see, she started something she couldn't control."

"I— I don't believe you."

"Then don't. Let me say this about Powell. He's been in the till for a few thousand, maybe because he's basically insecure, but he's made millions for this company. Now let's go to Lancaster. Delineate his Vegas debts to the board. Tell them his wife's a whore. Yet remember he's made this company his life, he's risked his nuts for it, and has given us the only real marketing program we've ever had. Now let's turn to you. Strip yourself, too."

"I have nothing to hide."

"No. Only the ambition under you. I haven't quite seen your insides yet, but I think I may. Let's see at this meeting whether or not you have a set of balls."

"Let me go right now. Because I don't think you're going to like to hear what I have to say before the board."

"What I think I'll see is that under your bullshit you'll show me you want it. You think you're the best man for it. Deep in you, naked and bareknuckled, you want it. You still want it. You'll join the club to get it."

"No."

Breedlove sat down on the bed. He put his feet up and leaned his head back. "Fetch me my gophers, Scottie," he said. "Let's get the sideshow on the road."

It was a duly constituted, legal board meeting of Breedlove International, Inc., a vitally important meeting, but conducted with such informality and disorder that it seemed to Scott a grotesque charade. Breedlove lay on the bed, occasionally closing his eyes and seeming to sleep, while the directors in narrow ties and business suits stood along the walls of the small room, twitching in disbelief. Breedlove opened the meeting.

"We're here for a single purpose, to elect from within this company a new president and chief executive officer who will replace me today," he said. "There are other matters before the board, but they can be tabled until later. I will make my recommendation to the Nominating Committee soon. Right now, however, I believe we have some final campaign speeches. Keep them short."

Powell spoke, at first with hesitation, but soon with steadily improving assurance. He expressed confidence that Mendenthal would be defeated, crediting his efforts on proxy-fight counteraction. He described BII's financial future in glowing terms and recommended an increase in the dividend. The company's corporate acquisition phase very possibly was over for a while, he said, but noted that every acquisition BII had made in the past decade had been profitable. Powell finished, receiving a small stir of applause, and Lancaster held the floor. He was terse and effective. He noted that the Drug Division, successfully test-marketing BII-2000, was experiencing its best year in history. The new advertising program in the Food Division had improved sales and lifted profit margins. Lancaster briefly outlined a five-year division-by-division marketing plan for BII, including budgets, sales forecasts, and profit expectations. Then he looked at Scott, a slight smile twisted on his lips.

Scott went to the window. He looked out at the Olen cannery. He turned, eyed each director individually, and spoke with his hands on the sill.

"What I have to say is something you will not want to hear, but it is what I must say. I hope it will be accepted as truth, for I believe we have long avoided truth in this company." He paused, looking at Clem Hawley. Hawley turned away. Lancaster grinned. Powell sucked on the stem of an unlit pipe. Breedlove's eyes were closed. Scott continued. "I want to say, first, that I oppose just about every policy and practice promulgated and created by Lewis Breedlove because many such practices border on corruption." He heard a murmur among the directors, but he did not stop. "I think we do not listen enough. We do go ahead, without thinking of the possible consequences. Do we listen to people like Ellis

Culvert? No. We laugh at him, call him a troublemaker, even a kook. Is he? I don't think so. I think he speaks the truth. We don't like to hear the truth, because we're afraid of it. Philip Mendenthal, in his own way, speaks the truth about us. He has awakened me, and, I think, should awaken us all. We think of ourselves as men of substance, honor. We are actually men of subterfuge and deception. We have been chasing willy-nilly after profits to the detriment of our employees, our customers, and ourselves. We risk devastation because of it."

Again he paused. Lancaster was still grinning. Powell's hands were trembling slightly. Breedlove had not moved. Scott stepped away from the window. Now they would see him, the Mark Scott he knew he was, see him perhaps for the last time, yet hear something they would remember. Would they pay heed? Perhaps not. Yet they would hear. They could not stop him. Not even Lewis Breedlove could stop him, because he was free of Breedlove. His voice rose as he continued.

"I'm going to cite specifics. I'm going to charge, to accuse. I do not exclude myself from the guilty. I knew and I condoned, I closed my eyes. I—"

"Scottie," Breedlove interrupted. All eyes turned to him, lying stiffly on the bed with his hands under his neck. "Are you sure you want to go on in this way, Scottie?"

"Yes," Scott said. The eyes shifted back to him.

"Then get to your point," Breedlove said.

Scott looked at Lancaster, who met his stare without flinching, a grin still crooked on his lips. "We've heard boasts about the effectiveness of our advertising program," he said, speaking not to Lancaster but to the entire group. "I suggest that the entire program, in addition to being in bad taste, edges precariously close to fraud. What it promises is not delivered. It seems to me to be predicated upon the proposition that the populace is a mindless beast and that the housewife is an imbecile."

"Not far from the truth," Lancaster said.

"Hank, I have the floor."

"Not to attack me. Not without a defense." The grin was gone. A snarl had replaced it. "I'm sick and fucking tired of listening to you already. This company does not need an impractical Don Quixote as consultant or adviser. Go chase after windmills. Don't tell me my business."

Breedlove's hands clapped sharply. "Hank, let him continue," he said. "Give him his rope."

"All right," Lancaster said. The grin had returned. "Preach on, parson. Have at us sinners."

Scott squared his shoulders. "You all know my position on BII-2000. I am not convinced we're test-marketing a safe product and I recommend that it be withdrawn until we are sure. I realize that I've been guilty of not pushing my opposition more vehemently. BII-2000 could destroy the Drug Division and seriously hurt BII. Hank, shall we risk that?"

Lancaster said, "You are a fool, Scottie."

"We're in enough trouble." Scott's voice had begun to snap. He must control it. He must not lose his temper. "We're in trouble with the SEC, the FTC, the environmentalists, the consumerists, and I think we deserve it. We asked for it. We could have avoided it. We've paid off overseas, rationalizing it by saying others do it, why not us? A committee of this board is supposedly looking into this, but I strongly suspect that their report is far from completed and perhaps never will be completed unless federal investigators turn more pressure on us. We should do it *ourselves*, before we're pushed into it. We pay off politicians, we influence-peddle in Washington, we have a lawsuit because of questionable kickbacks in our Food Division. I don't think we can hide any more." His jaw trembled. His shoulders were unsteady. He realized he'd been expelling emotional energy that left him drained. "Gentlemen," he said, "I leave BII to you—or, if not to you, to Philip Mendenthal's slate of candidates for directors. They well might guide BII with as much expertise as us and certainly with greater fiduciary responsibility to shareholders and to the public. I take with me only my guilt."

The room was quiet. Scott turned away and looked out the window. He saw the river, alive with green current, and, beyond, the black, level fields. From the street came the blended voices of milling people, auto-horn toots, and shouts of children. The air was balmy, thick with spring odors of awakening trees and moist earth. Scott thought of his free, happy days as a child and a surge of nostalgia warmed him.

He wanted Anne. He wanted home. He wanted the kids. It was over—the stress, the conflicts, the indecision, the compromises, the power war in the executive corridor—and his relief was total. He was on the edge of tears. He felt he had gained, not lost.

Breedlove stirred. "Scottie, before you go, one more matter. I asked you long ago for a recommendation on the plant here. Have you made up your mind about it?"

"It's your plant." Scott turned sharply. "You decide."

"Give me your opinion."

Scott hesitated. His eyes met Breedlove's. It was an electric moment between them. Finally Scott said, "My opinion is that it should be closed."

"When?"

"Immediately after the spring harvest. There are details on it in a report I'll leave."

Breedlove removed a pen from his breast pocket and scribbled something on a small piece of paper. "We convened this meeting to elect a president," he said. "Here is my nomination." He passed the paper to Powell, who looked at it without a change in his dour expression, and slowly it went around the room. Lancaster looked at it last. He crumpled it up. A sneer had replaced his grin. A sneer of triumph? He looked at Scott and smiled.

"Let's vote," Breedlove said.

Within an hour it was all over Olen that Mark Scott, the hometown boy, had been elected president and chief executive officer of Breedlove International, Inc.

36

ANNE GOT CONFIRMATION OF THE NEWS FROM SUSAN Powell. "My congratulations," Susan said. "Or should I instead extend to you my condolences?"

"I don't understand."

"You are now the first lady. First ladies share a crown that can be uneasy and troublesome."

"I keep hearing only rumors. I can't even *find* Mark."

"The rumors are true."

Anne stammered. "I—I simply do not know what to say, Susan."

"There is nothing to say, except goodbye." Susan raised her head. She drew on gloves. They were outside the big tent, where the annual meeting was about to reconvene. "We tried hard, but we lost. I think we have been wronged, but be that as it may, we have lost."

"Surely George will stay with BII."

"Surely George will not stay." Susan arched her eyebrows and regarded Anne with a piercing stare, like a ruffled hawk seeing prey. "May I be frank with you?"

"Be as frank as you like, Susan."

"Now we need pretend no longer."

"I have never pretended."

"Lewis Breedlove has made a mistake. I believe that his mind is gone. He selected the weakest of the three, simply because he sought a surrogate son, not an able and experienced chief executive."

"Are you finished now, Susan?"

Susan's lips curled into a cruel sneer. "A surrogate son with a bird of a wife. A bird of a wife."

"Susan," Anne said. Blood rushed to her brain. She calmed herself. Susan's eyes were wide, stark, insane. Looking at her in disbelief, Anne thought, *Her. She did it.* Anne knew. The anger dissolved and pity replaced it. "Oh, Susan," she said.

Susan Powell stalked away, her head high.

Scott returned to the annual meeting in a state of near shock. He'd slashed out at BII and specifically at Breedlove, yet Breedlove had nominated him, the board had rubber-stamped the nomination, and he had accepted. His reversal had been quick and complete. He felt weak, drained. His surroundings seemed to whirl around him like a surrealistic landscape of unnatural colors and blurred images. The ground under him seemed spongy and unsteady. Again he felt as if he had lost control, as if events determining his fate had proceeded apace without his sanction or knowledge. The web of Lewis Breedlove? No. He rejected that notion. It was melodramatic and unrealistic. Yet he felt the web almost physically, its silky threads imprisoning him, as he prepared to chair his first BII annual meeting. The stockholder group wavered unsteadily before him. Scott squared his shoulders. He was here, at the top after all the conflict and indecision, Breedlove's elect for reasons he'd yet to discover, and if it was a prison, he'd entered it willingly, for he could have rejected it. As always, Breedlove had been right, slashing to the truth; down deep, Scott had wanted it, wanted it very much. Now it was his, although he could not quite believe it yet. The town knew, the stockholders knew, soon the world would know. The tent was quiet, waiting for him to speak, following Carl Sampson's announcement of his election and Breedlove's retirement. Breedlove was not there; he'd disappeared into his hotel room, followed by Scoggins. Powell and Lancaster and their wives were not there. Scott searched for Anne, but he could not find her. He delivered a short, hesitant speech, forecasting continued financial gains for BII, yet noting that the gains, under his leadership, would not come at peril to the company's social responsibilities. His comments drew slight applause. Stockholders were looking forward to the main event, the election of directors. Mendenthal sat quietly, surrounded by his candidates. He seemed uninterested, almost bored. Ellis Culvert sat in the front row. When Scott announced that the next order of business would be the election of directors, Culvert leapt up. He protested loudly, citing Robert's Rules of Order, terming it "unjust" that directors be elected before the question-and-answer session. Scott found the meeting out of control, degenerating into shouting and bickering, and then he looked down to see that Philip Mendenthal had stood up and was asking the chairman to recognize him.

"May I come to the podium?" Mendenthal asked.

"You may," Scott said.

Mendenthal moved in slow strides, his shoulders back, his head erect. He stood before the stockholders, a figure of gray dignity, and waited for silence. Finally he spoke.

"Mr. Scott, I want to state that our committee—the Committee for Better Management of BII—supports your election to the presidency of the company. It is a step in the direction we advocated. It is also a factor in the announcement I am about to make to stockholders. I will state it simply. Our committee is withdrawing its campaign to unseat current directors of BII."

A loud buzz went through the tent. There were some cries

of "No, no!" Again Mendenthal waited for silence. "This decision was made at the noon break, but it is not a sudden decision. We have contemplated it for some time, hoping the company would voluntarily implement the reforms we have advocated. We have strong reasons to believe that this will occur. Therefore we do not withdraw in defeat. I thank you for your support and attention." He left the podium and slowly walked out of the tent.

The rest of the meeting was routine. Scott fielded questions for an hour, including a dozen from Culvert. He found himself giving terse and evasive answers, reminding his inquisitors that he was, after all, new to the job, inciting a tinkle of laughter. He was impatient to end the meeting and seek out Breedlove. The old man had a habit of abrupt departures. Maybe he had already left town. Scott found it difficult to concentrate on the meeting. It seemed anticlimactic and unnecessary. He fidgeted, snapped out terse answers, glancing at his watch as a hint to his interrogators that his patience was growing short. He told only one lie. When asked point-blank whether or not the Olen plant would be soon closed, he said the matter had not yet been decided. It was a technical truth, for it had not been voted upon by the board. Finally Scott resorted to a time-honored technique for closing a meeting. He said he'd take one more question. It came from Culvert.

"Mr. Scott, BII has suffered repeated attacks in recent months, apparently from terrorists, resulting in loss of lives and substantial financial losses. What has been done?"

"The attacks have ended," Scott said.

"Can you be sure?"

"We are positive."

BII's directors were reelected in an almost routine vote. Exactly at five o'clock, Scott tapped the gavel on the podium and declared the meeting adjourned. Stockholders began to file out.

"Scottie, you handled Culvert with fine finesse," Carter Mannering said, a wide grin on his face. "Yes, sir, fine finesse."

"Finesse suggests deception," Scott snapped.

"To me it means skill."

"I'm sorry, Carter. I didn't mean to bite at you. It's just that I've got to get to Breedlove before he runs out of town."

But still he was trapped, now by Cotton Meeks, who had J. B. Toms on his coattail. "Mark, you're a sight for sore eyes," Meeks said. He was twenty pounds heavier than when Scott had last seen him. Thick globs of fat hung from his neck. "Mighty glad that your first act as president of this great company was to live up to your promise to keep our plant here open and producin'."

Scott's eyes met Meeks's. Meeks turned away. Something came to Scott, a realization that apparently had not yet fully penetrated his consciousness. He *was* president, duly elected and absolutely in power. Yet he had hesitated, actually lied, when asked about the plant. Within the vastness of BII, it was not a major matter; it meant something, in fact, only to Olen citizens. Yet it was a decision to make, his first as BII president, and he had dodged it, afraid of the consequences, vacillating in lingering indecision. Yet he *had* decided. Now Meeks met his gaze.

"I didn't exactly say the plant would stay open," Scott said. "As a matter of fact, it will not stay open."

Meeks's jaw dropped. His neck fat trembled. Scott escaped him without pretense of diplomacy. Hurrying up the aisle toward the exit, he heard his name being called and stopped abruptly, recognizing the voice. It was Norma.

"Hi, Mr. Scott," she said.

A scar ran down one side of her face, giving her mouth a harelip appearance. It rushed back to Scott, the recent terror he'd so quickly forgotten—the bombings, the fear of the BII executive jet, Lawrence Breedlove and Clinton St. John, the chauffeur named Morris, and Anne's face white with apprehension. Now that it was over, ended by Lewis Breedlove's quick, avenging sword, Scott wondered if, after all, Breedlove's techniques were not the most effective and even just. Not long ago, he would have been horrified by such an attitude. Norma turned her scarred side away.

"Norma, will you look at me?"

"Bad, huh, Mr. Scott?"

"No. Not so bad."

"My Olen tattoo. It will keep me here, at that old plant."

"I'm sure we can find a better job in the company for a bright young lady like you."

"Scar and all?"

"I think we can do something about the scar."

"Life isn't all too hot, is it, Mr. Scott?"

He watched her go with mixed feelings of pity and guilt. He made a mental note to do something for her, but he wondered if he would follow up. The company had paid her hospital bills, and, to ward off a possible lawsuit, had offered her six thousand dollars, which she'd accepted. He'd thought it insufficient, but he hadn't interfered. Scott had thought about Norma quite often right after the Olen explosion, but she'd soon slipped completely from his mind. There was too much else to think about.

When he left the tent, Scott saw Clem Hawley outside, waiting for him. Hawley handed him a white envelope.

"My resignation," he said. "Effective immediately."

"Why? You were just reelected a director."

"So were Lancaster and Powell. How long will they stay? You know I have to go down. This makes it easy for you."

"You can stay on if I ask you to stay."

"But you won't. You know that."

"I have a question."

"Shoot."

"Why did he pick me?"

"I think I know, but that's got to come from him."

"I need you, Clem. For moral support if for nothing else. But a lot more. I need somebody I trust to tell me when I'm wrong."

"Well, I'll be around. It's not like I'm shuffling off to Buffalo." Hawley looked at Scott, his eyes misty. "Is it?"

He turned away. Scott did not call him back.

The day was still bright with sun and a humid breeze had begun to stir. Main Street stirred with heavy traffic. Scott strolled to the hotel, brushing off congratulations from people he'd never seen before, and tapped on the door to Breedlove's room. Scoggins opened it a crack.

"He is not feeling well at all, Mr. Scott," he said.

"Scoggins, for Christ's sake, let him in!" Breedlove bellowed.

Scott went in. The room was semidark, shaded. He smelled cigarette smoke. He made out Breedlove's dim outline, huddled in a chair by the window.

"That's close enough, Scottie," Breedlove said. His voice

was hoarse, almost a whisper, as if the outburst directed at Scoggins had drained his energy and left him gasping. "Whatever it is," he said, "make it quick."

"I have just one question."

"You want to know why I went for you. You really don't know the answer?"

"No. I really do not know."

Breedlove's voice was stronger. He spoke rapidly. "It's because you're clean. We need somebody to run it who's clean, or at least has that image. Who could look into your baby-blue eyes and suspect duplicity? Not only are you clean, but in the past few months you've learned the world isn't all fairy tales or anything else the way we'd like it to be, but instead it's the way it is. Tough and competitive. I picked you early on and I don't like to be wrong so I'm happy the way it turned out. I liked the change I saw in you. It took balls to batter away at us devilish old farts in that meeting."

Scott could not speak. A sinking feeling went through him as he peered at the dim image before him. It had been Breedlove's final maneuvering of Mark Scott. The old man had been far ahead of him all the way, turning and twisting him, leading him perhaps much in the manner he had tried to lead and manipulate Larry. He'd failed with Larry; he'd succeeded with Scott. Breedlove actually had goaded him into speaking out against BII. Scott felt some resentment, which he did not express; he also felt foolish, taking the edge off his earlier surprise and elation.

"You have Powell and Lancaster to send down," Breedlove said. "It should be a pleasure for you."

"No, it will not be a pleasure."

"Well, believe it or not, it's never been a pleasure for me, either, having to send a man down. It's an admission you made a mistake." He looked at Scott, his eyes tired, his shoulders sagging. "There's not much more I have to say. Except, as you know, there's a different mood in the country now, one that's been building since Watergate. You can't cut corners the way we did before and you can't hide if you do. It may last quite a while." Breedlove grinned. "You might even have to cut the perquisites, with this Jesus-lover in the White House jacking up the SEC. You might lose the 727."

"I won't miss it."

"Will you miss this town when it's dead?"

"I don't want to do it. But I see no alternative."

"I know it's lonely in your chair. But remember that you're not in a popularity contest. Look at it this way. We created this town, so we can ruin it too. If it bothers you, remember that in killing it you bring life elsewhere."

"That's one way of looking at it."

"The only way," Breedlove said. His clawlike hand stretched out. The shade snapped up. He sat slouched, grinning crookedly, his skeletal face drawn and pale. Only his eyes were alive. Come to me, come to me, the eyes seemed to say. Breedlove pulled the shade back down. "I just wanted to look at you," he said.

Scott went to his room and found Anne lying on the bed, her hands over her swollen stomach, her eyes wide open. "Well," she said. "Congratulations."

"That's all? Just congratulations?"

"I can't think of anything else to say, not right now." She sat up, patted the pillow, and held out her arms. "Mark? Come here?"

He went to her and held her. She was trembling and he saw that her eyes were streaked with tears. "I'm sorry," she said. "I am happy. I *am*."

"Then what is it?"

"You know. I think you know."

"The company has me, not you and the kids?"

"Something like that."

"Think we're grown up enough to work it out."

"All right. But now I want to go home."

"We'd better stay tonight. I have some unfinished business here." He looked at her, into the child-woman's face that had been soft with the loving of him for so many years, and he knew she was right. Their family times had shrunk from hours per day to minutes and would shrink even more. But he would not think about it. Not now. He said, "I think you have something else on your mind. What is it?"

"Well, I talked to Susan Powell."

"How did Susan take it?"

"Bitterly. To say the least. Mark, I think she had something to do with the attacks on us."

"You may be right. Breedlove said that, too."

"You don't sound very astounded."

"It might well be that nothing astounds me any more."

"I feel only sorrow for her. But it got me thinking. How horribly competitive this must have been for you. What did you have to do to win? And what will you have to do to stay on top?"

He stood up. "Anne, aren't you being a little unfair? Assuming I had to play dirty?"

"I guess I am. I'm sorry."

"Don't put pressure on me, Anne."

"I want the Mark I know. Not a different Mark."

"Now I think you're being childish."

"Maybe I am. I might be worried because I'm not sure I'm up to it, being your wife."

"Of course you're up to it."

"It will take some getting used to. The new us."

"Everything and everybody changes." He snapped out the words. "Anne, haven't we argued about this before? I don't think I want to discuss it again."

"Then we won't discuss it."

"Frankly, I'm quite disappointed in your reaction."

"Maybe it's just another mood. I'll cheer up."

He left, closing the door quietly, wanting to escape her eyes. Once she'd called the top job at BII an opportunity of a lifetime; now, the chair his, she'd greeted him coolly and had been almost accusatory. He had grown in the past few months, but apparently she had not. Her yearning for independence and lamentations over a lost career had been sham; in reality, she was a homebody, dependent, and capable of making him feel guilt. He did not want to feel guilt. He wanted to feel elation. He must go forward without self-doubt, without hesitation, without fear of the consequences.

Scott stopped. Philip Mendenthal stood by the staircase at the end of the hall. They gazed at each other for a long moment before Mendenthal spoke.

"I have been lurking here, waiting to waylay you. And I might warn you that another waylayer, Henry Lancaster, lurks at the bottom of the stairs."

"I'm looking for him, as a matter of fact."

"I congratulate you, Mr. Scott, but I do not envy you. You have a massive cleanup job ahead."

"You lose with dignity."

"As I told the meeting, I really did not lose." Mendenthal

smiled. "We think we've accomplished our objective. Our campaign against BII opened many eyes. I think your election to the presidency is at least in part a result of our campaign."

"I don't quite accept that."

"His way has been defeated. He is finished. I will say that seeing him as he is, infirm and dying, gives me no satisfaction. Once I admitted to Mr. Powell that Breedlove was a monomaniacal obsession of mine, and now I admit to you, Mr. Scott, that obsession is a very costly fault. I hope that BII does not become an obsession of yours."

"It won't. I won't allow it."

"I fear you will, if you're to stay at the top."

"No. I think I can maintain a balance in my life."

"Shall we part with a handshake?"

"Of course."

"I will warn you, Mr. Scott. We will be watching."

"I suspect many will be watching."

"A final question. Is he a man you admired?"

"He is a man I can never forget."

"Perhaps you, too, have the Breedlove demon in you."

"The Breedlove demon? Well, I won't admit it."

"My war is ended," Mendenthal said. "Yours begins."

Lancaster, waiting downstairs, a drink in his hand, raised his glass and said, *"Le roi est mort, vive le roi!* O king. O new and mighty king. What may we do to please you?"

"Start by handing in your resignation."

"It hath been done, O lord."

"Shall we be serious, Hank?"

"About one thing I will be serious, sport. That was good work in the hold of that airplane."

"I don't think I could have done it without you."

"All right. That's over. War buddies split up. I commend you on your pretty speech."

"I meant what I said."

"I am sure that you did. I shall sell my BII shares at tomorrow's opening."

"Be my guest."

Lancaster began to speak with small sneers, his eyes red. "You won't stop it. You can make pretty speeches, moralize, but you won't stop it. Soon you'll condone it, turn your back to it. If you don't, you'll get murdered on the bottom line."

"We'll see."

"You'll stop test-marketing of BII-2000?"

"Yes."

"You'll ruin the drug's chances, put it under a cloud."

"Hank," Scott said. "We could have had this together. If we had worked together just a few times, like we did on that plane, we could have done it."

"I work alone, sport. Three or even two cannot drink from the same cup."

"All right, Hank."

"You take care. You watch out for number one. I know you will. You're the new Scott. And now you have it all. You have the regulators, the investigators, the charity seekers, the childish scientists, the greedy workers, the unfriendly press. They will call you sir and knife you when your back is turned. You'll be tested and pressured every day. I think you might crack."

The words did not affect Scott. Breedlove had been right, he reflected as his eyes met Lancaster's. He was enjoying his triumph. He anticipated some resignations from executives faithful to Lancaster, but he was sure he could fill the posts by promoting those faithful to him. For the first time since his election, Scott felt his full power. It was a feeling of ultimate pleasure.

"Well, I'm off to Vegas," Lancaster said. "Ball a few whores, hit the tables, get smashed. Then I'll take an asset inventory and go back to work."

"May I go past now?"

Lancaster bowed, stepped aside, and swept his hands in a courtly gesture. "Man plans," he said, "God laughs."

Powell packed methodically, arranging the ties so they would not wrinkle, wrapping his shoes in tissue paper, putting his shirts into plastic bags. Susan stood beside him.

"You're going to New York?" she said. "To see her?"

"Not to see her. I have affected her life quite too much already."

"In a way, you realize, she was really responsible."

"Carol? For what is Carol responsible, Susan?"

"She was your weakness. She destroyed your concentration. Did you know she cheated on you? A guttersnipe."

"Do your worst, Susan," Powell said, sighing. "It hardly matters now."

"It does matter. Your business career is not over."

"I fear my life is over."

Her eyes hardened. She snorted. "You failed, yes, but it was not because of me. When I realized you were losing, I tried to help you. Shall I tell you what I did?" She became more agitated. She gestured, her eyes blazing. Veins on her neck stood out. She spoke rapidly, her words tumbling out in a shower of spittle. "I took a chance for you. I hired the detective agency that told me about Carol Reynolds to frighten that little fool, Anne Scott."

"Susan, you did *what*?"

"And they did frighten her. I'll tell you, oh, they did."

Her peered at her in disbelief. Perspiration smeared her makeup, revealing rough-skinned patches. Powell met her stare with a darker one of his own. He saw to the truth of her for the first time in his life. He saw a woman with a veneer of refinement that masked an inner turmoil so severe it approached savagery and perhaps even dementia. He fought inner rage.

"This was not a war," he said, trying to control his voice.

"It was a war. Your strategy, I might add, was self-defeating. You *needed* me." Her red lips twitched. "I was your strength. You were spineless without me. A jelly-fish."

A heavy rap came on the door. "I think that is Scott," Powell said. "I wish to talk with him alone." Again their eyes met. He was the first to turn away. He said, "I feel only pity for you, Susan. You are not well."

"Should I apologize? Fall to my knees and beg to be forgiven?"

"My only advice to you, Susan, is that you resume psychiatric care. I do not think you will, however."

"There is no need for it."

"Whatever happens to me, one matter is a certainty. I must escape from you."

"You would wilt. Wither and die."

"I have, Susan. With you. I have withered slowly."

"Failure," she hissed at him. She threw back her head. "Failure!" she screamed.

He regarded her calmly and spoke in a hushed voice. "I admit failure. I admit even to failure as a moral man. Yet I claim superiority to you, for there have been at least some hours in my life when I have felt empathy for others."

The rapping sounded again. Powell opened the door and motioned Scott in. Susan didn't look at Scott. She pushed past him without speaking and walked away, her carriage regal.

"Well," Powell said, closing the door. "Perhaps you would like a drink."

"No. Thank you."

"My congratulations."

"Thank you."

"You will have my resignation soon."

"I'm afraid I'll need much more from you than your resignation, George."

Powell looked out the window. "So you know."

"Yes."

"I suspected you did know." He turned and gazed at Scott, the sad George Powell gaze. "I'll restore the money."

"I'm sorry, George. That's not enough."

"Then you'll turn me in?"

"George, why did you do it? I can't understand *why*."

Powell's eyes widened. He spoke rapidly, gesturing wildly. "Don't you realize the very economic base of this country is threatened? This administration is *ruining* the country. It could all tumble, collapse."

"So we must protect ourselves?"

"Yes. Of course."

"I'm sorry, George. I simply do not accept that."

"You think it's a rationalization?"

"I don't know what it is. I know only that I cannot possibly shield you."

"Scott," Powell said, his voice unsteady. "Let me go."

"Oh, George. Don't beg." Scott clenched his fists. "Do you think I like this? Don't you know that if I let you go, knowing of it, I become an accessory to it? I've held the information too long already. Jinkens knows about it. Do you think I want to be under the thumb of that ambitious scheming young machine? But even if he did not know, I couldn't let you go."

"I see you have learned to protect yourself."

"Would you do it differently, George?"

"I suppose I would not." Powell's eyes showed a tiny spark. He sighed. "At least now I know my future. The race is ended. The prize is yours. The cost will be high."

"I know that. I know that only too well."

"It is useless to look back. Yet I wish that in my wanting years I had produced one single creative thing, something I could hold in my hands, like a volume of poetry."

"You have contributed much, and created much."

"I have created nothing, just as I have come to nothing. But I blame no one, only myself. The more of life I see the more I realize that once a person turns onto a certain path, it becomes impossible to escape that path." Powell turned urgently. "Scottie, don't take the job. Go home to your family. Profit by my mistakes. I've ignored that which really counts. Don't you do it."

"I need a drink," Scott said. "We both need one."

He found himself outside. A sinking orange sun hung over the cannery, pouring moist heat on the town, and insects hovered above, their diaphanous wings beating. He wanted to be alone, to escape Powell's haunting eyes, the taunts of Lancaster, Anne's doubts, and lingering questions about Breedlove. Perhaps he'd take a stroll in the woods, try to recapture childhood visions. But that was no good. He couldn't go back. He heard someone call to him, using his first name. He turned. Then he had his father by the hand.

"I came down for the shindig, but I had no idea it was to elect my boy king of the world," the elder Scott said, grinning. He looked younger than when Scott had last seen him, about two years ago. There was a glint in his eye and a spring in his step. "Your mother wanted to come, too, but the next-door neighbor is sick, and you know when that happens, she has to stay home and care for the person. She should have been a nurse. She ordered me to bring you back, however. How are the kids? Where is Anne?"

"Anne is in the hotel. Let's go surprise her. Seeing you will cheer her up."

"You're crowned king and she's moping?"

"I think she sees an uneasy reign."

"You don't look too thrilled about it, either."

"I'm still in shock."

"Well, come up north and see us."

"I will. Soon." They stood in the sun, looking each other over. Scott's mind drifted, taking him back to their long talks before a fireplace, to their fishing together and walking in the hills; vividly, as if it were yesterday, he saw them standing breathlessly still amid pinecones, watching a deer and her fawn come down to a stream to drink. "I know one thing. You're still the happiest man I know."

"Well, I never understood why anybody's unhappy."

"I envy you."

"You have work to do, Mark. I'll go see Anne alone."

"You're going to have dinner with us."

"Can't. I'll go talk to Anne, then head on home. You know I hate driving after dark."

"Or staying away from your fifty-mile radius."

"A man doesn't need the world." He gazed deeply into Scott's eyes. "I hear this plant will be closed."

"News travels fast."

"You're not the most popular person in Olen right now."

"Decisions have to be made."

"Mark, you got to do things, I know. When you get it all out of your system, c'mon home."

They shook hands. Scott did not want to let go.

The mighty of Olen clustered around Dorothy Lancaster in the Main Street bar, shielding her from the lustful stares of red raw farmhands who'd never seen anything like her, at least in the flesh. She was having a good time. It was a cute, loose place. She wriggled to the jukebox to play old-fashioned tunes, lively ones such as "C'mon to My House," sentimental ones such as "Moon River," one of her favorites. The ugly little fat man, Cotton Meeks, had assumed the role of her protector, drafting even uglier J. B. Toms into service as his assistant. She'd had four big glasses of strong red wine, and she was feeling just fine. The farmhands watched her from the bar, grinning.

"Don't let them grins fool you," Cotton Meeks said. "They're in an ugly mood around here."

"Why?"

"Around here, there's gonna be a ghost town."

"Why?"

"It's building up, I can tell."

"She smiled. She ran her fingertips over his fatty chin.

"Cotton's a cute name," she said. "J. B., don't you think Cotton's a cute name?"

"Reckon," J. B. said. He'd been drinking and he was morose and sour.

Dorothy felt free. Olen was a nice town. Maybe she'd leave Hank, take her alimony, and set up an X-rated theater here. Build a whorehouse in back of it. It would put a snap in the old place. The thought amused her. She giggled. She sipped wine. A hand gripped her shoulder tightly, hurting her; she gasped, looked up, and saw Hank above her, square-shouldered and frowning.

"Let's go," he said.

"Don't wanna go," she said. She *could* revolt. She would show him. "Wanna dance. Wanna dance, dance, dance."

He had her hand. "We're leaving."

"Let go. You let go. I got friends."

"What friends? These hicks?" He stared at the men along the bar. He snarled. "They fuck only their sisters."

He pulled her up roughly. Meeks shied back. Toms sat motionless, his eyes drooping. Two of the farmhands turned from the bar and shuffled toward them. One, in bib overalls, his face brightly red, said slowly, "She wants to stay, let her stay." He had massive bare arms. He kept his hands behind his back. "You like to stay with us, pretty lady?"

"I want to stay," Dorothy said. "I want to stay and have a nice gang bang."

Hank glared. "Go back to your beer, sonny. Have one on me." He scattered change on the floor by the big man's boots.

The man scowled, his face growing even redder. He took two quick steps toward Hank. Then he sprang. *Sic 'im!* Dorothy thought, a thought that amused her, causing her to issue little bubbling giggles, and then the scene flashed before her—a thud of boots, the quick flash of a knife in the big man's hand, Hank dodging, his eyes wide, his mouth open. He wasn't quick enough. Not this time. The knife slashed down. Hank clutched the side of his head. Thick blood squirted between his fingers. He looked at Dorothy, a look that sought something—perhaps understanding, pity—and then he took his hand away. He was grinning. His ear hung down by his jawbone from a flap of skin. He sank slowly to the floor, his hands over his head. Still he was grinning.

Dorothy heard screams and only when they stopped did she realize they were her own.

Scott could not sleep, and he surmised that Anne, lying motionless in the dark on the bed next to his, was not sleeping either. They did not speak. Activity in the street below was unusually heavy for night in Olen; he could hear murmurings and the shuffling of shoes on the sidewalk. He got up and went to the window. Below, under a streetlamp, was an assemblage of people, mostly men, perhaps twenty-five or thirty, a group that seemed to be growing. Scott glanced at Anne. She hadn't moved. As he turned back toward the bed, stumbling in the semidarkness, he heard a sharp crash and the tinkling of glass, and an object bounced on the floor. Anne gasped and sat up quickly. It was a rock, hurled through the window from the street below. Someone was pounding on the door.

"Mark?" Anne said.

Scott felt his heart jump. Blood surged in his veins. The heavy knocking rattled the door. Anne was up, reaching for the light switch.

"Don't!" he said. His voice was a hoarse whisper.

"W-what is it?"

"Just for God's sake leave the light off!"

He went to the door, moving silently. The knocking was even louder and the knob rattled and turned. "Mr. Scott, you in there?" a voice outside said. It was high-pitched, urgent. "It's Johnny. The sheriff."

Scott unlocked the door and opened it halfway. The sheriff stood in the hall, his face wet with sweat. "You'd better get your things, Mr. Scott, you and the missis. I got a car out back and I'd better get you out of town."

"Why? What's wrong?"

"Wal, that group's beer-logged and riled up. I can control 'em, but I'd feel a lot better if you'd get packed and outta town."

"Is it because of the plant closing?"

"More or less, I'd say. You hear what happened to the other one? Lancaster?"

"Hank? No. What happened?"

"Wal, he managed to get himself into a knife fight down at

the saloon an' from what I saw he come out second best. We got him off to the hospital at Indian Falls."

"Is he all right?"

"I think he'll be okay, but you check with them, at the hospital. But for right now, it's best you head out of town. Seein' some blood, I guess, set things off here."

Scott became conscious of Anne behind him. Her hand touched his arm lightly. He said, "No. We're not leaving."

"You'd best understand somethin', Mr. Scott," the sheriff said. "Them farmhands and plant workers are pretty independent people. Individual, they're okay, they help their neighbors. But together, with some booze in 'em, they can be somethin' to reckon with. They don't understand no big companies. They think that plant's theirs."

"Well, it isn't."

"I'd advise you to leave."

"I thank you for the advice, but we're not leaving until the morning, when a company car will pick us up. I'm not going to sneak out the back door."

The sheriff rubbed his chin. "Wal, suit yerself then. I'll go out, see what I can do. Don't expect much sleep tonight, you and the missis."

"I'm not sure we could sleep anyway."

"Wal, best of luck." The sheriff turned.

"Johnny?" Scott said.

"What?"

"Thank you."

"It's my job, that's all," the sheriff said, and shuffled away, his holster bobbing against his hip.

The Cadillac limousine came to the hotel at 5 A.M., easing through a crowd that now numbered perhaps a hundred. It was no longer merely a crowd. It was a mob. From it came a stirring and a loud, chantlike murmur. The faces of the men were like one face—tight-jawed and narrow-eyed, human as individuals but animalistic as a group. A headline in the *Record*, held up by some, screamed, "BII TO CLOSE OLEN PLANT." The sheriff, Johnny, flanked by two deputies in uniform, their pistol holsters unsnapped, guided Anne and Scott toward the car. Scott walked slowly, holding Anne's arm, feeling the tenseness. The chauffeur stayed inside the car. Johnny opened the door, put their luggage into the back seat, and motioned to Scott. Scott stopped. He looked at he crowd, searching for familiar faces; he wanted to go to the men, to try to calm them, to tell them that the company would relocate them and their families in other BII plants, but he knew it would do no good. They were Olen people, and they did not understand relocation. He had done it, he was the target, and he knew then quite fully both the consequences and the power of the decision maker's chair. He had condemned the town, judged it and sentenced it, and soon it would die. Grass and weeds would grow unheeded in its streets, and winds would howl ghost sounds through paint-chipped boards of the abandoned cannery. But he did not pity Olen. He felt, instead, a rising elation. Anne was right. He was a vastly different Mark Scott from a few months ago, perhaps from only a few hours ago. There would be more decisions, much more bitter and hurting to some, but he would make them. Briefly his thoughts fled to Breedlove. The twisted old man had left, perhaps to find a place to die, having found a caretaker for his offspring, and now in that offspring raged what Philip Mendenthal had correctly called the Breedlove demon. If not that, one thing was certain. He was a Mark Scott no longer innocent. He felt only a slight twinge of loss, overwhelmed by triumph.

The crowd shuffled closer. Scott saw an arm snake forward, and a clump of heavy mud splashed against a window. Anne winced. Scott helped her into the back seat. Now the car was being pelleted by stones and mud rocks, glancing off its roof, cracking its rear window. The sheriff slammed the door shut. Anne crouched in the seat, biting her lips, her hands trembling. Scott put his arm around her shoulder and she came to him with a small sob. The car was moving, slowly. The crowd pressed in, moving in a sudden surge, the men hurling whatever they could find in the street, their voices now raised in an uncontrollable rage. Looking out, Scott saw J. B. Toms's face distinctly, pressing against the window. A rock thumped the roof, followed by two more. A man darted in front of them, waving his hands. A streak of mud slashed across the windshield, obscuring the driver's iew. Yet he moved on, more rapidly, gunning the engine, aking and swerving, forcing the crowd away from the car. n they were free of the town, moving rapidly on a paved road under a tranquil sky streaked with the pink of dawn. Looking back, Scott saw the crowd stop in the road, the men standing in anger, their fists in the air. He heard Anne's gasps, and he touched her shoulder. He felt quite calm. He reached for his briefcase. There was work to do. Anne sat up and stared silently out the window as the telephone poles and sun-pinked fields fled past.

Pain thrust deep within Breedlove's body as the 727 banked. He had a fleeting glimpse of the black, newly plowed terrain below, and in a sharp, blinding flash, a microsecond of past-present-future, he saw himself standing in the center of a field with interminable boundaries, earth smells thick in his nostrils, under a sky so blue and dazzling that it caused his eyes to water. He was no age, he was all ages. The vision dissolved. He was lying on the bed in the stateroom, and for a moment he was in darkness and he did not know where he was. He fought back, his jaw set, his fists clenched. Sometimes the pains were sharp and then gone, but this pain, he knew, was different. It would last. It was not needle-thrust pain, but probing, twisting knife-thrust pain that fed alive on every nerve in his body.

"Scoggins," he said weakly.

He waited. He tried to call again, but no sound came out. Yet Scoggins had heard, for he appeared dimly above Breedlove, his mouth tight, his shoulders square. Breedlove pointed to his arm, indicating that he wanted his injection of morphine.

"No, sir," Scoggins said.

Breedlove couldn't understand. His lips moved.

"I will not give you an injection, sir," Scoggins said.

Breedlove's mouth opened. He could not speak.

"My daughter is dead," Scoggins said. "I have come to the conclusion, Mr. Breedlove, that you are at least in part responsible for her death."

He left, at first backing away cautiously and then whirling to depart abruptly. With great effort, Breedlove drew his knees up to his chest and lay gasping and trembling, his hands clawing stiffly, his agonized, vanquished body too weak to find a way to howl protest, to hurl rage at the gods that had denied him immortality.

ABOUT THE AUTHOR

ARELO SEDERBERG was Howard Hughes'
public-relations man. He is at present the
financial editor and columnist for the LOS
ANGELES HERALD-EXAMINER.